ALSO BY RANDALL WALLACE

Pearl Harbor
Braveheart
Where Angels Watch
Blood of the Lamb
So Late into the Night
The Russian Rose

RANDALL WALLACE

Simon & Schuster
New York   London   Toronto   Sydney

LOVE

AND

HONOR

SIMON & SCHUSTER
Rockefeller Center
1230 Avenue of the Americas
New York, NY 10020

For information about special discounts for bulk purchases,
please contact Simon & Schuster Special Sales:
1-800-456-6798 or business@simonandschuster.com

Designed by Karolina Harris

Manufactured in the United States of America

10   9   8   7   6   5   4   3

Library of Congress Cataloging-in-Publication Data

Wallace, Randall.
Love and honor/Randall Wallace.
p. cm.
1. United States—History—Revolution, 1775–1783—Fiction.
PS3573.A429 L685 2004
813/.54 22   2004051761
ISBN 0-7432-6519-X

To Thurman Wallace,
Andrew Wallace,
and Cullen Wallace
My father and my sons

LOVE

AND

HONOR

Chapter One

Northern Russia, 1774

TH E first howl sang across the night void and trembled the frozen air, a sound thin as the starlight poised on the blue plains of snow, with no more presence than the memory of a vanished loved one, and just as inescapable across the face of the world; and as with a ghostly visage rising before me, I might have denied that the cry existed. But the horses plunged.

Sergei Gorlov, the friend and fellow mercenary who had mentored me for the last two years in the art of cavalry warfare and who guided me now into the vast mysteries of his homeland, sat beside me, bundled beneath blankets in the open sleigh. Opposite us huddled a fat merchant, his back to Gorlov's driver, Pyotr, an ageless Russian peasant whose expert hands upon the reins had kept the horses moving briskly through the long night. And I, Kieran Selkirk, shivered beneath the sizzling stars, five thousand miles from America, and the colony of Virginia, and the cottage where my father warmed himself beside his fire at home. Or so I hoped. I tried not to think too much about him; I had learned it is not wise to dream of comfort when you dwell with danger, and have just felt the fear of your horses at the sound of wolves.

Pyotr growled the horses' names deep in his throat, and with Russian words I did not know but understood, he told them they were stupid beasts and full of perversion, yet he had a sentimental weakness for them and would consent to tighten their reins and sweep the whip above their heads. The horses did settle, and trotted on.

Their hooves fell muffled on the snow-packed road, and the sleigh's runners whisked. The tops of the trees drifted between us and the sliver of moon. The night, except for the wind sailing past, lay dead still, and I thought then that only I and the horses had heard the howl, until Pantkin, the fat merchant across from me, pulled the cloak from around his mouth, as if untroubled by the cold, and chuckled, as if unafraid, and said in French, "How much farther?"

"Shut up," Gorlov answered, without unwrapping the flannel from his own mouth, "or we'll let you measure the distance on foot."

Pantkin looked away and covered again his frosted beard, and his nose, with the twin ice rivers set in the whiskers of his mustache from the nostrils to his mouth; he covered all but his eyes, staring at the passing trees. When he had joined us two days before in Riga, I had thought Gorlov was giving him the best seat—back to the driver, screened against the wind—but I learned quickly that a swirl invaded the open sleigh when the horses were at speed; Gorlov and I, our heads against the high curved backing, sat in a dead calm, while Pantkin watched the road vanishing behind us and faced the breeze. That morning I had offered to change seats with him. Gorlov had laughed; Pantkin had only stared at me. I was glad now that he had not accepted. I had had no feeling in my feet since sundown.

Another howl rose from the darkness. Pantkin glanced at me.

The horses lurched again and threw their hooves faster. This time Pyotr did not gather them back. The sleigh seemed to grow lighter; the runners sailed on the road. I said to Gorlov, "I don't know how much farther we must go to the next station, but—"

"Twenty versts," Gorlov volunteered casually. Pantkin looked up into the treetops, as if he did not care.

I calculated the versts to be twelve miles. "I don't know your winter, or your wolves. But I know if he tries to run those horses the last twenty versts, he will kill them."

"They are Russian horses," Gorlov said. He did not uncover his mouth. He did not look at me.

When the master at the last station had shrugged and told us we could either stay or drive on with the horses we had used for eight hours already, because he had just turned out his last fresh pair, Gorlov had snatched him by the throat. The stationmaster had wept, and begged, and babbled something in Russian, repeating what I assumed to be the word for "early"—we had driven hard since crossing the border. Gorlov had cast the man into a corner, shrugged, and gone outside to order Pyotr to trace the same horses back up. While I sat beside the fire, drinking hot beer, the stationmaster grinned, said something to Pantkin, and laughed uproariously. Pantkin had walked to me and said, "The stationmaster remarks that we may catch the other sleigh. We can pick up the horses then. He finds this very funny." Then Pantkin looked at me with the same expression that had been in his eyes ever since.

The horses ran on. I stomped my feet on the wooden floor of the sleigh and felt a comforting ache. I stomped three times, and a barking rose far off, as if in response. Pyotr gave the horses' backs the lash and let them out into full gallop.

A shrill moan came from somewhere—the wood beside

us, I thought; and then it seemed the cries were everywhere: before us, beneath us, over us. The whip whistled back above the sleigh, then cracked between the horses.

Gorlov sat up. He raised his head to the wind. I leaned forward with him, and when his face turned slowly toward me, I saw nothing of his black eyes except a glimmer—not of snow, but of something hot.

Pyotr pulled back on the reins, and the sleigh stopped.

At first the noise danced—cacophonous barks and growls from a legion of demons, as if someplace distant yet far too close to the earth had opened a fissure to hell. But as the breeze of our motion died, no longer twisting around us the sound of the passing plains, Gorlov and I stood, raising our heads into that troubled calm, and I said, "Not behind."

"No," Gorlov said. "Before."

A tallow lantern hung on either side of the driver's perch. Gorlov stepped up onto the seat beside Pantkin, unslung one of the lamps, and held it aloft.

"Pyotr. *Yezdi.*"

Pyotr clucked, and the horses shambled forward. Gorlov steadied himself with his free hand, and the merchant slid into the middle of the seat as I stepped up into the corner opposite Gorlov and peered into the darkness of the road beyond. The gelding on the left jerked his snout into the shoulder of the bay mare, and she danced sideways. Pyotr tugged the left lead and urged them forward again. They went, slowly.

The mad voices grew louder, more numerous. Then they stopped. The horses halted. Gorlov raised the lantern higher and leaned forward into the night.

Circles of fire glowed ahead of us, a hundred pairs, all turned in our direction, all unblinking and still. Eyes.

A pistol boomed beside me, and the eye fires scattered, flowing across the drifts and through the ranks of fir trees. I turned and noted where beneath his cloak Gorlov replaced the pistol that I had not known he carried.

The report of the shot soaked into the hollow quiet, as if the whole dark world were an empty cathedral, and the black powder had shouted *Death!*—for all around the trees and snow and the black clouds with the moonlit edges expelled the last breath of life, and held still.

"*Yezdi,*" Gorlov whispered. The horses obeyed, feeling through the reins the wish in Pyotr's hands. Now we could hear the snow crush beneath each descent of hoof.

We came upon the rear of a sleigh; Pyotr, speaking in a reverent hush, guided the horses to the left and stopped when we were alongside the broken harnesses, where the other horses should have been standing. Pyotr lifted the lantern, the one on the right side, and I stepped out into the snow. Gorlov's boots banged across the floor behind me and crunched down at my side.

I cannot say I had any thought when seeing the clustered skeletons; in the way that I was speechless, I was thoughtless as well. The harness tracings grappled at the horses' bones and held them clustered, when no muscle or even gristle existed anymore to bind them into shape. The tongues of the sleigh led up to the box, and beyond that to the empty compartment. I knew there had been drivers, passengers, but somehow did not think of them; I realized, without reasoning, that some must have tried to run and had, like the horses, been pulled down. Others had been torn from the seats where they were clinging, stiffened already by cold and fear. Scraps clung everywhere—clothes ripped and even chewed apart in frenzy. But most of all there was blood, frozen in red clouds in the snow and churned up by paws scrambling to brace for a larger bite. I cannot say I wondered then at the number and strength and hunger of the wolves that could pull down a team of horses in full flight and strip their bones so quickly; I cannot say I calculated. But suddenly I felt no cold at all, no fatigue, no darkness. I felt the great still nothingness of the Russian night.

We stared, all of us, even Pyotr's horses. And then a cry rent that silence, a shrill howl sharp on the air, and we were grabbing at the sides of the sleigh as Pyotr cracked the whip and the horses bit their hooves into the snow and staggered back onto the road, and we were flying.

I was sure there was nothing in heaven or hell that could catch us, but the clouds still followed us, lazily, as if we did not move, and the cries—of many voices—rose up behind.

Pyotr swung his whip; the crack was not in the open air, but against the back of the gelding. Gorlov sat very still in his corner, I sat in mine.

The merchant looked from one of us to the other. To me he said, "There are wolves in the streets of St. Petersburg."

"On two legs, or four?" I said. The merchant stared, then threw back his head and cackled. Gorlov snapped his gaze to the seat beside the merchant—toward but not at him—and I understood Gorlov's feeling, that if he were to look at Pantkin too closely, his own fear would make him want to snuff out the spark of panic already alight on the merchant's face.

The cries were drawing closer.

We sat, all of us still except for Pyotr, who leaned so far over the reins that we could see only his rounded back and not his head.

The barks were snarling, wet. Behind us. Almost beside us. I felt them at my shoulder. I looked into the merchant's eyes. They were wide, frozen open, staring straight at the road behind.

I threw off the robes, baring the uniform of the Sixth Prussian Light Horse, and ripped the saber from its scabbard. The sound of sharp steel ringing into the open air had always honed my fear, so that I had the teeth to fight, and thus the sound thrilled me now. Gorlov rose beside me, delved beneath his robes, and fumbled to reload a charge of ball into his weapon. I looked at Pantkin, tore open the bag I had carried beneath the seat, and withdrew a dagger.

"Take it!" I screamed in English. Then I yelled again in French. He stared at me, and I wanted to kill him. Fear is the fuel of fight, but panic is its poison, and when I saw it on Pantkin I turned away, desperate not to look at him again.

The sleigh flew so smoothly that the noise outside became unreal. But as I leaned out I saw a wolf gathering his legs and stretching them forward, leaping through the snow beside us, closing on the bay mare's withers. I held hard with my left hand, stretched my right, and cleaved him through the skull. He fell tumbling, spurting; the racing horde behind us flowed around his scattering form and chased on.

Gorlov swung his pistol over the back of the sleigh and fired into another bundle of screaming gray fur. The ball tore a forepaw off the wolf, and yet he did not cease running, slid-ing only for an instant on his snout through the snow, then scrambling forward on three legs and a shortened stump, still running but receding into the pack.

I leaned again from the side of the sleigh and began to hack.

Then there were no beasts close enough for me to reach, and the horde began to fall back. I raised my saber and shook it in the air, saw the blood frozen on the bare blade, and stared at the still-howling wolves. I looked forward. My triumph van-ished. We had gained a long downslope that gave the horses speed; but now the road loomed ahead with a corresponding half mile of gentle climb.

At the bottom of the grade, the runners of the sleigh shuddered through deeper drifts of snow, and the horses' heads plunged and bobbed, and the brave animals bore on. Behind us, our pursuers howled with new lust.

I stood facing forward now, hearing the baying but looking no more, watching only the rippling backs of the mare and the gelding as they sprayed steaming lather against Pyotr's knotted form. He cracked the whip—no more into their flesh, but in the air above them, to tell them that they had done their duty, but more than duty was required.

I looked toward heaven—a habit I thought I had given up—and we seemed to have stopped beneath the glory of the stars; yet the wind still rushed into my face, and the icy lashes of my eyes clung in their sweating sockets. The top of the rise came slowly nearer, and the horses gained it, staggered, and galloped on.

Before us, glowing with the blue opalescence of snow beneath stars, lay an endless flat plain.

Gorlov stood beside me, staring ahead. I do not remember looking at him; but I recall the realization, coming to me with absolute certainty, that the next few moments upon that plain would tell us whether we would live or die—and that Gorlov, a man of battle, knew it, too.

The wolves poured over the rise behind us. I did not have to turn to look at them; I could hear them. And I could hear them gaining.

I did look at Gorlov then. He was staring at the bareness before us. And then he looked at the merchant.

Pantkin had not moved since I offered him the dagger, and had remained with his robes pulled tightly about him. I thought perhaps he had died that way, and frozen. But as Gorlov continued to stare at him, Pantkin's eyes quivered upward.

A sound came from within the merchant—not from his lips, but rather like a screeching inside his head. When Gorlov grabbed at him he did not move, yet the sound from within the merchant grew louder and more shrill, and when Gorlov lifted him the merchant's arms stayed clutched to his body, his knees drawn up and rigid, as if he were still sitting, though Gorlov hoisted him high in the air, and with one full motion threw him out the back of the sleigh.

In the shadowy vista behind us, the body pitched along the road into the shrieking pack—and the wolves swarmed about it, gnashing teeth into it and one another, pawing chunks of snow into the air.

And we sailed on, as away from a dream.

Pyotr cracked the whip no more and did not snap the reins, but let the horses run, knowing there was yet no real safety on the open plain, and that if he should allow the team to withdraw too soon from the frenzy of the first flight, there would be no hope of inspiring them again for a second. We bore swiftly across the powdered tract, then twisted through a section of wood, curling down at last upon what back in Virginia I would have called a hollow—an open depression of ground, where stood a hovel of notched logs encircled by a broken fence. A lantern shone beside its door, and an inner fire cast orange light upon the paper of its windows. The horses wobbled through another patch of drifted snow, clattered upon the bridge crossing a frozen stream, slowed of their own accord, and halted beside the lantern.

Pyotr sprang from his box, pounded with his hands— frozen to clubs within his mittens—against the latch of the shed doors, and finally threw them wide. Just then the door of the main house opened, and a fat man with hair growing from his chin, nostrils, and inner ears—but none from his head— appeared. He gripped a blanket about himself, and clearly had retired to his bed with the blissful assurance that anyone traveling that night was already dead; he yawned, probed with his tongue around his foul teeth, and turned back inside, leaving the door ajar.

I leapt down into the snow and barely caught myself from falling when my knees gave way. I was weak with the urge to regurgitate, though my stomach was empty. Gorlov gazed across the broken fence and snowy pasture, stretched as though he had been sleeping, and stepped down. Pyotr instantly tugged the horses toward the door he had opened for them.

I retrieved my bag from beneath the seat before the sleigh should slide away. "Well," I said in French to Gorlov, "my feet feel as if they shall kill me, so I suppose I will not lose them tonight."

"No, not tonight," Gorlov said. "Tomorrow."

Still feeling the urge to vomit, and challenged by Gorlov's bravado, I said, "You pledged to see me through to St. Petersburg safely. If I lose a toe, then I swear you'll lose a finger. If I a foot, then you a hand."

Gorlov withdrew from beneath the seat his own bag and that of the late merchant Pantkin. "What need has a cavalryman of feet?" He shrugged.

I was formulating some rejoinder as we walked toward the open door when something in Pyotr's voice stopped me. The sleigh had not yet moved; he was speaking to the horses in words I did not know, yet I heard the begging there. Bracing his short bandy legs, reaching up with his hands on the harness, he gazed at the bay mare, sang to her, tugged at her rein. The mare did not resist, she simply did not respond. Then her left foreleg gave way. She stumbled against the gelding, who pitched in his traces beside her and cried out, then she swayed back the other way, curved her neck around as if to bite at her back, and fell dead.

Pyotr, still clinging to the leather of her collar, sagged into the snow; the gelding, pulled down in his own harness, struggled and kicked. I ran to the gelding, freed his traces, and trotted him into the barn. He pranced gladly to leave the dead mare, and if I had had Gorlov's pistol in my hand, I might have shot him; compared with hers, his chest was clean of froth and chafing. She had pulled us through.

And now we pulled her. With ropes around her neck and forehooves we tugged her into the barn, leaving no bait for the wolves. The stationmaster, despairing of ever getting any rest in this perpetual winter night, threw down his rope and trudged back into the lodge as soon as we reached the straw. Gorlov at least stood with me for a moment. "See?" he said, looking down at the carcass of the mare, already stiffening with cold. "A Russian horse. She dies only when her task is done." Then he, too, dropped his rope and walked out of the barn.

"Tankoo, Myaster!" Pyotr said, in the few words of English he knew. "Morrow—go, go!" He sat down at the mare's head, and began to loosen the nooses from her.

"Yes, Pyotr," I said. "Thank you."

I wanted to put my hand upon Pyotr's head, but instead I patted the mare's. It served as well. When I walked from the barn, Pyotr was holding the mare's head in his lap, and was weeping.

Chapter Two

IT was that night, in the reeking hut that served as way
station, that I allowed myself to ponder for the first time
since entering Russia the secret that sent me there—a
secret I had forced far from my thoughts, as if to keep it
hidden even from myself. Inside the one-room hut, Gorlov
snoring in one bed, the stationmaster snoring in another, and
Pyotr snoring on a pile of blankets in a corner near the fire, I
sat before the stone hearth, unable to sleep, staring into the
low flames, and I heard again those words, spoken to me three
months before. . . .

"It will not be easy."

The warning took me back to London, and the gloom of
that city's harbor, and the night when I stood at the rail of a
wooden ship tethered to the fog-shrouded dock. All around
the cockney voices of the sailors and dockworkers called out
in their work, but I spoke to no one, and stared across the
water.

Still I noticed the slender sailor who moved silently up
the gangway and stopped in the shadows near me. From the

corner of my eye I saw him studying me, as if wondering who I might be; in my cavalry boots, with the saber outlined beneath the cloak, I was clearly not a man of the sea. Finally the man approached and quietly spoke. "Are you Kieran Selkirk, of Virginia?"

"I am."

"Someone wants to meet you. Another American—like us." His accent was of the middle northern colonies: Pennsylvania, I thought.

"I've booked passage home," I said. "The ship sails in an hour. And I don't know a soul in London."

"Someone knows you. He is a patriot." The man lifted my bag and turned toward the gangway; as he did, I drew my saber and tucked its razor edge to his throat.

"That's a dangerous word, friend. And I don't go down any dark streets with you until you tell me this patriot's name."

He held his neck cocked back from the blade and his body frozen; his eyes shifted left and right before he whispered, "Benjamin Franklin."

A N hour later I sat at attention, waiting in a rich man's London apartment, all the curtains drawn, the sailor sitting in another chair beside me.

The door opened and Benjamin Franklin entered, in all his glory: spectacles balanced below his sparkling eyes, a distinctive fringe of straight hair skirting the broad bald dome of his head, rich clothes fitting tightly around his formidable girth. He barged in without ceremony, already talking. "Good evening! Thank you for coming," the great man said, and I noted that he did not speak my name, even as the sailor who had only whispered it now quickly slipped from the room. I jumped to my feet and accepted the hand Franklin extended. "Please do sit down," he said. "My valet will bring you food and drink if you are hungry." His English valet had drifted through the door behind him.

"Thank you, no."

Franklin could tell I was excited to meet him; at least he seemed amused. He waved his valet away, waited for the soft closing of the door, and then asked me a blunt question: "Do you know who Catherine the Great is?"

Clearing my throat, I answered, "The Empress of Russia?"

"They call her the Tsarina. That's Tssaarr—ee—nah," he pronounced, trilling his tongue with the *r* and crinkling his nose. "The Russians are particular about how you pronounce it. But I understand you have a facility for languages."

"I speak some French and German, sir."

"The Tsarina is a full-blooded German, having been a minor princess there when the royal matchmakers discovered her as a wife for the heir to the Russian throne. And the Russian court speaks French." He said this in a way that told me my qualifications had been carefully considered. "Have you heard anything else about her?"

"No, sir," I answered, after a slight pause.

Seeing through my hesitation, Franklin laughed. "Of course you have! But Voltaire tells me that story about her and the horse is an exaggeration." He heaved himself into an embroidered chair, wincing as he sat; yet it was not the pain of gout that stole the smile from his face but something else, something that frightened him. "Catherine is brilliant. Beautiful. Utterly ruthless. Shortly after she and her husband rose to the throne, he was found strangled. Now all the power of the Russian empire is hers—and the fate of America rests in her hands."

At first I thought Franklin was joking; how could the ruler of a country on the other side of the earth from ours, and with scarcely any ties to our past or present, be crucial to the future of America? But I saw that the man was dead serious.

"I have friends among certain societies you joined while at university," he said carefully, "and from those sources I hear you have reason for hating the British."

"I prefer to think of myself as loving liberty, Mr. Franklin."

"Touché! And yet when your friends went on to gentler trades—to the study of law, to the clergy, to commerce—you came to Europe to learn the art of war. You could have chosen a more peaceful outlet for your passions, for I understand you are an eloquent man."

"No man is as eloquent as the soldier who stands his ground."

Behind his spectacles, Franklin's eyes danced. He took pleasure in my reply, not just for its passion but for something else; it was as if I were a puzzle piece, but I would not know for many months the picture he was assembling in that brilliant mind of his. He said, "We have discovered that the British are plotting a secret bargain with Catherine the Great." Before I could absorb that pronouncement, Franklin's valet entered with a tea service and placed it on the table between us. Franklin, who missed nothing, noticed my glance at the valet, and said, "Don't worry about Berwick; I trust him with my life."

"And with mine, sir?" I said.

"You are a wit! That is most encouraging! Berwick, prepare a purse with funds for passage to Paris and from thence to St. Petersburg." Berwick bowed and left the room, having scarcely raised his eyes, and Franklin went on to me: "I understand in Paris you have a Russian friend, who trained you as a soldier."

"Sergei Gorlov. But what—"

"The British are asking Catherine to provide them with

twenty thousand Russian soldiers to go to America and put down all resistance there," Franklin said. I must have paled, for Franklin emphasized that he had spoken correctly. "Yes, twenty thousand. For American independence to have any hope, we must rely on the fact that the British are stretched thin throughout their empire. They are short of infantry. But twenty thousand Russian troops, unleashed in America, fresh from their brutal victory over the Turks . . . Well, I see that the possibility disturbs you as much as it does me."

"What do you want me to do, Mr. Franklin?"

"We have no advocate in Russia. Our British masters will not permit that. So I want you to go to Russia, not as an American patriot but as a mercenary who happens to be a British subject. Ironically, Catherine has need of foreign mercenaries, for the Cossacks are rebelling inside Russia, and her own soldiers are reluctant to fight them, having an almost mystical reverence for the Cossack cavalry." As a newcomer to the mercenary units in the Crimea, I had encountered Cossacks, and had even shared a campfire with them in the company of Gorlov, my Russian friend and mentor. The Cossacks, tribal horsemen from the Ukraine, were both fearless and deeply emotional, and I had seen in Gorlov the odd combination of contempt and respect for them that Franklin was describing. He continued, "So I want you to go and volunteer for every danger, especially against the Cossacks. The British will see you as an ally and may even help you, for the sooner Catherine settles her own little rebellion, the sooner she might help them with theirs."

"If I fight to help Catherine, and the British, how does that help America?"

Franklin's face, I thought, went blank. "Boldness, skill, confidence verging on the edge of arrogance—these stand out in a place like Catherine's Russia. If you are brave enough, you will come to the Tsarina's attention. And when you do, speak for America. Show her our side of the story."

"You want me to go to Russia . . . as a spokesman? To an empress?"

"Why not? Back at the College of William and Mary you were noted for your skill in debate. And you were the leader of your class in discussions of French progressive thinkers like Voltaire and Diderot, philosophers Catherine greatly admires. You have both wit and eloquence."

"Then why do I feel so speechless?"

Franklin smiled again, then just as quickly frowned. "The task I send you on is dangerous, my young friend," he said. "At stake is the future of the American continent, and though the British can't hang you as a traitor while you are in Catherine's Russia, they would certainly have no hesitation to murder you if they distrusted your motives. So you must go there quickly, before the Russian harbors unfreeze and British ships start bringing in the news of fresh revolts in America. The overland trip is nearly impossible . . . but the right man might make it. The right man might get to Russia, become noticed, and fall under the protection of the Tsarina before the British delegates there become suspicious. The right man—a man with a keen sword and a keener mind—might infiltrate the Russian court, and, when the opportunity came, speak, with passionate conviction, for America. The choice lies with Catherine. The right man might reach her and plead our case. Are you the right man?"

I don't remember how long I sat there without replying. Franklin sat back in his chair and answered for me. "Your eyes are fierce," he said, "and bright with the challenge."

I had been staring at the fire. Now I looked at him and saw that he was smiling. I was not sure what made him smile, but of this much I was sure: Franklin knew more than he was telling me.

Chapter Three

WHEN I awoke the next morning, Gorlov had already stoked the fire, and my boots were smoking beside it. He had his back to the blaze and his nightcoat hiked up to warm his backside, but stood insensible to the heat. He was staring at me, his black eyes steady beneath the brows that had always reminded me of the bristle of a cannon brush.

"Damn you, Gorlov!" I said, stirring from the blankets. "Do you expect to save my feet from the cold by setting them on fire?" He turned distractedly to the boots and swatted them from the hearth. I arose fully dressed, not having wanted to associate too closely with the bedding the stationmaster had thrown me the night before. "Why are you watching me that way?"

Becoming aware then of the odd attention he had focused on me, he turned away suddenly, plunging his face into a basin of water that could have been for shaving, had we not given up on razors a week before. Gorlov's chin was now nearly as dark as his mustache, while mine bore only an irritating blond stubble. Tossing his head, slinging the water, he began to dress himself. Having been so oddly perused by Gorlov—who had in the past displayed the soldier's ability to ignore a comrade so thoroughly that a kind of privacy is possible even in the most miserable and immodest conditions—perhaps I cast a more watchful eye in his direction; as he pulled on his shirt I noticed the welts on his left wrist. Catching my glance, he bared his teeth in a grin and said, "The merchant!"

So Pantkin had resisted, had not frozen completely after all, had clung to life, if the only purchase life offered was the arm of his executioner. Somehow I felt better toward him, knowing that he had possessed some instinct to fight back. It was something I needed to believe—that all men possess, somewhere, the dignity to value their own lives, if only enough to scratch the arm of the man who throws you to the wolves.

Pyotr joined us at the table and we breakfasted on slices of black bread soaked in hot animal fat. My first three days in Russia I had refused the fat, but had finally tried it in order to stave off the hunger of the journey, and discovered then its powers of warmth. During the meal, the stationmaster, as he served us, glanced at my uniform—the cavalry boots, the brown riding trousers with yellow stripe, the green tunic— and made some comment to Gorlov, snickering.

Gorlov, sopping a final corner of bread around the last grease in his bowl and stuffing his mouth, mumbled, "The stationmaster says that the German officer wears a colorful nightgown." Pyotr put down his wooden mug of grog and stared most intently at his empty plate.

"He does, does he?" I said. "Tell him that this is my traveling uniform, that I have a formal uniform preserved clean in my bag. Tell him that I am not German, but merely served with a German cavalry unit when I fought in the Crimea, though I was born in Virginia, the greatest dominion of the

British Commonwealth. But nevertheless, he is correct: I do wear a German uniform. Tell him that if he insults this uniform, or any uniform I choose to wear, I will kill him. Tell him that, Gorlov." Gorlov merely continued what he had begun doing during my speech, namely sucking first one greasy finger and then another; so I leaned forward and said hotly, "Tell him!"

Gorlov turned lazily and muttered something to the stationmaster. It was a phrase of extreme brevity in comparison with the oration it was intended to translate, and, not believing the Russian language to be one of such economy, I assumed Gorlov had been something less than literal. The stationmaster busied himself removing cooking utensils from the fire, and looked at me no more.

Pyotr rose, pulled on his hat and coat, and went out to the barn. Gorlov stood, fished in his pocket, and tossed three copper coins onto the table. The stationmaster shuffled quickly over and reached for the coins; when he grasped, he found my hand between his and the money. He shifted a glance to the ax leaning beside the door.

"Tell him he gets two coins, not three," I said to Gorlov, while looking at the stationmaster. "Tell him he has the horse, which he will butcher and sell for beef. Tell him the next time an officer, or any man paying good money, stays beneath his roof, to give that visitor clean sheets."

Gorlov sighed and held out a hand palm up, in a manner that conveyed to the stationmaster: *See for yourself; I can do nothing with him—either kill him or let him go.* The stationmaster took his hand from mine, and I put one coin into my coat pocket and left him the rest.

Outside Pyotr had drawn the sleigh from the barn. We boarded, and covered ourselves with the warming furs. Pyotr leaned down, scooped up a handful of snow, and buried his face in it, scrubbing; when he emerged his visage glowed red with the circulation, his ears a cherry pink, his round ball of a nose bright as a Christmas apple. He hurled a spray of snow over the new horses, leapt into the box, clucked, and we were away.

A brisk wind blew gamboling fairies of snow across the blinding steppe and up into a crystalline blue sky. I took the coin from my pocket and dropped it in Gorlov's lap. "Give it to Pyotr. Tell him to buy gloves."

"I don't know why you make such a fuss," Gorlov said, tucking the coin away. "Not every jest is an insult."

"You know me not as a man who despises jesting. The question was not of insult, but of respect. The man showed no respect for Pyotr at the death of the horse, and no respect for me, with the sheets he gave me. Someone who gives me clean sheets can jest with me all he likes."

"Clean sheets, you say! When we have not bathed for a week!" He made no mention of having received a clean bed himself.

We drove on, nearing St. Petersburg. The land rolled and pitched, the trees reached higher and grouped into sheltering forests. We began to encounter villages—first a trading post only, with a cross painted on its otherwise bare side, later two wretched houses next to a crooked shelter bearing a cross, then farther along a broader knot of houses, with a larger, less-crooked church. We stopped before noon at a half-built inn, where we changed horses and had what passed for a meal before setting off again, hopeful of reaching St. Petersburg before darkness.

JUST after leaving the hamlet, when topping a rise that overlooked a long flat valley of forest, we saw a plume of smoke floating into the clear bright sky. Pyotr, who had been singing, fell silent. We descended farther along the road into the valley, still watching the brown plume curling toward us. Halfway between the apparent source of the smoke and the village from which we had just come, Gorlov spoke suddenly to Pyotr, who pulled off the road and into the trees.

The wood stood thick, the trees growing so closely together that there seemed no possible lane for a sleigh; but Pyotr never let the horses stop, turning them tightly around this cluster, about that fallen trunk, moving us steadily across the snow frozen hard within the shade, so that we were soon deeply hidden, glimpsing the sunny road only through sparse angles between the trees. Pyotr alighted from the box, scurried back to the spot where we had entered, and brushed drifts over the tracks where we had left the hard pack of the road. It was this precaution that most put me on my guard; I swung out of the sleigh and stepped to the heads of the horses, to keep them quiet.

When Pyotr joined me there and saw me with the horses' heads turned away from the road and their noses tugged down from the wind, he shut one eye, peered at me with the other, and smiled, approving of my horseman's knowledge. Gorlov remained seated in the sleigh, his hands beneath his coat.

We did not wait long. Through the first slit in the trees we saw a horseman pass along the road, and then another, and then others, two and three abreast. They slouched beneath smocks of horsehide tied at the waist with rope belts, wolf-pelt shawls upon their shoulders. Their leader, whom I glimpsed again through another gap in the trees, wore upon his skull a hollowed wolf head, the snout cast out above his eyes and still baring the sharp white teeth; the fur that once warmed the wolf's neck now covered the neck of the man. The entire band, as nearly as I could tell from my limited vantage, carried curved sabers at their sides and iron knives thrust into the ropes at their waists, and they sat thoughtlessly upon their horses, as if they might fall asleep there at dusk, ride all night, and wake at dawn fully refreshed.

Pyotr, stroking the neck of one of his own horses, and staring in the same direction as I, whispered one word: *"Kazaki!"*

The last man—the fifty-third, for I had learned in the Crimea to count everything I saw—passed us, and we waited ten minutes before I remounted the sleigh, and then we waited five minutes more. While I had encountered Cossacks before, these bore scant resemblance to the formal cavalry units I had seen fighting in the Crimea. This group had all the motliness of outlaws, yet there was a disciplined manner to their movement, if nothing more than in the common expertise with which they sat their horses. Further, I saw in them a strategy: brigands, I thought, would burn only if they believed their smoke would not bring enemies upon them, but these men had torched a town on a clear morning and ridden slowly toward the next prize, giving the citizens a chance to ponder what ransom they might pay to be spared. And all this within a day's journey of one of Russia's two capitals.

Since Franklin had mentioned Cossacks to me, I had read everything I could find about them, but that was precious little. I had gleaned that they were descendants of runaways, a wild-born mix of fugitive serfs and escaped Tartars, and were happiest to be living on the run and taking whatever pleased them. They were piously religious or relentlessly profane, as it suited them. They frequently sold their swords to the highest bidder and were known to be utterly loyal, right up to the moment when they weren't. They might demand huge payments for their talents; just as readily they might fight you for nothing, as, apparently, they were fighting the Tsarina's rule from their homelands, deep in the Don River regions of southern Russia.

When Pyotr had us back on the road again, skimming through the burned-out village and then beyond, I said to Gorlov, "What are Cossacks doing this close to St. Petersburg?"

"Cossacks live in the Ukraine," Gorlov said. "There are no Cossacks here."

He lied so definitely that I might have thought my impression was mistaken, had I not heard what Pyotr whispered. We rode for another half hour in silence. "Gorlov," I said at last, "I have never known you to have borne a pistol within your coat. Not on a battlefield, and not in a brothel. But here we are in your own country, and you carry one now."

He did not look at me. "So what?"

"Should I have one, too?"

He turned his head toward me then, his brows rising parallel to his mustache as he grinned.

I looked away, and then said, "I want you to teach me Russian."

"Russian!" he boomed. "Nobody worth talking to speaks Russian in Russia! The Empress herself understands it poorly, and writes it worse! Russian! Hah!" He laughed as if I were a great fool, insulting me so that I would tell him my reasons.

"I expect it will be convenient for me to know what lies you are telling about me in my presence, and how much you are cheating me when I ask you to make purchases on my behalf."

Gorlov smiled again, this time without affectation. "Well," he said, "Russian is not without its beauty. In fact, I would say this: If I had to choose one language for whispering into a woman's ear, it would be French; to write an artillery manual, I would choose German; to make a speech, I would use English—if I could speak it, which I cannot, yet I have heard it, and I know how the English love speeches, so it must be the best. But if I had to choose one language for all purposes, that language would be Russian."

"Then teach me," I said.

He thought a moment, sucking down on his upper lip until his lower lip was in the place of his mustache. "Perhaps I had best begin with words you might need for a specific purpose. Now suppose . . . just suppose you have met the Tsarina, and she sends a handmaiden to visit you, a young but experienced girl, and you would say something to the lady to prove that you are a gentleman. Well, you might say, softly, something like . . ."

And in this way we passed the miles, until, as night was falling, we crossed the bridges into St. Petersburg.

Chapter Four

I S A Y we entered the city, though I cannot state that I had yet seen it, descrying only lamps burning occasionally through the darkness, hazed throughout by a fog rising up from the endless canals and floating over the snow. We stopped before a clapboard inn so tall the fog hid its upper stories. The light from its leaded windows warmed the mist upon the street. A painted sign above the door proclaimed the house as the Duke of Holstein Inn, but the setting was more British than Saxon, and the fat form of an enameled bird affixed to the wall beside the entrance gave the place the name by which we would know it, the White Goose. Gorlov and I dismounted from the sleigh, and Pyotr, without another word, drove away into the night. "Where is he going?" I asked Gorlov. "I wanted to give him something for his service."

"He has family here and stays with them. You will see him again."

On the main floor of the inn was a tavern room; Gorlov and I walked the length of this room and took a table beside the blaze. The only others in the room—two Hollanders speaking French with Dutch accents at one table, and three Germans speaking German at another—looked up as we passed, but they quickly resumed their conversations.

Dropping into the chair nearest the fire and throwing open his coat to let in the heat, Gorlov said, "Do we get drunk first, then eat, or eat first and then get drunk? Or do we get drunk at dinner? Or just get drunk and forget dinner?" He slapped his head and said, "Oh, I forget you are too young to behave as a man. Perhaps we will have dinner, with milk."

A sallow waiter, coming quickly over, stared at us for a moment and said to me, "*Speissekarte?* . . . Menu? . . ." Then he looked at Gorlov and said, *"Menjek?"*

Gorlov erupted from his seat. Banging the table back, he shouted in French, "You speak Polish to *me*? You dare call *me* a Pole?"

Grabbing Gorlov's arm as he raised his fist at the retreating waiter, I laughed and said, "Stand easy, Gorlov! The man was only having a joke."

"A joke?" Gorlov bellowed. As I gripped him back he shouted to the waiter, "That's a good way to die poor, my friend! First I remove your family jewels, and then I remove your head!"

The waiter approached again, head lowered, but with the calm of having faced angry patrons before. "I meant no disrespect, sir, I had only to establish that you were indeed Russian. You see, we do not allow Poles here. It is bad for business."

Gorlov's blood rushed from his cheeks to his ears. He laughed. The Germans and the Dutch chuckled, too. The waiter brought us wine and a roasted fowl.

As we ate, the room began to fill. Roughly a third of the men entering wore uniforms, in colors I took to be Russian, though I noticed them, from their accents and languages, to be Scottish, Prussian, English, Swedish, and other of the

Scandinavian blonds. Among the rest of the company, wearing the latest in stylish European dress—waistcoat and jacket and ruffled shirt and even slippers like the French wear—were Dutch shipbuilders, British surgeons, German engineers. By the time we were finishing the last of the smoked sturgeon Gorlov had insisted upon, tobacco smoke rolled along the ceiling in billows, stirred by polyglot tongues.

When the waiter had cleared our table of the last dish, and we had sent him to instruct the concierge to prepare us rooms for the night, a freckled man in a cavalry major's uniform brought his tankard over to us, and said in the English of a Scotsman: "My greetins to ye, gentlemen. Ah couldna help b' notice tha' one o' ya is wearin' cavalry boots and a captain's uniform o' the Burgessmeir Campaign. There was a young colonial wi' a Scot's name who distinguished himself mos' harty in tha' bit o' fightin', and Ah'd jus' like to say, sir, tha' if tha' be you, then Ah drink to ye, sir. And if i' be not you, than Ah drink to ye anyway, for wearin' o' the uniform Ah once fought in meself!"

"Kieran Selkirk, sir," I said, standing and offering my hand; he shifted his tankard to his left, wiped his right quickly on his coat, and shook my hand most heartily. "If I am the one you mean, I thank you. And if not, I thank you anyway, and lift a glass back."

"Selkirk?" the Scotsman said. "Selkirk it was! Barman! Full glasses to the Highland Horseman and his friend! A toast to Kieran Selkirk!" The barman sent his boy scurrying to fill our glasses, and when we and the Scotsman toasted, others around the room joined in the draught.

"Tam MacFee!" our visitor said, accepting the chair I offered him. Most of the others in the room went back to their own conversations, while several rose and drifted over, within the glow of the fire and within earshot of our table. I sat again and introduced MacFee to Gorlov, who shook hands with the Scot quietly and made no indication that he did not understand English.

"Have ye arrived tonight only?" asked MacFee.

"Two hours ago," I said.

MacFee wanted to introduce us to another professional cavalryman, a Norwegian named Laarsen, whom we not only knew already but had fought beside in the Crimea. That reunion brightened Gorlov and shifted the conversation to French, in which tongue Gorlov regaled the company with battle legends and delighted in telling MacFee why he sometimes called me "Svet," a nickname derived from the Russian word for "light"—because, Gorlov claimed, of the mad glow that came into my eyes just before a mounted charge with sabers.

We remained in the room amid further toasts and revelry. I met numerous soldiers, artisans, and merchants, all called from faraway places to the riches of Russia. Gorlov had a jolly time and told more tales, stretching the truth beyond recognition and ultimately devaluing the believability of all that he had said, until I must certainly have seemed a coward, to have been called courageous by as grand a liar as Gorlov.

Gorlov remained boisterous throughout the evening, and was thoroughly happy when at last we took leave of our company and accepted two keys from the innkeeper, who bade us, "Good night, Count Gorlov. And good night to you, too, sir."

We had climbed halfway to the second floor when it hit me.

"Count?" I said to Gorlov. *"Count?"*

"You never asked me," he said sleepily, stumbling slightly on the stairs.

Chapter Five

OUR rooms stood adjacent, off the central part of the wooden corridor. I bade Gorlov good night at his doorway and walked down to my own.

I found a chamber more hospitable than any accommodation I had had in Paris or London. An iron brazier hung in the corner, warming the room with orange charcoal of a smoky and pleasant aroma. The bedding lay turned down, exposing a proper pillow. Beside the bed on a three-footed table stood a candle, its light reflecting against a narrow frosted window, which revealed, upon my scraping away a porthole in the icy mist of its panes, a view of the street. I sat down upon the bed and through the froth of my fatigue drank in the heady brew of having crossed the world, arriving at a destination I had thought I might never see alive.

I opened the bag beside me, and from its depths I withdrew my writing case. Strapped beneath its tin cover was a packet of scribblings of my own authorship: letters begun and never completed, jottings of thoughts that I would share with souls beyond the reach of human postage, the fragments of a diary. But it was not these that I sought. Lying precisely in the middle of the stack of clean sheets at the bottom of the case lay another paper, concealed thus among its fellows. It was a letter of introduction from Franklin to the French ambassador to Russia. Now, having arrived in St. Petersburg, I did what I had not done since the night three months before, when the letter and writing case first came into my hand: I withdrew the epistle and read it.

I replaced the letter in the stack and set the paper back into the writing case.

I undressed, put the dagger beneath my pillow, lay down, and stared into the low flames, unable to sleep.

I felt the weight of my own importance. The responsibility itself did not frighten me; I could do this, I had believed so immediately. Benjamin Franklin himself seemed so sure of it, and twenty-four-year-old cavalry officers do not tend to doubt their abilities.

But now the enormity of what I was attempting stretched before me like the endless forests of Russia. I had made it into the country only by the grace of God and the saber, and that initial step was nothing compared to the distance I had still to cross.

And yet, as I lay warm within that bed in the inn at St. Petersburg, and stared at the wooden ceiling lit by the blue light of the star shine reflected through the frosted window by the Russian snow, I believed I could accomplish it all. I believed because . . . well, because I believed. I believed in America; I believed in myself as an American. I believed that the child of a king or a queen was not likely to be healthier of spirit, mind, or body than that born of a farmer (in fact, I confess to a prejudice in the opposite direction). Like all men, I believed God thought as I did.

More specifically, I believed that Catherine of Russia also

believed as I did, for though she was a queen, she was not born one. She had risen to her position through intelligence and talent, and that fact alone reassured me that she could hear my simple statement, *America will prevail,* and would believe it.

I burrowed deeper into my bed and tried to take comfort in such thoughts. Soon I was fast asleep.

Chapter Six

T H E next morning I rose early, rang for the chamber boy, and washed and shaved in the hot water I had him bring me. Having sent the boy to the laundry with my traveling uniform and soiled linen, and wanting to save my formal uniform for such time as it might be necessary, I dressed in the civilian clothes I had carried in my bag, locked my room, and tapped at Gorlov's door, intending not to wake him if he were slumbering deeply. Hearing no stir, I left him to his rest and went downstairs.

In the dining room I breakfasted on tea, cheese, and black bread; and, as I had the night before, I felt strangely buoyant, alone and alive in a vigorous world. I returned upstairs to fetch my coat and, still hearing nothing at Gorlov's door, wound back to the lower floor and out into the street.

Lying as it does in the earth's northern latitudes, St. Petersburg greets the sun late in winter and loses it hardly at all during the summer—so I had been told in London. It was now eight o'clock, and early April, here on the brink of the Gulf of Finland. The frozen ground whispered forth a mist in promise of thaw, and the yellow morning light colored these vapors like buttermilk. Sleighs slithered through the street.

I was surprised to see Pyotr waiting in his sleigh at the front door. "Good morning!" I called out, trusting my smile to tell him what the words meant. He looked at me expectantly, clearly hoping to be of service, so I happily stepped in. "Tnanski Prospeckt," I announced. He turned, smiled, and clucked to the horses.

All cities have two faces—their countenance of hauteur in their architectural landmarks, and their grimace of misery in the squalor of their slums—but nowhere had I seen the masks so jarringly juxtaposed as in St. Petersburg. Seeing the ordered architecture of many fine homes, churches, and public buildings, I thought at first that St. Petersburg could be taken for any European city—Vienna, Berlin, Stockholm—but as we skimmed across a wooden bridge spanning the main canal that bordered the German suburb, I saw that we had left Europe behind and had entered Russia again. Unpainted gray houses squatted like solidified fog on the icy ground, their lower halves stained by repeated flooding; rot showed in the planks at the bases, though the structures were not old enough for the saw marks on their upper members to have weathered away. Tsar Peter I, wishing a port for his landlocked country, had beaten back the Swedes and founded this city in a swamp on the shores of a frigid gulf, and for the last seventy-five years the workers who lived in these common hovels I now passed had continued to wage the war against nature that their great Tsar had begun, digging canals, rechanneling streams, draining marsh, erecting great structures. Builders toiled everywhere along the main canals, and they set up a din as if they believed that they could force back the sea and the cold with noise alone. Crews of men, chained together, dragged masses of timbers and stone up to sites where carpenters and joiners sawed and hammered. Engineers shouted orders in German, and supervisors responded by whipping the chained men and shouting in Russian. I assumed these workers to be prisoners and so was shocked to glimpse a group of them, reaching the end of a long pull, shake loose their chains and drag them back to another great bundle of lumber, only to truss themselves up again; they bore the bonds placidly, just as they accepted the lash.

Pyotr drove me to a broad lane that lay beside the Neva, the sky reflecting blue upon the solid mask of ice hiding the river's deep flow. Between the lane and riverbank rose great houses, square as German town halls, ornate as French snuffboxes. *"Nomer pyat,"* I said to Pyotr. Number five.

I soon found myself stepping from the carriage, out onto a snowy lane lined by mansions. I stood before a fine residence from whose rooftop flew the flag of France, marking the home of that country's ambassador to the Court of Catherine the Great.

I approached the door and knocked; as it opened, I began the speech I had prepared: *"Bonjour. Je suis Kieran Selkirk. Je voudrais présenter une lettre à Monsieur . . ."*

Then I faltered as I saw that the door had been opened not by a house servant, but by a woman whose tumbling curls of auburn hair framed eyes of luminous green. Her lavender dress ought to have clashed with her coloring; it did not. Her expression, one eyebrow lifted higher than the other, was fixed from the moment I first saw her, and she had chosen it, I was sure, before she spoke to me; but her eyes studied me closely. "Mademoiselle," I said quickly, and bowed. She stepped back, admitting me into the mansion foyer, and sighing as if she had been welcoming men all day.

"You say you have a letter for my father?" she asked in English that made it clear her native tongue was French. "I will take it," and seeing me pause, she went on impatiently, "Oh, come, my father is with his mistress. You may trust me!"

With laughter in her eyes, she reached out her hand. I realized then that my embarrassment was a delight to her, and increasing it was a game she was quite used to playing. I said, this time in English, "My name is Kieran Selkirk. From America."

"Charlotte DuBois," she returned, with a flirting curtsey that involved scarcely more than a bob of her head. She extended her hand again. "The letter?"

"It is only that it was sent confidentially—"

She plucked the letter from my hand and snapped it open, then read aloud: "'Please help this young man, Kieran Selkirk, and his friend Sergei Gorlov with necessary introductions for the mutual benefit of our nations.' Signed by Benjamin Franklin! My, that is impressive!"

She paused at the arrival, visible through the foyer windows, of a carriage discharging a gangling young man with pomaded hair and a Russian uniform. Prancing up the walkway, he entered the foyer without knocking, then seemed confused by my presence, but Mademoiselle DuBois greeted his appearance easily, like the delivery of a piece of furniture. "There you are, Rodeon!" she said. "Go into the parlor and I shall join you in a moment." She took his arm, tucked him through the parlor door, and shut it behind him, then turned quickly back to me. "I wish I could visit you now, but as you can see I am occupied with a prior appointment. But I will give this to my father. You may . . . rest upon me."

She gazed at me for a moment, as if to be sure I took the full meaning of her last phrase, then tucked the letter into her bosom and popped into the parlor, leaving me to let myself out.

❋

A N hour later, Gorlov, Pyotr, and I sat at a window table in the dining room of the White Goose. Gorlov was gobbling food as I sat berating my own stupidity. "I am such a fool! My glorious letter of introduction—and I let it end up between a girl's breasts."

Gorlov looked up. "Her breasts?"

"I didn't put it there, she did."

"She put it there?" he mused. "Beautiful girl?"

"Gorlov, you don't understand at all, you great hulking idiot! I'm a bumpkin, I've blundered, I've thrown away any chance we have to—"

I broke off as a magnificent carriage drawn by four white horses thundered up and slid to a stop directly outside our window. It was made of padded velvet, with blue tassels flying from its top and along the traces of its team. An envoy—I know not what else to call him—in a cardinal coat with a ruffled collar stretched around his neck like the feathers of a fighting cock emerged and trod delicately through the muck, onto the steps, and into the inn.

This dignified personage moved to the innkeeper's clerk, who sat at an anteroom desk visible to us in the dining room, and spoke to him quietly; the clerk, struck dumb at the appearance of the envoy, gestured toward the dining room, and the envoy moved to its door.

"Messieurs Selkirk et Gorlov, s'il vous plait!" the envoy sang in a majestic treble, and the whole roomful of diners gawked toward him. The innkeeper's clerk had scrambled to his feet and now pointed toward me. Walking in a fashion that kept his feet far ahead of his chin, the envoy strode to our table. Gorlov was as mute as I; but worse, he was shocked into immobility, for he sat rigid, hunched over the joint of fowl from which he had just bitten a long tear of roasted meat, his eyes wide and upon the envoy, the meat hanging from his teeth and dripping savory juices down his chin.

With his white-gloved hand the envoy withdrew an envelope from an inner pocket of the cardinal coat and held both hand and envelope above his head. After an eloquent pause, he bent at the waist as if his body possessed that single hinge, and caused the envelope to land on the precise edge of the table. Swinging back up, till the hand was again at its former height, he then found a swivel in his shoulder, and moved the palm down to his waist. "Count Gorlov," he sang, accenting his parting bow to that worthy with a click of his heels. I admit that I was not entirely unrelieved that this tower of respectability had correctly assumed the man with the half pound of roast chicken dripping from his lips to be Gorlov instead of me, and I was feeling even a bit superior when the envoy said, "Monsieur Selkirk," made another click and bow distinctly to Pyotr, and let his heels precede him from the room.

Gorlov had not moved even yet, and still held the meat stringing from his teeth. I noticed one small, tentative movement of his jaws, then another, and another, until with a gradually accelerating chewing he sucked the meat up into his gnashing mouth. With each movement of his mandible he seemed to recover his wits a little more, so that by the time he swallowed he was the old Gorlov again. Wiping his lips with his sleeve and taking a quick gulp from his tankard, he cast an eye toward the envelope and said, "From your acquaintance on Tnanski Prospeckt, eh?"

I picked up the envelope and withdrew from it an invitation, engraved in a flowing hand. I read aloud: "The Marquis DuBois requests the honor of your presence for a ball, to be held—" I looked up at Gorlov. "This is for tomorrow night!"

He paused a moment, sniffed, and said, "Ah, well! We aristocrats move quickly! Don't we, Monsieur Selkirk!"

Of course he said these last words directly to Pyotr.

IMPRESSED, even smug, with the pace of my progress, I returned to my room, telling Gorlov I wanted a rest. But as soon as I entered, something seemed out of place—or, more accurately, everything seemed too much in place. The room had been dusted, the water pitcher beside the washbasin re-filled, the bedsheets smoothed. I noticed, too, that the floor had been swept, and my bag returned to the precise spot where I had left it beneath the table. Something about this precision troubled me. I retrieved my writing box and checked the stack of letter paper.

To alert me to any tampering of the box, I had formed the habit of placing a single sheet of the writing paper out of line with the others. I was sure I had done this again when I han-dled the box that morning, though I was removing the letter. I saw immediately that now all the pages were in a neat row.

I wondered if I had been wrong about the misaligned page. And yet the possibilities disturbed me greatly. Had someone gone through the box looking for money? For information? Where were my enemies? Who were they?

Wondering at my own steadiness of nerve, I lay down upon the bed. I questioned whether I was letting fear stimu-late my imagination. My optimism of just moments before had so suddenly evaporated, and I felt truly tired. I spent most of an hour lying in a dark lethargy, telling myself that the rigors of the journey had caught up to me at last, that I would soon identify the paths through the forest before me, that great opportunity would soon be mine—and doubting it all. When I was nearly asleep, the last vestige of discipline in my thoughts dissolving, I surrendered myself to anticipa-tion of the coming ball, and like a schoolboy began to sort out what I might wear, to imagine whom I might encounter, to wonder how I might present myself and if I might create the proper—

I sprang upright on the bed, paused, and then leapt to my feet. I touched the dagger hanging on the wall peg beside my saber, thought another moment, and ran for Gorlov. Fetching him from his own slumbers, I brought him in bewilderment back to my room. I locked the door and turned to face him. "I'm going to ring for the chamber boy, Gorlov. I'm going to ask him some questions he will not want to answer. I know he speaks French and German. But he is a Russian. And I think we can get at the truth better if we use his own language."

"The chamber boy? What could—"

"Someone has searched my room. I am sure of it."

"For what purpose? You carry your money—what little you have—on your person."

"I do not like snooping!"

Gorlov twisted his brows, squinting as if he thought me carried away. "Listen to me!" I insisted. "Yesterday I gave the chamber boy my traveling uniform and linen to have laundered and pressed." I pointed to the stand beside the window. "There is the uniform, hanging here now! He came back. He has a key. He could have helped anyone get in and out without discovery. I'm going to ring him up here." With that, I gave a pull on the bell cord.

Promptly a knock came upon the door, and I opened it to the chamber boy, who said, *"Oui, monsieur?"* with what I thought special politeness. I told him to come in; he hesitated, then stepped inside, faltering when he saw Gorlov. I locked the door behind him, and he spun round. Then he stood quite still.

I stared at him. He had straight sandy hair over a square Slavic face with a small up-bent nose in the exact center. He could have been no more than twelve. His expression changed as he stood there; he began to look sleepy and stupid.

"Yesterday," I said in French, "I gave you my laundry. You brought it back clean and left it here. But you let someone else in when you came."

"Oh, no, monsieur!"

I lifted the dagger from the peg, slowly stripped off the sheath, and tossed it to the bed. I touched the end of my left index finger to the dagger's point and twisted the blade back and forth. "Yes. You did. And you let someone into Count Gorlov's room as well."

The boy looked toward Gorlov, who watched without expression. The boy looked back toward me, and I thought I saw his lip quiver. "Didn't you?" I insisted.

He had opened his mouth without making a sound and had just begun to shake his head in denial when I jumped at him, clapping my left hand to the back of his head—not snatching hair but merely holding, for I thought that more sinister—and pressing the point of the dagger to the boneless flesh under his chin. My nose an inch from his, I whispered, "I am not afraid to kill boys. Turks are just boys to me, and I have killed many Turks. Who was it? Who did you let into our rooms?"

Through the hand at the top of his spine I could feel his legs quake. He no longer tried to look stupid. He stared straight into my eyes and said, "No one, sir."

In the periphery of my vision I could see Gorlov shaking his head. He stepped forward, pushed the dagger away, and began to beseech me not to kill the boy. His pleas were so fervent and so at odds with my intention (as I not only had no desire to hurt the boy but was even at the point of accepting his innocence), that I gathered Gorlov wanted me to play up my bloody desires. I did so, stepping back as Gorlov argued, brandishing my dagger as Gorlov spoke to the boy, and casting butcherous looks at both of them. Suddenly Gorlov snatched up the lad himself, lifted him in the air as he had lifted Pantkin, and deposited him sitting upon the bed. Stepping back, Gorlov wiped a hand down his own face and began to speak in Russian.

The boy sat rigid, staring. Gorlov continued steadily. The boy's eyes darted from Gorlov to me, back to Gorlov, to me again. Gorlov's resonant voice rose and fell upon the Russian syllables like the dirge of a solitary cello. The boy's chest heaved, and he began to cry.

The weeping became bitter, uncontrollable; Gorlov, who was bent over with his hands upon his knees, applying some last few phrases to the distraught boy, now raised up, walked slowly over to me, and said, so the boy could not hear, "I told him that you are angry with him not because he has lied to you and betrayed you, but because he has disappointed you. I told him that while all the other foreigners in this inn treat him like garbage because he is a Russian, and of peasant birth, you like him, and said to me—me, Count Gorlov, a Russian you have honored with your friendship—that you thought this chamber boy had promise and might even someday make a soldier. I told him that it was this sense about him that caused you to entrust your uniform to him in the first place, because, whereas other soldiers passing through this inn have hurled dirty uniforms at him, and tossed him filthy boots, expecting him to lick them clean like a dog, your uniforms are special because you are a great soldier. You will allow no one to touch your uniforms, but you put them in his care because of your faith in him. He has betrayed you and that is what has hurt you so deeply."

Looking at the boy crying, I felt wretched. Gorlov added in my ear, "But I have told him that you might forgive him, if he could only show that he is not a common, worthless cur, fit only to be whipped and used for a liar, but has rather the makings of a soldier, because he can stand before his captain and tell the truth."

He walked back to the boy, asked a question in Russian, and straightaway received an answer. "He says the owner of the inn came into your room to search for hidden money. He always does this, not to steal but to know your ability to pay, should he get you drunk and charge you for his most expensive wines." The boy sobbed, and choked; he had barely gotten the words out.

I paced to the window and stared out. I strode back before Gorlov and the boy as imperiously as I could. "Gorlov, you will tell this boy that I forgive him absolutely for everything he has done, and that I will not hesitate again to put my trust in him. He has, in telling us the truth, justified my initial opinion. No one will know that he has revealed anything. And I will take it upon myself personally to kill anyone who should threaten him." I found my bag and withdrew my dress uniform—the blue one, with the silver epaulets. As Gorlov, for the sake of effect, relayed the first part of this address in Russian, I handed the boy the tunic and breeches. "This," I said, "is my finest uniform. I need it pressed for the ball tomorrow. I entrust it to him."

The boy rose, needing no translation. He bowed low, and I was ashamed, but I took comfort from the joy in his face as he lifted it again. He turned to leave, and I was pulling my purse from my pocket when Gorlov tapped my hand and frowned.

When we were alone, I said to Gorlov, "He knew I would not hurt him."

"Oh, no. He believed you would kill him. He had no doubt of that. He has seen other boys killed, crushed like roaches. He continued to lie only when he thought it his only hope."

"I should have given him money."

"No. You have his absolute loyalty, forever. If you give a Russian boy respect, he will give his life for you."

That evening Gorlov and I dined quietly. Once or twice I thought he had fallen uncharacteristically silent and seemed to be studying me, but perhaps that was only my imagination.

I retired for the night with the dagger again beneath my pillow; still, I did not sleep soundly. The long silent hours of night trembled with thoughts of Russian horses, Russian chamber boys, Russian men like Gorlov, and my dreamy puzzling over the question: If these are the mysteries of her subjects, then what must the Tsarina be like?

Chapter Seven

THE dawn brought sunlight fierce, a new south wind blowing stiff and steady enough to chase the fogs to the earth's pole.

I had risen earlier than Gorlov, as was my habit, and apparently earlier than Pyotr, for he was not waiting outside in his sleigh as I stepped from the White Goose. But there were many taxi sleighs in St. Petersburg, and I approached a parked single-horser that seemed to be for hire. *"Gahvahn?"* I asked the driver. He removed the pipe from his mouth and nodded. I mounted into the box behind him, and we started off. The word I used was one I had asked Gorlov about, and now I hoped I had indeed directed the driver to the harbor and not to some local prison, convent, or colony for the insane. Imagining the destinations possible from a misunderstanding, I laughed aloud, for my mood had brightened with the morning.

The tops of the buildings gradually became visible in the strengthening sun. The sharp smell of tar, hot and smoking, swabbed my nostrils, and the clatter of wood mallets rattled my ears. We reached the edge of an icebound harbor and saw the hulls beached up and heeled over as teams of fitters patched holes, replaced planking, and hammered in chinks. I noticed first the scent of the sea and gazed out toward the gulf, where the wind had broken the waves from the grasp of winter. Ruptured islands of ice pressed against the shore so tightly that the surface pack seemed intact, but far off shore the waves heaved up frozen boulders and danced in white caps.

The driver slowed and turned to me. I motioned toward a row of inns and public houses, and he complimented me by stopping before the best.

I went into the tavern and took a seat in a back corner opposite the door. Ordering a small breakfast of stew and ale, I sat quietly and listened to the talk. I overheard a German navigator saying the Russian winter was a visitor reluctant to leave, and untrustworthy even in its warmest promise. The sea captains near me asserted to one another, over and over, that it would be two more weeks at least before any ship could cast off without being battered to splinters by the jagged ice clogging the harbor.

I took this to be good news. In taking the perilous overland route into Russia, I had made the right decision. A ship leaving London and sailing free of the winter-clogged roads of northern Europe might make most of the journey faster than I had, but the clogging of the harbor meant I had gained time. For two weeks I would be without any of the communications that Franklin had promised to send me by sea. But if America's agent in Russia was cut off, then so were any possible agents from Britain, and the precautions of secrecy that Franklin had taken with me were enough to make me grateful for the time I would have, free of any danger from them.

After listening for an hour, I was so convinced of the harbor's remaining icebound for at least the next half month that

I decided to return to the Goose; I had just paid for my breakfast when a breathless young ship's officer burst into the room
and shouted one word that brought the entire assembly to
silence: "Sails!"

Suddenly all were clamoring into the street and down
toward the piers. I joined in the crowd, moving with their
momentum. At first they walked as if slowed by their disbelief, but soon they were moving faster and faster as the public
houses emptied and even the fitters and chinkers and tar
moppers left off their work.

The gathering—the entire seafaring community of St.
Petersburg, it seemed—washed out upon the piers, whose
great supports stood still encased in a bed of ice. "Nowhere, I
see nothing!" men around me shouted to one another; but at
the edge of the dock, standing high upon a stack of mast timber, a young man kept pointing with the authority of one
who has been the first to know what everyone else has wondered. Amid the jostling, arguing, and contradictory pointing,
I strained my eyes toward the water and glimpsed there, above
the heaving waves and tossing ice blades, a billowing sheet of
canvas. The mast that held it aloft swayed slowly, and shuddered, and came on.

"How does he keep from smashing his sides?" a German
beside me demanded to know.

A Dutchman nearby answered, "There! See? He has stood
to the south, and beats in with the wind! He has trimmed so
he drifts with the ice—it moves along beside him!"

"I see it!" another navigator said. "He keeps his canvas too
lean to the wind, then slips when he comes about!"

And they said other such things as I could not understand,
beyond that they were full of admiration and envy of the man
who drove his ship to fortune and glory through dangers that
had defied them all. "Can anyone make out a flag?" someone
else wondered. We all peered as the masts drew closer, and one

of the captains withdrew a glass from his coat and sighted, then passed the glass around; each man took it and grew silent in his turn, and I had made out the colors already before a naked-eyed English seaman, perched upon the timber stack, shouted out, "The Union Jack! The Union Jack! God save the King!"

Reaching the shelter of a landfall that stretched out into the gulf and cut off a shearing current, the ship dropped sail. The British sailors ran a string of banners up the lines to the masthead and fired from the foredeck a single cannon charge.

The assembly returned the salute with a loud but formal "Hurrah!" Then rowboats flew from the piers, and in short order they had drawn the ship snug against the dock.

One of the sea captains standing near me said grudgingly in French, "No one in God's whole world can sail like the English." Not a man in the harbor would have disputed that opinion then, in any language.

I stood at the dock and watched the ship's sailors rig a gangway to the side of this vessel as the dockworkers, prostitutes, and souvenir hawkers surged forward to welcome their new arrivals. First off was the captain; stepping down immediately after him came a man who in his haste brushed the captain aside and strode directly across the dock, waving for a taxi carriage. It was an act of astonishing arrogance, affronting an able sea captain who had commandeered his ship through such danger; the captain glowered but voiced no protest, and his recent passenger, a tall, slender figure with eyes so dark they seemed to absorb rather than reflect light, took no notice of him or anyone else and climbed aboard the first carriage that responded to his call.

I hurried back toward the tavern and the driver I had left waiting for me; I intended to follow the dark-eyed Englishman. But by the time I reached my driver, having fought my way through the crowd, the other carriage had disappeared.

I directed my driver to return me to the White Goose.

I was not at that moment aware of the fact that along with all I had noticed, I had missed something, too. Aboard the *Conquest* was not only the mysterious Englishman, but also a sailor, a man I had met. He went by the name Hiram Marsh, though that, too, I did not know at the time. He was the American seaman who had found me in London and had taken me to meet Franklin. Marsh had watched as the Englishman stepped off the ship and hurried away. Marsh had seen me, too; but he had remained hidden, waiting for his chance to find me again in secret.

Chapter Eight

T IKHON, the chamber boy—after the events of the previous day I insisted upon knowing and using his Christian name—stood before me, holding the dress uniform out at arm's length and glancing back and forth from my face to the blue tunic. "It is satisfactory, Tikhon," I said. "It has never looked better."

I was hoping to find just the right compliment and seemed to have failed; his face fell for a moment, and he stammered, "Sir, I . . . I . . ."

"What is it, Tikhon?"

"I . . . habba eet repeered!" he blurted, mixing in German, which he spoke well, with the English he tried in my honor, and rolling his *r*s from the Russian.

"What?"

"Dee boottons!" he said, indicating the row of gold-plate buttons crossing the blouse from left shoulder to right hip. "Loose were few. Seamstress iss mein mutter!"

"You took the uniform all the way home, just to have buttons sewn on tighter?"

"Nyet, sir! Mutter comes here!"

"Yes. I see."

Recalling Gorlov's injunction against paying money for what is intended as a gift, I knew not how to thank him, and not only for the buttons; he had blacked my boots till they gleamed like a hound's nose, had buffed my buckles and braid, had even braved to nag Gorlov for me, that we might be on time. "Where do you live?" I asked the boy.

"Nearly, sir."

"What? Oh. Yes. Well take this coin," I said, fishing one of the last two from my purse, "and buy from your mother a strip of ribbon as long as you are. Hurry, we leave in twenty minutes."

He returned, panting, with a bright crimson band, just as we were entering Pyotr's sleigh. "Thank you, Tikhon," I said. "Now go in and tell the innkeeper that you are to have a soldier's dinner, to be put upon Captain Selkirk's bill." The boy marched off, and I handed the ribbon to Gorlov. "Give this to Pyotr. Tell him to tie it to his hat. Tell him he deserves a decoration."

Gorlov, with a bored sigh for such sentimentality, did as I requested, taking, I am sure, the liberty he always took with my translations. But Pyotr sat the box like a prince, his greasy cow pie of a cap plopped upon the center of his head, the ribbon ends snapping behind him as he drove through the early darkness to the Tnanski Prospeckt.

THE skip of violins and the gush of a harp met us as we turned off the main way onto the Prospeckt itself. Before us crept a string of sleighs and carriages, depositing celebrants at the gates of the estate DuBois. The moon brightened the branch tips of the bare trees upon the lawn and seemed to illuminate the notes themselves as a chill breeze spread the music to the other estates lining the river. The horses and coachmen before us, though richly attired, appeared gray in the moonlight, but the ladies they delivered glistened in scarlets and blues and flashed of jewels set in silver. The gentlemen who alighted before them and squired them to the house glowed from collar and cuff, their jackets replete with military colors or the deeper sheen of satin. This procession floated endlessly toward the house's door, thrown open to cast a yellow aura down the walk, a mouth receiving glowing food into a belly of light. Gorlov and I took our place in this line and moved up the stairs, past the regal envoy who had fetched us our invitation the day before and whose twin now bowed with him on the other side of the doorway. We strode through the foyer in which I had stood on my first visit, passed tables set with food in the front parlor, and beheld the ballroom.

If I have said that the ladies in attendance glimmered in the moonlight alone, I need not describe how vividly they shone with the light of a dozen chandeliers crashing above their heads. Handkerchiefs waved and fans fluttered (however needless they might seem at the end of a Russian winter, they found constant employment), and every lady fixed a smile upon the man with her, without ever looking at him, while each man pretended he was alone for as long as it took him to smooth his hair and adjust his trousers. The orchestra hammered vigorously though no one had yet begun to dance, and the servant who announced the names of the entrants boomed to make himself heard. As we were waiting for the several others before us to file their way into the main ballroom, Gorlov and I had a moment to pause at the doorway. It was here that he said to me, "An acquaintance. You say a mere . . . acquaintance, of an acquaintance in Paris. And he has invited you here, when you only called upon him yesterday as a courtesy."

"Exactly."

Gorlov knew I lied, but this did not trouble him. He glanced about, pushed his lips forward, and nodded his head in general endorsement of the furnishings. When the chanter at the doorway sang out, "Count Gorlov and Monsieur Le Capitain Selkirk," Gorlov threw back his head as if to expose his mustache to the most favorable rays of the chandeliers, then strode across the ballroom in cadence with the music.

While everyone else in the ballroom either watched the swaggering Gorlov or ignored the announcement of our arrival altogether, I scanned the whirl of faces and caught three pairs of eyes glancing to me. The first belonged to an elegant gentleman of raven pompadour and silver goatee, whom I knew instinctively to be the Marquis DuBois; the second lurked within the sunken sockets of another gentleman, shorter, grayer, even more slender than DuBois, and wearing, like the Frenchman, a diplomatic medal about his neck; the third pair, green and already familiar, were those of Charlotte DuBois. She was giving orders to a group of waiters and serving maids, and she glanced up for a moment only; when she saw me staring back at her, she held her gaze on mine just long enough to show that she felt no timidity in having been caught looking, and turned again, casually, to the servants.

I followed after Gorlov, toward where he was already introducing himself to a Prussian general too old to fight but too young to stoop his spine, and, as Gorlov had, I swaggered.

I paused for a moment beside Gorlov, then walked straight to Charlotte DuBois. She pretended not to see me at first, then abruptly flicked the servants away. "Thank you for inviting us, Mademoiselle DuBois," I said crisply.

"You are welcome, I am sure," she said. "But I did not invite you. My father did."

"Yes. I know. I . . . wanted to thank you anyway. And I have." I bowed and turned to walk away.

"Monsieur Selkirk! I am not sorry that he did invite you, I only meant . . ."

I snapped another short bow and returned to Gorlov's side. At least I had ascertained that her father had wanted to see me, and soon. I wondered what he had told her.

The orchestra, with an enthusiasm befitting the opening dance, burst into a louder and more buoyant melody, and some mysterious force cast the ladies in their gowns and the gentlemen in their uniforms and evening jackets to the far perimeters of the dance floor, pinning their backs to the walls and leaving them to face an empty, open expanse of parqueted brilliance, the eye of the social storm. The perfumed, pow- dered, and pomaded heads twisted to Charlotte and her father. She blushed, her father's face blazed with a smile, and he, with a hand lofted above his head, paraded from the top of the room where the orchestra was playing and met her with a bow in the center of the floor. She curtseyed, and they began to dance.

They followed the path a top might, careening off the periphery in short arcs, then twirling straight down the length of the room. As an ensemble they were not so graceful as I at first thought; as I watched I realized the charm of their danc- ing lay not in their grace but in their conviction that they made a captivating spectacle. I envied them, and yet felt cold, too, as if I and all the others had been summoned there that they might have an audience for this very moment when they gloried in the display of their devotion.

I suddenly felt lonely beyond the reach of woman and God.

It was an awareness so desolate that it caused me to won- der whether my past, my current dangers, or some flaw of heart poisoned me against the unmingled joy everyone else in the room exhibited. I glanced around, searching, I suppose, for a sign that someone else might feel as much an alien to this as

I; everyone I saw appeared quite happy. As for Gorlov, he was watching the dancing and tossing his head as if he himself held Mademoiselle DuBois in his arms.

Marquis DuBois applauded vigorously with the others as the dance ended. He returned to his former place among the distinguished elder gentlemen who grouped at the punch bowl near the orchestra. Charlotte immediately set about urging people onto the floor, and soon a number were dancing. She continued to augment this group by forging her way along the periphery, dividing existing pairs and introducing gentlemen and ladies in such sudden fashion that the new couples, being totally unacquainted, had no choice but to dance.

With Charlotte thus occupied, I found myself with the perfect opportunity to approach and greet her father without arousing particular notice. He was speaking with two other gentlemen as I approached, and I paused until he might see me and break away. I saw only the other men's backs, but was sure that one was the pale diplomat who had peered at me as I entered; the other was a burly fellow stuffed into his evening jacket, who stooped as if embarrassed to be so much larger than his associates. DuBois, seeing me in the periphery of his vision, stepped a few paces from the men, as if to give directions to one of the serving maids. I approached him.

"Marquis DuBois. Thank you for your hospitality."

"Captain Selkirk! So nice of you to come!" He shook my hand firmly. He was a handsome man, shorter than he had appeared out upon the parquet floor with his daughter. "Have you eaten? Are you hungry? Here, I must show you where to eat!" As he led me through the doors into the front hall, where the tables sagged beneath the food, I felt, upon my back, his hand—and the pale diplomat's eyes.

The marquis stopped beside one of the tables and positioned himself so that he faced the open door and ballroom

and no one within that room could see my face. With the
same light expression of amusement as he had worn when
first greeting me, he said, "You are quite young. How old are
you?"

"Twenty-four."

He continued to smile. His voice was grave and low. "I did
not expect you here so soon."

"We drove hard," I said. "And already a British ship lies off
the ice pack in the harbor."

"How well I know it! Earlier than anyone else.
Shettlefield is so proud of that." He gazed upon the table as if
interested in the salmon roses with mint leaves. "Did you see
those two with whom I was talking when you came up? The
smaller is Shettlefield, my counterpart—as I am head of the
trade delegation of France, he is chief trade minister from
England. The big Russian with him is Prince Mitski. He is
trade minister for the Court of the Empress Catherine."

I reached for an hors d'oeuvre and glanced through the
door. The two men he mentioned were facing each other,
both in profile to us, with Mitski bent over and listening
intently as Shettlefield emphasized some point with a genteel,
palm-up gesture. "Shettlefield has had the grace *not* to mention the ship's arrival here in my own house," DuBois said,
and laughed. "He does not need to; everyone else does it for
him. But even now he is telling Mitski what profits he can
reap if he will increase his country's trade with the British
Empire. I must not leave them alone for too long."

Now DuBois turned his eyes to me—green eyes, like his
daughter's. "Franklin told me that he would send a good man.
Are you a good man, Captain Selkirk?"

I simply looked at him.

He smiled. Then he stopped smiling. "Catherine the
Great," he said, "Empress of All the Russias. Not one drop of
Russian blood in her, a German princess ascended to the

Russian throne. A virgin until the age of twenty-three, now making up for lost time. Patron of humanists, the special friend and correspondent of Voltaire and Diderot. Do you think you can—" he searched for the word "—impress such a woman as this?"

I perceived that this was no idle question from an envoy of France, whose power struggles with England could be drastically affected by Russian actions.

"Doctor Franklin has charged me to convince her of but one thing."

"Oh? And what is that?"

"That if Americans have a war, it is a war we will win."

"Ah. Yes." DuBois picked up an hors d'oeuvre. "Russians understand nothing so much as strength. And do not be misled. Catherine is a German by birth, but she is a Russian to the depth of her soul." He popped the morsel of bread and caviar into his mouth and licked his fingers. "Come," he mumbled, chewing. "I will introduce you to my friends. Our friends."

We threaded our way back into the ballroom, DuBois speaking and laughing with everyone we passed. He made a display of showing me the house as we walked, pointing to the murals on the wall, the plaster sculpturing of the ceilings, the French doors lining the opposite side of the room reflecting in their faceted panes the images of the swirling dancers. Shettlefield noticed us approaching and ceased speaking immediately; he smiled and called, "Claude! Who is your young friend?"

DuBois feigned surprise at the sight of Shettlefield and Mitski, as if he had forgotten they were still there. "Gentlemen! Excuse me for having left you so long, with nothing to talk about! My friend? Oh yes, this is Captain Selkirk! He comes from Paris, where we have many mutual acquaintances. Captain, Prince Mitski and Lord Shettlefield." And with that introduction, DuBois suddenly showed pleasurable astonishment at some face he had glimpsed in the crowd and, calling the name of that guest he hurried away, leaving me alone with Shettlefield and Mitski.

The Russian took no notice of me; he reached out a docile paw for me to grasp but did not look at me at all, and he appeared disinterested in the whole ball, sleepy even. Shettlefield, however, gripped my hand with firmness, and said in a voice of surprising depth, "Selkirk! That is a Scottish name, is it not?"

"Yes," I said, answering in French, as he had addressed me.

"And when were you last in Scotland?"

"I have never been in Scotland. I was reared in Virginia."

"You are a long way from home."

"We all are, aren't we? All except Prince Mitski." Still Mitski did not look around; he sipped the champagne he had just lifted from a serving maid's tray.

"Why aren't you a planter? I thought all Virginians owned plantations." Shettlefield had switched to English, and though he had watched me steadily for some moments, I noticed his eyes more now.

"I was not fortunate with agriculture," I said.

"Please forgive me for asking so many questions," he said, smiling without altering his stare. "It is so rare for me to encounter a fellow member of the British Empire here, some-one with whom I can converse. You seem an educated man! Did you attend school in England?"

"I studied at the College of William and Mary, in Williamsburg."

"What?"

"The College of—"

"No, no! I am aware of your colony's college. I meant what did you study."

"Mmm. Philosophy and art, language and theology. When

I was there, it was commonly believed that a man ought to be broadly educated in the liberal arts."

"Oh, and that has changed?"

"More of a premium is now attached to the military sciences."

"And so you, too, are now a military man!"

"Merely personal fate. As I said, I had no luck as a planter."

He plucked at the lace of his cuff. "Marquis DuBois tells me you come with letters of introduction from friends of his that you met while in Paris. How long were you there?"

"Not long."

"Isn't it a bit strange for a career soldier to visit and befriend people in the capital of a nation that competes so hostilely with the interests of the commonwealth to which that soldier owes allegiance?" He was smiling.

"One can often learn more from enemies than one can learn from friends," I said, "though I have not found the French to be hostile, unless they hear their language misused. Besides, that is a strange question for a British gentleman to ask, while he enjoys entertainment in a French gentleman's home."

"Touché!" Shettlefield declared, returning our conversation to French, in which we chatted for a few moments about St. Petersburg and the impending spring. When Mitski, who had been standing by stiffly in what I took to be boredom but later understood to have been anxiety, heard the triviality of this new talk, he broke in, speaking to Shettlefield in Russian, and I excused myself.

I immediately ran into Charlotte, who greeted me with, "Monsieur Selkirk! Are you not dancing?"

"Oh! Uh, not as yet, Mademoiselle DuBois." I did not blame the stupidness of this answer on her question.

"Then we shall have to find you a suitable partner immediately! But you have not yet introduced me to Count Gorlov!"

Gorlov—who had been facing away from us, with the knuckles of his right hand pressed to the point of his right hip, and his head cocked back—forced me to tap him twice on the shoulder and address him by his title before turning suddenly, acting surprised, bowing, and saying, "Count Gorlov, at your service, my lady! But I must disappoint you. I will travel all the way from Paris with young Selkirk here, will ride for two months bundled in the same carriage furs, and will even sleep with him in the same bed. But I cannot be his partner in the quadrille. People might talk."

As Gorlov said this he bored into her with his black eyes, and she tossed back her head and trilled an arc of laughter toward the chandeliers. It was an unrehearsed and natural outburst, but she instantly recovered her hauteur and said, "Delightful to meet you, Count. You seem to know our topic, though you pretend not to have overheard our conversation." She extended her hand coolly, and Gorlov, entranced, kissed it.

A young suitor, driven by her laughter in the company of intruders, said, "Charlotte! You must come with me! I would like you to . . . to—"

"Oh, Rodeon!" she said, as if she had just discovered a pet puppy at her feet. "You must meet Colonel Selkirk and Count Gorlov. Gentlemen, meet my friend Rodeon Dmitrovich Roskov, ah, Prince Roskov."

"*Captain* Selkirk," I corrected her, extending my hand to the scowling Roskov.

"Captain, colonel . . . aren't they the same?" Charlotte said, smiling.

Roskov shook our hands without ever looking at us, and he struggled to finish his hanging entreaty. "Charlotte, I would like . . . Would you please allow . . . Take the next dance with me!"

"With you? That would be delightful, Rodeon, but I have promised this dance to Captain Selkirk."

She took me by the hand and led me to the center of the floor, leaving the dark young man in furious silence beside Gorlov, who pursed his lips and lifted his chin to stare down his nose at us. In fact, as I touched my right hand to the starched lace at the waist of Charlotte's gown, and held her gloved fingers in my left, and began to step with her across the floor, having had to remind myself to lead, I felt as if everyone in the room were watching.

My impressions of the interval of that dance were as blurred as the faces of the spectators and other dancers who swirled across the field of my vision, with only the features of Charlotte crisply visible before me, and my mind too jumbled to take her in as much as I might have wished. I remembered the social finishing classes at the College of William and Mary, where my humiliation at not knowing how to dance scorched deeper still when I was forced to take instruction partnered with similarly ignorant freshmen males, as no ladies attended our school; I thought of the one whom I had promised to take to a ball someday, making the vow not to her but secretly to myself, and how that promise must forever be broken; I thought of how far I had come, and why.

And amid all those thoughts and sensations I had reason to pause: I saw behind and beyond Charlotte a porcelain face, with eyes of Wedgwood blue, looking at me.

The eyes snapped away so quickly that I began to doubt my initial certainty of having been stared at. I turned back to the open floor, then looked at her again, just as her face came around once more and her eyes met mine. Her gaze had an intensity and a steadiness, and in the moment it lasted it had a fearlessness too; and then in haste she glanced back to the dancers, then down to the floor, as a blush soaked into the china of her cheeks.

Unsettled, I fixed my eyes upon Charlotte until the quadrille ended and she conducted me off the floor, remarking about my grace and delightful company. Roskov's face darkened even more as we approached, and he was about to say something to Charlotte when she dropped my hand, took up Gorlov's, and led him out beneath the chandeliers.

In the progress of this minuet, Gorlov tossed his head so that a black lock of hair separated from the others and bounced upon his forehead, and I could feel Roskov growing ever more still beside me. He said, "Count Gorlov tells me you fought together as mercenaries, against the Turks."

"We were paid for fighting," I answered. "Every soldier is. But we fought to learn the art of war, and we learned against a cruel and vicious enemy." Gorlov, I knew, had never used the word "mercenary," not in his and Roskov's language, or in any other.

"The count tells me you went together to Paris."

"Yes." I knew Roskov was trying to draw me out in some way. I intended to volunteer nothing.

"I suppose you were quite a hit among the Parisians, being so fashionable as you are. I noticed your elegant sleigh and driver the other day. I even caught sight of him again this evening, in festive attire."

I thought of the ribbon I had bought Pyotr, and how ridiculous he looked with it in his hat, and how proud of it he was; and I looked at Roskov's smile. "The driver is Count Gorlov's servant, not mine," I said. "If you insult his sleigh or his driver's dress, then Gorlov will kill you. And if you insult the driver, then I will kill you."

Roskov took a step back, his lower jaw yanking up and down. "Do you mean to challenge me, sir?!" he rasped.

I trusted my look to tell him that mainly I meant to remove the smile from his face, and would be happy to kill him if I had to, and was certain he had not the courage to make me.

"And what is this?" Charlotte said, like a peeved

schoolmistress, marching up with Gorlov in tow behind her.

"This . . . this . . . he insults me!" Roskov sputtered, his face purpling. The orchestra was still playing, but several people nearby had heard and were looking over.

"Oh, *everyone* insults you!" Charlotte scolded, and with an exaggerated sigh she tugged him toward the center of the floor. He put up a dramatic resistance and finally succumbed, staring into her eyes as they danced.

"Did you insult him?" Gorlov said casually.

"No. I simply offered to kill him."

"Why?"

"He insulted my dancing."

"Impossible. You are not the most graceful man I have ever seen upon the dance floor," Gorlov said, sucking one cheek and nodding with the lowered eyelids of an expert, "but you are adequate. You must be lying. Why did you quarrel with him?"

"All right then. He insulted your dancing."

I left Gorlov blinking at this remark and walked along the perimeter of the room toward the orchestra. I separated from him not only because I did not want to explain the real substance of the offensive comments; whatever the details of Gorlov's pedigree, and his family's reduced circumstances, I knew without question that for an insult to Pyotr's livery he would indeed kill Roskov, or anyone else.

I glanced once more to the place where I had seen the Wedgwood eyes. I could not find them again. I saw that one of the double French doors lining the far wall lay open, revealing a veranda.

I cannot say exactly how I knew, yet as I gazed out at the moonlight falling on polished stone beyond the door, I conceived the notion that there I would find the girl with the Wedgwood eyes. When I stepped from the ballroom and saw no one standing outside the doorway, I was disappointed.

I filled my lungs with the night air, frigid and fresh. I walked out to the balustrade and stared across to the other estates lining the frozen river. I looked back toward the ballroom, and through the doors saw the dancers. I turned to stroll down the length of the veranda. She was there, standing at the end.

It was as if I had pursued her, and could not turn away now. Perhaps she heard my boots upon the stone, or perhaps she saw me come through the door; but she turned her face slightly toward me, and then looked back across the ice.

Halfway to her, I stopped and turned to the river myself, and stood trying to formulate what I might say. The longer I waited the more humiliated and stupid I felt, until at last I walked up to her and said, "I am sorry. Twice tonight, when I have felt apart from everyone else here, I have seen you. I . . ."

The sentence began so wonderfully, and left me at a chasm. I could not find another word. She had just turned to me, and I, watching the moon settle into the china of her eyes, had opened my mouth to try to continue, when someone screamed, "There she is! There! *There!*"

I whirled. The shouter—a French officer who with his female companion had drifted outside for a breath of air— was pointing not toward the lady and myself but out across the river. The coquette beside him joined the cry, calling, "Here! Out here!" Moving to the open doors, elicited by the excited couple, a mass of guests streamed out onto the veranda.

While at first the calls reminded me of the shouts of the seamen for the approaching sails, the presence of the crowd gathering upon the veranda reminded the French officer of the need for calm—for social grace is a restrained goddess— and with a suddenly assumed detachment he directed attention to a point across the river. There a line of torches moved through the darkness, dozens and dozens of flame points, becoming hundreds, collecting on the far bank. Then into their illumination something golden gleamed, and a hush came upon the spectators on the veranda. Moving reflections of gold—harnesses, of horses!—bounced in pairs through the night, pulling a sleigh that by its brilliance lit the air above it.

The sleigh and horses—ten in all—drew up beside the bank and stopped. Reflections smeared out toward us in the ice of the frozen river, and the sound of laughter floated across in the stillness. A mass of adoring peasants were trailing the sleigh on foot, and they were humming a melody in soft soprano, supported by rich basses.

Suddenly Marquis DuBois, pressed against the balustrade with the rest of his guests, burst into a shout, "Three cheers for the Empress of All the Russias! Hurrah!"

"Hurrah! . . . Hurrah! . . . Hurrah!" the crowd upon his veranda erupted, in the essence of refined lustiness, as if the Queen, wrapped somewhere beneath a mound of white sable, could pick out each voice and know which admirer to reward, and which to banish.

DuBois waved for the musicians to play, and the guests began to dance and continue the party out in the cold air, as if the Tsarina would hand out promotions based on who had enjoyed himself most. I stared toward the torchlit carriage, reflecting fire in the gray ice of the Neva.

I glanced again at the beautiful young woman beside me; sensing my confusion, she said, "The Tsarina. She comes to celebrate the thaw. Russians give spring a long welcome, having missed it for so long."

"You . . . speak English quite well," I said.

"So do you. For a German."

"I am not German; I only trained with the Prussian Army."

"Is that where you learned to dance?"

I glanced at her and saw that her eyes were laughing. That made me smile—suddenly, easily, I could smile.

"I've never been to a ball in my life," I told her, and it was true; but then I thought I should not have admitted it.

"That explains it then."

"My dancing, you mean?"

"No. Your face. You are the only person at this whole gathering who feels anything."

Caught off guard, I muttered, "Everyone . . . seems . . . quite happy."

"It's one thing to seem. Quite another to feel. In Russia, the only people who feel are the ones with empty bellies, who follow a golden carriage for a glimpse of glory."

I realized she had just told me a secret thought; in two minutes beneath the stars, both of us had revealed something of ourselves.

"So you have met my daughter," a voice behind me said, and I pivoted. The speaker was Shettlefield.

I looked back to the young woman, then back to him. "Yes," I said.

"I was wondering how you had arrived in Russia," Lord Shettlefield said, "as travel here is so difficult. Marquis DuBois tells me that you and your friend crossed the frontier, in an open sleigh no less! You must have been in a terrible hurry, not to wait for a ship."

"I suffer from seasickness. So I preferred to come by land."

"But the frontier is more dangerous than the sea."

"Except for the wolves and the Cossacks, the trip was no problem."

The music had not been loud, as the orchestra was inside and most of the guests were on the veranda. And I was certainly not whispering. Franklin had urged me to be bold to the point of arrogance; assertiveness was, he said, a trait the fashionable admire, as they themselves are cowardly and timid. But I had not been loud, I was sure of it. Still, the veranda went quiet, not all at once but in waves, first of whispering and then of silence, as guests reacted to the mention of Cossacks. Gorlov, whom I saw standing beside Charlotte DuBois, seemed to be trying to will himself invisible.

Lord Shettlefield gave a laugh that sounded even sharper in the sudden quiet. "They have no Cossacks in Virginia, my young friend!" he said. "You surely don't know what one looks like!"

The whole crowd laughed and shook their heads, as if I were a great fool.

"They were in wolf-pelt shawls," I said, more loudly than I needed to, "sitting on their horses like they were born there. And their leader wore the head of a wolf, as a cap."

This time the silence on the veranda was deafening.

"Let us have another minuet!" DuBois called. He motioned sharply to the orchestra, and they began to play; people started laughing and talking and dancing again, with vigor, the more to pretend that nothing had happened.

"Pardon me, gentlemen, but I have an early day tomorrow," Lord Shettlefield said. Bowing, he moved quickly away.

I looked around for his daughter, but could not see her anywhere.

Gorlov approached, nodding in mock approval. "Silver tongue," he said.

"Cossacks are some kind of stinking secret?"

"Cossack raiders do not exist because they are an embarrassment to the Tsarina."

"What kind of country is this, that to be a good citizen, you must be blind?"

"Which world do you live in?"

"I hope to see a better one."

"You are a bumpkin. I'm going to get drunk and be a bumpkin with you." Gorlov headed off, moving past DuBois, Mitski, and Shettlefield, who were leaning close together and whispering.

I turned once more to stare across the river at the golden carriage, surrounded by the torches of adoring peasants.

I FOUND Gorlov inside at the banquet table, pouring down a prodigious amount of liquor. "Let us go," I told him. "I have damaged our prospects enough for one night."

"You're going about it wrong," he said, draining in one draught a crystal goblet full of a clear liquid I knew must be vodka. "Drinking and brawling is the way to success. One cannot rebound until one has hit bottom!"

"Come on," I said, and helped him toward the door.

We were wobbling together toward our sleigh when DuBois's servant caught up to us. "Sirs? The marquis wishes to see you."

The servant led us toward a small hut, tucked into the shadows on the dark side of the house. I glanced at Gorlov. "A trip to the woodshed?" I wondered aloud to him, and he shrugged. When Gorlov was sober, he was beyond fear; when he was drunk, he was beyond caring.

The servant tapped at the door, then opened it without waiting for a reply. We entered what was no more than a gardening hut, lit by a single candle casting orange light upon tools for digging, pruning, and cultivating. DuBois and his friend Mitski were there expecting us, having passed their wait by pacing, smoking, and drinking from a bottle of vodka. The servant left, closing the door as he did so.

DuBois spoke first. "Tomorrow, we, and some friends of ours, must send a shipment to Moscow, on personal business of the Royal Court. The shipment is valuable to us. And presently the royal policy is that no danger from the Cossacks exists. We cannot send an armed escort, or anything that appears to be one. But if you saw Wolfhead—"

"Claude!" Mitski interrupted, alarmed that this name should even be mentioned in his presence.

"—or anything you thought was Wolfhead," DuBois went on, "prowling around St. Petersburg, then we cannot ignore the possibility of danger."

Gorlov leaned to me and whispered so loudly that no one in the room could have kept from hearing, "I'll handle this." Then he staggered over to our hosts and took the vodka bottle from Mitski. "May I?" Gorlov asked. "Thank you. Mmm, Russian vodka, very nice. So you want us!"

"Two men only," DuBois said. "New arrivals to St. Petersburg, who might appear more as traveling companions than as guards."

"Sounds dangerous," Gorlov observed. His words were stumbling, but his thoughts were still erect.

"Not at all. The sleigh we are sending is exceedingly fast; it could outrun almost any trouble."

Gorlov took a swig, slammed the bottle down onto a wooden tool chest, and waved me to follow him as he moved to the door, saying, "Come on, he could get anybody."

"We need . . . men of courage!" Mitski said quickly. "One might say, reckless courage."

"To guard a private shipment from a danger that doesn't exist."

"The cargo is quite precious to us!" DuBois admitted.

"So we must guard it with our lives." Gorlov cocked his head away from the noblemen and pretended to rub one eye, while he winked at me with the other one.

"We will pay you a thousand gold rubles," Mitski said. Gorlov coughed, then tried to conceal his surprise. Mitski, sure that such a rich payment guaranteed our acceptance of the mission, sighed and added, "We will send a sleigh for you at dawn, to collect you to my home, from which our shipment will depart. Horses, all necessary provisions, and letters of introduction to the various estates at which you may stop along the way will all be provided."

Gorlov picked up the bottle again. "Well, Prince, it looks like you've found your men!" And with that Gorlov took a huge swig of the pure Russian vodka.

"No. Piss on your money," I said.

Gorlov blew a mouthful of alcohol across our hosts, and sputtered at me through his coughing, "A-a thou-sand g-gold—"

I stepped to face Mitski and DuBois, and looked from one to the other. "In public, you laugh at me. Then you ask us to defend against a danger that you pretend I only imagined. And you offer to pay us a handsome sum. We will guard your precious shipment. But if we keep it safe, then you will help us get commissions in the Royal Cavalry."

Mitski and DuBois looked at each other; then DuBois looked back to me and smiled with what I took to be admiration. "Done," he said.

"And you will pay us two thousand, not one."

"Also done," Mitski said. I turned to Gorlov and winked.

As I helped him to the front of the mansion and our sleigh, Gorlov was effusive. "That was . . . the greatest thing . . . I ever saw!" he boomed.

"Be quiet! Don't let them hear you gloat."

But he would not be restrained. As he fell onto the floor of the sleigh and Pyotr clucked the horses back onto the frozen lane, Gorlov bellowed so loudly they could have heard him across the river. "I have returned to Russia with a genius!"

Chapter Nine

WHEN Pyotr drew the horses to a stop in front of the Goose, Gorlov rose from the floor of the sleigh, brushed himself off with dignity, and strode out—his foot missing the metal step entirely so that he fell face-first upon the ice of the street. Pyotr noticed but did not comment, clucking the horses away and leaving me to help Gorlov to his feet.

Gorlov wiped the blood from his nose with the side of his hand, then noticed the cheerful noises spilling from the brightly lit tavern room of the Goose. "Ah," Gorlov said. "Ah." And he barreled up the steps, in search of another drink. I did not try to restrain him, having long before learned the futility in that; I myself was so aroused by the evening's events that sleep seemed an impossibility.

As we entered the tavern room our acquaintances there noticed us and called out; when we removed our cloaks and revealed our formal uniforms, they applauded rowdily, and we accepted their good-natured howls. Gorlov announced a round for the room, and we sank into the comfort one feels while surrounded by comrades.

When we had been there less than a half hour, the innkeeper approached and handed me a note, saying quietly into my ear, "This just came." He retreated before I opened the note, apparently having been warned of its confidentiality. The note said, "Come now. Alone. White house, end of main street. Burn this." The note was signed, "Lord Shettlefield."

TH E footing was difficult upon the sideways of the street. The fresh cold had frozen malleable slush into hard, jagged swells, and I would have preferred to walk upon the road itself had not the ruts there been so deep. Everyone else upon the street had trouble walking normally—or no one did, depending upon one's outlook, for everyone else out at this hour was drunk, from the two Swedes who stood before the dark window of a long-closed bakery and argued, apparently about which cake they should buy, to the three Germans who swayed along happily shouting orders to two prostitutes who staggered with them and sang bawdy airs in French. (Every whore in St. Petersburg, whatever her true nationality, pretended to be French—this according to Gorlov.) I moved away from the Goose, from which, for some distance, I could still hear the boom of Gorlov's voice in the front dining room as he told war stories.

Far ahead, I could see the lights of houses at the end of the street, structures three stories high and apparently fashionable; and yet between those houses and the genteel group of inns, taverns, and shops surrounding the Goose there squatted a motley row of decidedly less reputable establishments. A chorus of shouts and threats, mixed with raucous laughter, spilled through the thin doors of a dimly lit public house as I passed. From the opposite side of the street, and the upper floor of an

unpainted hotel, I heard more shouting, a man's vicious curs-
ings in German, and a woman's shrill and even more vulgar
reply. "Are you lonely?" a voice said to me in French, and I
peered into the darkness of a doorway to a candle shop and
saw only the painted face of the woman huddled there, the
rest of her enshrouded by the cloak she gripped around her. I
walked past, stopped, dug into my pocket, and found my last
coin, then went back and extended it into the murkiness
where she stood. A narrow hand came out from the bundle of
clothes, closed around the coin, and receded into the dark. I
walked on.

I was not fearful of passing through this section, having
seen others like it in my time as a soldier, but I was surprised
at its presence, and surprised further that Shettlefield had not
told me of it. I began again to ponder Shettlefield's purposes
in summoning me in secret.

Behind me glass shattered, and I jerked around. The sound
had come from the hotel far down the street, where the man
and woman had been calling each other names. I lowered my
arms—having raised them in a posture to fight—and resumed
walking, thinking that the tunnel of buildings along the street
and the cold, still air had accented the sound. But I knew, too,
that I had lied to myself. I was fearful.

Recognizing this caused me to doubt my impression of
having glimpsed a man's silhouette as I spun around, a figure
disappearing into the shadows behind me.

I reached the gate of Shettlefield's house, and glanced
again suddenly back down the street, but I saw only the pools
of darkness as the clouds moved across the moon.

The gates, unlatched, were heavy black iron. They
shrieked as I pushed them open and sang again as I closed
them. Upon the porch beside the door glowed a lamp, the
wick trimmed so that it marked but a point to walk toward
while revealing no detail around it. The house itself was

stately, with plaster pillars and carved window facings. Only two upper rooms appeared lit, yet as I drew nearer I saw that the main floor was illuminated also, light slipping through the windows past the edges of heavy curtains.

I reached the door and knocked. I waited for some moments, and was about to knock again when the door swung open and Shettlefield himself admitted me.

He did not speak until I was fully inside and the door shut fast behind me. But then he was especially courteous and animated. "Captain Selkirk! How nice of you to come!"

I caught the faint fragrance of the floral scent I had encountered at the ball in the presence of Lord Shettlefield's daughter, and I heard a rustle of silk from somewhere near the top of the staircase, which ascended directly from the entry hall. I glanced up involuntarily, saw nothing, and hastily shook the hand Shettlefield offered. He took my overcoat, hung it himself on the mahogany stand by the door, and led—I might say he pressed—me into the front sitting room.

My immediate impression was that the house wore a brown garment of masculinity. Beige paint and oak wainscoting encased its walls. Framed pictures of English gentry riding to the hounds were the only ornaments, and those sparse. A low fire hissed in the sitting room grate, and added to the undertone of tobacco. Shettlefield closed the sitting room door, ushered me to one of the high-backed chairs beside the fire, and sat down in its twin opposite me. "Did you find the house without difficulty?" he said.

"Yes."

"Did you tell anyone else you were coming?"

"No." *But you did,* I thought, *since I was followed.*

"Would you like something to drink? I have dismissed all the servants for the evening, but I have brandy right here." He pointed to a richly carved sideboard.

"Thank you. No."

"Perhaps a pipe, then. The *Conquest* brought me Virginia tobacco, and of course I don't have to tell you that it is the finest in the world."

"Thank you, but not now for me, I think. Do go ahead yourself."

"You don't mind?" he said, already filling his briar, then lighting it with a wand from the fireplace and sitting back down, puffing out blue smoke.

He was stalling for some reason. "Sir," I prompted him, "the circumstances of this meeting have left me quite intrigued."

I heard the turning of an oiled latch. A door beyond Shettlefield's back opened quietly, and striding into the room came the same dark-eyed man I had seen step off the *Conquest*.

I don't know if my face registered surprise. I tried to mask that reaction; and if I displayed it I hoped it would look not much different from the face of anyone meeting that man for the first time, for his was a presence designed to intimidate. Shettlefield, I was sure, did not see my first response, as he had turned at the sound of the latch to say, "Ah, Mr. Montrose! Percival Montrose, meet Captain Selkirk."

Montrose advanced to me and gripped my hand. His fingers were long and powerful; he had a soldier's hands. "I'm sorry, Captain Selkirk," Shettlefield added, "but I have forgotten your given name."

"Kieran," I said.

"Yes, of course, Kieran." Shettlefield was watching me closely, and Montrose's dark eyes never left me, even as he stepped back to the sofa and sat down. In fact, through the rest of the interview neither his eyes nor Shettlefield's ceased to study me. "Mr. Montrose," Shettlefield went on, "advises us on matters of trade, specifically in the issues of the transportation of goods."

I said nothing, trying to avoid the awkwardness of one who is conscious of being watched.

"When Lord Shettlefield told me you had crossed the frontier, I was most keen to talk with you," Montrose said. His voice was deep, his accent polished on the fringes but coarse in the body of his words, like one born low and then educated—not unlike myself.

"Any intelligence we can gather that might give us an advantage in trade routes is crucial to us," Shettlefield added smoothly. "That is why we've arranged this meeting in such a discreet way."

"Never hurts to keep the competition in the dark," Montrose added.

I nodded, as matter-of-factly as possible. "Well, gentlemen, I'll be happy to help you if I can."

"I am delighted to hear that, Captain," Shettlefield said. "These days not all of our American colonists are as loyal to British interests as you seem to be."

"I haven't been home in a long time. Have matters grown that bad?" I looked at Montrose as I said this, since he was staring so fixedly at me.

"I wouldn't know," he said. "I have been in Russia all winter, and have not paid attention to political news." He lied badly; he knew it, I think, for he quickly added, "I do not concern myself with such matters."

This, I knew with sudden clarity, was not the truth; in fact, it was the very opposite of the truth. Montrose was no more a trade adviser than I was pope. What he was, most surely, was lethal. Everything about him said so. I saw the danger in him, and yet I was not frightened; I had caught him off guard with a question, and he had lied—instinctively, and unnecessarily.

Shettlefield seemed to know this; he took charge of my subtle interrogation. "So you are not political, Captain?"

"On the contrary, I am as interested in the peace and stability of my homeland as any other Virginian my age might be. But the more I see of wars—especially those of other people—the less I wish to see war among my own people."

"Well said." Shettlefield continued to study me, as did Montrose. But the former analyzed me as he might a laboratory specimen, while the latter seemed to be measuring me for a coffin.

And yet I say again, I was not frightened; if anything, my confidence grew. The men before me were on the lookout for American agents in Russia, and clearly they were suspicious of me. But all they had was suspicion; if they had evidence, I would already be dead, with no one, not even Gorlov, knowing how I had been drawn to my death.

For a few minutes more Shettlefield played out this ruse, asking me to delineate the specific route I had followed in traveling into Russia, pressing me for details about the width and condition of roads as if to satisfy themselves that the overland route presented no real challenge to the supremacy of British shipping. It struck me that they considered me stupid—or perhaps they did not care if I saw through their charade. Finally Shettlefield said, "It grows quite late, and I know you must have some preparations to make before your journey tomorrow. Thank you for indulging our curiosities in this matter."

"It was my pleasure, I assure you. Good night to you, Mr. Montrose."

Montrose nodded stiffly to me and remained behind as Shettlefield stood and ushered me into the foyer. I was sure that it had been Montrose who had followed me from the Goose; Shettlefield had been stalling at the beginning of our meeting to provide Montrose the chance to circle to the rear of the house and to enter as if he'd been there all along. I felt certain that he would not trail me on my return.

As I donned my cloak and scarf, Shettlefield said, "I hope you understand our need for discretion in these matters, Captain. I apologize for the trouble it has been for you."

"Not at all."

"I know Marquis DuBois considers you a friend, but I hope you will consider me one as well. And if you should need anything, do not hesitate to ask."

"There is one thing."

"Name it!"

"I would like a pouch of that Virginia leaf you offered me earlier."

"Of course! Do take it now!"

He stepped back into his sitting room and quickly returned with a small pouch of Virginia leaf, a treasure in this part of the world. I thanked him and stepped out again into the night, and wondered, in the fresh cold air, why my cloak seemed to carry the fragrance of Lord Shettlefield's daughter, even though I had not been wearing it when I met her at the ball.

BACK in my room at the Goose, I sat upon the bed for several minutes, trying to collect my thoughts. Then I rose and went to the wall rack where my cloak hung. Reaching deep into the pocket to retrieve the tobacco I had intended to leave for Pyotr, I felt not only the pouch but a slip of paper. I withdrew it and found vellum, softly fragrant, exuding the scent of Miss Shettlefield.

Upon the paper were three words, written in an elongated, feminine but bold hand: *"Beware the provers."*

I undressed and lay upon the bed, but had no hope of sleeping.

Chapter Ten

THE knock did not startle me; I had heard the careful approach of the footsteps up the stairs and down the hallway. I tugged on my trousers quietly, lit a candle, and saw from my watch on the bed table that it was two hours past midnight.

Pulling on my boots as the knock came again, I stepped to the door, wedged my foot behind it so that it could open but two inches, unlatched it suddenly, and swung it that much ajar. A single, bareheaded man, his face in shadow, stood beyond it. "Yes?" I said.

"Cap'm Selkirk?" he said in a low voice.

"Yes."

"I be Hiram Marsh. From the *Conquest*. And I would be warmer if I could sit beside a Franklin stove."

I smiled, admitted him, and bolted the door. He stood in the center of the room, gripping the circular brim of his hat and watching me warily. He was no older than I, shorter, stockier, with skin that would have been fair if not reddened by the cold and the brine spray of the sea. I ushered him to a chair and took one opposite. He rubbed his hands beside the brazier.

"I make your accent to be of New England," I told him.

"Rhode Island! Newport!" He smiled, then just as quickly frowned. "Though I have not been home for four years, since being pressed into the British service."

"And what do you hear of home?"

He turned and looked toward either wall before he leaned forward and spoke. "There has already been shooting. British regulars firing into unarmed crowds—"

"Where?"

"In Boston."

"Were the British provoked?"

"Provoked? By the Almighty, yes! Integrity provokes them!"

"Don't misunderstand me, Marsh, I don't take the Royalist side. But I need to know what the British version might be, for that is the account I shall encounter."

"The crowd were throwing paving stones, then. And bricks too, I suppose. And *refusing to disperse,* if you take the word of the British officers I heard speaking of the incident. Most recently, patriots got up as Indians marched on a British ship and tossed a shipment of tea into the harbor, in protest of the Tea Act."

"And what has been the American reaction?"

"There are calls for full revolt."

"Open calls?"

"Open calls." He answered proudly, with defiance.

"And what does Franklin say?"

He frowned, bunched his shoulders up, pursed his lips, and squeezed out the words that he had doubtless thought through every day since he had received them, yet kept buried far from speech, so that it took such an effort for their unveiling. " 'Hostilities unpredictable but inevitable. Waste no time.

But put discretion above haste, effectiveness above discretion.' " Having discharged himself of his burden, Marsh relaxed and stared at me to see whether the words were more comprehensible to me than he had found them.

"When do you sail again?" I asked.

"We'll be in port another week, two at most. The cap'm's a whapper, he'd like to be back to London before the others have had the guts to sail. Do you have a return message?"

"Are you to deliver one?"

"I will, if Franklin is still in England when I get back."

"What do you mean?"

"He's been poking fun at the government with his articles in the paper. Published a piece called 'Rules by Which a Great Nation May Be Reduced to a Small One.' "

"Another of his satires."

"Satire, yes, and many of the local citizens agree with his points. But Lord North and his friends are iron-headed old murderers, and they'll have Franklin out of the country, and war in the colonies, before they give up office, you can believe that, sir."

"I believe everything you have told me, Marsh. And I appreciate the knowledge you have brought me and the risk you took to bring it."

"So will there be a message then?"

"I have nothing to give you in return. Except that the British are looking for American agents. So be careful."

"Oh, I will be, sir."

Marsh rose, shook my hand gravely, and we bid each other farewell at the door. "By the way, Marsh," I said, "how many times have you been to Russia?"

"Four."

"Would you know what a 'prover' is? In some particular sense, either British perhaps but most probably Russian?"

"No," he said, shrugging. "I have never heard the term."

"Very good," I said casually. "Again, farewell. And thank you for coming."

I bolted the door behind him, blew out the candle, and scraped frost from the windowpanes to watch him cross the street, his sailor's hat catching the heavy snowflakes dumping from the black sky. He walked toward the livery stable, and I wondered if he intended to find a ride back to the harbor or to stay at one of the cheaper inns that stood on the side canals.

As I pulled the covers of my bed around me for the second time that night, and closed my eyes again, a chill crept up the back of my neck, not from snow falling outside but from this question: if Franklin told this young sailor who I am and why I am here, who else might know my secret?

Chapter Eleven

T H E first gray light of dawn settled on the snowy street, which was empty except for Gorlov and me standing in the shelter of the White Goose's doorway with our traveling bags and sabers.

"What do you think we are guarding?" I wondered aloud.

No answer from Gorlov. When I looked around, I found he had stepped into the alley for a quick vomit. He returned as if nothing was wrong, and frowned through his hangover. "Fine morning to start a trip. You were saying?"

"What is so important to these men that they hire guards?" I said.

"Who knows, who cares?" Gorlov then noticed a group of four Russian constables, tall men in even taller caps the same official blue of their overcoats, all huddled at the mouth of the alley twenty paces from where we stood. They were conversing in grave whispers, arousing Gorlov's natural curiosity, even in his present condition. He drifted toward them, and I followed, pulling up short as I saw the object of the constables' interest: a body lay in frozen, twisted form upon the snow between two barrels in the alley. Gorlov, oblivious to any inhibition from official authority, asked the constables a question in Russian, then translated their answer back to me. "A man was eaten by wolves."

"Inside the city?" I wondered.

"The wolves are all around, but they would only come if they smelled blood. He must've been drunk and cut himself when he fell."

A chill seized my soul; I moved closer and looked down at the bloodless, frozen face of the dead man. It was Hiram Marsh.

THE sleigh came for us exactly as promised, and we stepped up into it without exchanging greetings with the driver. Gorlov was sullen, while I was grim. And yet the morning, whose first light had revealed such a grisly death, was delicately beautiful. Dawn filled the Russian sky like a rose opening at the edge of the world, pinkening the reflection of its cloudy petals. In the blush of its half-light we sailed through the empty streets, past the boulevard of the estate DuBois, across a bridge, and down a line of mansions on the far side of the Neva. We turned in at a circling drive, at the apex of which, before the pillared entry of a house, sat an astonishing sleigh.

It was twice larger than any sleigh I had ever encountered, larger even than the hack coaches that carry mail and passengers throughout England. Unlike the open sleigh Pyotr had piloted for us across the Russian frontier, this one was completely enclosed by a domed top, of the same polished wood as its flattened bottom. Planked and hinged ports covered the window on its right side; a tile chimney emerged from its top on the end opposite the driver's box and even now wafted smoke into the still air. The whole huge arrangement, carved, painted on the panels, and gilded at the edges, perched above graceful steel runners, and before it stretched a double line of horses, ten in all, twitching and steaming.

The sleigh that brought us from the Goose, a child's toy by comparison, stopped not beside this grand conveyance but at a door of the guard booth appended to the front corner of the house. Gorlov and I entered this booth and found DuBois, Prince Mitski, and Lord Shettlefield all waiting for us. "Gentlemen!" DuBois said, and pressed our hands. Mitski left off twisting the French silk handkerchief around his red fingers and pinched our palms distractedly. Shettlefield greeted us both with what struck me as forced calm. I suspected that he too had played a hand in our employment.

"Everything is ready," DuBois said. "All the ladies have entered the sleigh, except for the Princess Mitski, whom we expect momentarily."

"Ladies?" Gorlov and I both said at once.

"Yes," DuBois said. "The cargo . . . is our daughters."

How long Gorlov and I stood there without the power of speech, I cannot estimate. It was, I can vouch, a formidable surprise. In that moment it became clear to us why the fathers had been so concerned, and were willing to pay any price for protection against dangers no one in Russia seemed willing to admit to.

"How many ladies are there?" I wondered in English, having reverted to it in my shock.

"Five," Shettlefield answered. "And two attendants. The Princess Mitski must be in Moscow to celebrate her betrothal to a royal relative. It is a date that must not be missed."

Gorlov, following this exchange with his eyes, said nothing. "Where are our horses?" I asked, and Mitski motioned us outside, where grooms had just led up two sleek grays and were tethering them to the brass rings at the back of the sleigh.

"They lack saddles," I pointed out.

"Packed into the luggage locker," Mitski answered. I looked toward the sleigh. The grooms left, having made no further preparations for the horses. As I turned back to Mitski he cut me off: "You will not be mounted. Not until you are well out of St. Petersburg. You are not an armed escort."

"If you expect us to ride on top, with the driver and his lackey—"

"I do not. You will ride as passengers."

I explained all this in French to Gorlov, then said, "All right, gentlemen, we will do this as you wish, as long as we are within the city, and safe. But I tell you now that whenever we feel it necessary we will behave as the soldiers we are, and will not endanger the others or ourselves in order to keep up these appearances."

"If we thought you would do otherwise," DuBois said, "we would not have hired you."

The front doors of the house burst open and Natasha Mitski appeared, a girl no more than eighteen, tall, black-haired, and broad-featured like her father, and with his potato nose, attended by half a dozen seamstresses and assistants who lifted her skirt off the walk, fussed with her lace, and patted her curls as she swept toward the sleigh. Her father rushed forward and caught her, fell to his knees, kissed her hand, wept upon it, and rose beaming and sniffing. The driver's lackey, working pulleys connected to the sleigh's top, lifted the great hinged hatch on the sleigh's left side, and from within spilled a chorus of feminine adulation for the princess, who turned her back on her father and began chattering and laughing as she climbed the mounting steps and ducked into the compartment.

"Farewell, gentlemen," DuBois said, and walked from the booth out to the portico, to stand beside Mitski. Gorlov and I followed, looked toward the fathers—Mitski standing at attention, DuBois relaxed and confident, Shettlefield a pace apart from the other two, his hands clasped behind his back, his eyes downcast—and stepped into the sleigh.

The mellifluous conversation, flowing so happily the moment before, ceased as we entered. The chamber startled our senses—perfumes so flavored the air that each breath bore taste as well as scent, and jewels sparkled amid silks and ruffles, all tossed about and framing delicate faces peeking out from the piles of furs blanketing the chamber floor. Among the faces was that of Lord Shettlefield's blue-eyed daughter. The lumps beneath the furs squirmed closer together and bunched around the fire glowing in the copper slotted stove on the back side of the sleigh, leaving half the total space unoccupied in the front.

"Welcome, noble sirs!" squealed a voice far higher than any of the others I had heard, and up from the piles sprang a figure with the face and contour of a woman but the stature of a child. "Oh, great knights of the Tsarina! We await you, our maidenheads all aquiver!" the dwarfess trilled in French, her voice high and reedy as an oboe. Giggles filtered up through the furs. "We shall endeavor to—agh!" she screamed as the fur flew suddenly from beneath her feet, and she plopped upon her already flattened face to an explosion of laughter.

"Oh, do shut up, Zepsha, or we shall tie you to a horse's tail!" The speaker was Charlotte DuBois, who dropped the edge of the pelt she had snatched to spill the little creature and now smiled placidly at my gawking. "Captain Selkirk, Count Gorlov, good morning."

"Good m—" I began.

"Not I!" Zepsha interrupted, popping back upright. "I am too small for a horse's tail. But not too small to be tied between his legs!"

The maidens gasped, and Charlotte hurled a hairbrush toward the offender, who dodged and scurried behind the stove. "You may take the place at the front, gentlemen," Mademoiselle DuBois said, motioning toward the pile of rugs and furs already laid there. "I trust you will be comfortable, and warm enough as we will not be traveling at night." As we took up the places Charlotte indicated, she finished her general introduction. "My friends, these gentlemen are also my friends. And our . . . protectors," she added, watching me and mouthing the word with a slow and deliberate movement of her arched lips.

"Yes!" hooted Zepsha. "They protect us from the Cossacks—who would rape us! Rape us all!" And with that she dove full length back onto the lumps bunched beneath the furs, bouncing off first one and then another and another, eliciting squeals, threats, and giggles.

I caught a last glimpse of the pained, pale faces of the three fathers as the hatch banged down beside us. The ten-horse team broke into full stride, and the sleigh lurched, again tearing Zepsha's footing from beneath her and cartwheeling her across the furs to crash against the back wall, an event that delighted her companions immensely.

T H E ride within the enclosed compartment was smooth. The sleigh's weight bore it softly through bumps, and only during the first few minutes, when the driver was negotiating turns around city corners, did we roll beneath our coverings, Gorlov and I knocking shoulders and the ladies bouncing together. But as the way straightened, and the runners beneath us whispered, or beat across the wooden bridges spanning the canals, we grew comfortable within the enclosure, so cozy in fact that we sat up out of the furs. Charlotte made more specific introductions. Immediately to her left sat Princess Mitski, whom Charlotte announced simply as

Natasha. "And I believe, Captain Selkirk, that you may have already met Anne," Charlotte intoned, in a voice of musical detachment. Miss Shettlefield's eyes held me fast, and she nodded once, never looking away. Charlotte then went on to introduce the Contessa Bellefleur, and lastly the Lady Nikonovskaya, these latter two being the only members of the company older than eighteen. Nikonovskaya's dark mane bore strands of gray, though she could barely be thirty. The contessa, I thought, must be a year or two beyond that. Her hair glowed red, and that may have been the cause of the chill in Charlotte's voice when she spoke her name, though the older woman's hair was too orange to be natural. Charlotte made no mention of the attendant who sat in the corner between the door hatch and stove and remained hidden beneath a plain bonnet; she concluded her introductions by nudging the toe of her slipper into the ribs of the dwarfess sprawling in the space before her and saying, with a roll of the eyes, "I think you already know Zepsha."

"Know me? Of course they do!" the mite screamed, snapping to her feet like a puppet whose strings are snatched. "Everybody knows me, too well and too soon to suit them! Behind the Tsarina—or beneath her, I should say—I am the most famous woman in all of Russia! See how I travel about with these fine ladies in my retinue! And what do you say, gentlemen? Is this status due to my charm, or simply to my beauty?" With that she hopped in profile to us, jerked her hands to her hips, and cocked back her shoulders. Her left cheek glowed pink and swollen from her recent disagreement with the compartment's back wall, and her blonde curls, which I saw now to be a wig, sat slightly askew on her skull. Her lips buckled in contempt, and I found her stance before me annoying, a reaction she recognized and aggravated by shouting, "Well? Am I your female fantasy, or not?" When still I failed to answer, she kicked at the lump of Gorlov's feet beneath the covers and said, "Perhaps the American is too large to take advantage of me. But how about you, eh Gorlov? You should be the right size!" Unleashing a cascade of shrill giggles, she bent double, propping her arms against her knees and thrusting her face, contorted in laughter, right into Gorlov's.

"Get the little bitch, Beatrice," Natasha Mitski said, and the attendant in the bonnet stirred, but hesitated.

I myself sat frozen, having seen Gorlov, in a Crimean tavern, break the nose of a serving girl who tried to steal his watch, and I trembled to imagine what a blow from the same hand would do to the dwarfess (the serving girl having been as large as Gorlov). But before any catastrophe could occur, Charlotte had stretched out, grabbed Zepsha by the rear ribbons of her dress, and pulled her onto her back among the ladies. Cradling her like a doll, Charlotte said, "Oh, but you are not nearly so beautiful as befits you, silly girl, your coiffure is misarranged!" She snatched the wig around so that its curls obscured the pinched face. Suddenly three more pairs of hands alighted upon the writhing Zepsha, dousing her with perfume, dusting her with powder, smearing her with rouge and other female implements of male destruction produced instantly from hidden troves.

Zepsha made a pretense of resisting. She kicked and cried for help, encouraged by the delight such struggles elicited in her attackers. Through the entire episode only the silent attendant and the Lady Nikonovskaya remained apart. The attendant sat with her hands pressed together beneath the covers and her face obscured by the bonnet, but the Lady Nikonovskaya, just to Gorlov's right, watched us intently. Swoops of her rich hair pressed in upon her cheeks and framed a strong nose and heavy lips that on some other face might have stood out unpleasantly but combined on hers into a look both exotic and sensual. Her eyes lurked behind veils of thick lashes, and she made us wait for some moments, even after our repeated glances showed that we had grown aware of her staring, before she spoke. "So gentlemen," she said in a voice quiet and yet so definite that it cut through the commotion beside her, "you must be experienced travelers. Besides all the wars you've journeyed to, you have crossed Europe, all the way from . . . Paris, was it?"

At this Anne Shettlefield, who had been the least enthusiastic of Zepsha's tormentors, now ceased tickling the dwarfess entirely; the others followed her lead, heeding my answer.

"Together from Paris," I said. "I was in London before that." She continued to stare at me, and caused me to add, "Of course I have also crossed the ocean by ship. But I count that more as a disease than a journey, as I was seasick the entire time."

Nikonovskaya smiled, yet seemed unamused. "You met in Paris by accident, or design?"

She was looking now at Gorlov, so he answered. "By accident, I suppose. We had left the army after campaigning against the Turks, with no plans other than to take the Grand Tour. I was sure Svet would need me as chaperone, as he is but a child. Then he went to London—a den of iniquity—but Paris was as far as I dared go on my bonus money from the campaign. He returned from England just as I had exhausted my funds, and we decided to make our fortunes as Russian soldiers for hire. He provided the money for the journey, and I the expertise."

This was more information than I had ever known Gorlov to voluntarily reveal. But there was something about the lady's approach—a blend of softness with intense attention—that drew out such candor.

"But you are more than mere acquaintances, are you not?" she pressed. "You are, in fact, close comrades, having done battle together in the same regiment?"

I did not know where she had acquired her knowledge of us, and began to grow uncomfortable. She glanced to me and then back to Gorlov, who told her, "More than the same regiment! We shared the same tent! I took him under my wing, once I saw how mad he became in battle. A soldier is safer to surround himself with the craziest men he can find. God protects the insane."

She nodded, as if gleaning something profound from this banter.

Natasha Mitski seemed to tire of this talk. "Let us have some of your special tea, Svetlana!" she said, and the Lady Nikonovskaya opened one of the cabinets set into the wall beside the stove. She withdrew a hamper and produced a samovar that connected to a clasp upon the stove's top. The samovar must have contained heated water, for in only a moment it was steaming. In that time I glanced once at Miss Shettlefield; feeling my eyes upon her, she looked at me, then immediately glanced down.

"Tea for you, gentlemen?" Lady Nikonovskaya said as she produced tiny cups for the others.

"Thank you, but not now for me," I said. "We must be going outside directly."

"Brandy, then?" she said. "I brought some especially for you, to keep you warm during your exposures."

As it was but early morning, I declined. Gorlov accepted a cupful. She never took her eyes from him as he drank it down.

I rose and banged with the bottom of my fist into the wall beyond which the drivers sat. The sled stopped. We heard the lackey climb down, and the door came open. The cold and light suffusing in caused the ladies to burrow back beneath their robes. Bundling my cloak about me, I stepped out, and Gorlov followed.

The air burned my nostrils, and the bright overcast

watered my eyes. We had left the city behind already; the sleigh was even swifter than I had thought. Gorlov and I walked to the back to look at the tethered horses. The lackey followed, his bare face and hands crimson. We found the animals warm and blowing mist, yet still fresh and spirited. Gorlov gave an order in Russian to the lackey, and said to me, "I have to visit the necessary." I started off with him to the thickest clump of trees in view, just back up the road. Removing my gloves as we walked and feeling the sting of the cold, I said, "How do they do it, those lackeys, without even mittens?"

"Do you see how red his skin is?" Gorlov answered. "The blood circulates and keeps him warmer than if he covered himself."

"My fingers would fall off!"

Gorlov snorted. "Yours, probably—as you are so delicate. And speaking of falling off, there is a danger. I knew of a whole regiment in the Crimea who lost their manhood to frostbite." We reached the trees, and drew out together. Gorlov launched a steaming stream, shivered, and said, "Whoo, it *is* cold!"

"You call this cold? I remember days in Virginia when your spit would rattle when it hit the ground."

"I only meant cold relative to what we have seen lately. I have seen nights in Russia when a man with a full bladder could saw through a broomstick, if he could only go long enough."

We finished in silence and walked back toward the sleigh, where the lackey had finished saddling one horse and was starting on the other. We stopped halfway and surveyed the road. The snowy, rolling plains dotted with bare trees stretched lifeless to the horizon. "Who is that woman, that Lady Nikonovskaya?" I asked. "Do you know her?"

"I do not know her, but I know who she is," Gorlov

answered, keeping his voice low. "She is the concoctor, mixing up teas, soups, and other such things to keep the royalty healthy."

"You don't believe in surgeons here?"

"Of course we believe in surgeons," Gorlov said, impatient with me. "A surgeon is perfect for sawing off an arm or leg that has been shattered in battle, but you would be amazed how seldom such an operation is necessary for kings and queens. No, a concoctor makes the pampered feel better. But not through superstition. The good ones study books."

Gorlov spat, noticed no rattle, and added, "But I do not know of her because of her herb teas. I know of her because she is the mistress of some foreigner. I forget who."

"But how do you know this about her?"

"One learns many things in St. Petersburg, if one listens to the whispers in Russian. At the ball, and even at the Goose, when the conversation moves to Russian it is either about God or adultery. I noticed Nikonovskaya at the ball, when I was dancing with the large-breasted woman. Women, when they desire you—and all women, as you have noticed, desire me—will speak of other women only when they think it will make them look better by comparison. You haven't seen this? How could you be so stupid?"

Gorlov pressed at his forehead with the back of his gloved hand, then held a palm to his stomach as if uncertain of his digestion. He scowled toward the sky, and though he could not locate the sun there, he said, "It grows late. We must go."

"Wait, Gorlov. One more thing." He stopped and frowned back at me. "Do you know what a prover is?"

"Prover?"

"Yes." I had given him the word in French, but the word was a direct translation, no more or less obscure than in English.

"I have not heard the term," Gorlov said. "Why, to what does it refer?"

"I don't know."

"Where did you hear it then?"

"I'll tell you later. Come on, it's nothing pressing. We must go."

The lackey had both horses saddled and ready, but when I began to mount, Gorlov reached out and stopped me. "Hold a moment, Svet. Only one of us need be in this cold. You take the first hour inside."

"If anything happens, we both should be mounted."

"There will be time for that. I will ride a quarter verst ahead of the sleigh, and if there is any cause for alarm I can easily get back in time for you to mount." He saw me hesitating and added, "We could see fires long before we reached any sacked villages, and if we do get ambushed, do you really think the two of us could stop them? Hah! Those girls in there can just go ahead and mother a few dozen Cossack babies!" He laughed, then scowled again and touched his stomach.

"You look unvigorous," I said. "Why don't you let me ride the first hour?"

"It is nothing. I had Tikhon bring me a sausage roll this morning, and it was too seasoned; I'm fine. Besides, for the next hour I shall be thinking how good it will feel beneath the furs, while you shall sit beneath the furs and dread the cold."

"All right," I said, and released the reins I was holding.

Gorlov handed his reins to the lackey, stepped to the same horse I had been holding, and, swinging into the saddle, said, "I also thought I deserved the better horse, and knew you would select it for yourself."

"Oh, I did. The one you are on now is bigger, but only in the neck. His chest is smaller, and his foreleg shorter. This one that you just passed over will be much faster. I knew you would want to switch, so I started on the lesser horse."

"Heathen!" Gorlov growled, and spurred his animal off down the road. I laughed after him and reentered the compartment. The sleigh started again on its way.

Chapter Twelve

INSIDE, the ladies had begun to partake of breads and cheeses as well as wine; the aromas of the meal, mixing with the scents they had splashed over Zepsha, contrasted so sharply with the winter air I had just left that I felt as if I had fallen into some olfactory well. They offered me food when I had snuggled back down beneath the furs, and I accepted a wedge of Stilton upon a circle of bread. "Tell me," said the Contessa Bellefleur, tilting forward her thin face and licking her tiny lips fixed in a perpetual pucker. "Are you one of those American Puritans who will drink no strong spirits, or dally in other vices?"

I suddenly felt watched by them all, and wondered if they had not used the interval of my absence to discuss me. As I was just in the process of taking a cup of Bordeaux extended me by Anne Shettlefield when the contessa asked the question, I gestured with the cup and said, "I drink wine."

"Yes, but the Puritans do that," Charlotte DuBois said, grinning.

"If you are asking what religious doctrines I hold—"

"We are," the Princess Mitski broke in.

"Well, then. I was reared within a community of Presbyterians. I once embraced all their teachings. Since then my personal theology has undergone countless mutations, which I think are not worth mentioning."

"They are more interested in your moral code, Captain Selkirk," Anne said, and fixed her Wedgwood eyes upon me.

"More specifically, in the vices in which you are prone to dabble," the contessa inserted, and laughed aloud.

"Awk, he has dropped his cheese!"

"See how he blushes!"

"Fetch him another, Beatrice," Princess Mitski ordered sharply.

The attendant in the bonnet scooted to where I sat and knelt to place another piece of cheese upon the bread I still held. Then we both fumbled for the wedge I had dropped, and grasped it simultaneously. Involuntarily she raised her head, and for an instant I was face-to-face with her, and it was a face as much in contrast with the others around her as the wind outside to the scented atmosphere of that compartment. While they were rouged and powdered, perfumed and bejeweled, she bore not a trace of decoration; I noticed her features for their simplicity: the straight nose, pale lips, tapered chin. Most of all, amid this elegant starkness, I noticed the eyes, neither green nor brown but both at once, alive, darting, yet deeply anchored, like a tree on a windswept hill. I do not say that the others in the sleigh suddenly became unlovely; yet the face beneath the bonnet, in the first moment I beheld it, altered the way in which I beheld the others.

What had Princess Mitski called her? *Beatrice.* She lifted the lint-covered cheese from my fingers and returned to her seat behind the princess.

I forced a smile and said, "Well, ladies, if you wish to know about the moral code of a soldier—this particular soldier—"

Zepsha the dwarfess interrupted me. "Why don't you just speak English?" she croaked in that language. "We all understand it, and I can certainly translate for anyone who does not! We wish you would speak your native tongue, as your French is simply abominable!" She tossed her head in emphasis of this last adjective, and glowered at me. It angered her that I had turned from the group's plaything to its lecturer.

"All right," I said to Zepsha, slowly and in my own tongue. "Then allow me to tell you this. At the university, where I studied the French I speak so badly, I also studied religion, thinking I might someday enter a seminary. I was taught to believe that I should keep my body as a fit temple for God. I do not feel like a temple, and fear that God, wherever He resides, would no longer be God if He took up residence in me. From lingering habit, I take care of myself. I avoid strong drink, having acquired no taste for it. I avoid smoking tobacco, yet find its aroma pleasant. The discipline of a military life suits me."

"But you say nothing of *vices,* Captain," the Contessa Bellefleur cooed.

"Vices?" My resentment at being treated as a boy caused me to behave more boyishly.

"Of course you do know of what I speak," she said, wagging her head. "We have heard stories of the women who follow armies around."

"The ones with sores," Charlotte inserted, wrinkling her nose. Natasha Mitski groaned in disgust, then tittered.

"Come, come, Captain, do tell us of those," the contessa prompted, arching her back, lifting her chin, and cocking her head slightly. The others leaned forward, spectators to the joust. When I did not answer, the contessa said, "Why do you hesitate now? Did you hesitate *then*? See how he looks away! Ah, now, see how he flashes!" Her voice dropped into velvety alto. "Were you afraid of disease? Or were you, perhaps . . . a virgin?" The ladies gasped and held manicured fingers to their mouths.

"I am no virgin," I said.

"Oh, no?" The contessa's eyebrows arched to her hairline.

"No. I am a widower."

The luster drained from the contessa's face. The whisk of the sleigh runners filled the compartment, grown suddenly hollow.

Not another word was spoken until Gorlov, stiff with cold, came in to warm himself, and I went outside to ride.

THE gelding traced down the road sideways at first, and pranced, as if he found the feeling of a rider on his back as pleasant a sensation as I found his back beneath me.

I was surprised again by the swiftness of the sleigh. At times I had to break my horse into full gallop in order to stay sufficiently ahead, as when we passed along a section of road through heavy woods, where the sheltering of the trees had prevented drifts and given the surface a uniform depth. The driver, a long, scrawny man in tailored purple livery, cleverly chose the pace of his team, running them when a density of forest or hills beside the road offered possibilities of ambush, calming them to an easy lope on safer open spaces, though the long expanses of new snow tempted his whip.

We reached rivers and streams, all lying frozen in solid ribbons of ice. On the first crossing we made I rode directly out into the center of the rough wooden bridge and found my horse knee-deep in a treacherous ice rubble; I dismounted and led the gelding carefully to the other side. I was just about to shout back a warning when I saw the sleigh team veer off the road and down a broad smooth path beside the bridge, then flash across the ice and up the bank on the other side. At the next stream I shunned the bridge and found that the ice itself provided surprisingly good footing for the horse as long as I kept his pace steady and path straight.

We encountered little local traffic—an occasional pair of walking peasants, and one leading an oxcart, who bowed and removed his hat when he saw me, then fell to his knees and pressed his bare forehead to the snowy road when the sleigh passed him.

We reached another river, the widest yet, and I stopped on the bank to watch the several parties of peasants and trades-men moving up and down the ice in either direction. I paused to wait for the sleigh to reach me, and the driver swung the team out and then straight up the ice, using the river as high-way. As we were meeting other travelers with ever-greater frequency, I rode alongside the team. The driver now showed a tendency to overuse his whip, for the benefit of those who gawked at us as we passed.

Before the day had quite begun to wane we had reached Berenchko, an estate surrounded by bare fruit trees, and whose great wooden house was studded with crooked gables, like a stump covered with toadstools.

Chapter Thirteen

T H A T night the owners of the estate, cousins of Natasha Mitski's father, provided us with a feast. The Countess Berenchkova had donned her finest dress, but kept frowning down at it, picking at its lace, tickling disgustedly at its sleeves in a way that suggested she found it greatly inferior to the outfits of her guests, a tragedy for which she apparently blamed her husband; she snapped at him each time he dared comment about anything at all. Their servants, too, did not escape, being shouted at to refill (with vinegary wine) the already full glasses of all of us who sat at the long rickety table. But her sharpest words and glances she bestowed upon her spouse.

He received her barbs, her comments on his stupidity and ignorance of "anything two versts from him," with smiles, as if such attention made him quite happy.

I thought he might at last stop smiling when his wife led the women to the drawing room and we repaired to his study, but he beamed only more broadly, and said, "Well, gentlemen! How do you like country life?"

We pronounced it exceedingly fine, and declared ourselves envious of the delight in which he lived.

"Yes, ah yes!" he exuded. "The country cannot be sur-
passed. No, I say it cannot even be equaled. Its great peace
places it above all other possible environments."

I might have thought peace was the attribute most singu-
larly lacking in the Count Berenchkov's domestic arrangement, but I nodded in deep agreement, as did Gorlov. "Ah,"
said the count, "but I do not in my own satisfaction mean to
diminish what situations give others satisfaction. Let them be
as happy as they can!" We likewise endorsed this generous
sentiment. "So! How are things in St. Petersburg?" the count
said, while pouring us each a few drops of cognac.

Having no idea what aspect of the royal capital the count
would find most interesting, I delivered myself of the brilliant
answer, "Fine."

Gorlov, when the count turned to him, closed one eye in
reflection and added, "Typical."

"Yes. Yes," the count said, nodding gravely. "I see what you
mean." Slowly seating himself in the chair between those
already taken by Gorlov and myself, and staring sadly into the
fireplace, in which a few sticks burned, he repeated, "Yes. I see
what you mean."

He uttered these words with such conviction that Gorlov
and I both awaited some further enlightenment from our
host as to just what we had meant. We were yet waiting, and
watching the Count Berenchkov twist the bowl of the
brandy snifter between his fingers, when the harsh cry of the
countess preceded her into the room. "Grigor Ivanovich!"
she tooted, sweeping in. "We have not the rooms!"

"Room for what, my heart?" the count said, beaming as
he stood to face her.

"Room for all our guests, you idiot! Even with putting one
of the girls in the cook's quarters, we are one room short!"

"Please don't trouble yourself over that, madam," I said. "I shall be happy to sleep in the barn."

The countess stood there blinking for a moment, then flittered out again without another word.

As the Count Berenchkov slipped into a silence, which, rather than the peace he praised, struck me more as a painful isolation, I made conversation with, "Your estate seems similar in some respects to the plantations of Virginia, sir. Which crops do you find most profitable here?"

"Profitable? Here? Profitable? Profitable . . ." The word stumped him completely. "The happiness of my family—and my extended family, my serfs—is the great blessing of my investments each year." He looked up and showed me that same smile, now grown thin as water. "I have undertaken new reforms to improve the lot of my serfs, reforms for which the Tsarina has lobbied for several years. I have allotted each his own parcel of land, and allow each to keep his produce. They are to pay rents in the form of a percentage of their crop." Here the count lost the thread of his thought and drifted into a puzzlement.

"And . . . they produce well?" I asked.

"They scarcely produce at all," he answered. "They say they need equipment—a harness, a plow. So I buy them the finest. In a week they have taken the tool I bought for fifty rubles and sold it for three to buy vodka! Profitable? Profitable? Oh. Yes. Mmm . . ."

I was regretting having asked, seeing that my inquiry confused him. "However," he said, "I am happy for my reforms, not just for the happiness they have brought my serfs, but because they shall remain steadfast, no matter how far the Cossacks spread their revolt."

I looked to Gorlov. He shook his head.

The count looked at me—not harshly, and not with his smile; he merely gazed at me plainly. "Yes, I see," he said. "It is really that bad in St. Petersburg. They have blinded themselves that far."

He had turned away from me again when his wife broke back into the room. "A shame!" she cried. "A terrible shame to be forced to treat one's guests so!"

"Has . . . it all not come right, my dear?"

She glanced at him, the pupils of her eyes shrunken with contempt. "The ladies were shocked when I told them the German would sleep in the barn. They did not say so, but they were shocked, I know it."

The count found this a great joke. After a hearty laugh he corrected her: "No, my dear. Captain Selkirk is an American!"

The lady shrugged as if there could hardly be a difference, squinted at my uniform, then shrugged again. Relapsing into distress, she said, "But I am in quite an impossible situation."

The count was grinning himself into danger of facial cramp, unable as he was to suggest anything.

"Perhaps I can help you then, madam. In fact, I know I can," I said in German, causing the countess to peer at me in a confusion as great as her husband's; not liking the lady, I could not resist this small torment, even as I sought to deliver her. But then I translated my words into French, adding, "I would like very much to sleep in the kitchen tonight, on a pallet of blankets by the fire. It is where I slept as a boy, and I would enjoy the experience again. You may even tell your staff and other guests that I insist upon it."

Now Countess Berenchkova grinned at me.

THIS hearth was huge, large enough for me to have stood upright within it, or to have stretched out to my full length across the bed of orange coals hissing hickory smoke. The cook had stacked the fire skillfully, so that it might glow in the same way through the long night, never breaking into blaze but always emitting its dry heat, and still retaining enough life to flower into vigorous flame when stirred the next morning. The servants had removed the spits and kettles from their various hooks within the hearth, pushed back the carving tables, swept the warm brick floor, and spread out a mat of straw. Upon this the last servant to remain, an ancient pantry maid, placed the stack of folded blankets that were to serve as my mattress. It made the coziest of beds; the old woman winked at me as she left by the back door for the servants' cottages.

The kitchen itself was an annex, a house unto itself, separated from the manse by a ten-foot open space that served as a firebreak. It had two rooms: the large cooking area—overhung with knives and utensils, a water pump and trough in the corner, copper pots all about catching the glow of coals, and the whole place suffused with the echoed aroma of a thousand sizzling roasts—and the cook's sleeping quarters. Of how that looked or smelled I had no idea; the door had been shut fast since I entered.

I was just beginning to unbutton my tunic when the outer door flew open and Gorlov walked in. He was grinning. I was beginning to suspect that the estate Berenchko bore some curse that caused continuous grins in its inhabitants. Looking around he said, "Seems a perfect place for you, Svet!"

"Are your accommodations adequate?"

"That's what I came to tell you. My room is right next to the Contessa Bellefleur's." He grinned again. I perceived that it was not because of the Berenchko curse.

"Well, if you should grow cold in the night, you're welcome to bring your bedding down here."

"Oh, if I should grow cold, I should ask your assistance, you can count on that." Suddenly, as he had done too many times already that day, Gorlov winced and grabbed at his intestines. He actually bent his body across one of the carving tables, pressing his face against the scarred surface. As he squeezed back a groan, I grabbed his forehead.

"Gorlov, you're fevered!"

"It passes," he said quickly, forcing himself upright and knocking away my hand.

"It worsens," I said.

"No. It has come and gone throughout the day. Cramps and griping, it's nothing. The attacks were weakening, but have gotten worse after I overate at dinner."

"Why have you said nothing?"

"Bringing fever into a home is no way to ensure hospitality. And indigestion after dinner is even less gracious, wouldn't you say?" With that Gorlov stepped calmly to the back door, threw it open, went out into the frigid night, and vomited. I winced at the sound of his retching, but he marched cheerfully back inside. "Ah. All better," he said. "Good night, my friend."

"Call me if you need me," I said as he opened the other door, the one back to the house.

"I shall call you if the Contessa Bellefleur needs you," he said. "But she won't."

With Gorlov gone I walked back to the hearth. Unbuttoning my tunic, I stretched high my arms, pressing my palms against the chimney bricks above the hearth opening and leaning down to face the fire. I had stood thus for some minutes when a voice behind me said, "Captain Selkirk?"

I whirled. It was Princess Mitski's attendant, Beatrice. She stood two feet outside the sleeping chamber, and retreated back into the doorway as I turned on her. Fumbling to rebutton my tunic with one hand I held the other up to stop her and said, "No, wait, I'm sorry, you startled me. Excuse me, I was unprepared. . . ."

She hesitated, then stepped forward again as I finished the buttons at the collar. "Can I help you?" I asked.

Her lips paused open; she watched me so closely it was as if she had forgotten to speak. She had removed her bonnet, and I saw her for the first time without the heavy cloak that had enshrouded her all day. Her dress was plain, a thin beige; but in that garment, without the mounds of petticoats, ruffles, and paddings that the noble ladies wore, she looked more feminine than I had remembered women to be. Her hair was chestnut, tied in a bundle behind her neck. She seemed to be storing up the will to speak, but when the words broke loose, they came clearly. "I wanted only to tell you that your French is not terrible."

"Are you . . . French, Beatrice?" I asked. She had an accent, so slight I could not place it.

"No. I am Polish."

A Pole! In my surprise I must have mouthed the words, or even spoken them aloud, for she answered me:

"Yes." Not *oui,* but *yes.*

"And . . . so you speak English, too."

"I do, yes."

"And German as well, I suppose?"

"Yes. Why do you smile? Do you laugh at me?"

"No, no, Beatrice, I do not. I laugh at them. I know what they think of Poles. And now I know what you must think of them."

Her eyes lingered upon me for a moment, as if in disobedience of her own will, and she said suddenly, "I must go. I wanted only to tell you that . . . that Zepsha merely sought to be cruel, and—"

"Stay, please. Only a moment, but stay."

"For what?"

"To talk. I would love just . . . to talk. Sit with me here and let us just talk." If she was surprised by the fervor of my invitation, I was equally so. In that moment I was disposed even to plead with her to stay, so great was the mingled draft of loneliness and desire that ambushed me as I stood there with her. On that estate full of beautiful, noble ladies, single and available, charged with flirtation, on that night when Gorlov and the Contessa Bellefleur were sure to have at each other, I wanted nothing more than that Beatrice not return to her room and shut the door, leaving me desolate in that place that before her entrance had seemed so hospitable and complete.

She walked slowly to the hearth and with an unmatched grace sat down upon one end of the pallet before it. I took the opposite end, and, like her, pulled my knees up below my chin, clasping wrist in hand around the shins and staring at the coals. I was searching for some polite, conversation-beginning question, when she asked, "What do you know of Poles?"

Nervous as a schoolboy, I spoke like one. "Poles? I know that their country lies between two nations that perpetually lurch between partnership and hostility. The embraces have been as destructive to Poland as the wars, because the foundation of every treaty between Germany and Russia is an understanding that the Poles not be allowed to unify and determine an independent path. As for the people themselves, they are called cruel and stupid, and they laugh at the jests made about them, and do so, I think, because no Pole believes in his heart he deserves the reputation the world bequeaths him. On the battlefield Poles are reckless and brave. Desperate, too, and quite resigned to death if it comes."

She nodded. However she digested my dissertation, she showed no reaction. Not looking from the fireplace, she said, "Is it true you slept in the kitchen as a boy?" When I did not answer, she turned her face to me. "The Countess Berenchkova came into the drawing room, where I had been allowed to join the ladies after dinner. She was troubled and amused that anyone so common could become an officer."

"I see. Well. Yes. I did sleep in the kitchen, though it was not a large separate structure like this, but an end of our house where my father cooked—what cooking we did."

A tap sounded on the door.

Beatrice crossed the floor in a running float, closing her door behind her, all without sound. I looked to the outer door, from which the tap had come. I stalked to the door and opened it.

Anne Shettlefield stood in the moonlight, pale shafts of lunar silver glowing at the tips of the gray fur bundling her against the bitter cold. She was casting a glance back toward the house as the door opened, then she turned to me. We both paused, an instant only, and she hurried inside, with another glance into the darkness as I shut the door behind her. "Anne," I said.

She held a finger to her lips, then whispered, "Is Natasha's attendant asleep?"

"She is very quiet," I said.

She moved deeper into the room, but only a few steps. She now stood between me and the closed door of the small annex where Beatrice surely stood listening. Anne turned to face me, and I could see that she was anxious, ready to fly back to the main house at any instant. The glow from the fire now burnished the tips of her fur, the side of her cheek, and her blue eyes. "I . . . I come to warn you, Captain," she said.

"Against what?"

"Against everything." She saw me trying and failing to make sense of such a warning. "There are more dangers here than I can name."

"Dangers to everyone—or to me personally?"

"Some are to everyone—but some are yours alone. And I fear you are too . . . innocent to see them."

"Miss Shettlefield, you confuse me."

"You confuse me, Captain."

"Anne . . . I don't understand what you mean to tell me. Are you trying to help me, or do you need help?"

"There is no help for me."

Those words, uttered by a beautiful eighteen-year-old woman, might make any man protest; but she spoke with conviction. And when she moved toward the door, I stepped away. She started out. "Anne!" I called suddenly. She stopped, her eyes snapping up to me. "What is a prover?" I asked.

She closed the door again behind her and turned back to me. Her Wedgwood eyes were brittle, unblinking, as she said, "There is a rumor about the Court. It is a rumor I believe. The Queen loves to play at love—because of her past, when romance was denied her and her suitors exiled, or because of her own inclinations, I do not know, but I do know, of a certainty, that she is deeply romantic, and desires for herself and for everyone around her to be in a state of constant courtship. The rumor is that when a young man is identified as a possible lover for Catherine, a prover is selected—a woman who will try the prospect for his prowess at lovemaking. It is unthinkable that a man should enter the Tsarina's bed and prove to be . . . unvigorous."

Her gaze drifted down to dart back and forth across the floor, and then she opened the door suddenly and stepped out again. "Anne!" I called, and she stopped, the door half open, her face in shadow. "Is there a prover among the women of your party?"

She stood very still in the cold and the darkness, then closed the door and was gone.

I turned to one of the carving tables, leaned against it, and tried to organize the thoughts and feelings Anne's visit had stirred in me. After a moment I stood upright and went to Beatrice's door. I tapped. No answer came.

"Beatrice!" I whispered loudly, tapping again. "Beatrice! Are you yet awake?"

She said something on the other side of the door.

"I'm sorry," I said in a normal voice. "I could not hear you."

Then her voice came plainly through the door. "I am no prover," she said.

Chapter Fourteen

E departed the Berenchko estate the next morning, leaving our hosts standing beside each other and waving until we had turned out of the lane; the countess was tilted toward her husband and unleashing a stream of reproach, while the count grinned in joy to see us off, that he might resume in undivided bliss the peace of his country life. The horses were refreshed, the road hard frozen and smooth, and I should have had an outlook for the day's journey as rosy as the dawn clouds. But Gorlov's condition instilled me with foreboding.

We rode side by side; in light of the Count Berenchkov's mention of the Cossacks the night before, we had decided both to remain mounted as long as we could, and then to switch off only in short shifts when cold or fatigue forced us into the compartment. But Gorlov, as soon as we were out of sight of the estate, slumped from the jaunty posture all cavalry officers hold when riding in the presence of spectators. The hunched position he now adopted made me doubt he could cover ten miles. "The Contessa Bellefleur has returned you to us somewhat the worse for wear," I said.

"She would chew you off to your eyeballs if you'd let her," Gorlov growled, trying to straighten. "Of course, I can only blame myself, for having aroused such passion." He was not smiling, and he struggled against the canter of the horse— a terrible sign in a rider as skilled as Gorlov. "But how about you, you young rooster. Two women at once. My God!"

"What do you mean?" I said, smarting already.

"I know who visited you last night," he said, sitting up straighter in his saddle as the spasms in his gut relaxed. "We watched from Antoinette's—the Contessa Bellefleur's—window. In fact, you were our pretense for getting together. Antoinette came to my room whispering and giggling and led me back to hers. 'Anne has left her chamber!' she said. So we peered out from the second floor and saw her enter the kitchen—where you and that quiet little Polack already were. I assume Beatrice shared in the fun, as it would be hard to be so close to the acrobats and not want to join the circus, huh?"

Gorlov knew me better than that. But he wanted me to tell him what did happen. He joked this way also because he was worried about himself.

"So the Contessa Bellefleur knows Anne paid a call on me."

"Every woman with a room on that side of the house watched her. By now they all know! Those merchants who pay printers to post advertisements on streetlamps are the greatest fools of all; they have only to find one woman, whisper whatever they want broadcast, and tell her it is a secret."

I said nothing. This annoyed Gorlov, but the cramps seized him again, and came and went until, less than an hour out of the Berenchko estate, I convinced him to ride awhile in the sleigh, and I was left on the road alone.

T H E solitude I welcomed, as I had the day before. My uncertainties were growing, multiplying one another. I thought of Anne Shettlefield's visit, of my visit to her father, of Marsh, and Franklin, and of Beatrice.

"Be patient," Franklin had told me in London. "A man who walks through open doors is thought to be but rational; a man who presses against closed doors will attract attention and make his intentions plain to everyone."

Riders! Many riders! I reined my horse back so hard he reared; when his forehooves landed, he spun in a circle. I cursed myself and brought him under control. I had my hand upon the handle of my saber, but before I drew it I saw the uniforms. And they were not uniforms only, but the rider at the head of the others wore a tunic exactly like mine; he was a Prussian mercenary.

Instead of galloping back to the sleigh to turn it, I waved my hand high to tell the driver to slow down, and trotted toward the contingent as they closed on me. I saw perhaps twenty men, all professional soldiers—German and Dutch, Irish and Swedish. I pulled up before their leader and found his uniform bore the bars of lieutenant. He was a classic Prussian: thin in the chin, lips, and bridge of the nose, rigid of face and posture. He was older than I, but only by a few years—Gorlov's age. He actually wore a monocle, and as I waited for him to salute he eyed me through it. I kept my hands folded across the saddle horn and let my horse nuzzle his. The monocle popped out, and he snapped his hand up as if he had not waited at all, as if he had not tried to intimidate me. I returned the salute casually. "Out hunting, Lieutenant?" I said in German.

He was about to answer when he saw the sleigh approach, and his steely eyes pulsed wider for a moment. The driver tugged back the horses, and they halted with a chorus of snorting, the sleigh sliding to a stop directly beside me and the Prussian. The other mercenaries neither made way nor moved toward the team; they eyed our horses, the fine livery of the driver and lackey, the gilding of the sleigh itself, and held their ground.

"We are not hunting," the Prussian said to me. "This is a training mission. But I am ordered to investigate anything I find suspicious."

"Then I hope you will train your men to be disciplined soldiers . . . Lieutenant," I said.

"You may trust me for that . . . Captain," he said. "What are you escorting?"

"I am no escort, but a traveler, doing a favor for friends. This is a royal carriage, as you can see. It contains a Russian prince, who is an embarrassment to his family, for he is quite mad. The good monks of a certain monastery, whose name I may not divulge, have agreed to accept him for the rest of his natural life, to keep him from harming himself and shaming the Crown. He is a bastard, you see." I spoke this last sentence leaning forward and in a soft voice; and I prayed the whole speech was sufficiently hushed to be convincing and loud enough for Gorlov to have heard with his ear pressed to the sleigh's wooden window.

"We would trouble you to let us see him." The words came from a man at the Prussian's right, a horseman of indeterminate national origin who wore a Russian uniform with sergeant's rank. His fur cap listed to the right, down over the stump of a missing ear, and like other disfigured fighting men I had seen, he wore a smug smile.

"Shut up!" the Prussian lieutenant snapped, but then he turned his gray eyes back at me.

I might have told them to go to hell, and ordered the driver to send the team forward, but our fates would have turned on a single, unpredictable moment, when the mercenaries would have been either cowed enough to let us pass, or aroused enough to snatch the harnesses of our horses. And I did not care to trust in the rationality of twenty armed men who were brawlers and debauchers on the best of days, and who had not seen an attractive woman in weeks; with no one else in sight for miles, I knew our party could be robbed, raped, or murdered, with the Cossacks blamed for the crime. "If you have orders to inspect us, then you must," I said slowly. "Come with me, Lieutenant. And why don't you come along, too, Sergeant?"

We dismounted, the three of us, and walked around to the side of the sleigh, where the door was. "Prepare yourselves, gentlemen," I said. "He is not a happy sight." I unlatched the door, and gave it a slight tug. It came open, then slammed shut again, pulled from the inside. "Come now, Prince!" I called, as if to a spoiled child. "These gentlemen wish to see you." To the gentlemen in question, I said, "I am sorry, sometimes he is recalcitrant." Tugging lightly again, I pleaded, "Come now, Prince, please!"

"Let me help you, sir," the sergeant growled, and, seizing the handles, he gave a nasty jerk. The door flew up, carrying the sergeant's arms high, and a terrible roar and a scream split the cold air. The sergeant, from whom had come the scream, toppled onto his back in the snow, spouting blood from the side of his head, and Gorlov, still roaring, emerged slashing with his saber, one swing backing off the Prussian and myself, several more cleaving phantom enemies, and then a final few flying over the fallen sergeant. The sergeant howled, and Gorlov reciprocated with slobbers and ravings of his own.

"My God!" the Prussian said. "He's cut off his other ear!" And sure enough, there on the road between us and the fallen sergeant lay a stray ear. Gorlov saw it when I did, I think, and snatched it up, took a bite from it, spat the piece at the sergeant, threw the unchewed half at the Prussian; then, to apply the coup de gras, he vomited onto the cowering sergeant's chest.

This last improvisation, inspired no doubt by Gorlov's illness and his rancor over having been disturbed, was a bit too much for the Prussian; he staggered beside me. "Prince, please go back inside!" I called. Gorlov rolled his eyes toward me. "Go back inside, and I shall ask the monks to give you that puppy I promised!"

Gorlov smiled, waddled docilely back into the sleigh, and pulled the door shut behind him.

Biting hard on my own tongue, I turned to the ashen-faced Prussian, who said, "My God, these Russians are wild. Even the sane ones are mad, but the mad ones . . . my God!"

"There is no accounting for them," I agreed.

The sergeant staggered to his feet, snatched up his cap, and used it to try to stem the flow of blood from his new stump as he ran, hunched over, back to his horse. "Sorry to have detained you, sir," the Prussian said.

I'll bet you are, I thought.

"You must be careful here," he said, now full of helpfulness and concern. "There are Cossacks about."

"Have you seen any?"

"We have pursued the same band for over a month. It is led by a man who wears a wolfskin cap. The peasants call him 'Volchaya Golava'—Wolfhead. We have been within a few hours of him. But as we pursue his band divides, and divides again—and we keep dividing, to follow them. Most of our teams find nothing; it's as if the Cossacks disappear into air. But when we regroup, some of us are always missing, and these we do find, mutilated. I have lost a dozen men already, and I will divide no more. We will continue our charade of being a training mission."

"So as not to alarm the populace," I said.

"We need more men. Better men," the Prussian said tightly. "The looting and rape of a few villages doesn't alarm the government. Nor do a few dead mercenaries. But wait until the Cossacks march on Moscow. Then the charades will stop in St. Petersburg."

We walked to our horses, mounted, and exchanged salutes. He waved his men forward, and I preceded the sleigh away. I looked back once, to see the sergeant in the rear of his column, slumped over and bleeding down the wrist of the hand he held to his head.

Chapter Fifteen

SHORTLY before noon we reached a frozen river, and the driver stopped, explaining in broken French that he wanted to rest and water the horses. He set the lackey to chopping a hole into the ice, while I reconnoitered the opposite bank and found a stand of spruce thick enough to conceal the sleigh and to give the ladies shelter should they wish a respite themselves.

"Oh, what a fantastic spot!" Charlotte exclaimed when I had drawn the sleigh up behind the trees and opened the door to the ladies. "Captain, you have an instinct for tasteful surroundings."

"The spot does look magical," Anne said, disembarking behind her. I was surprised by the sprightliness in her voice; she seemed to have lost her aloofness from the others.

"Yes! Perhaps there are Snow Spirits here!" Charlotte called happily.

"We don't have Snow Spirits in England," Anne said brightly. "What do they look like?"

Princess Mitski, wrapping her fur cloak around her as she

emerged from the warm compartment, quickly joined in: "Oh, they are enormous, with giant blue faces and white whiskers all about, even on the women."

"Whiskers on the women? Ah, something like the Countess Gellnikova, you mean?" Charlotte said, and all three burst out laughing.

"No, not her," Anne said. "She has only a mustache."

"Yes, and Snow Spirits have full beards," Natasha Mitski added.

"The Countess Gellnikova is growing one," Charlotte said, and they all laughed repeatedly as Charlotte insisted it was really true.

"Who has a beard?" Zepsha demanded, running from one lady to the other and frowning; having come late to the conversation, she did not understand the joke and was irritated that the laughing continued. "What are you talking about?"

The ladies stopped and looked at her. "Snow Spirits!" Charlotte whispered.

"The little, tiny, obnoxious kind," Anne said. And suddenly the three ladies were chasing Zepsha around in the snow, the dwarfess tumbling and rolling and sliding in and out beneath the sleigh.

"No, not all at once!" I screamed at the lackey, who had come up from the river and was unharnessing the horses as they stood in their traces. "Two at a time! Two only!" The man stopped and peered dumbly at me. "Look, you— I want—"

Beatrice was just climbing from the enclosure, and as I reached out to help her, I said, "Here, Beatrice, could you make this fellow understand that he is not to unharness the entire team at once? I want him to unhitch and water two at a time, in opposite pairs, leaving the others prepared to run if they have to."

She raised her face and said, "You'd better get the Princess Mitski or one of the other ladies to translate for you. The lackey would take the order better." The princess was then beside us, giggling and kicking at the hands of Zepsha, who was mixing herself up with the struts of the sleigh runners. Beatrice curtseyed low to her mistress, and in a whisper she explained the situation. The princess turned directly to me.

"My, Captain, how vigilant you are! Yes, I shall certainly tell the man!" And she marched off and did so, quite proud of herself.

"Is there fresh water?" Beatrice asked.

"Yes. Would you like some? I'll walk you down."

"No, please, let me go alone." I halted and watched her walk away, cradling the crystal pitcher she had retrieved from the sleigh.

Not having seen Gorlov since his appearance as the mad prince, I looked in upon him. What I found unsettled me greatly. Gorlov lay with the back of his head propped against the wall opposite the door. His face had lost all color, and the paleness stood out in the dimness of the compartment. Contessa Bellefleur and Lady Nikonovskaya sat on either side of him, the contessa pressing the knuckle of her forefinger against her lips and looking baffled as well as worried, while the Lady Nikonovskaya spooned an aromatic herb mixture between Gorlov's heavy lips. "Gorlov!" I said, and moved to kneel beside him.

He raised his eyelids, stared at me a moment, and then lowered them in shame. "Is it fever?" I asked the contessa.

"On the contrary. He is quite cold," she answered. I felt his forehead and found it damp and chill as a raw oyster. "It is just a digestive problem," the contessa said, as if she believed it.

The Lady Nikonovskaya, who obviously had been the source of this diagnosis, added, "It will pass soon. Would you like some herbal tea, Captain? It will warm and improve you." She held the large cup toward me.

Ignoring her in my concern, I felt Gorlov's neck for his pulse. He reached up and pushed my hand away, grumbling but not opening his eyes. "He needs a surgeon," I said.

"The nearest good one is in St. Petersburg, if you want to go back," the Lady Nikonovskaya said. "And by now we must be almost as close to Moscow. But I assure you, Captain, a physician could help him no more than I can."

"Can you bleed him?" I asked her.

"Bleed him? Don't be ridiculous."

"He needs medical attention."

"Captain, have you ever been bled yourself?"

"Not medically so, no. But I have seen it done many times, and heard its benefits attested to."

"By those who recovered! What did those who died say? I promise you, Captain, the lancet will not help him."

"What has he been eating?" I asked the contessa.

"Breads and cheeses," she answered. "And quite a lot of brandy, I'm afraid, both before and after he became the 'prince.' "

"Well, keep him reasonable, won't you?" I said hotly. "No more brandy at all! And if he is not himself tonight, we go for the nearest surgeon no matter where he is!"

I stormed from the sleigh, angry with Gorlov for having drunk brandy when he was already out of sorts, peeved at the ladies for having urged it upon him, and unsettled with vague suspicions I could not yet name.

The ladies outside, heated by their games, were now sharing water from the pitcher Beatrice had brought up from the river. The driver had condescended to help the lackey with the horses, and they were making quick progress leading the pairs down to the hole in the ice. I walked to the cluster of ladies and accepted a drink myself. Beatrice poured, but Princess Mitski handed me the cup, and it was she I thanked.

"How is your friend?" the princess asked.

I shook my head.

"If he is in the care of Bellefleur," Charlotte said, "then you can be sure he's in good hands—in fact, that they're all over him!"

At this the princess and Anne snickered, covering their mouths with their hands, as if fearing I should be offended by too much laughing; but Zepsha collapsed backward into the snow, throwing up her tiny feet and kicking as she cackled. Charlotte herself was embarrassed by this overreaction, and winced at me, blushing; but it was clear the ladies considered Gorlov's distress to be but an affectation for the contessa's attention.

The lackey was just leading the last pair of the sleigh horses back up the bank from the river. Since my horse and Gorlov's had yet to be watered, I untied both from the back of the sleigh and led them toward the river.

The wind was rising, and as I reached the slant of the bank I felt its full gust, funneled through the channel of the river and carrying the crisp odors it had swept up—the scent of wet bark, of spruce needles, of leaves in a stray patch of thaw—but it was the sound it bore that gripped me. I froze, and strained to hear, but could not find it again. Yet it was such a potentially dangerous sound, and one so familiar to me, so unlikely for me to mistake—the whinny of a horse—that I led my own animals back from the bank and waited.

At first I made out only the hiss of the wind through the spruce needles and the distant dull clatter of branches clashing. I waited so long hearing nothing more that I began to suspect my imagination. Then, starting back toward the hole in the ice, I saw them.

Four mounted Cossacks came down the frozen river, moving slowly and cautiously, but with that ease I have seen in every Cossack to sit a saddle. The horse of one was croupy, in fact, dying—he snorted with a wheeze and coughed with a wet rattle—but his rider managed not only to quiet him, through distraction with the reins, but to keep him moving. I shrank back into the trees, slowly at first, turning the heads of my own horses to keep them quiet and unexcited by scents, then, when screened by the bank and trees, fairly yanking them back to the sleigh.

"Get in! Now!"

The Lady Nikonovskaya and the Contessa Bellefleur, who had stepped outside the sleigh for a few moments of fresh air, gawked at me, then paled as I seized them by the arms and shoved them back into the compartment. Looking in after them I saw Beatrice attending Gorlov, who would have appeared asleep but for the grimace on his white lips, and the others sitting in a circle. They gaped up at me as I said, "We fly! If the sleigh stops, and the door is opened from the outside without me first calling that it is safe, the first man to enter and everyone after that must be killed, by Gorlov if he is able, and by you if he is not!" I snapped the door shut upon their startled faces, and ran to the driver. "Be ready! There are Cossacks!"

"Where?"

I did not like the look in his eyes, and thought him ready to crash off that very moment. "All around," I told him, as calmly as I could. "We are encircled. But they don't know we are here, and I see a way out, if you will be silent and do exactly as I say." He tightened his grip upon the reins, and tightened his teeth against one another. "Stay here until I come back, and watch for me; I will signal the direction you are to go, but you must move in silence. Do you understand?"

He nodded. I tied Gorlov's horse to the back of the sleigh, led my horse halfway back to the riverbank, tethered him to a sapling, and waded the rest of the way on foot through the deep snow within the shelter of the trees. I crouched behind the largest.

The party had moved down the river almost to the spot where we had crossed. Their stealth was so natural that I could not distinguish casualness from fatigue in them; from their appearance, they were likely full of both. Only the man in front, a short rider whose stubby legs stuck straight from the sides of his horse, appeared at all watchful.

I do not recall a moment's effort at deducing who they were and how they came to be there. I was aware instantly, perhaps from the first moment I heard the sound of the sick horse, that they were part of the main band, dispersed through the pursuit of the Prussian's mercenaries, now regrouping and heading back to the main body. It was clear to me that pre-arranged rendezvous points supported their entire strategy, as they had been able to lure the mercenaries into dividing in pursuit of what seemed to be inferior numbers, but which were, in fact, coordinated groups, ready to pounce. I could not know how far they were from their next point of collection, or how far removed they were from the main body. But I knew for certain that the question of our immediate safety or danger lay with how sharp-eyed the squat leader of this group was.

They drew even with the spot where we had crossed and the hole the lackey had chopped in the ice. They kept moving, watching, it seemed to me, only for any random traffic to appear upon that common fording point. The leader held up his hand. He squinted, then urged his horse closer to the hole.

I started to back away from the tree, but forced myself to hold my position a moment longer. Below me, the little leader dismounted and poked his finger through the crust that had formed on the surface of our watering hole. He spoke to the others. They began to look around and converse quietly. Then one of them pointed to the scars of the sleigh runners. They spoke more, and faster. One of them, jabbering, pointed to where the runner marks ran up the bank. I slid away from the tree upon my belly and raced back to my horse.

Slipping into the saddle and pressing the gelding forward in a trot, the gait I had found to be his smoothest and quietest, I gained the sleigh and swung alongside the driver, tapping a finger to my lips and motioning that he follow me. I led around the grove, forcing my own horse to walk, for the team at that pace would make less noise than at any other. Thirty yards across the field we reached the wooded road toward Moscow, and I broke us all into a canter, hoping the wind would carry our noise from the Cossacks or that, if any sound did reach them, the combination of hooves would jumble like the whoosh of breeze in a forest—a scant hope, but my only one. Any moment I expected a shout from behind as the Cossacks topped the bank, followed our fresh tracks, and caught sight of us.

Still no shout came, and a hundred yards down the road I found what I was looking for: a way back to the frozen river. Winding off the road and into the trees again, we maneuvered to our right, upstream, the sleigh plowing tracks in the virgin snow that the Cossacks could miss only if they were in such a panic to pursue us that they would ride in full gallop right past our entrance.

We broke from the thin woods and out upon the river, several hundred yards above our original watering place and out of sight of it, but I paused. The wind was in our faces, and if it could carry the sound of a cough from a single Cossack horse down to me when I was at the hole, then how might a team sound to the Cossacks, now that I had reversed our positions? I spurred my horse, and he plunged down the bank quietly enough; but the team, all harnessed together, clattered out onto the ice, and the sleigh boomed onto the surface like a wooden cannon. "Run them!" I called to the ashen driver. "Not full gallop unless I signal, but make them run!"

He raised his whip, had the sense to hold it back, and lashed the reins. The horses snapped forward, making brisk way along the flat, winding ice.

I fell in behind and cast wild glances as I rode, searching the trees for the ambush, or jerking to stare backward at the pursuit from downriver. The sick grip of battle was already upon me, the apprehension so close to panic that it whips itself higher into a whirlwind rush of blood, gut to head to gut. Had I seen an adversary then I might have done anything, however senseless, such as screaming or hurling my saber at him; I was that taut.

Struggling to control myself, I forced questions through my brain. Would they follow us at all? Would four tired Cossacks have the alertness, the curiosity, the confidence, the very savagery to pursue and attack us, when they themselves were evading a pursuit? And if they had not seen us, how good were they at tracking? Could they judge from the markings on the ice the number of horses in our sleigh team, and know from that and the depth and gauge of the runners that they had come across the marks of a massive vehicle, one substantial enough to be royal? And if they came on, would it be like frightened, cautious men, or like wolves? *Volchaya Golava. Wolfhead.*

The driver's thoughts must have been like mine; he had lashed the horses into full flight. The pace was as perilous to the passengers as the Cossacks, for the river was narrow in places and the banks steep, so that the whole sleigh could overturn as it swung round any of the tight bends, or catch a runner if we reached a section of frozen rapids, ripping off the metal and turning the whole structure into a gangling mangle dragged by the panicked horses. It took me most of a mile to draw even with the driver and motion him to a stop.

"Go easy!" I said, gasping. "You'll kill your horses and your passengers!" He stared at me, and it was a moment before

I could believe he saw anything at all. "Now move forward," I ordered him, "but slowly, no running at all! Look for a way off the river, but by a road, not just a clearing in the trees."

"The banks are too steep to get off! We are trapped here!" he hissed through clenched teeth.

I sneered, and tried to look bored. "Did you see any Cossacks? I saw the only Cossacks, and they were moving away from us. Do exactly as I say and you'll be safe, both now and when we get back to St. Petersburg." I stared at him long enough to convince him my threat was in earnest. "Now move forward. Slowly! If you must gain speed to climb a bank, do so, but only for a road! And keep your lackey looking back for my signals!"

They moved ahead. The sound of the sleigh team diminished greatly as they drew away, but the runners had tracked a glazed silver trail upon the otherwise white ice. I trotted back to a tight bend at the end of a long straight stretch of the river, rode in among the trees, and peered out at the open ice on the other side of the curve.

They came.

And the way they came was as unsettling as the fact they came at all. Narrow as the river was, they were spread upon it to protect from ambush, one rider skirting either bank and two coming in tandem down the center of the ice. They rode quickly but did not hurry. I had maneuvered against them as if they were animals, and they met me with tactics.

I felt a tingling heat within my ears. It was like ringing, but there was no sound.

Screened by the bend of the river, I chased after the sleigh, trotting at first, then cantering. I dared not cry out, for the yell might carry back and reach the Cossacks above the sound of their own horses' hooves; but I waved at the lackey. He waved back, and the sleigh was suddenly at top speed.

"Damn you!" I cursed beneath my breath. "No! No!" We

could outpace them if we but held steady, moving briskly until we reached a road and the safety of a town or the Cossacks gave up the chase. I waved again, frantically, and the lackey waved back. The driver cracked the whip.

Still it might not have been so bad. The sleigh sailed so swiftly upon the ice that the Cossacks would have been hard-pressed to catch us within miles. But at that moment the driver saw what he must have thought a great opportunity—a bridge, where a road crossed the river.

He reined back on the team, and I, a hundred yards behind him, relaxed. But then he saw that the bridge itself was covered in snow, and the smooth-packed, worn-down bank the travelers used was on the side away from us. The bridge was far too low for the sleigh to pass beneath, and the banks nearest us lay deep in drifted snow. The sleigh seemed to pause, as if the driver meant to stop. Then the whip cracked, and the horses hurtled toward the bank.

The lead pair piled into snow up to their chests, broke through for a moment, and staggered as the second pair hit the bank and lost their footing. The sleigh behind them darted in a lateral skid, then flipped onto its side. The crack I heard was not the sleigh itself, as I first thought, but was rather the yoke, twisting in two. The lackey flew free and slid against the bridge; the driver, still holding the reins, was jerked down among the tangled traces and mixed among the hooves of the colliding horses. One runner of the sleigh jutted out toward me, as high as my head as I pulled my horse to a halt beside it. The other runner lay hooked upon a branch jutting from the ice-encased fallen tree that had tripped the top-heavy sleigh.

Screams soared from within. As the lackey stumbled to his feet and ran to steady the horses, I climbed upon the side of the sleigh—now its top—and broke open one of the windows. "It's I, Selkirk!" I called. "Is anyone hurt?"

Charlotte's voice came back at me. "Not for want of trying! Do you mean to kill us?" Inside lay a jumble, elbows and
feet thrashing out from the great wad of furs sloughed upon
the compartment's side, the whole heaving pile sprinkled over
with hairbrushes, broken hand mirrors, jars of lip rouge,
clouds of powder, and wine goblets, all of which rattled about
as more heads appeared. Someone was crying—the Contessa
Bellefleur, I thought—but it was Anne who emerged with a
bleeding nose. Beatrice was seizing coals with her hand
wrapped within her bonnet, tossing them back into the overturned stove. Gorlov, standing upright upon what had been
the door, held his saber. His glazed eyes flashed toward the
light of my open window, and I was unsure he recognized me.

I looked back down the river. Except for the erratic scars
of the sleigh runners upon its dull surface, it was a vista of
country desolation. The wind had dropped. The trees rising
from either bank were still in the cold. I calculated two minutes, at the most three, before the Cossacks rounded the last
bend and saw the overturned sleigh.

The lackey had seized the more overwrought of the
horses in the lead pair and was hanging his full weight upon
the neck harness to keep the stallion from rearing. The other
animals surged within their mangled traces, but they were all
on their feet and unstrangled within the lines so that I could
hope they would at least grow quiet. The driver lay motionless, trampled into the snow of the bank, the right side of his
skull crushed with the imprint of a hoof. Gorlov's horse was
still on his feet, saddled and tied to the rear of the sleigh. He
appeared unhurt. "Who can ride?" I called in to the ladies.

"I can." Charlotte again.

"We all can," Anne said. She was pale, yet spoke calmly.

"If it's sidesaddle," Princess Mitski added, as if willing to
put aside the recent inconveniences and join into whatever
party we were planning. But her qualification struck me, and

the other noble ladies as well. None had sat upon a horse except under the most proper circumstances. I paused and looked at Gorlov, gawking now at the women.

"I can ride anything." That was Beatrice. She unwrapped the bonnet from her hand and watched me.

"Gorlov!" I said. He looked at me. "Give me your hand!"

He reached out, seized the arm I offered him, and helped me tug him up through the window. He collapsed to his back upon the side of the sleigh and said, "I don't know if I can ride. But I can fight."

"Yes. I know you can. Now you, Beatrice!" I reached back in and withdrew Beatrice. She came out in one motion, lifting her own weight and alighting in a crouch, darting her eyes about as if she could sniff the danger. Charlotte and Anne poked her coat up after her. "No, not that one!" I said, rushing my words. "Give her a cloak, she must look like a man. And that fur hat there, Nikonovskaya's—it could look like a hussar's at a distance!"

Gaining these articles, I rattled to Beatrice, "Put these on. Poke up your hair! And take Gorlov's horse, that one there. Ride up the opposite bank and into the trees. When I charge them, then you let them see you, but not so much to see as to hear, it's the noise we want. Crash through the brush, loud as you can, do you understand?" She nodded.

"And you, Gorlov, you just sit here, atop the sleigh. If they see only you, and you looking casual at that, they might take this for a military party, and doubt their advantage. Now go, Beatrice. But wait! If you see me go down, then don't wait to see anything else, and don't interfere! You ride, do you hear me? To safety, anywhere you can find it! Now go!" She slid down onto the ice, untied the horse, stepped into his saddle, and was away.

Leaning back down into the compartment, I said, "All is well, ladies. Please keep calm, and quiet. And—" A thought hit me. "Anne! Hand me that rouge pot, please!" She did so, and I straightened up again, sitting on the sleigh side. Gorlov, hunched over as if his innards were one great agony, watched me silently as I smeared broad streaks of rouge upon my cheeks, and leapt down upon my horse.

I had meant to make the bank, hiding in the trees opposite Beatrice, but as I reined around and faced downriver, I saw the first rider appear at the bend.

He popped back, out of sight, and there was a pause. Then all four riders rounded together, in a tight bunch. They bore on, slowly, steadily, their horses' heads rocking as they walked.

Behind me, Gorlov began giving orders to the lackey. He spoke in French, which the Cossacks would not understand, nor did the lackey for that matter; but Gorlov presented a confident air. The riders drew on.

I knew they were not fooled. Had they been suspicious, they would have come in separately, from all directions, or not at all. But they kept coming, and their stumpy leader urged his horse a bit ahead. *Any second,* I thought, *they will charge.*

I screamed. I threw back my head and howled. I kicked my horse, and he ran at them.

Across the ice, I saw them hesitate, their leader's wrists surprised and stiff upon his reins. I screamed again, a hundred yards away, but I could not hear the sound from my own throat, so great was the pounding in my ears. I felt my horse beneath me, but I could not hear his hooves upon the ice; the whole world, except for my heart, had gone silent. I had a stray awareness that Beatrice should be moving then, but my eyes were so fixed upon the four Cossacks before me, my field of view so narrowed, that I could not see the trees, much less Beatrice among them. The Cossacks, looming ever larger, gaped at me, at my wild Indian face. Then the trailing two balked. Their leader shouted to them, and raised his short curved sword into the air.

I snatched from its scabbard my own saber. I heard it ring.

Two of the Cossacks—the leader and one other—spurred forward of the other two, who were facing the woods, and came at me. Irregular as they were, they formed a perfect battle line, one behind the other, for the classic saber attack is to close with the enemy head-on and then veer to the left, meeting right arm to right arm for a single slash before wheeling to rejoin for the random hacking. Abreast, they would have lost the advantage of their numbers, as I could have darted by to encounter one upon one. But in a line they could hope to unbalance me in the first clash and finish me in the second before I could recover.

The leader drove in first, waving his sword, his lips peeled back. I spurred in and cut before him—not to his right, as he expected, but to his left. Before he could shift over his horse's neck for an awkward cross slash, I was past him and on to the second rider. I dropped him with a chop to the neck. My cross slash is not awkward.

Still at full speed I drove past the backs of the other two Cossacks, who were hesitating as they faced the woods, the one with the wheezy horse holding a short sword like his leader's, the other gripping a bent saber in his right hand and a knife in his left. They flinched and twirled around as I crossed behind them, and the one had to bite his knife blade to free a hand for the reins as his horse shied sideways.

Twenty yards past them, I reined back and slid to a stop. The top of the ice was crusty and gave the horse's hooves good purchase, but the short slide reminded me not to make my turns too tight. I wheeled and saw the Cossack leader had done the same. We charged each other again.

His first pass he had ridden carefully; this time he came at me full tear, his mount kicking up a plume of ice chunks behind. I slowed, then raced at his left, as if to clash on the cross side. Just as he began to shift I feinted as if to veer to his right, and he hesitated long enough for me to flash by him again in a straight gallop, without clashing. I was on to the other pair before they were ready. The man with the wheezy horse raised both arms across his face and shrank away, almost falling out of the saddle. The other Cossack dropped his reins again, snatched the knife from his teeth, and was trying to balance himself as I reached him.

When I had first gone to the Crimea as a green volunteer anxious to learn the ways of war, I already possessed skills of riding and swordsmanship, but it was Gorlov who had taught me the true arts of fighting, he who had told me what no one else had—that in combat I should cease to allow my brain to give my body instructions, and allow it to react on instinct alone. I did that now, letting eye and hand choose the target, my body loose and uncoiling, so that the saber sped like the end of a whip. It caught the Cossack below the chin, and his head fell from his shoulders, bounced upon the rump of the horse, and rolled across the ice.

For a moment all was silent, except for the hoofbeats of the now-headless Cossack's fleeing horse, muffled on the snowy ice. The shock of what had happened gripped everyone upon the frozen river, and in that sudden stillness I heard a human noise, like an involuntary burst of prayer, as someone terrified might speak the name of God. I realized that somewhere in the woods, on the riverbank opposite of the one to which I'd sent Beatrice, was another unseen Cossack. A scout? A wounded man? Since he had not joined the fight, he must have been frail, or frightened; but whatever the case, he was there, looking on.

The lanky partner of the man I had cut in two decided he no longer wished to fight; he snatched the reins of his own horse, and the wheezy beast struggled off under a barrage of spurs.

But the stubby Cossack he left on the ice did not flee. I

think he knew that I would not let him go unchallenged, and he felt less exposed showing me his face than his back. Having seen his numbers go from a four-to-one advantage to even, he was desperate and wild-eyed. And his odds were worse than he knew.

He came at me again, but this time there was no charging, no waiting to clash. His horse moved slowly, barely in a trot, and he stood in his stirrups slashing back and forth above the horse's head, as much, I thought, to keep me away as to challenge me. His lips pinched forward and rolled out into a florid ring around the gray of his beard, and he sucked breath in pants. His bright eyes locked upon me, and bugged huge, as if I had suddenly grown so large that they could not contain me.

I parried two of his slashes as he drew close enough to reach, then knocked back his sword as he made a cut at the head of my horse. I would have killed him then, but he backed off, hissing breath and flailing the air. He began to circle, his eyes still full of me, and I cut him off, and backed him.

Breathing faster and faster, he raised his sword. He was much too far from me to slash. I think he actually meant to throw it, but I would never know. As the Cossack was perched in his stirrups, with his sword cocked overhead, Gorlov's saber pierced him.

The Cossack dropped his sword gently. His mouth gaped open, and his eyes rolled down to stare at the ten inches of steel curving up from beneath his breastbone. With great deliberateness he clutched the blade with both hands. A dry gurgle came from his throat, like the rasp of an unprimed pump, and as Gorlov snatched the saber back, the Cossack's fingers grasped the trickle of his own blood. He dropped off the horse without bending, dead.

Gorlov, upon the bare back of one of the sleigh horses, the severed traces dangling to the surface of the ice, twisted the fingers of one hand into the horse's mane, nodded, and bent down in cramp, pointing with his saber toward the last flee- ing Cossack.

I spun round to pursue, and caught the pitiful sight of the wheezy horse plodding along as his rider lashed and spurred him and bounced as if through pantomime alone he could make the animal fly. The Cossack, a hundred yards away, shot a frantic look back, saw me coming, and turned the laboring nag toward the bank.

Beatrice! She charged down the bank, straight toward the Cossack, who panicked and reined around so hard that his horse stumbled upon the ice and fell. Clawing to his feet, the unhorsed Cossack fled back out to the center of the ice, run- ning as badly as his mount had, slowing with each step.

I thought Beatrice would wait for me, or I would have called to her. But she kicked her horse in the flanks and tore so swiftly after the Cossack that I was caught speechless. She rode the man down, driving the chest of her horse into his back and galloping straight over him as he fell.

There was a faint rustle of branches and crunching of snow from among the trees on the other riverbank, as the remaining Cossack who had hidden there, if Cossack he was, fled back into the forest.

When I reached Beatrice she was sitting with her hands folded across the saddle horn, the Cossack prostrate and whimpering at her horse's forelegs. "Beatrice, I . . . Can he stand?" I at last managed to say. She said something to the Cossack in Russian, and it was not a question or a request. The man got to his feet, one leg threatening to crumple and one arm limp, clearly broken. "Come on, then," I said, and we marched the prisoner back before us. As the horses walked I looked at her, and she felt my eyes upon her but did not return the stare; she looked down, and then fixed her eyes straight ahead as we rode.

We found Gorlov hunched down over his horse's neck, but he lifted his shoulders as he saw us and reined in beside me, even swatting the hobbling Cossack once with the flat of his saber to speed him along.

When we reached the sleigh, heads went popping back down inside, both at the window I had broken into and the second one the ladies had opened themselves. They shrank back like some embarrassed hydra turtle, then slowly bloomed forth again to gawk at the Cossack, and gasp, and whisper.

Gorlov, sliding off his horse as the lackey took the traces, staggered and fell. The prisoner dropped to his knees and pressed his head to the ice, as if he wished to become invisible. "Gorlov!" I said, dismounting, "are you wounded?"

"Not from the Cossacks, Svet. But, God! Whatever gnaws my gut has teeth worse than steel."

"You hold on, we'll soon have you to help. Ladies— Charlotte, Anne, and you, Contessa Bellefleur! Climb down here, and bring some blankets with you! In fact, all of you must come down, and hurry, please! Hurry!"

Gorlov gripped my leg and rolled his eyes up to me. "You may take your time. When they find that Cossack with his head missing, they won't follow us."

I gripped Gorlov's hand to try to reassure him I was calm, but still felt a powerful urgency. "Beatrice, find me something with which to truss up this Cossack, would you, and tell the lackey to rig up any four horses he can, in whatever makeshift harness, with a trailing lead long enough to lash round that upper runner."

We soon had Gorlov wrapped up and reclining in the snow beside the bridge, fussed over by the zealous ladies. When they had emerged from the compartment, they were quite useless; but their shared fright at the proximity of the captured Cossack, and the bout with fainting Princess Mitski experienced when she stumbled upon the dead trampled driver, quickly organized them into attentiveness and tractability. The Cossack we strapped like a roasting pig and stood against a tree. The lackey and I, aided by Beatrice, who steadied the extra horses, took a team of four, lashed them to the runner in the air, and tugged the sleigh. It righted with a great crash, but seemed sound enough, and the runners appeared straight. Pulling the sleigh away from the bank and out so that it faced down the ice was harder, and reattaching the team was harder still; having to cut out broken traces and knot together what we could, we were able to jury-rig harnesses for only eight of the original ten in the team. So the two most battered we released, knowing the wolves might have them. But they were fine horses, and still sound enough; I had not the heart to destroy them.

The entire process consumed an hour. We worked frantically, distracted only occasionally by Zepsha, who made a game of running to touch the Cossack, then screaming and fleeing behind the coat of one or another of the ladies. At first she squealed only slightly, but on her third or fourth sortie, when she had gotten everyone's attention, she saw the Cossack roll his eyes down at her when she put her fingertip to his knee, and flailed backward, howling all the way to Anne's skirts. "Shut up, would you?" I said hotly. "We are exposed enough! Would you call trouble upon us?"

"Where will we go?" Charlotte said, as I went to help Gorlov back into the sleigh and told the ladies to reboard.

"Back to Berenchko," I said. When this response drew various looks from them—a confused frown from the princess, and an especially thoughtful glance from Anne Shettlefield—I explained, "We have a partial team and makeshift harness. Our driver is dead. One half of our escort is ill and in grave need of a physician. We have encountered brigands and might reasonably expect more. It is closer back to Berenchko than it is to the next estate, which I am not sure I could locate any-

way, nor could the lackey. I am sorry to disrupt your sched-
ule, ladies, but my directions are to see to your safety before
all else, and I intend to do that. Now please come quickly."

"But . . . what about the prisoner?" the Contessa Bellefleur
wondered. Of all the ladies, she had grown the palest.

"I will strap him to the top of the sleigh—beside the driver's body. I have no place else to put him, and I can watch
him there."

"You do not ride inside with us, Captain?" the Lady
Nikonovskaya asked.

"I ride in the box, and help the lackey with the team.
Now get inside! Beatrice, would you wait a moment, please?"
Beatrice, without looking at me, had been just about to reen-
ter the compartment, and she stopped now beside the door.
She stood there waiting as Nikonovskaya, the last to enter,
popped inside and then back again, with a small flask.

"Here," Nikonovskaya said, "would you like just a sip to
keep you warm?"

She handed me the flask, but kept the stopper. I hesitated
a moment and said, "Thank you, no. But if you don't mind I'll
keep the brandy, to taste it as I need on the road."

She handed me the stopper and climbed back into the
compartment. I put the brandy into my coat and turned to
Beatrice. I took a step back with her, away from the door.
"You must do me one more favor," I said softly, "and it is a
grave one, as your other favors have been. You must see to it
that Gorlov consumes nothing more, neither food nor drink,
offered to him by anyone, all the way back. Be as subtle as you
can in denying him, spill tea cups or make diversions as you
will, but if you must, forbid him to eat or drink outright, and
say openly that it is my order. Understand?"

She raised her eyes, beneath her reluctant lids, nodded, and
began to step back to the door. "One more thing, Beatrice," I
said, catching her arm. "You were magnificent out there. I am

alive because of you." She turned quickly to the door, but stopped once she was inside to look back at me.

THE way back to Berenchko was uneventful, yet bitterly cold and desolate. We saw not one other living soul, nor living animal or bird that I can recall. The team itself was slower and awkward in their unorthodox traces, but they pulled well, and the lackey was a competent driver, swerving only once, and that when we were first starting back down the frozen river; he swung the team to the side, that we might skim past the severed head of the Cossack, lying on the ice. The lackey looked down at the frozen face, but did not look at me.

And there was once, when we had returned to our original road and left the river some miles behind, that I thought I heard the distant cry of wolves, and my mind swam in images of gnashing teeth. But the sound could have been the wind only, rushing by my numb ears.

Every hour or so I would wait for a straight stretch of smooth road and then leave the box, crawling back along the flat perimeter of the sleigh dome to where the driver and the Cossack prisoner lay end to end, like matching Yule logs. The driver's face was already frozen a blue-white, and the Cossack's nose, protruding from the wrappings, was almost the same color. But each time I went to him he raised his head, batted open his eyes, and accepted the sips of brandy I poured down his throat.

Just as the sun was setting, we reached Berenchko.

Chapter Sixteen

WHAT, back so soon? This is a capital surprise!" Count Berenchkov shook my frozen
fingers, and beamed. I had climbed painfully
down from the box by the time he came scurrying from the house, and I took my first steps toward him
like a leper, numb as I was with cold, but he took pause at
none of that, nor the scraping on the carriage, nor the deple-
tion of the team and defacement of the traces; he slapped me
on the shoulder as he would to celebrate seeing a long-lost
friend in the pink of health. "So you've decided to stay with
us another day. This is capital! Stay two if you wish. It's clear
you love the country as much as we!"

I believed the man actually thought we had spent the day
in sightseeing, and had returned to Berenchko because we
could not bear to pull ourselves from the peace of its surroundings. His wife, however, held no such impression; she
scowled at me as she came from the house, and without stopping she ran right up to the door of the sleigh as the lackey
opened it up. "What is the matter? Something terrible, I

know—who is dead?" As a dozen or so serfs who had been digging out a cistern at the side of the house shambled over to surround and peer at the sleigh, I drew Berenchkov aside.

"Count," I said in a low voice, "you may want to ask your wife to step back into the house. We encountered Cossacks on the road. The driver is dead. And we have a prisoner. I thought perhaps you might wish to spare your wife the shock of seeing a corpse and a Cossack, all at the same time."

The count listened to me with the same steady expression he had worn when—and only when—he had before mentioned the Cossack danger. Now he looked at his wife, then back to me, and his face appeared as I could only describe as sly. "Why don't you show her?" he said.

"All right. As you wish." I tapped the lackey on the shoulder and pointed to the top of the sleigh. He climbed back up onto the box. Berenchkov spoke to his serfs; several of the less muddy ones drifted over and stood at the back of the sleigh, from which the lackey had already unhitched the horses. They waited, apparently expecting to receive baggage. The lackey looked at me, at the ladies gathering and chattering outside the door, and back to me. I gestured to him with a circling motion of my finger, and he rolled off the body of the driver, stiff as a log.

The serfs caught this burden—baggage it was, indeed—and carried it to the front steps of the house, where they laid it down, and in that weary walk common to serfs they moved back to the rear of the sleigh to receive the next parcel. The Countess Berenchkova glanced toward the corpse once, twice—and on the third look she screamed. This encouraged the other ladies greatly; they seized the countess by the hands and arms, leaned forward, and accelerated their narrative.

The serfs themselves, as Berenchkov and I watched, were utterly undisturbed by the corpse or the countess's reaction to it. They waited with arms outstretched and received the

Cossack as the lackey rolled him off the side. But being not quite frozen, the prisoner bent in the middle and opened his eyes face-to-face with one of his erstwhile pallbearers. The serf screamed. His partners screamed. *"Kazaki!"* they cried. All four serfs dropped the Cossack, though he was still quite trussed up, and a frail man to begin with, and wounded and half frozen, and they fled from him, back to their muddy group. Then all the serfs retreated twenty yards.

The Countess Berenchkova bettered that: she flailed to the steps, tripped over the body of the driver, fell, clawed her way up, bounced off the closed door, fell again, pulled herself back to her feet by tugging on the door latch, threw the door open—screaming all the while—and fainted halfway across the threshold.

Berenchkov looked at me. "The country is not all peace," he said. "I would not want to give you that impression. But its prevalent tranquillity serves to accentuate life's little adventures when they come our way." As his household servants rushed to the attendance of his wife, the count walked toward the discarded Cossack and gestured for his serfs to come back. But the count's small glory at that moment over one woman, his wife, was preempted by another—the Princess Mitski, who strode to meet him and said imperiously, and much to the attention of the cowering serfs, "Good Berenchkov, we accept your hospitality once more! We shall leave for St. Petersburg tomorrow. In the meantime, please see to the custody of this prisoner, whom we have taken in the name of the Tsarina Catherine, Empress of All the Russias!" With that the lady gave the Cossack a shove with the toe of her boot, walked back to the sleigh, and called in to Beatrice to fetch nightclothes for all the ladies "without delay."

I then approached the beaming count myself and asked him as gently as I could to provide us further with care for the horses, repairs to the harnesses, decent and secure containment for the prisoner, and, most important of all, a proper place and medical attention for Gorlov.

THE doctor was a German. He arrived looking sleepy and had gravy on his shirt. But he brought a clean china bleeding bowl and a bright steel lancet. He inspired confidence in me with the way he fitted the scoop of the bowl to Gorlov's elbow and turned the white flesh of his inner forearm upright.

"Are you sure about this?" Beatrice whispered to me, as we watched from the foot of the bed.

"Of course," I reassured her. "Gorlov knows it's for the best." This opinion was a liberty I took upon my long acquaintance with Gorlov, for at that moment, strictly speaking, Gorlov could not have been said to know anything. In the hour it had taken for Berenchkov to send for the doctor and the doctor to arrive, Gorlov had experienced two separate bouts with spasms—whole contortions of face and body; he now lay propped by pillows, limp, in and out of consciousness. He did not move as the doctor opened the vein in the crook of his elbow.

Beatrice watched, fascinated. I, however, had to turn away, with a warm wateriness suffusing my stomach. Blood on a battlefield is one thing; it is quite another in a bedroom. A half tankard of Gorlov's Russian fluid drained into the china, and I bore the sound of the spattering for the sake of my friend's recovery. The doctor tied the slit in a dry cloth, cleaned his lancet upon the knot, and stood. "Too much vodka, night air, and other poisons," the doctor declared to me in German. "He will spend a restful night now, and be much better tomorrow. A second treatment then is advisable."

"Thank you, Doctor." I gave him a gold coin, from the expense money.

"Very good," the doctor said, slipping the coin into his empty watch pocket. "I shall be available if you need me." He left, with his bowl.

For a few moments I observed Gorlov, lying quietly, and sat down beside the fire burning opposite the bed. Beatrice, too, watched the patient, then came and took the chair opposite me. We sat some while before she said, "Why did you tell Count Berenchkov that Count Gorlov's disease could be contagious?"

"You heard me say that?" I had held a tight conversation with Berenchkov beside the carriage while Beatrice was unloading it.

She nodded her head, her chestnut hair shimmering in the firelight. "And I also heard it repeated."

"By whom?"

"The Princess Mitski. She announced that we were all to stay away from this room, until it was clear that Count Gorlov had no catching fevers. I, of course, was excepted."

"Did she seem upset?"

"Oh, yes."

"For Gorlov, or herself?"

Beatrice looked down at her hands in her lap.

"I wanted to make sure that the count provided us with a room like this," I said. We were in a back corner bedroom, the most isolated within the house. The kitchen would have been better still, of course, but no one would want a sick man there. "I wanted us alone, so I could protect him." Beatrice's gaze shot up to mine. "I also wanted to find out which ladies took the threat of contagion seriously, and which did not."

"You think your friend is being poisoned."

I did not speak. I watched her. Gorlov moaned suddenly, and we both looked at him, frowning in his stupor.

"No one fed him today," she said. "But everyone tried. Everyone but Zepsha, she ignored him. But he ate nothing, and drank nothing. I wet his lips once with water from the common jug."

"Did you make yourself noticeable in guarding him for me?"

"No. He was unconscious most of the time."

Gorlov groaned again. He convulsed, quick spasms that pitched him left and right. He lay quietly for a few minutes. We sat watching him, then the floor, then the fire.

Gorlov thrashed again, throwing his blankets to the floor. We hurried to him, and as Beatrice covered him I took him by the shoulders. "Gorlov! Gorlov! Do you hear me?"

"Of course," he grunted, but kept his eyes squeezed shut. "It bites me. It bites me!" The wave of pain drained away from him, and he fell back into a tortured slumber.

"Beatrice," I whispered, "I need to go out for a moment. Would you be all right to keep watch alone, just till I return?"

She nodded. I assured her I would not be absent beyond five minutes, took up my cloak, and left the room.

Down a long corridor, I found the door exiting onto the grounds behind the house, the same door Anne had used the night before; once through it I went not into the kitchen, but turned and made my way past the servants' cottages, into the barn, to the corn crib with the Cossack locked up inside. Several peasant men stood about, speaking loudly, and though their words were in Russian I recognized the bravado in them, their swagger in the presence of this enemy. A number of peasant women and children also milled about; they grew silent suddenly when I entered, and a man who was holding a boy up to peer through the wood slats at the prisoner lowered the lad and stepped back as he saw me. I looked into the crib. The Cossack lay facedown upon the husk-covered floor. Close to his head glistened a revolting pile of food scraps— vegetable tops, molded potato peels, a few bones from some unidentifiable animal—tossed in beside him as one might feed a dog, but there was no sign that he had eaten any of it. The barn was warm enough, insulated by bales of straw and heated by the cattle in nearby stalls, but still the pale Cossack looked cold to me. "Does anyone here speak French?" I said to the peasants, thinking that a more likely language for them than German.

"I do. A little much," one old man answered.

"Ask the Cossack how he feels."

The old man, looking back and forth from me to his fellows, at last shuffled to the crib, as if it contained poisonous serpents, and shouted something. The Cossack looked up, and squinted as the peasant haltingly strung some words together. The Cossack looked at me as the old man spoke and finally answered something. He and the old man made several exchanges, as if they did not fully understand each other; I drew the impression that their languages were merely cousins. Finally the old peasant turned back to me. "He says his stomach hurts."

"Has he eaten anything?" The old man started to turn back to the Cossack, but I caught his arm. "No, you tell me, you know."

"Anything? Ah, anything . . . no much, me thinks."

I turned and started quickly back to the house. But I stopped at the barn door. "Do you have bad apples here, moldy ones, full of worms?" The old peasant stared at me, and I did not wait for him to nod. "Find some, and bring them to me! And salt, too, with warm water. Lots of it. And a pail. And a wooden tub. Get it now, and bring it to me in the house. I'm in that room there, on the corner."

I heard Gorlov's cries while I was still in the corridor. Reaching the room I found Beatrice standing over the bed, the worry in her eyes. I threw off my cloak, removed my tunic, and rolled up the sleeves of my shirt. "Thank you, Beatrice," I said. "I think you should leave now."

"What are you doing?"

"Gorlov has been poisoned, slowly and steadily. I was unsure of it myself because of the way his disturbances would come and go. I think his collapse was meant to be slow and gradual, so that his murder would not be apparent. God! Where is that man?" I frowned at the door.

"Where is who?"

"The old peasant! He's bringing some things. Listen, it is this. Gorlov has had several great exertions in the last two days, times in which he forced himself to action, and became quite agitated, after which he would vomit. I think that has saved him so far! He must be purged."

"I will help you."

"It will not be pretty."

"I know."

Chapter Seventeen

THE old peasant, with two boys for helpers, brought the articles I had demanded. They carried them in—the apples in the pail, the pail in the tub, the salt water in separate wooden pitchers—set them down in the center of the floor, and left hurriedly, their eyes diverted as if afraid—fearing not the man who lay groaning in the bed, the sick man, but rather the insane one, the officer who had given them such orders. I stoked the fire into a hot blaze, shoved the tub to Gorlov's bedside, removed the pail, poured the putrid apples from it onto the floor, and filled the pail with brine from both water pitchers. "Are you ready?" I said to Beatrice.

She nodded. "But why so much water at once? Why not give it to him in a cup?" she asked, with such gentleness that it troubled me for her sake.

"Because he must drink. He must. He will do so willingly at first, but will soon resist, and then we must force him. We will engulf him, so that he drinks by instinct, in preference to drowning."

She nodded again, and placed a hand behind Gorlov's neck,

lifting him off the pillows. I put the pail of brine to his lips, and he sipped. Beatrice let him sag back. "No, no!" I said. "We must fill him up, while we can! He's barely noticed yet!" As she pulled him back upright, I shouted, "Drink, Gorlov! Drink!"

He accepted several more swallows, then balked without seeming to wake. I tipped the pail higher, spilling the warm brine down his cheeks and over his nose; he choked, gulped, coughed, gulped more.

He tossed himself back upon the pillows, and his eyes fluttered open. Beatrice tugged him upright again. "Drink!" I ordered, and sloshed him again. He chugged down a pint before flailing with his arms to knock both Beatrice and me away. He fell back and gasped.

"Are you all right?" I said to Beatrice as she stepped back up to the bed. She answered by slamming her palms into Gorlov's shoulders and pinning him against his pillow. I put down the pail, grabbed the vilest of the rotten apples, and shoved its softest, most putrid side into Gorlov's nose, driving the matter directly up his nostrils. His eyelids, at first clamped closed, suddenly snapped open. Coughing, choking, snorting, clawing at his head, he bolted upright. A blush exploded onto his face, his cheeks ballooned, and I jerked his shoulders so that his head fell over the side of the bed and above the tub as he regurgitated.

"A fine blast, Gorlov, old cannon!" I said. "Come on! Let's reload you!" Sagging exhausted and sweating upon his pillow, he raised his eyes to me, as if he comprehended my words— or feared that he did. We were upon him quickly, and he batted back, striking me upon the cheek and knocking Beatrice to the floor. She sprang back to her feet and dug her fingers into his throat. Gorlov's eyes popped.

"No, Beatrice, don't kill him yet, leave him for me!" I shouted, on the mad edge of laughter. "Here, you pour and I'll hold him."

Throwing my full weight upon Gorlov, I wrestled his arms to his sides and pinned them there, as Beatrice dosed him with the brine and then, with a vengeance, administered another decayed apple into his sinuses. We both leapt back as he purged.

We repeated the process for perhaps an hour, perhaps three; through that night, I lost track of time. Gorlov's resistance grew more animated and vicious. He called us both the vilest of names, damned us each to everlasting hell, and swore, with blazing eyes, that he would see my heart fed to the wolves. I tried to discern in him some clearing of the mind, some lessening of his delirium. But I could not tell. Having fought him for such a time, and breathed the stench that he had begun to expel from every orifice, I felt delirious myself.

Later, deep into the night, he ceased to battle. Beatrice and I besieged him no more. We stood away from his bedside and watched.

Gorlov lay still. He thrashed. He snapped over upon his side and screamed. He fouled himself. He moaned for it. He bounced upon his back. He batted his head against the pillow. He twisted his neck and vomited. He fouled himself again, without caring. He lay sunken in weakness, still once more.

BEATRICE and I, as drained as Gorlov, sat now in chairs on either side of his bed, awaiting new convulsions. Then we were no longer waiting, simply watching, too tired to move.

Our eyes met.

"He sleeps," she said.

"Beatrice, you were . . . for the second time today—"

She waved me to a stop and shook her head slightly. I was trying to tell her again that she had been magnificent, and she told me with her gesture that she wanted not to hear the words, and for me not to say them. I realized then that I did not want to mutter the sentiment again myself, that something wordless had already passed between us.

For perhaps five minutes we sat in that loud silence.

Through that time I stared at the floor, she at the wall beside Gorlov's bed. Finally I looked at our patient and said, "He does sleep. Are you cold?" She did not answer, and was no more cold than I was, but as I stood and lifted my chair, she rose and picked hers up also, and we moved to sit before the fireplace. Quietly, so as not to disturb Gorlov, we took up positions neither side by side nor opposite, but angled to face the low flames.

Perhaps because I felt she was about to speak, I spoke first. "Beatrice, how did you come to ride so well?"

Whatever she was about to ask, she put aside, and smiled at me, and then at the fire. "My father," she said. "He was a soldier. Like you."

"A cavalryman?" I asked. She nodded. "The Poles are excellent riders. Hard and fierce."

She laughed softly. "He wasn't a Pole. He was a Swede. He fought with Charles the Twelfth, against the Tsar, Peter the Great."

A Swede.

Without further prompting from me, she released her story.

"My father was twenty years old, and a major of cavalry, when he followed his king through Riga and into Russia, to fight the Tsar. He—"

"Twenty, and already a major?" I interrupted. I did not fear to break her narrative. In our wordless exchange, we had already pacted to tell each other everything. "He must have been a serious soldier. Or else a noble. Or both."

"Both," she said. "But less of a noble, and more of a serious soldier. He loved to ride, and to fight, too, I think. But when he spoke of being a young man, in Sweden, he said only that he was wild, with the hunger to see war. He said this as if to call himself stupid, but without conviction. He . . . was confused, later in his life. But the love of riding he never lost. In our village, everyone said that Ulvaeus on a plow horse was swifter than a Russian on anything else. He was captured at the Battle of Poltava, along with three thousand other Swedes. The Russians sent many of them to Poland, as punishment to both peoples. He worked for ten years in a labor camp in the forests, and was released because the Russians started using a different kind of wood in the ships the Tsar was building. He met my mother, who was twice a widow already, and married her. They had the rarest of things in Poland . . ."

"Love?" I ventured.

"Love is not so rare in Poland. I meant they had a successful farm."

"Ah."

The room was completely still. Gorlov lay without motion other than the slow rise and fall of his chest, and the fire whispered, crackling softly, like the echoes of broken dreams. Beatrice sat tilted toward the fire, her spine straight, the light catching her from hair to stomach and from knee to toe.

"My father died of consumption," Beatrice said, "when I was ten. The rest of us—I had three brothers and two sisters— were unable to keep up the farm. But it was just as well, the Tsarina claimed the land for Russia soon after. The Mitskis were awarded an estate that included what had been our property, and I went to work for them and became Natasha's assistant."

"Do you still see your family?"

"None are left. My mother died of the consumption also, and my brothers were conscripted into the army, to fight the

Turks. We were told they died also. I used to get letters from my sisters, but no more." Lifting her eyes to me, Beatrice said, "I have told you all there is to tell about me, and now you must tell me about you. How did *you* come to ride so well?"

And then I wanted to tell her everything. Or not everything, for the details did not seem to matter then, but I wanted to tell her the truth.

"My father raised horses, and trained them for the people who had the money to buy them but not the skill to master them. He came from Scotland, and crossed on a ship with a load of Presbyterians, bound for Virginia and religious toleration. My mother . . . came from Scotland on the same ship, but she did not survive the crossing—or, I should say, my birth, for she died after a labor of three days tossing through the waves. Our neighbors—the ones who made the crossing at the same time and still lived near us afterward—said she refused to die until she had heard me cry, but my father never spoke of it, and I don't know if that part of the story is true. They buried her at sea, and for her sake the Presbyterians accepted my father's coolness to their faith and always saw to it there was some woman—a very old one—around to read the Bible to me. You see, he was not really part of their community when they set sail, though my mother was, and had 'worked on' him—that's what they called it—since they were married. She left Scotland, so they said, for the religious freedom. My father left, I know, because he hated the English. 'Scotland's true export is her sons,' he always told me. 'The British have taken all opportunity and replaced it with one chance—to be a sailor, or a soldier of the British Crown.' So from my father's work I had horses, and from the Presbyterians I had study, mainly the Bible. When I was fifteen they surprised me: the church had collected money for a scholarship so that I could attend the College of William and Mary. My father was against my going, though he never said a word."

"Against study?" she broke in, surprised.

"Not so much that. I told him I wanted to become a minister. He wanted something finer for me. He wanted me to become a gentleman of Virginia, and whatever the learning and polish and manners, all of which he wanted me to have, that dream was impossible without the money. And my intentions for the clergy rankled him, but he didn't take them seriously. Nor did I, I suppose, not deeply enough. I never told my father that. Nor even my wife."

"What was she like?"

"Pretty. Happy. Like a child. She was seventeen, and I was eighteen."

"And why did you marry her? I know, I know, you loved her. But why did you love her? What did she have that . . . ?" She was embarrassed to be asking the question, but she did not withdraw it.

I had to stare at her a long moment before I could answer. "Faith. Faith, I suppose. You know, I think that's it, if I could name one thing. She believed in God, and truth, and the goodness within everyone. I had trouble with those beliefs. She accepted me with my doubts, and her acceptance, so complete, made it easier for me to share the faith she had." I had kept the doors within my mind sealed against memories of Melinda, but somehow the presence of Beatrice—a woman I respected, whose openness and strength were so like the qualities of the one whom I had lost—caused those doors to open without resistance, and the ghosts of my heart strolled in. I saw Melinda as I had first seen her, in a pew of the Bruton Parish Church, sitting beside her father, who had sent for me to meet him after services to discuss the training of horses he had newly purchased. (Most Virginians would not have done such business on the Sabbath, but her father was not one to let technicalities interfere with business, and my father could not spare me on any day except Sunday, so I promised to attend services with the Episcopalians and sat in the balcony.) My eyes found her, and during the singing of a hymn she looked up at me. Her eyes were the green of grass in May, her hair the yellow of those same blades in August, and breath had left my body when she looked at me.

But it was not the angelic qualities of that moment that caused me to fall in love with her, or the way she watched from the porch when I walked with her father to their barn and rode the stallion no one else could even saddle. I fell in love with Melinda because she had something beyond beauty and character. She had laughter. When I would tell her that our society was unjust, and that it was wrong for hardworking and generous-hearted commonness in America to be ruled solely in the self-interest of nobles across the Atlantic, she would nod in sober sympathy. But when I expressed my darkest fears, forebodings sickening my stomach, that the opportunities in our country, the endless resources of land, water, and climate, were breeding a new race of people who would spill blood to have freedom, she would laugh at my anxieties and hold me in her arms, affirming a life that had a future. A family. Peace. Since the day she died, I had been unable to think of such things.

I pulled myself back to Russia.

"Her father owned a tobacco plantation outside Williamsburg, and he thought I wasn't good enough for her. I thought he was right, but not for the same reasons he did. His resistance to our relationship may have driven us to marry so quickly, at Christmas, the same year we met. Before the winter was over, she was with child.

"We lived in a cottage that was always cold and damp, and when her time came near, her father called on us and said she should go back home to have the baby. I thought he was right. It was the period of my examinations, but her father promised to send a messenger at the first sign of her labor, and

I promised to ride like the devil to reach her in time. And she believed me, believed me with a smile. She always believed.

"When the messenger came, he was not from the plantation; he was a friend of my wife's father. 'Your wife broke out in sores two days ago,' he said, 'and gave birth this morning. The baby had pox, too.' They uh . . . uh . . ."

I had to stare at the fire before I could speak again. I was unprepared for the difficulty I found in talking of this. I had never told anyone before.

And even now there was something I was leaving out. I could not tell Beatrice that when my wife lay suffering, her father had sent to Williamsburg for a physician, and the royal governor there, aware of my rebellious politics, had instead dispatched the doctor to more loyalist subjects—a fact that fueled my hatred of royal authority, as well as fed my guilt, that my wife and child had died because of me.

"They had buried both of them before I could get there. Afraid of the pox. I went home and stayed awhile with my father, until we were both about to hate each other. I told my father I would not go back to school, but I would not raise horses either—I told him I would be a soldier. We had a neighbor, a man to whom my father had sold horses, who told me America would one day need officers of its own, and he encouraged me to train in Europe. My father paid my passage."

She nodded and seemed to understand more than I did. "The rest," I said, "the rest is typical. I learned to fight. I look for wars."

"I think not."

"What do you mean?"

"Do you dream?"

"Dream? You mean . . . fantasies of the daytime, or visions in the night?"

"In the night."

"What have dreams to do with anything?"

"You do have them, don't you?"

"Like anyone else, I suppose."

"The same dream frequently, or always different ones?"

"Dreams are random ravings, a passing night madness, incited as the body, recuperating in slumber, releases the poisonous humors it has collected during the daytime. This is plainly known."

"Do—"

"Please don't tell me you are superstitious!"

She paused. "I make you angry."

"No! Of course not."

She stared at me with such honesty that I felt shamed, and then she turned back to the fire.

"Beatrice," I said, "listen. Nothing makes a person angrier than being told by someone else that he is angry when he is not!" I chuckled, a laugh so forced and artificial that it grated my own ears. "Now what is this . . . fixation you have on the subject of dreams?" I heard then the aggression in my tone, the bite in my choice of words.

She lowered her head for a moment, but when she looked up and faced me, it was with strength. "I have not wanted to offend you," she said.

"Beatrice, I . . . I would . . . I wouldn't . . . Thank you, I mean. I would not offend you either. I . . . yes, I am angry, I admit it, I'm sorry. But you act as if you know something about me, something you won't say, and that does anger me; it insults me. It implies that you think me too weak to bear the truth."

She fixed me again with her magnetic stare.

"Last night," she said slowly, "after Miss Shettlefield left, and I had been in bed for some time, I heard noises from the main part of the kitchen. They were . . . strange sounds, moans and sobs. I listened at my door, and kept hearing them, off and on. I slipped on my dress and peeked out. You were lying by the fire. I tiptoed toward you and saw you still slept, but . . . I crept closer to the hearth anyway. And I saw you were making the noises, and I watched you as you slept."

She stopped. Our eyes locked.

"Yes?" I said; it came out as a whisper.

"You were weeping. What I heard were your sobs. It was not the steady crying of one who has given over to grief. It was more the kind of moaning of some pain to wish away, or a longing after something lost. And at the very moment I watched, you pitched over upon your back—you had been sleeping with your face toward the fire, away from me—and then you actually reached up, your arms out straight, your fingers trembling and grasping. Your eyes were puddled in tears. You sobbed again, you—" She broke off, and wiped unsteady fingertips across her lips.

"Suddenly you cried out so loudly I thought it would wake you, and then you clasped your arms to you, they . . . hugged, but found nothing, and you . . . sobbed again. You stirred, panting, and seemed to wake without opening your eyes. I was certain you would, and see me. But you shook your head—consciously, I believe—and rolled over again, and lay still."

She had not taken her eyes from mine during all this she told me, but now she did, looking far away.

"It is not always the same dream," I said quietly. "Sometimes the faces and situations I see are quite vivid, sometimes vague. And yet in that vagueness I am swept with definite and undiluted emotion. At times the scenes and faces are familiar to me, and other times I encounter faces, faces I know and yet have never seen in wakefulness. And these faces can be the most vivid of all. I have seen my mother. I see my father. I see my wife. I have also seen my child. And . . . and no, the dreams do not come often to me. When they do come, it is usually after something has happened. I have had a rare conversation—an honest, simple one, as with you last night. Or they come after I have seen death, or been moved some way." *As when the mare died,* I thought, remembering another night I had spent intoxicated in slumbered emotion. When I awoke the next morning in that wretched livery station, Gorlov had been staring at me. I wondered if he had seen what Beatrice had, and what he must have wondered about me. I looked at Gorlov now, and watched him as he slept, breathing ponderously in the bed across the room.

I looked back to Beatrice, and said, "The dreams are not torture. They often begin with an elation unlike any I have experienced in life. The anguish comes on as I feel this happiness receding, and I struggle to keep it, and lose it, and grieve. Whether I weep openly each time, I don't know. But then I didn't know before how much I might show to anyone who saw me when these dreams take me."

Looking into the fire, she nodded.

"Thank you for telling me, Beatrice," I said.

We said nothing more. Together we stared into the fire until the flames died, and sometime during that night I fell asleep in my chair. When I awoke the next morning, I found myself covered with a blanket I had not put there. But that was later.

During that night, I did not dream. But I slept as if encased in a cloud of warmth and peace, rising into a sky of anticipation.

Chapter Eighteen

G ORLOV. Gorlov. Wake up! Gorlov. Gorlov! Wake up!"

His head rolled loosely as I shook him; his body remained limp. He still breathed steadily, as he had all night. "Gorlov!" I jolted him back and forth, then slapped him with such vigor that his eyes rattled open. The lids remained thrown back, giving him a countenance of surprise. Then his jaw dropped, and the words rumbled up: "I accept. Sabers, or pistols at ten feet. I'll kill you as soon as I've had a bath."

He tried to close his eyes again, but I shook him. "Gorlov! Gorlov! How do you feel?"

"Eh, unh? Mmmmahh late for starting?"

"Yes? Yes! We must go! Can you rise with me?"

He stood like a new colt. As he rose he released from the mattress a buried pocket of sick stench. "God! Is that me?" he said. "Where are we?"

"Back at Berenchko!" I said. "And there is a bath waiting."

The sun was up and shining, reflecting fiercely off the

softening snow as I led Gorlov around the back of the house and toward the bathing hut, perched on the bank of the frozen stream that curled beyond the barn. He wore only his boots and a wrapping of blankets, while I stank inside my soiled and bloodstained uniform. We thus presented an ideal opportunity for the proving of that social law which mandates that a chance encounter always catches us at the most embarrassing possible moment. The ladies, having risen and dressed in the expectation that we would leave at dawn, were breakfasting with the Countess Berenchkova in the estate's morning room. This room adjoined the greenhouse, and just as Gorlov and I passed, the Contessa Bellefleur looked up from her croissant, squinted through the windows past the scrawny tomato vines, and shouted, "Glory be to God! Count Gorlov has recovered!" And suddenly all the ladies had streamed out to watch us as we hobbled across the snow.

Lacking wraps, they stopped just outside the greenhouse door and called to us from their huddle. "Yoo-hooah! Sergei!" the countess called to Gorlov. "Are you feeling good this morning?"

Gorlov, his bare calves a blue white, with the black hair standing out from them like bristle, tossed a salute toward her and tried to hobble faster.

"Captain, will we be leaving soon?" Charlotte DuBois called.

"Yes!" I shouted. "In an hour! Please be ready!"

I thought we had escaped, but I heard a giggle from the group and turned to see Zepsha waddling along behind us, her dress hiked up, her already-bowed legs bowed out even farther as she marched along in a mockery of Gorlov. As I looked she saluted toward the ladies as Gorlov had done, and they howled. I tried to keep Gorlov moving, but she overtook us and screamed, "So, Count, recovered from your bout with overdrinking, I see!"

Gorlov did not look at her; he kept striding along, hunched over from the pain still in his gut. But she hunched over too in perfect mimicry and shrieked, "Need another diaper for him, Captain? You may use one of my bedsheets; I have an extra! I'll even help you put it arou—"

Gorlov suddenly had her throat in his hand, and was carrying her at arm's length, her tiny feet thrashing in the air; he never broke stride, simply changed direction, marching straight toward the cistern twenty yards away. Holding his fluttering burden aloft, he was unable to keep a proper grip upon his blankets; his wrapping slipped from one shoulder, then from the other, and he finally released them entirely so that they dropped at his feet. He continued to march across the snow in nothing save his boots. The ladies squawked, covered their mouths but not their eyes, crowded back toward the greenhouse, and gaped toward the cistern. Reaching its edge, Gorlov chucked the squealing dwarfess into the foul hole like a turd into a privy; the muddy serfs who had been down below cleaning the cistern came scurrying out over its edges like startled roaches. Gorlov turned upon his heel and, leaving me to pick up his blankets, stalked straight out to the bath hut and slammed its door behind him.

At almost the same time, from the door to the lady's section on the hut's left side stepped Beatrice. Her hair, washed and brushed back, gleamed in still-damp luster. She wore a clean dress and a cloak thrown loosely over that; the steam wafting up from her glowing face made merry of the cold. She cast her eyes down at first, but then raised her chin and smiled at me. "I have put your uniforms into the dressing closet there in the gentlemen's side, along with clean linen," she said.

"Thank you, Beatrice, but you've done too much already today. After rising too early."

I believe she blushed.

I was just stepping in to join Gorlov when I heard "Halloo! Captain Selkirk!" I turned to see Count Berenchkov trotting happily toward me from the direction of the barn. He wore the tailored, completely impractical work clothes of the country squire, with gaiters and a plumed felt hat, and he was beaming. "We have fixed your harnesses, and even repainted some of the scrapings upon the sleigh itself! We've resecured the compartment's stove, and—merciful Saint Gregory! What is that?" He pointed toward the cistern, where Zepsha, covered from head to toe with slag from the bowels of the excavation, was just emerging, screeching mortal curses at the spattered peasants who were trying to help her.

"Oh," I said, "that's Zepsha. She just accepted an invitation from Count Gorlov to explore the bottom of your cistern."

"Count Gorlov? Is— . . . wha . . . ?" Our host gasped again and pointed toward the door of the greenhouse, where the ladies were patting the fingers and fanning the face of his wife, the Countess Berenchkova, who had apparently fainted at the sight of the naked Gorlov. The lady looked quite secure to me, however, lying as she did across the doorsill; but that may have been because when I had last seen her she collapsed in the process of entering the house, so her fainting upon emerging struck me as natural. The count himself was equally sanguine, raising his eyebrows and remarking, "I say, she's done it again, hasn't she? What could have caused that?"

I explained as plainly as I could the circumstances of Gorlov's parade across the snow.

"Without a shred of clothing but his boots, you say?" the count responded. "Oh, my! Oh, my! Hee hee! Completely, utterly naked you say? Hee hee hee. Well! Just a little garnish of the unexpected upon our salad of serenity, no?"

"Well put, Count."

"And good morning again to you, my lady," the count said to Beatrice, taking his hat off to her. I don't think I ever could have liked him more than I liked him then.

"Good morning, again, Count," she said. "And thank you for having the water heated for the bath. It was perfect."

"Excellent, excellent!" he said. "And now, you say that Count Gorlov has recovered? This is marvelous news. Oh, and I was just about to say, the sleigh and harnesses are all mended, at least in the best manner we can accomplish here in the country. And is there any other way I could possibly be of service?"

"There is one," I said. "I must send a messenger ahead to St. Petersburg. Do you have anyone who could go?"

"Anyone? Anyone. Yes, well . . . my cook's son is a good rider. He could go!"

"I'll need paper."

"Excellent! Excellent!" the count said, and trotted off toward the house. His wife stirred as he approached, and, seeing him, she began to scream. "My dearest!" he cried in response. "Whatever could have happened?"

Beatrice, to provide me with privacy and to fulfill her feminine obligations of attending to the fallen, followed the count. I entered the bathing hut. Gorlov was fully undressed now, which is to say, he had removed his boots. He stood, feet wide apart, upon a spruce grate as two peasants on a shelf above him tilted an iron kettle to pour water directly upon his head. The water washed down his body, combing the dark hair of his arms, chest, and legs into a uniform mat, pressing the hair of his head into a slick cap, drooping his mustache, making him smile; the water splashed through the grate down onto the ice and sent up gouts of steam, until we were enveloped, as among the clouds. I undressed at the bench and stepped out on the grate with him. The peasants doused me, too.

Gorlov called to one of the men on the shelf, who tossed down a loaf of soap. Gorlov lathered himself until he looked like a snowman; the peasants doused him back to the brute he was. He broke the loaf, handed half to me, and lathered again.

"Bathing is for healthy men," I said. "It's good to see you do it so enthusiastically."

"This is nothing!" he said. "Nothing! See the spot there, where the water melts the ice? Plunge in there! That is a real Russian bath!"

I laughed. "Is the ladder there for climbing down to swim in the stream in the summer?"

"Yes. But don't try to change the subject. What, it's too daring? Your American bones too brittle?" And suddenly he plunged straight into the frigid water, submerging completely, then sprang back up and the peasants doused him off again.

I, of course, had no choice but to plunge in as well, and Gorlov, of course, kept laughing and shouting in Russian at the peasants, who pretended to be out of hot water, so that I had to stand on the grate shivering and screaming threats in German until they finally doused me again.

Gorlov and I had soaped and rinsed our final time when we heard the door to the women's section slam, and a voice shouting orders. "Look alert! Prepare for me!" It was Zepsha. The dousers on our side began poking pots through slots high in the wall, where their female counterparts received them. The dousers continued to hand across pots, originally handed to them from the warming annex beside our hut, as Gorlov and I dried ourselves within enormous Turkish towels. "Soap! More soap!" we heard Zepsha screaming; Gorlov grinned at me.

But as we were dressing in the clean uniforms Beatrice had placed in the hut wardrobes for us, we heard Zepsha begin to call out as if being molested. "Keep away from me!" she cried. "Haven't you done enough? Oh, sires, have pity on poor Zepsha!" Gorlov and I frowned at each other, until we realized the charade: Zepsha was continuing to entertain the ladies, who were within the greenhouse, in range of Zepsha's shouts. "Oh don't rape me, *please!*" she sang, like some heroine in a carnival melodrama. "I know I am small and weak, and naked before you, but don't rape me, nooooo!"

The partition separating the sexes in the bathing hut was as strong as any of its outer walls, and this the ladies in the greenhouse surely knew; but we could hear them filtering outside again, to gasp and chuckle as Zepsha continued her barrage. "Come," I said to Gorlov, "let's walk outside and prove our innocence. After which, we'll toss our accuser back into the cistern!"

"Wait," he said, buttoning up his shirt, "I am not yet decent."

"Decent?" I said. "Decent?" I was starting to laugh at Gorlov, when something Zepsha was screaming snatched all my merriment away.

"No, no, not two at once! Take Beatrice, if you must. Beatrice can make love to any number of men! Beatrice *enjoys* it! Take Beatrice, not me!"

I stiffened, aching each time Zepsha screamed out Beatrice's name. I might have stormed over into the lady's section and dealt with Zepsha myself, but I hesitated in the fear that any too public defense of Beatrice could do her no good among the others. I was still hesitating, and smarting under Zepsha's continued barrage, when I heard the door of the women's section suddenly bang open. The barrage stopped.

Then a voice—Beatrice's voice—came through the wall. "Listen to me!" she hissed at Zepsha, who must have been startled, for she made no further noise. "You say my name again, and I'll claw out your black little heart and eat it!"

There was silence, as the two must have stared at each other; the door to the lady's section banged again, and, after a moment, a knock came upon ours. I stepped out and met Beatrice. "If you'll hand me your soiled uniform, I'll see that it's washed," she said. I felt the eyes of all the women at the greenhouse upon us as I looked at Beatrice. I wanted to say something to her, but I knew not what it was. Gorlov stepped out beside me, with the bundle of our soiled clothes in his hand. Beatrice reached for them, but I took them instead.

"No. You'll not carry my dirty laundry," I said.

"Nor mine!" Gorlov said, so loudly the ladies at the steps could hear.

"Don't be ridiculous!" she said, smiling. "Do you think I am ashamed to carry laundry?" She took the bundle from me; I yielded like a child. She glanced at Gorlov, then at me, and walked off toward the kitchen, straight and proud.

I WROTE this message on the paper Count Berenchkov provided me:

Attacked by Cossacks, south of Berenchko, north of Yolkova. All women safe. Driver dead. Two horses lost. Returning to St. Petersburg today. Will enter by Kaskov road.

(signed) Selkirk

The road was one Gorlov had named when I asked for the most discreet route into the city; I felt such a quiet entry advisable since we had encountered a definite Cossack threat scarcely a day's ride from the northern capital. I sealed the note, addressed it to Prince Mitski and/or Marquis DuBois, gave Berenchkov's peasant messenger instructions to ride as fast as caution would allow, and sent him off.

Berenchkov himself would accept no recompense whatsoever for all he had provided us, not even for the mattress Gorlov had slept on, which I advised should be buried or burned. The country count merely asked me if the money came from the Crown or my own pocket; and though I assured him the payment stemmed from my employers, when I withdrew my own purse he refused to receive anything from it. He then even insisted upon providing us with another of his retainers, to serve as replacement coachman.

So with two of Berenchkov's horses added to our team, the harnesses repaired, the sleigh repainted, our Cossack retrussed and bundled on top, and Gorlov and me in the saddle, we left the estate Berenchko again, and rode back toward St. Petersburg.

Chapter Nineteen

"WHICH way?" I said to Gorlov.

"I don't know. Take your pick."

"My pick? This is not my country, is it?"

"Don't worry! Either of these must be right. This close to St. Petersburg, every road leads into it."

"So none lead away? Damnation! I'm too miserable for this!" Halfway back to St. Petersburg we had actually run into rain. It began as sleet, turned liquid long enough to soak us, then hardened again to sting us. The exertions of our riding kept us hot in the dampness beneath our clothes, but my face—the part uncovered by the bearskin cap Gorlov gave me—felt foreign. Now we were stopped at a fork of the road, five minutes or five days from the center of the city, for all I knew—and for all anyone else knew, apparently. The lackey at the reins of the sleigh only shrugged when we asked him the way. We had left the main highway to enter by the discreet route Gorlov had suggested, and I had followed Gorlov for an hour, only to discover that he thought he was following me. "This is the end of the city we first entered by, when we were with Pyotr!" I shouted at him. "Don't you remember any-thing?"

"You were with me."

"It's not my city!"

"It was dark then."

"Wait a few minutes, and it will be dark again! Will that make it all familiar?"

Gorlov yawned. "Go any way you like."

"*I* like? Why must *I* choose?"

"Do you think I intend to take the blame for getting lost with five of the noblest maidens in Russia? You made this arrangement. You choose."

I blindly spurred my horse onto one of the forks, and we had barely started along it when we saw a rider approaching from the opposite way. Before we could hail him he reined back, thrust his neck forward, whirled about, and galloped away, yelling something neither Gorlov nor I could decipher. But, as this bizarre fellow was clearly no Cossack—he was attired, as best we could discern, as some sort of household servant—we pressed on.

We broke from the wood into a clearing, where miserable houses stood. "Ah! Good choice! You—" Gorlov began, then hushed. In front of a few of the scattered shacks stood people, families, in fact—a woman holding a baby, a man with chil-dren clinging to his pant legs, various couples and individuals, all gazing as we passed. I looked at Gorlov; he frowned and shook his head, bewildered.

We drew toward a bridge spanning one of the St. Peters-burg canals. On our side of the bridge there was no one. On the other side waited several hundred people. They pointed at us. They watched. They made no noise until we crossed the bridge, and then began to cheer in waves: "Hurrah! Hurrah!" We stopped; it was that or ride over them. They pressed so close that the horses shied and pranced, the people forming a tight circle about us. At first I was concerned for the safety of the ladies in the sleigh, but the throng kept away from it, swirling about, still yelling.

Then we saw the rich carriage, parked beside the road, with Prince Mitski already emerging, followed by the Marquis DuBois.

As the hatch of our sleigh opened and the ladies began to emerge, the fathers dashed to their daughters: Prince Mitski to Natasha, Marquis DuBois to Charlotte. Natasha first turned her face toward heaven and made the sign of the cross, then offered her hand to her father, who covered it with kisses as his daughter sat beaming, while Charlotte dove directly into the arms of her father, who snatched her to his chest and covered her cheeks with kisses—which made her squint and wrinkle her nose.

Gorlov and I dismounted and walked—staggered, actually, so stunned were we, and wearied to the saddles—toward the men who had employed us to protect their daughters.

"Gentlemen! Gentlemen!" Mitski cried, seizing my hand in both his, then grasping and shaking Gorlov's, then my hand again, then Gorlov's. The onlookers seemed delighted by all of this, as did the august gentlemen, who stopped at the edge of the circle of bodies and smiled.

Then I saw a second carriage, disgorging other distinguished gentlemen, who rushed to attend to the other ladies; the Contessa Bellefleur had not one but three gentlemen of the Court inquiring after her welfare. As she answered them she opened the fan that hung from her wrist and actually employed it, there in the snow. Lady Nikonovskaya, and even Zepsha, had richly dressed men in royal hats there to welcome them home.

A third carriage clattered up, its driver pulling a team of four snorting horses to a stop, and out of this carriage leapt Lord Shettlefield and a tall, slender man whom I realized I had met once before, Montrose. Now both these gentlemen pressed their way through the crowd, toward Anne.

Marquis DuBois was near me; I inclined my head to him and said, "What can all this be? I did my best to enter secretly."

He lifted his eyebrows and smiled, glancing at me sideways as if we shared a secret—which, to some degree, we did. "Sending a herald before you to proclaim your arrival? You declared it to everyone!"

"What herald? The messenger? He was meant to convey our route! Quietly! I meant to enter without notice!"

"No need to pretend naïveté with me, Captain. You have used this little mission to gain reputation, exactly as it was intended. We both are to be congratulated," DuBois said, with that same knowing smile; it was as if he claimed not only to have foreseen the events of our recent trip, but also took credit for them.

Irritated by his air, and the accusation of it, I looked to Gorlov, who wore the expression he always adopted when thoroughly surprised: that is, the cocked-eyebrow, cheek-sucking sneer of one who is so superior to events around him that he knows not whether to spit or fall asleep. Mitski was snatching the hands of each of the ladies now, even Beatrice's; Zepsha he patted on the head. "Oh, my dears, my dears," he said in French. "I was so happy to hear of your safety! I read your note with tears, I tell you, with tears!" He said this not to me, but to his daughter.

"You wrote?" I said to Natasha. "When?"

"From Berenchko, of course!" she said. "When you sent the messenger! I composed a quick letter to my father, telling him all that happened!"

"Which . . . was what?"

"The fight! The driver! The wreck of the sleigh! All the Cossacks you killed! The ones you beheaded on horseback!"

She said *all* as if it meant hundreds; I dared not guess how many men she perceived had died upon the river.

At Natasha's words, so loudly proclaimed, the crowd buzzed, and her father threw up his hands, atwitter. " 'A prisoner!' you wrote! 'A prisoner!' "

The princess raised her arm, her hand, her finger in a slow whip, until the tip snapped up to point at the top of the carriage. The lackey, taking this cue, grinned—I had never noticed before that he had green teeth, where he had them at all—rose in the box, grabbed the trussed Cossack by the shoulders, and held him up. The crowd stuttered for a moment, awed by the courage of the lackey, and broke into laughter and shouts, hurling sharp spurts of words into the Cossack's blue face. To keep him from freezing I had ordered his arms bound across his body, with his hands free, and his legs untied below the knee, that he might exercise these appendages and get some blood into them; I looked for him to move somehow now, to twitch in defiance or fear, but he showed nothing, just hung there from the lackey's hands.

I understood then why the crowd had come into the cold to cheer us. We brought violent, blood-spurting death to them, and we made it look as harmless as an empty corn sack trod into a road.

I turned and saw that Lord Shettlefield had reached his daughter, and their reunion had been more reserved, if no less heartfelt. They stood at a close and yet I might say respectful distance from each other, her hand outstretched to her father and his patting her fingers as a way of giving comfort. But as I watched I found myself astonished; Shettlefield glanced back at Montrose, as if aware that by attending to his daughter he was delaying the attentions of someone even more important; he stepped away from Anne, and Montrose moved to her, placing his hands upon her shoulders and touching his lips to her forehead. He moved alongside her, wrapping an arm about her waist, and ushered her back toward their carriage, Anne moving docilely, as if she actually needed his protection. She did glance back at me just once, a blue flash of longing and regret, and then they were lost in the crowd.

I turned quickly to look for Beatrice, and saw her then, still inside the open hatchway of the sleigh. She had seen me look at Anne. Now I tried to say something with my eyes, but she turned away from me and busied herself with picking up the hats and shawls that the noble ladies had left spilled on the floor behind them.

One of the court ministers began to shout a phrase in Russian, over and over. The people took up these words, all together: *"Rischari Tsarini! Rischari Tsarini!"*

"Gorlov!" I screamed. "What are they saying?"

He faced me with his same expression of indifference; but his eyes were twitching. "Knights of the Tsarina," he said.

I AWOKE in a down bed, to the tap of refined knuckles upon a door of ebony. "Yes?" I said to the tapping, trying to sound alert, though I had slept so deeply; it seemed the gracious way to rise.

The door opened an inch, and a gray-haired English manservant—he kept his head down so I saw only his hair—said, "It is eight o'clock, sir. Your breakfast is laid in your sitting room."

"Ah. Yes. Thank you."

"Shall I open the shutters for you?"

"By all means."

He crossed the parquet soundlessly, drew back the double draperies, and swung the shutters open to a flood of sunlight. I squinted at the window, and through it to the arctic blue of the sky. The manservant glided back to the door and stopped, his head still bowed, to say, "Prince Mitski will be expecting you at nine, I believe, sir. Will that be all?"

"Yes. That will be all."

Gorlov was already seated at the table when I entered the parlor adjacent to my bedroom; apparently, we were coproprietors. He was cracking the top of the shell of a soft-boiled egg and looked up with a smile. "Ah! Without a hangover, I see!" he said. I had drunk no spirits whatsoever at the celebration Prince Mitski had held for us in his ball-room the night before, while Gorlov had consumed his usual quart of vodka; it was his joke that he always awoke more jovial than I.

"Has the prince given you his house as well, or only all his servants?" I said. One serving maid had just brought Gorlov a plate of peeled apples, another I could see through the open door into his bedroom brushing his uniform tunic, and a houseboy had just come in with his boots, polished to a gloss. Gorlov received the boots without comment, pulled them on over his wool stockings, and said to me, "The mark of a great leader is that he knows how to employ his troops."

"Yes, I see." I sat, accepted a hot loaf of molasses bread from the serving girl, and began to butter it as she left. Gorlov had already cut his loaf into narrow strips. These he inserted into the hole he had excavated in the top of his egg, and withdrew them sopped with yolk.

"Your appetite is hearty," I said.

"My appetite is always hearty!"

"Do you have any particular sense of what might have caused your illness on the road?" I asked as casually as I could.

He buried another brown and yellow soldier in the tomb of his mouth, licked his fingers, and said, "I've been thinking about that. Thinking very seriously. And I think it may have been the cherries."

"Cherries? What cherries?"

"Antoinette—the Contessa Bellefleur—had them. From France. Dipped in chocolate. She gave me some—slyly, for she had not many to spare."

"I see."

"Sweets can be very disruptive to the digestion. I'm sure it was the cherries. Of course, it could have been the brandy that didn't agree with me—it seldom does—so you may have noticed that I avoided it entirely at the party last night."

"Yes, I saw how scrupulously you looked after your health."

"Well, I am a fanatic about these things. Only the purest vodka will do for me. And no more brandy! I swear it off! Ah . . . it was a small distress, anyway."

"Quite small," I said, and tucked a napkin beneath my chin. "Do you know what Mitski wants to see us about this morning?"

"I suppose to discuss our reward. The serving girl told me that Lord Shettlefield is coming."

I fell to eating.

Chapter Twenty

P R I N C E Mitski was seated in a velvet-embroidered chair in the parlor where he had held the celebration for us the night before. Then the room was filled with tobacco smoke and drinking men—it was a gentlemen's night—and the talk rang loud, the laughter louder, the toasts the loudest of all. By the end of the evening shards of smashed glasses glistened on the firebricks and heaped at the back of the hearth. The Cossack activity, unmentionable before we left, had suddenly become the only topic of conversation. In our absence, the government had announced the treason of their revolt and declared its decision to deal with it; detachments were moving south already. As the ministers drank to the death of the Cossack leaders, it came out that troops had already been operating against them unofficially for some months.

But now the parlor was clean, the rug swept, the ash bowls polished, the fireplace emptied. And Prince Mitski, so nervous in other surroundings, appeared quite at ease in his own home. He closed his book slowly, stood, and extended his hand as we approached him. "Good morning, sirs! Slept well, I see! Sit down, sit down!"

We took seats, and Mitski invited us to share in some of the Virginia tobacco remaining from the huge tin Shettlefield had brought over for the party. I declined, Gorlov accepted, and Mitski received the pipe Gorlov handed him and filled it sparingly with the precious leaf. "Lord Shettlefield will be here any moment," Mitski declared when he returned the pipe, as if to apologize for its lightness and reassure Gorlov that more of the brown gold was on its way. "So, sleep well, did you? Oh, I asked that already, didn't I? Where is my brain?" Mitski laughed happily at himself. "Ah! There's Shettlefield now!"

A carriage rattled up outside—even this early the ice was already melting on the road so that the wheels bit down to the cobblestones—and Shettlefield strode inside, tossing his gloves to the harried servant who could barely keep up with handling his hat and coat. Shettlefield left the man fumbling at the door into the parlor, said, "Good morning, gentlemen," and took a seat near Mitski, across from Gorlov and me.

Mitski appeared surprised at Shettlefield's abrupt behavior, but he resumed his cheerfulness quickly, saying, "Count Gorlov. Captain Selkirk. The Marquis DuBois has excused himself from our meeting this morning since, as your sponsor here in Russia, he might seem overly biased, so the pleasure of this moment falls to Lord Shettlefield and myself. Have we failed to thank you for the service you have performed us? For protecting our daughters at the repeated risk of your own lives? Of course we have not. We have thanked you continuously. Yet we thank you again now. Thank you, gentlemen. Thank you." He smiled at each of us, and took our hands in turn. Shettlefield nodded and waved his concurrence, with the manner of wanting Mitski to get on with it.

Mitski, however, was in no hurry. "Thanks are one thing,

gentlemen, and thanks you have. But gratitude is another. Thanks are nice, but they do not buy food or clothing, or houses, though I assure you that what is mine is yours, and you are welcome with me as long as you choose to share my home! Absolutely! As you have saved for me my one treasure greater than home!"

Shettlefield glanced once at Mitski; not doubting, I believe, Mitski's reverence for his daughter, but sensing the man was saying rather too much, preliminary to setting a value on services rendered.

"Nevertheless," Mitski continued, "it is gratitude, not thanks, that oils the axles of personal affairs!" He seemed pleased with this metaphor. "Yes, it oils the axles!"

This was too much for Shettlefield. "What he's trying to say," he broke in, "is that we owe you money. What he's trying not to say is that we're not ready to pay you."

Mitski's eyelids fluttered, but he sat stiffly and did not dispute this summary. I glanced at Gorlov for some sign of his understanding all this, for I was baffled; but Gorlov was only staring toward the corner—never a good sign. "So . . . what are you seeking here, gentlemen?" I asked. "Are we negotiating what our reward will be? Do you want to arrange for payment later? Or both?"

"Neither," Shettlefield snapped. I looked at him, but he looked away.

"Please, please!" Mitski laughed. "You are surely getting the wrong impression! We want to tell you today that word of your bravery over the last few days has reached the ears of the Tsarina herself! She wishes you to come to the palace tomorrow evening. I do not wish to presume, not at all, I could never begin to presume of the Tsarina. But it is not impossible, not altogether impossible at all, that she might wish to make some recognition of thanks, and even of *gratitude* herself, to you. And we, Lord Shettlefield and I, simply do not wish to . . . to *soil,* if you will, such a pure and wonderful event as the expression of the Tsarina's gratitude by the common-place expression of our own."

Still confused, I was frowning at him when Gorlov rumbled, "What both of them mean is that they're afraid to pay us." Mitski and Shettlefield stared at Gorlov, and he glowered back. "That's it, exactly," he insisted. "It happens that we have killed Cossacks at the very moment the government has admitted there are Cossacks to be killed! Now no one knows just how much the Tsarina approves of us, and until they know that, they are terrified of showing approval of their own. They will give us *thanks,* yes, but not *gratitude!*" Gorlov looked at me. "If they reward us lavishly, while the Tsarina only pinches our cheeks and tells us what good boys we've been, then they will appear as fools—or worse, as men who have strongly expressed a personal opinion in military matters, which is dangerous. And if they are stingy, and she is generous . . . Well! This is bad, too, for all the wealth they possess in Russia comes directly or indirectly from her, and she might be displeased to learn you have been mean with your rubles, might she not, my fine gentlemen! And she would know what you have paid! Catherine, they say, always knows."

"Count Gorlov, you—" Mitski tried to inject. But Gorlov would not be interrupted. "You see, Svet? This is the way it works here. Everything is done with the hope of pleasing the Tsarina! Debts are paid or not paid, gifts are sent or withheld, accepted or refused. Marriages are made, daughters are bought and sold—"

"You go too far!" Shettlefield shouted, rising in his seat.

"I go not far enough!" Gorlov exploded back, ready—there was no doubt—to strike Shettlefield down should he actually dare to stand; and the Englishman, seeing this, kept his seat, but his eyes were aflame.

"Oh, I understand it all," Gorlov boiled on. "I know all the rules. Sell anyone, or anything, for you've already sold yourself. Say nothing if your daughter's fiancé is a cretin, not if he's rich! Say nothing if the priest is a pederast, he might be the Tsarina's favorite! Don't object if your wife takes a lover, oh, objecting, that's in the worst of taste! That's . . ." Gorlov's words came so fast they clogged in his throat. His fists quivered in the air, his face flamed, and then his anger consumed itself and burned out. He lowered his fists slowly, took deep, rapid breaths, and stared again at the corner.

"Well! Dear Count! I see we have been misunderstood!" Mitski said, smiling like a man who has taken shelter in a cave and emerged after the storm to welcome the sunlight. "If a delay in our gratitude causes such distress, we shall be glad to give you a written promise—"

"Without stating the amount," Gorlov broke in.

Mitski's hesitation proved Gorlov was right about everything.

"Ah, that is so very glib," Shettlefield said. "It quite ignores the fact that part of your responsibility—all of it, really—was to protect the virtue of our daughters, which virtue is as to be treasured as their very lives."

"I don't take your point," I said.

"My point is that you can hardly expect gratitude from me, as you have enticed my daughter to your very bedchamber and attempted there to seduce her!"

Mitski, who had appeared as baffled as I by Shettlefield's line of attack, jerked around and gaped at me. He then flushed red. Gorlov even swiveled his head around again to squint at me. I was about to launch into vigorous denials, but I held my peace for a moment, then said, "I had no bedchamber. The first night at Berenchko I slept by the hearth in the kitchen. The second evening I spent in Gorlov's room, nursing him from intestinal distress caused by bad brandy."

"In the kitchen, then! You drew her there and made love to her!"

Again I thought before I spoke. "Lord Shettlefield, you bait me. You do not believe what you accuse me of, or else you fear it so that you want me to convince you of its impossibility. I will not sink to this. It insults your daughter, as well as me."

"You deny that she came to the kitchen?" He spoke loudly, and he was straining to be harsh, but his face had already softened and that assured me.

"I deny nothing. Wherever you get your information, no one can tell you that what you intimate is true. And if you have interrogated Anne, she has not told you anything of any encounter with me." We locked eyes. It was I who smiled, he who looked away. "Now. Prince Mitski. I see you are distressed by all of this. Would you please ask your daughter to come into this room, before us all?"

Mitski lifted from the table beside him a silver bell, rang it, and dispatched the servant who answered to fetch his daughter immediately. Natasha entered directly, followed by Beatrice, who was bent over, holding up the excessive hem of her mistress's dress. "What? What is so urgent?" Natasha spouted. "Papa, I must finish this! I hear the seamstress is coming, and I see I must change all my dresses! They are simply wrong! The new—"

"Natasha! Natasha, please!" Mitski broke in. "We . . . we wanted to . . . About your trip, your recent . . ."

"What about it?" She was as bright and abrupt as he was dark and hesitating.

"Well, we . . . ah . . ." Mitski frowned at me.

"Princess Mitski," I said. "It would be a great favor to all of us here if you might answer a simple question."

"Gladly, Captain. If you make it very simple." She giggled, then turned and snapped, "Beatrice, quit following me whichever way I move, you distract me! You can drop that—the hem, drop it! I'm having that part cut off anyway, you goose!" She turned back to us and smiled, as Beatrice dropped the hem and stepped back several paces, her face lowered.

"Princess," I said, "will you tell us please whether anyone, anyone at all, committed any action, or spoke any word to you or in your hearing, that would in any way threaten your virtue or your reputation, from the moment the sleigh left your front door to the moment it returned?"

"No, more's the pity! And I was so disappointed!"

"Natasha!" Mitski said, trying to sound mortified but conveying more relief than rebuke.

"Well, it was certainly not the trip that every girl wants!" she spouted. "These men you hired did not do . . . their . . . jobs!" She accented these last words with three taps of her fan against Gorlov's pompadour, then said, "Look! My fan! He oils his hair! Oh, men do the most curious things!"

"Natasha!" Mitski said again, getting the mortification more right this time.

She giggled at the look Gorlov gave her. "What else do you want to ask me?" she said.

"I believe that was the only question we had," I said, looking at Shettlefield and Mitski. "We won't trouble you any more, Princess. Uh, but wait, please. There is one other thing I'd like to say." The princess paused, and, behind her, so did Beatrice. "Prince Mitski, there is something else you ought to know."

"Yes?"

"Gorlov and I are not the only ones who defended your daughters. Beatrice protected them, too, and not merely from having their dresses or their reputations wrinkled." Beatrice, I saw from the corner of my eye, had raised a hand to cover her mouth, and I feared I blundered; so I forged on, all the more boldly. "She saved my life and Gorlov's as well, because the distraction she created on horseback confused the Cossacks and gave us advantage. And she rode down the prisoner herself." I looked up at Beatrice, pale, and the Princess Mitski, before adding, "She was not mentioned in your daughter's letter, Prince. So I tell you this now."

Mitski sat still, even impassive.

"You have offended the order, Svet!" Gorlov rumbled, standing. "Don't you see that there is an order? They will not pay us before we see the Tsarina. And servants cannot have courage. That is the law of the only nature they know. Are you coming?"

I rose with him, and bowed to the ladies.

"There is no need for rancor, gentlemen!" Mitski pleaded, jumping to his feet and pressing our hands. He even smiled. "Let us have no misunderstanding. We may all respect one another, may we not?"

"Absolutely," Shettlefield said, too quickly.

"And gentlemen, please . . . Stay! I have sent for a special seamstress who will measure you for Russian uniforms we will present you for your dinner with the Tsarina."

Gorlov and I looked at each other. "If you insist," Gorlov said. "We will stay long enough to be measured—as long as it is by a seamstress, and not by a coffin maker! Ha!"

Mitski laughed, too. We began again to leave the room, when Shettlefield said, "By the way, Captain. An American was found dead near the White Goose the night before you left. You wouldn't know anything about him, would you?"

"An American? I—"

"A sailor. He came on the *Conquest,* in fact."

"Dead near the White Goose? Is that not unusual? How did he die?"

"Not so unusual, actually. He apparently indulged excessively in drink, then passed out in the snow. When he was found the next day, he had been gnawed on by the wolves."

"That is tragic," I said. "Quite . . . quite tragic."

"Yes. Tragic," Shettlefield said.

I turned upon my heels and left, Gorlov behind me. Out in the hallway, I had taken several steps before Gorlov called, "Svet? Our rooms are this way."

"What? Oh yes . . ." I said. Blindly, I had hurried in the wrong direction. My face was burning, my hands cold.

Gorlov stopped, and said in a low voice, "You knew that sailor."

"I—" I wanted to deny it, even to my friend, yet clearly my discomfort was obvious. Shettlefield had tricked me brilliantly; his accusations about Anne had distracted me completely, had caused me to lower my guard, and I realized that this had been his very purpose. I was a rank amateur, in contest with a master. I had been so smug after that first interview with Shettlefield and Montrose. But anything I had obscured then I had made obvious now.

I had to sort this through. Gorlov stood before me, his eyes penetrating. What could I tell him? Just then we were interrupted.

"Excuse me, sirs," said a tradeswoman who stepped from the hallway alcove where she apparently had been sitting, waiting for us to pass. "Would you follow me please for your measuring?"

"In a moment, woman!" Gorlov burst out. "The prince and the lord are not the only important men in this house! We, too, are important men, and you will not hurry us!"

"No. And I will not have your sewing completed either. But if you wish to go to the palace with the seams of your trousers undone, then I am content with that." She turned and, with her spine straight as a needle, walked back into the alcove and sat primly down.

"Come then. We are ready," I said, stepping to the doorway of her alcove.

She rotated her neck only, and looked at Gorlov. "And you, sir? Are you quite ready?"

Gorlov pushed me aside so that he could glare more openly at the woman. "Ready? Ready? Yes. I am quite ready!"

"Oh. Wonderful," she said, reaching for her sewing bag and standing. Her French was like her stature: not altogether classical, a bit too exaggerated in places and pinched in others, but vigorous, robust. She appeared to be about thirty and wore a flat straw bonnet upon the exact top of her head. From this disk of a chapeau dangled broad ribbon behind and the wisp of a veil in front—for decoration, not concealment, as her face was fully visible. I did not think her pretty at first.

She passed us at the doorway, quite refusing to look at the withering gaze Gorlov tried to give her, and proceeded down the hallway to a bright feminine parlor that had been prepared for her use, the damask curtains thrown back to admit the sun. From her bag she withdrew shears, gloves, and a roll of cloth tape. These she placed casually upon a small round table. Her hat she removed carefully, with both hands, and hung it upon the upholstered corner of a wing chair. About her neck she hung the shears, suspended from a sturdy loop of yarn threaded through one of the grips. She drew on the gloves; they were knitted, old, the fingers all gone, with a pin cushion stitched to the back of the left one. After all these preparations she turned, placed her hands upon her hips, and said, "Well, gentlemen? Are you going to remove your jackets or not?"

We responded, quicker I think than either of us intended, and draped our tunics across the arms of another chair that stood in the corner of the richly appointed room. The seamstress began with me—thereby ignoring Gorlov completely, leaving him to cross his arms, tap his feet, and sigh audibly as he watched. She first placed one end of the cloth tape exactly at the point of my shoulder and, holding the tape down with the fingers of her left hand, withdrew a pin from the cushion with her right and fastened the end to the fabric of my shirt. She then rolled off a section of the tape to the very point of my opposite shoulder and made a precise clip with the shears. This process she repeated carefully but quickly, again and again, pinning one end of ribbon and clipping the other, until I was soon trailing strips from every girth and angle of my body. Thus trussed, I was then discarded to stand like a wrecked schooner, my sails in tatters, as she went to Gorlov.

It was while I was thus so unceremoniously disengaged that I moved to glance idly at an Italian oil painting and heard filtering through the wall on which it hung the sound of shouting in the adjacent room. It was not an argument; only one voice—Natasha Mitski's—quivered the paneling. The subject of her shrill complaints seemed to be her dresses; I caught the mention of fabrics and lace. But I had no doubt that the object of her displeasure was Beatrice, and I knew I had wrought this mood by praising the handmaiden before her mistress.

"Oww!" Gorlov cried out. The seamstress kept pinning and snipping.

Pretending grave interest in the Tuscan landscape, I moved my head closer to the wall. But the commotion within my own room kept me from distinguishing the words from the other. "My God, woman!" Gorlov shouted, with threatening fury, "you skewer me with those pins! Stick me one more time, and I'll . . ."

The seamstress stood slowly and faced him eye to eye. With great deliberation she clipped off the strip she had just pinned and measured about his waist, and pressed the severed end to the side of his left buttock with her thumb. She plucked from her cushion a pin, held it up between Gorlov's face and hers so that he could see the full bright inch of it sparkling between her pinched fingers, and then—staring again at Gorlov's eyes as she did so—she plunged it into his buttock.

He did not cry out, or make any motion I could perceive except to clinch his teeth harder, raise his brows, and then knot them. Her brows rose, even higher I think than his, and she cocked her head to the side, waiting a moment, and then another, before withdrawing the pin and placing it back into the fabric of his trousers. Then, quite gracefully, she went back to work.

In the quiet that followed, with no more sound in our room than the *whoosh* of Gorlov's breathing and the snip of the seamstress's shears, I heard through the wall, distinctly, "Why do you just sit there, with no opinion? Of course! Wedding dresses don't matter to you anyway, do they?"

The seamstress took a final dreaded measurement upon Gorlov, clipped off the strip, and began unpinning and winding up the separate strands in some frantic but definite order. She did the same to me, took one more measurement around our bare throats, and then tossed the two balls of cloth strip, one for each of us, into her bag with her other instruments. She replaced her hat carefully upon the top of her head, and walked to the door.

As she was almost through the portal Gorlov called, "Well can you . . . do you . . . think you can possibly make us clothes that can fit?"

She stopped and turned. "I can make nothing more shapely than the body I must work with. But I assure you it will be no great task to make garments that fit better than those you at this moment wear. Good day, sir. Sir." With a second nod to me, she was gone.

Gorlov was silent as we donned once more our old tunics. He seemed not to know I was there with him.

" . . . more of the scarves!" we heard, as we stepped into the corridor. "And the tighter corset!" Turning, we saw Beatrice emerging from the ladies' sitting room, carrying a bundle of clothing. She glanced at us and averted her eyes quickly. The door sprang open beside her, and Natasha added shrilly, "Hurry! I don't have—"

The sound stopped suddenly; Natasha must have realized we were there, and she covered her embarrassment simply by slamming the door again. Discarded thus into the hallway, Beatrice blushed; but then she raised her eyes once more to me, held them there an instant, and was gone.

Gorlov and I went back to our rooms, gathered our things, and rode back to the White Goose in the droshky Prince Mitski provided. On the trip back, Gorlov asked me nothing about the dead sailor from the *Conquest* and sat lost in thought.

Chapter Twenty-one

OUR return to the Goose created haunting changes in the atmosphere there. When we dined, our fellows in the tavern main room no longer called over to us, or asked us to toss them bread, or threw back to us cheese, or did any of the comradely things they had so lately done. They were quieter in our presence, as if we were too important to disturb.

The innmaster, too, progressed beyond hospitality, all the way to arrogance on our behalf. My room had remained un-rented in our absence, but Gorlov's had been let by a Finnish clockmaker who intended to stay two weeks. The innmaster explained to him the situation; the Finn protested that he had paid in advance and wanted the best room, which Gorlov's was, and refused to be transferred, whereupon the innmaster recruited the barkeep of his own taproom and a blacksmith from down the way and tossed the clockmaker into the street, to be bashed by his baggage and further assaulted by the bal-ance of his account, delivered to him directly in—one might say—hard currency. We did not know of this treatment of the

Finn until Tikhon told us, after the clockmaker had already found his way to another inn; at that point we thought it best not to interfere. Perhaps an appointment with the Tsarina had already made us more haughty men.

Tikhon's reaction to our return was strangest of all. He was overjoyed, and yet whatever thrilled him contained him; he tiptoed around us, pondering before he said anything to us, and plainly deliberated every action, as if some butterfly of great delicacy was unfolding its wings before his eyes, and he dared not startle it into fluttering away.

Gorlov was sullen. His outburst with Mitski and Shettlefield buffed my curiosity to know more of the past he never mentioned, for his outrage seemed to stem from his dark well of yesterdays. Yet I would never press him, and even forgot the incident quickly, so submerged was I in mysteries of my own.

On the other side of the world, my country was becoming a nation, seizing freedom by force of arms. And in this country lay a power that could write in blood the verdict of that struggle. I drew close to that power, close to within touching, yet I was as far away from helping my country as my country was from helping me.

Able now to go to my old room and reflect upon my solo progress, I began to grasp the extent of the mess I had made, and the danger I was in. Shettlefield and Montrose were looking for American agents in Russia. Marsh, the dead sailor, had come directly from his ship to the White Goose to see me; if they had possessed any uncertainty of that fact, my reaction to Shettlefield's clever ambush had just removed all doubt.

But Marsh had not been drunk. They had killed him. Not Shettlefield, he could not do it. But Montrose—absolutely.

THE next day started sunny; then a storm blew up from the northwest, hurling snowflakes like wads of cotton in swarms dancing down the streets. I stared at that snow a long while from my room, and finally lay down again and slept.

A thump at the door roused me. I awoke to find the sun out again, but setting. Disoriented, I called, "Who's there?" I was answered by more thumping, as if someone kicked rather than knocked.

I opened the door to a mound of packages. Tikhon wobbled beneath them, and he tottered in with both hurry and delicacy; I helped him place his burdens upon the bed. Then he backed up, all the way against the wall, and watched me.

The largest bundle was rectangular, wrapped in brown paper and string. I undid the knots, stripped off the paper, and found a plain box. Tikhon sucked in his breath before I opened it. When I removed the lid I found something worthy of the boy's gasp; I beheld a tunic, snowy white, gold buttons down the center, scarlet epaulets with cackle frays on the shoulder points, a high choke collar, black enamel eagles emblazoned on either side of its central clasp. It was a tunic of the cavalry. Of the Russian Cavalry.

The other boxes contained the rest: trousers in one (the same eye-stinging white, with scarlet stripes), belts and sashes in another, even new linen in a third, gloves, a cape (blue, with crimson lining), a tall fur hat, and, in the last box, boots—richer than mine, not quite so serviceable, but with a mirror gloss.

I looked back to Tikhon. His eyes were glowing. "Does Gorlov have the same as I?" He nodded; I thought he might never speak again. "Then go tell him I will wash, and dress, and meet him in his room as soon as I can." Tikhon dashed out the door.

Putting on a uniform is an experience that quickens the heart. It is as if one is climbing a flagpole to become the flag itself, to fly in unknown and testing winds, to be measured and appraised, saluted or trod into the mud. It was not the symbol of my own country; my country had not flag or uniform, but please God it would have, and I would wear any uniform I had to that it might. Nevertheless, I succumbed to the sin of pride when I put on those Russian colors—not pride for whose colors they were, but that they were so fine, and I had won them in battle.

When I had donned the entire outfit, cape and all—when I snapped in full furl, as it were—I walked down the hallway to Gorlov's room. I found him bedecked as I. He stood motionless before the looking glass that Tikhon must have fetched from someplace; it now lay tilted against the mantel, and Gorlov had his back to me. Tikhon stood beside the bed, wide-eyed as before.

"Gorlov! I think our boot sizes must have been confused. Mine are too wide and a bit short, and I see yours seem to pinch. Will you trade?"

Gorlov did not answer. I walked farther into the room and tried to catch a glimpse of myself in the glass, but Gorlov blocked my view. I looked back to Tikhon. He, like Gorlov, remained frozen. After an awkward interval I looked at my watch and said, "Well, I suppose Mitski, or someone, will send a carriage for us."

"No," Gorlov said. "Pyotr. Tikhon! Send for Pyotr. He will take us to the palace."

At last Gorlov turned from the looking glass. A tear slid down his cheek and poised, glistening, on the thatch of his mustache.

＊

Chapter Twenty-two

A

S Pyotr snapped his closed carriage and four-horse team up to the steps of the Goose, whereupon we waited, he did not at first recognize us in our capes and new uniforms; he glanced about, looking for us, and as his eyes swept past and then returned to us, the pipe fell into his lap.

Gorlov and I climbed up into the carriage. Pyotr turned round to me, grinned, and held up his pipe. I smiled and nodded, but was, in fact, baffled, for Pyotr had never initiated conversation. But as he looked back to the horse and drove on, I caught the wafting aroma of his leaf. *"Tabak? Tabak oo Virgeenskou?"* I asked.

"Da!"

"Novou?" I thought he was telling me he had somehow acquired a new supply of Virginia prime.

"Nyet!" he answered, turning and grinning again. *"Vash!"*

Mine? And then I understood that Pyotr smoked it only in my presence, as if to do me honor. I was touched by this, and even embarrassed by his devotion; I wished to thank him for his sentiment, yet was incapable of devising a way to do so. It did not occur to me until some time later that this had been my first conversation conducted completely in Russian.

Shut up with Gorlov in the carriage's interior as we sped away, I found my comrade in a lusty mood. He sucked a great draft of air in through his nostrils, pursed his lips, grinned at me with a glint in his eyes, and said, "So here we are. Off for dinner with the Empress of All the Russias!"

"Congratulations, my friend."

"And to you!"

"Gorlov, what should we expect here?"

"Expect?"

"Someone has something in mind for us. These uniforms are too fine."

"No wardrobe is too fine for the Tsarina. But I take your point."

ACROSS bridges spanning frozen creeks and canals, onto ever-broader boulevards, we flew, a formal tandem. We swung down along the Neva, its ice grown darker beneath the lowering sky. Initially the other traffic had shown us deference, pulling aside for us to pass; but now, on this broadest of ways, the other carriages and even the pedestrians who crossed from one ministry building to another cast hardly a glance in our direction. Perhaps it was this casualness that dulled the bite of our arrival, and made the appearance of the palace itself less imposing than I had expected. The gates possessed mass alone, and not the overblown elegance that marked the other royal dwellings I had viewed in touring Europe. The same dogged construction as I had noted on the ministry boulevards was slaving forward here within the palace compound itself, infusing the entire structure with a sense of utility emphasized above style.

Pyotr deposited us before a pillared entry, and we told him we would find him at the stables. Armed doormen, bundled in furs, jewels winking from their sable hats, ushered us into a cavernous foyer. Dark British-style tapestries hung from the stone walls, and thick narrow carpets spanned the depths of a black marble floor. Rather than an energetic courtliness—or the type of pomp I had always assumed was indigenous to the royal atmosphere—the company here exposed an attitude that I, upon reflection, recognized as the courtliness of kings, the assumption that nothing need be proved, that the self-importance is obvious.

The fur-hatted guards dispatched one of their number down the hallway. He returned with some kind of sergeant, who led us through the corridors. I recognized this man. He had been with the contingent who had come to receive the Cossack prisoner we had taken. As I was not only curious to hear news of this Cossack, but was also growing steadily more nervous, I struck up a conversation with our escort, and asked him as we walked what had become of the prisoner.

The man seemed not to understand my French and looked to Gorlov, who translated the question into Russian. The sergeant grinned, answered Gorlov, then tossed me a few words of bastard French that I can translate only as: "He good! Want see? Time plenty!"

So he turned from his original route and led us through another series of corridors. A further twist to my expectations came from the variance in the quality of the rooms and corridors through which we passed. Some were stone, well fit and polished, with bright portraits hanging on the walls and embroidered upholstery puffed upon gilded furniture frames; other rooms were wooden, and that wet and warped, with dirty lamps barely able to push back the chill gloom. The entire structure seemed in a stage of upgrade; the sprawl had come first, and the effort to improve had followed pell-mell and at random.

We found ourselves in a short stone hallway, all damp and cold; but even above its mustiness, I could smell the blood. Our guide knocked casually at a metal door. Laughter rang inside, and the door swung open. We entered.

In the room were three men, and one other thing that no longer looked like a man. Of the three identifiable creatures, one was dressed like the sergeant, while the other two were bare to the waist, though, as I have said, the room was cold. The less recognizable object lying in the center of the floor was naked except for the blood that covered him like a sheet. A double chain, knotted into a holding ring anchored in the far wall, ran up through a pulley in the ceiling and down again to iron hooks that bit through the heels at a midpoint between the ankle bone, the sole, and the tendon of Achilles. The pulley in the ceiling was movable; the inquisitors could thus haul their subject up to better abuse him, or swing him over so that he hung above a heap of coals that had blackened one end of the floor but had since gone out. Various clubs, whips, and knouts lined the walls, and the sturdiness apparent in the bare chests of the men gave testimony to how vigorously these instruments had been applied. The object on the floor emitted a faint and too familiar wheezing sound; it was my Cossack.

I looked at the sergeant who had brought us here.

He grinned again and said something to Gorlov first. When Gorlov, who stood between the sergeant and myself, did not answer, the sergeant lifted a spruce rod from the corner, pantomimed a few strokes, and said, "Want you? Kack kack?"

"You bloody . . ." I made a lunge at the man, which surprised the sergeant but not Gorlov, for he caught me and hurled me toward the door. I had forgotten Gorlov's strength—I may fairly say I had forgotten everything at that moment—but I met a clear reminder as he seized me again and thrust me through the doorway and into the corridor. Still I surged back against him and found myself bounced against the stone wall, then pinned, with his hands enveloping my shoulders and his eyes glaring into mine. "Svet!" he screamed at me. "Remember yourself!"

I had no reply. None of the eloquent and noble replies I have thought of since came to my tongue at the time. Vomit was closer than elegance, rage nearer than nobility.

"Have you seen a village after a full Cossack sacking?" he breathed into my face, his nose not an inch from mine. "Not the smoke we saw when we first came into Russia, or the people's faces after a small raid, but the real result? For they don't leave people, they don't leave faces to show fear! Have you—?" Here Gorlov choked on his own words, and released me a little; but still he glowered and said, "Don't you judge. Don't you judge until you have seen it."

He stepped away and called the sergeant out, to lead us to our dinner.

A S M A L L dinner for a Tsarina, I discovered, falls upon a somewhat different scale than that envisioned by a Virginia cavalryman. We entered a hall a hundred feet long with fireplaces at either end that I might have stood within or lain full across had it not been for the blazes raging there. Through the length of the room ran a table covered by a white embroidered cloth that appeared to be of a single piece, topped all over with gold plates, silver utensils, and crystal goblets catching the light of the room's three chandeliers. Around this humble table milled an equally cozy gathering of guests—no more than eighty when we arrived—all besashed and bejeweled to fit the informality of the occasion. At first I believed that every gentleman present wore a uniform, so great was the splash of color; but I then saw that several were in diplomatic sash and braid. Shettlefield. And Mitski, too, with his daughter beside the near fireplace. Someone touched my arm, and I turned to see the marquis and Charlotte DuBois. They were beaming.

"Marquis DuBois! Mademoiselle! Good evening—" I began, and Charlotte startled me by grasping my hand and offering me her cheek, which I pecked with a kiss. She smiled brighter and took my arm. "Captain, you shall be mine tonight, all mine! How you do blush! You absolutely glow! And you must have a mind of the lowest sort, for I mean you are my companion at dinner!" She laughed and squeezed my arm tighter; glances shot to us from around the room. I looked for Gorlov and found him equally entwined with none less than the Contessa Bellefleur.

Charlotte took me about, introducing me to a stream of luminaries.

A bell tinkled somewhere, and this faint sound brought the whole room to silence. The great doors on the far end of the room swung open, and the Tsarina entered. Catherine the Great.

For some strange reason, I first noticed her hands; they were graceful, and confident, and slender, too, though she was a robust woman, broad in the shoulder. Her face was narrow, however, long in the nose and chin, high in the brow. Her best features were her eyes and hair. Her hair was thick and lustrous, brushed back from her face and wavy, as if it might have curled much more if left to itself. It was equally mixed in black and gray, both colors setting off the blue of her eyes. Catherine, I later learned, was born in the year 1729; and this being the spring of 1774, she was nearly forty-five. But she looked younger than that; and whereas I could have by no means called her beautiful, I give my testimony that she was attractive, and cite as my evidence this observation: while the woman was covered with jewels, having them about her neck and bosom and gleaming upon her dress and sparkling in her hair, her most noticeable attributes were personal—her gestures of hand and face and her eyes.

Behind her paraded a gentleman in a uniform much like Gorlov's and mine, but one spangled with medals and ribbons. He wore the rank of adjutant general. He was not a handsome man—quite the contrary; he had an overlarge head, an even more disproportionate nose, and a puffed, awkward body. He bore the grace of ease with power; he walked behind Catherine as if he were her reinforcement, not her lackey. I thought him to be several years older than the Tsarina, but I discovered later that he was nine years her junior. Still I did not mistake his identity: Grigory Alexandrovich Potemkin, the Tsarina's favorite. They came the length of the table, Catherine smiling and looking at everyone, he walking with his chin up and looking at no one. As she sat at the head of the table, he stepped to the place at her right and led the company in the muffled but vigorous applause of gloved hands. When he stopped, the guests stopped; when he sat, everyone sought a seat.

Not knowing where to take a place, I held fast to Charlotte's arm. A legion of waiters appeared suddenly throughout the room and one of them steered me to my place card, indeed next to Charlotte, directly across from Gorlov and the Contessa Bellefleur, and but a dozen places from the Tsarina herself. As we were settling in, and the waiters were filling everyone's goblet with champagne, I was surprised to catch sight of Anne Shettlefield, halfway down the table, seated between her father and Montrose. Opposite them was the Lady Nikonovskaya. Next to her was a gray-haired, stoop-shouldered general in a uniform only slightly less decorated than Potemkin's; he was patting her leg beneath the table—he made no effort to disguise it—and grinning as he whispered in her ear. He broke off whatever he was saying as someone cried, "God save the Tsarina!" and like everyone else took up this call, raising his glass and toasting.

Gorlov passed a look across at me. He was as quivery as I.

We had scarce put down our glasses when the doors boomed open and double-quicking in came a troop of soldiers, not one less than seven feet tall, all in enormous boots to make them tower even higher. Their uniforms were the green of spring ryegrass; the tall fur hats they wore menaced the chandeliers as they streamed around the table. Many of the ladies, who had jumped so when the doors first sounded, now screamed; many of the gentlemen, who had been equally startled, now laughed.

"The Giant Corps! The Giant Corps!" Charlotte sang, clapping her hands.

Their boot heels, striking in unison upon the polished floor, sounded like a barrage of cannon; they surrounded the table and slammed to attention in a thunderous closing stomp. I had not noticed until then that each was carrying a small white saucer in his right hand; on an order from their leader, they leaned and placed the saucers before each guest. In the exact center of each dish was a minuscule bread square bearing a single fish egg, purporting, I supposed, to be an appetizer. Another command sent the soldiers double-quicking out again, leaving the hall echoing. For a moment the chamber lay dead quiet; then the company burst into laughter, everyone applauding the Tsarina. "She . . . she has a Giant *Corps?*" I said into Charlotte's ear, through the uproar.

"All the crowned heads of Europe have them, silly child!" she answered, as a trio of violinists entered and began to play. "They trade them among one another, and send them as gifts, like snuffboxes! Russia has the best! The Tsar Peter started the collection; he was a giant himself, you know!" As she said this, she nodded toward a portrait hanging on the wall opposite us.

The painting showed in full, enormous length the figure of the Tsar, and I might have thought this stature an imaginary attribution, a fantasy of adoration, except that the face depicted was more homely than heroic. Yet the majesty of the figure was undeniable; he stood beside a harbor, gazing at ships. Peter the Great, the Tsar, a giant, a legend of Russia. I turned to look toward the end of the table, to the diminutive lady who . . .

The Tsarina was looking at me. Our eyes met for a moment only; I glanced away, and when I glanced back, her gaze was turned elsewhere.

I do not recall in any detail the elements of a dinner I should have expected to be so memorable. The food was good, certainly, and richly prepared, with sauces and butter, nuts and spice; yet I was secretly disappointed, I see in retrospect. I believe I imagined that royalty dined on a kind of ambrosia, and—for all my democratic ideals—that the apple upon a king's table must surely be sweeter than that upon a Presbyterian's. So what I had drawn already to the account of expectation, I paid off now in the currency of reality. My strongest impressions of the next two hours around that table were of the transactions among the diners—the exchanges between the sweating Gorlov and the smiling Contessa Bellefleur; the attentions of the old general upon the Lady Nikonovskaya; the joyless face of Anne Shettlefield as she sat and pretended to be listening to the discourses of Montrose, directed not only to her but to all around him; he sat back in his chair, his chin lifted, casting his opinions into the air and finding them too fascinating to allow himself to be interrupted. From time to time he touched Anne's arm as if to soak in the pleasure of her enjoyment. I say she only pretended to listen for several times, when he was looking away from her to those he was enthralling at the opposite end of the table, she glanced at me.

Lord Shettlefield sat quietly at her other shoulder, ignoring his daughter's boredom. He seemed oddly distracted by the flirtations of Nikonovskaya and the general across the table from him. The more Shettlefield tried to ignore them the more obvious it became that he could notice little else. I marveled that Nikonovskaya, so keenly observant on the sleigh journey, could now be so oblivious to the discomfort she was causing—

I realized it like a bolt of lightning; she was not unaware of Shettlefield's squirming: she was anything but. She flirted with the old general precisely because of the discomfort it caused Shettlefield, at a time when he could say nothing about it.

Nikonovskaya was Shettlefield's mistress.

A week ago I had been too naïve to imagine such a thing; now it was obvious, along with its implications. With the sudden realization of her hidden connection to my enemies, another conclusion followed: Nikonovskaya had been the poisoner—and her target had not been Gorlov, it had been me.

They had wanted to be careful, killing me outside the royal city, in a way that would have caused no questions. Their weapon was imprecise and had struck my friend instead of me; once the poisoning had begun she had tried to finish him to keep her attempt secret—but I was sure it was me, not him, they had tried to kill. They would keep trying; but the higher I rose in reputation, the harder it would be.

I looked around at the other guests, swept up in the sense that some intrigue bubbled in every breast. Every person there harbored a private agenda, a desire for more—more power, more money, more attention—and, in this moment, so close to the most powerful ruler upon an entire continent, they felt the fulfillment of their desire almost within their grasp. If they could but please the Tsarina, delight her with their laughter, please her with a compliment, whatever they lusted for would be theirs. They all pretended not to look at her, and yet not one person there, including myself, was unaware of her presence for an instant.

The Tsarina was conscious of the impact her every gesture had on those of her court—this I saw unmistakably demonstrated when she clapped her hands and brought the room to instant silence. "I would like you all to see something," she said. "Especially those of you whom I've just appointed to direct the various public projects we will begin in the spring—and particularly my new minister of agriculture." She clapped her hands twice and two palace guards entered, carrying between them an emaciated form, strapped to a wooden chair. It took a moment for some in the room to realize what they were seeing, and they gasped when it struck them that the nearly naked collection of bones held together by parchment-pale skin, topped by a head of bulging eyes and protruding teeth, was a living man. The guards lifted the prisoner higher for all to see. He drooled, his eyes rolling about; he had, I believe, been a guest himself at many such state dinners, and that, in fact, was the Tsarina's point.

"Behold my previous minister of agriculture," she said. "He spent the last planting season drunk, and now there is famine among some of my people. So I'm having him starved." She waved, and the guards carried the prisoner quickly away. Catherine looked down the table at the stunned faces of her new ministers, and, smiling brightly, said, "I wish you all a successful spring."

The group of palace musicians struck up a lively tune, and the diners reached for water or something stronger.

At the end of the musical interlude, Potemkin rose and held up his glass. The room once again fell silent. "To our

Ruler, our Protectress, our Guide and Eternal Companion, our Friend, our Mother—"

"Tush! I'm not that old!" the Tsarina said, slapping his waist. Everyone laughed.

Potemkin feigned insult. "All right then," he called out, and raised his glass again. "To the good lady who paid for this meal!"

We all called *"Bon fort!"* and lifted goblets to lips, only to cough at our wine when the Tsarina said, "Oh no, dear General, I mean to charge this to your stipend!"

Potemkin bowed and kissed her hand, clearly to her delight. He straightened himself again, and transformed himself instantly from a figure of intimacy and playfulness to one of imperiousness. He squared his shoulders and lifted his chin.

"My friends," he began, "the spring is almost come. The ice is thawing upon the Neva. To the south of us the packs have already broken, and the rivers of Russia run again. But these are only the rivers of water. There are more rivers in our country now—rivers of blood. A Cossack chieftain named Pugachev has declared himself the true Tsar and is leading an army across the Ukraine, sacking towns and estates and pressing peasants into his own army, doubtless with the aid of the Turks, the Poles, and possibly with the encouragement of the Austrians and various other plotters. This renegade has undertaken a campaign, the clear purpose of which is to commit as much murder and destruction as possible."

Women gasped; men choked. What Potemkin had just disclosed was treason that struck not just the political but also the religious underpinnings of Russia's whole society. God, they believed, had ordained the Tsars, in whose line Catherine reigned. But the threat of all this was more immediate than simple heresy; for every noble in Russia, there were hundreds of peasants, downtrodden wretches kept in servitude through ignorance of any other possibility, along with awe and fear of royal power. For these great masses of people to be mobilized into revolt by leaders as warlike as the Cossacks was a desperate danger indeed.

"He has raised large groups of fellow criminals and inflicted terrible atrocities upon the peaceful citizens of the land. The government had hoped local authorities might solve the problem, as local solutions are always helpful; but the outside influence has been too great, and the suffering has reached a point that we must now take coordinated action."

Potemkin went on in this fashion, never mentioning the size of this Cossack-led rebel force (and around the Goose I had heard the number rumored as close to thirty thousand) and never referring to them as an army, but rather as a "rabble" and "horde."

The speech lasted close on an hour. This proved something of an ordeal for heavy stomachs and wine-soaked minds. For my part I had stayed away from the drink, and still found Potemkin's harangue numbing. But then his tone brightened, and I came starkly awake, as he said, "I have an announcement to make. We have as our guests two gentlemen who have served us, perhaps without knowing that it was us they were serving. They have risked their lives to protect ladies of the Court—favorites of ours—from the very brigands and traitors General Potemkin has spoken of this evening. Gentlemen! Might you stand for us? Our friends, we give you Count Sergei Gorlov and Sir Kieran Selkirk!"

This attribution of the British knighthood to my name struck me only vaguely, so befuddled was I by nerves and self-consciousness; I deduced later that he had erred intentionally, in order that my appellation not seem so unequal to Gorlov's. But now I was simply dry-mouthed and short-breathed as I lurched to my feet.

I can assume that I looked no better than Gorlov did, and he was flushed, with sweat beaded upon his forehead. We stood through the patter of applause, glancing continually from the tabletop to each other, that one of us not sit before the other, and finally sat again, hurriedly.

"Gentlemen," Potemkin went on, now dropping the royal plural he had been using, and speaking in the first person singular of a prince, "I appreciate what you have done. I know how you performed; I have heard it firsthand . . . and secondhand, and thirdhand for that matter—in the last two days the ladies of the Court have been willing to speak of nothing else!" At this there was a titter of feminine laughter around the table, and the Tsarina twinkled a grin toward the various ladies Potemkin was embarrassing. Catherine seemed not in the least troubled by Potemkin's familiarity with the inner circle of ladies. "Now what you did, gentlemen, you could have done for reward. The fathers of the ladies are not without their ability to show gratitude, nor am I. But I am convinced that when life itself is at risk, and the enemy is near, and his numbers superior, and all manner of individual escape is possible, from personal flight to bargaining with the virtue and lives of those one might protect—then at such a time, the truest qualities display themselves. And the qualities you have displayed are qualities I admire and wish to honor. And so, in the name of Catherine, Empress of All the Russias, I commission you as generals in the Imperial Army!"

At this a clamor arose—much cheering and toasting, even kisses upon Gorlov and me from the ladies at our sides and shouts from the men. Gorlov, from the look of him, was as stunned as I, and as incapable of reaction. In the periphery of my vision I saw that Anne Shettlefield gazed at me steadily, while her father gazed at his lap, utterly unsurprised.

Potemkin, for his part, said with a self-satisfied smile as he settled back to his seat beside the Tsarina, "I assume, gentlemen, that you will happily accept these commissions."

I looked at Gorlov and rose to my feet. "For my part . . . no."

There was a sudden intake of air around the table, and then an utter silence. DuBois, I think, actually convulsed in his chair; the color drained from Gorlov's face. The expressions of the other guests, so approving moments before, now burned with hostility, with the exception of the Shettlefields—Anne was breathless and mystified, while her father watched me with the suspicious squint of a chess master whose opponent has just conjured up a novel move. I looked back to Potemkin and the Tsarina. "General, sir . . . Your Highness . . ." I nodded my head to her, in the best bow I could manage. "It is the greatness of this honor that prevents me from receiving it— the greatness, and the fact that my performance could not appropriately match the recognition it bestows. Please under- stand that I would not refuse your appreciation or . . . your gratitude, but . . ." She was watching me so intensely that I became aware of her attention and faltered. I glanced to the tablecloth to collect myself, then looked up and went on: "Count Gorlov is a Russian; he understands the Russian land and people. He will make you a wonderful general. I am an American. And I—"

"This is all very nice and humble!" Potemkin broke in, smiling, yet with an air of impatience. "We find you capable. So there will be some place you can—"

"It is not humility that prevents me, sir. It is arrogance." That stopped him. I met his eyes for a moment, then looked back to Catherine. "So many generals, especially young, hon- orary ones, become secretaries and messengers for the senior staff. This would not happen to Gorlov, he is too experienced, and too bold, and too familiar with the Russian manner, for his abilities to be wasted. But it could happen to me. I am an officer of cavalry. I have never met my equal on horseback. Forgive my impertinence, it is true. If you wish to reward me, I want no other thanks than what I have already received here tonight, with the sincere expression of your gratitude. But if you wish me to be of real use, then put me on the battlefield. Make Gorlov my general, and place us at the head of a corps of mounted men. And we will meet your enemies wherever they are."

I glanced again at Gorlov. The color had come back into his face, and his eyes were glowing.

Potemkin opened his mouth, but the Tsarina spoke first. "Count Gorlov, then, is not the only one at our table who is bold, Mr. Selkirk," she said. "You have given us much to think on. General Potemkin will let you know the outcome of these thoughts. In the meantime, we would like to propose a toast."

Raising her goblet aloft, the Tsarina said, "To bravery."

The adjournment was through a series of parlors, into the main gallery.

If I had doubts as to the effects of my remarks, the congratulations and smiles of the other guests around me did much to relieve them. Gorlov himself approached me, kissed me upon either cheek—something he had never done—and without a word went back to the side of the Contessa Bellefleur. Charlotte waited until I was the center of attention of a virtual queue of well-wishers and then pressed her lips fully into mine.

Gorlov received equal attentions from the contessa, and equal flattery from the others. DuBois was beside himself with delight, embracing every other diplomat he encountered and missing no opportunity to squeeze my arm and whisper, "Formidable! Formidable!" Charlotte's liberties with me seemed neither to embarrass him nor make him jealous; if anything, he encouraged them.

A S I was within the palace, among a throng who seemed to feel that I was now possessed of some magic that might become theirs if only they could press close enough to me, Beatrice was living a different experience. She stood in the cold outside the palace where the sleighs and carriages were arrayed and the coachmen, lackeys, and other private servants warmed themselves around lively fires and enjoyed their own drinks and laughter. They, too, felt themselves charmed to be in such proximity to the palace. But Beatrice, wrapped in a thin coat, her bare hands stretched above the blaze the Mitskis' driver had built, had no chance to join in the high spirits of her companions; Natasha appeared at her shoulder and ordered, "You must recinch my waist! Charlotte looks bustier than I!" Natasha said this as if the condition were due to some inadequacy on Beatrice's part, and stood huffing and trying to rearrange her own breasts as Beatrice hastily retied her corset. "That's enough!" Natasha snapped. "Are you trying to strangle me?" She scurried back into the party.

Left alone in the shadows beside the carriage, Beatrice looked up to the palace just as I stepped out onto the second-floor balcony.

I did not see her there; at that moment I may fairly say I saw nothing. The royal guests had swirled about me, and yet none of them, it seemed to me, had seen me at all, so preoc-cupied were they with how they themselves were being per-ceived; I had looked for a place to gather my thoughts and had found this small balcony. I breathed in the cold air and won-dered at the past that had led me here, and the future that lay before me, without signpost or landmark.

My exit had not gone unnoticed; I heard the door open behind me and turned to see Anne Shettlefield step out. She closed the door but stopped beside it, remaining several paces from where I stood. "You withdraw," she said. "I thought per-haps you needed a friend."

"Life has moved quickly since I came to Russia," I admitted.

"And even blessings feel like curses, if we have no loved ones to share them with."

"You see a great deal, Miss Shettlefield."

"I find it intriguing that a man who seems so brash at one moment could be so private at another." She joined me at the rail, and we looked out together toward the river.

Beatrice, in the shadows below, could not hear what happened on the balcony; she tried to look away but could not.

I did not know what to say to Anne; I felt sure her father or Montrose, or both, had sent her out to talk to me, and yet I felt she carried within her a private self that neither of those men understood. That part of her seemed eager to talk. "In Russia," she said, "time itself seems to stop. Then changes happen in the blink of an eye. I have seen the Tsarina's workmen build her an entire wooden palace in a single day, for a party such as this one."

"In a single day?"

"It's how they do things here."

"But if the wood isn't seasoned it will twist and split."

"Of course. They don't expect it to last."

"This country!" I sighed. "Great dreams spring up one night, and wither the next morning."

"You're beginning to understand Russia."

"I like things that remain."

At one of the fires below us, coachmen and lackeys began to sing. Group by group the others took up the song, and its music drifted up like the swirling embers of the flames. Anne listened for a moment, then said, "A Russian ballad . . . They are singing that it's better to live a single day than to be dead for a lifetime. I envy them."

I studied her face, before asking, "Are you happy with your life, Miss Shettlefield?"

"I was. Until I met you," she said.

My surprise at her answer was interrupted as Potemkin

stepped through the doorway. "Captain—I mean Colonel Selkirk," he said with his distant smile. "I will see you at the palace tomorrow. Come alone."

He stepped back inside, and immediately Lord Shettlefield appeared to say, "Anne. We must go."

Anne followed her father inside. I watched her through the glass, and she did not look back. But Montrose, trailing behind Lord Shettlefield and his daughter, did glance in my direction, just once, before stepping through the main corridor that led out of the palace.

I turned back to the stars and the singing, unaware that Beatrice was watching, even now.

Chapter Twenty-three

L A T E the next afternoon, Gorlov rapped on my door and said, "Come on. Bring your cloak. Pyotr waits for us in the sleigh."

"Where are we going?" I asked, following him. But he answered nothing.

A fresh snow made the going slow. We drove the length of the city, crossing canals and sliding past bare sections where workmen had drained marshes to form dry tracts for further building. Crossing a bridge wide enough for three sleighs, we reached an area where the confluence of the Neva and one of its straying branches formed a peninsula, within sight of the Winter Palace. The houses upon this peninsula dated, I thought, to the time of the city's founding. Not so grand as Prince Mitski's or the Marquis DuBois's, but grander than Lord Shettlefield's, they stood windblown and watermarked. Their walls sagged, yet columns with carved capitals supported their roofs. All featured stables and other outbuildings, but the estates stood close together upon the dry land so scarce now in St. Petersburg and rarer still when the Tsar Peter the Great first set his subjects to wresting land from the frozen swamps.

We turned in at a circular drive. Ahead rose the largest of the houses upon the peninsula, and surely the darkest. Three stories of windows faced the open river and the palace beyond, but not one bore a light or even the wisp of color of a curtain. Starlings flew in and out of one upper chamber through the broken panes. I looked to Gorlov, but he kept his eyes lowered to his hands in his lap; when Pyotr stopped before the front doors, he stepped from the sleigh without glancing up at the facade, strode to the double front doors, threw them open, and entered. I followed.

Furniture clogged the entrance hall. Chairs, tables, clocks, and lamps jammed what I took to be the dining room on our left and what had once been the front parlor on our right. Most of the pieces lay uncovered; some bore a layer of dust and others were nearly clean. Gorlov led me from room to room; that is, he drifted about without speaking, and I, feeling unnoticed, went behind him. He spent but a second or two in each chamber, yet I thought him determined to visit them all, until he reached a room upon the third floor, turned abruptly, and strode back down the stairs.

There Gorlov stopped and sighed again. "This was my father's house, Svet," he said. "I grew up here."

I knew not what to say, and yet I wanted to converse; I was sure Gorlov did.

A high-pitched wail filtered up from the lower rooms and drew nearer, the sound punctuated with fast jolts as if whoever made the noise was running and bumping through the obstacles in the rooms. A portly woman, with white hair poking from beneath her red scarf, appeared at the bottom of the stairs, just below us. She gasped back her own scream as her eyes beheld Gorlov; she clapped her hands before her mouth, clutched her heart, and emitted a new sound that was a blend of laugh and cry, indistinguishable as either. The Second Coming of Christ could not be greeted with more reverence and joy. There was, in fact, a religious rapture in the old lady's face as she again and again pressed her sputtering lips to the crucifix hung 'round her neck, crossed herself, and watched Gorlov's descent. As he reached the last few stairs she threw herself upon his feet.

Gorlov grinned easily. "Magya," he said—to me, not her, and bent to put his hand upon her head. He tried to raise her. She came only as high as his knees, where she snatched at him again and wet his trouser legs with tears.

I then saw Pyotr, standing in the doorway to the dining room, sucking contentedly upon his unlit pipe. Gorlov at last got the woman to her feet, and he gave her a hug, smiling brightly and patting her round shoulders. As he released her she clasped the newel post and clung there, choking and clutching at her heart. Then she suddenly looked to heaven, trilled a prayer of thanksgiving, and crossed herself again before beginning to dance about and chatter an unending stream of Russian. Through this torrent—for he was able to speak without causing her to interrupt her jubilations—Gorlov said to me, "This is Magya, Pyotr's wife." In Russian he introduced me to her, and she grasped my hand and dampened it with kisses.

She led us, with Pyotr, through the maze of furniture toward the back of the house, where we found a kitchen brightened and warmed by a fire. Here she sat us down to a table, fed us bread and marmalade, and only ceased arguing with Gorlov—about how much more he should eat—to beam upon him in pride. Pyotr sat with us, biting happily on his pipe stem. After a half hour's audience in the kitchen, Gorlov was allowed to depart with me back into the main part of the house, but not without more kisses, prayers, and tears. I also believe he swore to return to her table for at least the next two dozen meals.

Gorlov's mood when we returned alone to the front parlor was greatly altered. He was again inward and thoughtful,
but now he was relaxed; he pushed aside the several ottomans
to take a place upon the oldest sofa in the room, and
motioned for me to find a seat on any of the chairs clustered
adjacent. "So!" he said. "How do you like the old house?"

"It's wonderful. And . . . it has no shortage of furniture."

He laughed. "My wife has a soft bottom. It often requires
new furniture."

"And she has moved about frequently, I see."

"Why do you say that? Has someone been whispering to
you about me?" Gorlov said, reddening.

"Gorlov, can you think anyone would dare do it, or I listen?"

"Then how do you know my wife has moved about?"

"It shows—"

"Where?" he demanded before I could tell him.

"There is a redundancy of items—too many dinner tables,
several mantel clocks. And the furniture is in clusters, some
new, some older, some older still. And the styles don't all
match. It simply appears to me that she has bought furnishings for every place she has lived, then moved the contents
here when she went elsewhere."

He studied me, his eyelids half shut. "You frighten me
sometimes, Svet. Your brain is too busy." He shook his head,
sighed, smiled. "Yes, my wife has gone from place to place.
From man to man. She didn't want to stay in this house."

Gorlov kicked his boots out upon one of the ottomans,
and he sprawled back upon the couch. "Magya was mother to
me. I had tutors and governesses and the like, of course, but it
was Magya who crept back into my room after the German
mathematics tutor had screamed at me and blown out the
candles, to hum me a Russian tune and whisper prayers into
my ears."

"Your mother died when you were small?"

"I suppose so." He paused; I was hard put not to press such a mystifying answer, but I waited, and soon he recommenced. "My father was also in the cavalry . . . in the Preobrazhenskoe Guards, the proudest force in Russia, an elite founded by Peter the Great. My father sent my mother to a convent. I remember nothing of her, only that as far back as I can recall, everyone told me she was dead. But when I was twelve or thirteen, Magya told me that my mother was not with God in heaven, but was with God's Holy Orders on earth. A few years after that I found Magya crying in the kitchen. She always told me every sorrow, but she would not explain this one. I always assumed it meant my mother had died."

Now Gorlov's hesitation was too much for me, and I said, "A convent? That makes no sense! What could it possibly mean?"

"On the contrary. The meaning is quite clear. In Russia it is a banishment for infidelity."

"I'm so sorry, Gorlov, I didn't—"

"You could not know!" He smiled gaily. "Besides, the best people are in them! Only a noblewoman could deserve such leniency—a peasant would beat an unfaithful wife to death. And whenever there is a scramble of royal succession, the unsuccessful claimants, the ones left unpoisoned and unbeheaded, are cast into monasteries and convents to rot." Gorlov's face changed again; he stared distantly at his boots. "Magya told me that I must not think evil of her. She said that all my mother had done was to correspond fondly—and secretly—with another officer in my father's regiment. That this was a mistake, Magya admitted—though she could hardly bear to judge anyone wicked, and could well have been trying only to soften the future realizations for me. In any case, my father was a passionate and unforgiving man, and the exact truth will never be known. My father, when he found the letters, sent my mother away, never to see her or accept communication from her again; the officer he challenged and killed in a duel.

"My father lost standing, however; my mother was related to the Menshikovs, a family of importance at Court, with various royal cousins. My father refused every appeal that he relent and recall my mother—I say this on speculation, though I am certain of it, based on my knowledge of his character, and what came after . . . which was that many of his lands were reclaimed by the Crown, for various reasons, and his estates were diminished. He faced all this without a flutter. He smiled twice in my presence; once when I graduated from the military academy, and once when he received orders to command a force against the Turks. He died of pneumonia, in a room upstairs." Gorlov lifted his eyes, toward the memories.

Gorlov turned to me and said easily, "When I married, I went away for long periods, as my father had done, as every soldier must do. I left my wife in possession of whatever I owned, whatever was left of what my father left me. There is this house, and one in Moscow. My wife is there now—or at least, she is in the city, and uses that house as a warehouse, as she does this one."

I nodded. I was too affected to speak. Gorlov stood, stretched, and seemed buoyed. I rose also, and walked with him as he ambled about again aimlessly. He stopped in the study. His eyes shifted to a display table crowded into a corner. Wiping the dust from the glass top with the sleeve of his uniform, he peered down, and I saw below him, glinting in the half light of the shuttered room, ordered rows of medals and battle ribbons, lying like decorated tombstones on a field of red velvet. Gorlov straightened. "My father was a colonel. And now I am a general. He would smile again, I think." Turning to me, he said, "We must go, I am not supposed to be here."

"What? What do you mean? This is your house."

"No, it isn't. All of it belongs to my wife, my ex-wife. They gave it all to her when I was stripped of my possessions for having fallen from official favor." He looked at me, his brows like storm clouds. "Remember, Svet. The Tsarina giveth, the Tsarina taketh away." Gorlov opened his watch, glanced at its face, and then at me. "So," he said, "it's time for you to meet Prince Potemkin."

Chapter Twenty-four

F O R my return to the palace, I donned again the Russian uniform in my room at the Goose, then went downstairs and took leave of Gorlov, who sat interviewing the stream of professional soldiers eager to accompany us south to fight the Cossacks. I waved to him from the door, then stepped out to Pyotr's waiting sleigh.

A civilian met me upon the steps at the palace entrance, introduced himself as "an assistant to His Highness Prince General Potemkin," and preceded me into the foyer. "You have been through the palace before, have you not? You are familiar with it? The library here . . . the Italian sculpture gallery here . . . that single piece cost eighteen thousand rubles. . . ." And so he led me on, directing my attention to various riches as if he owned them himself. When we reached a section of living quarters, he stopped and compelled me to look into the chamber where Diderot had stayed on his visit; and he mentioned various other celebrities as if they were personal friends. "You know, we correspond with Voltaire," he told me.

Deeper into the palace we reached another door. He knocked, received a soft answer from inside, opened the portal, and sang out, "Sir Kieran Selkirk, into the prince's presence!" As the assistant did nothing more, merely posing there in the corridor, I entered the chamber, and the door closed behind me.

The air was heavy with incense and the smell of candles, burning everywhere. I had never entered a room so ornate, so covered with layer upon layer of carpet and tapestry, fringe and cushion. Even the furniture lay beneath stacks of embroidered pillows so that I could scarce make out the style or shape of any piece. It struck me as I had always imagined a Turkish pasha's lair to look. And indeed touches of the Orient spiced the room: in the silks festooned from the ceiling, the golden candleholders, the silver water pipes with their multicolored tubes. "Monsieur Selkirk," a sleepy voice said, "won't you sit down."

Not only did I see no proper place in which to sit, I saw no speaker either. But then a form I had taken to be another pile of pillows upon the damasked bed stirred itself and sat up. His face had been hidden by the curtains, and he was dressed in a glimmering silken garment something like a nightshirt; it extended to his knees, and there exposed bare legs as he swung his feet out to the floor and fitted them into a purple pair of slippers. He dropped onto the bed a sheath of papers he was holding, but his eyes appeared too slumberous for him to have been reading, at least with any enthusiasm. He stood and pointed. "There is fine." I walked to the mound of cushions he indicated, beneath which I found a chair. He sank into another one across from me and reclined as if to sleep. We were five feet apart, separated by a small carved table containing liquors in crystal. "A drink?" he said.

"No. Thank you."

"No . . . sir. For I am a general."

"Yes, of course! Sir! I beg your pardon!"

"You find my attire unmilitary, is that it?"

"In the privacy of one's own quarters, I should think one might dress in whatever attire one wishes, sir."

"Oh, but you were unselfish enough with your judgments last night! Tell me openly: Do you find my appearance unmilitary?"

"Well, sir . . . I would have to say that it does not match with my military experience."

He threw his head back and laughed. "Ah! So I am different from the other generals you have known! We have established that! Though I do not suppose you have known a large quantity of generals, being so young. But you are frank, so tell me this: do you find me decadent?"

"Decadent, sir? I couldn't—"

"Don't turn suddenly discreet; tell me!"

"It is not my place to—"

"Not your place? But you are an honest man! You showed that last night, before everyone! Now I ask you for an honest opinion. Give it to me! I desire it!"

I cannot say his voice was angry; but it held heat, and threat. I paused, and met his stare. "My opinion, sir, is this: you will likely be happier if the judgments you desire of me concern military, not personal, matters—for it is only upon those matters that I feel competent to speak."

He appeared delighted with this response, but he continued to watch me with a strange, askew stare. "Excellent, good sir! Noble knight! For is that what you want? You want to be the Tsarina's American knight? Yes, all bold and brave and noble. She loves that in a man, did you know that? Oh yes, but that is not a military question, is it, so I must not ask you that!"

He put his fingertips together and sprang his hands back and forth a few times. He grinned at me. "Your request is honored. Gorlov shall be a general. Shall be? Is! And you are his senior colonel. Senior, I say! But not so senior that you shall avoid the battlefield with all of us old cowards on the general staff. No, you and Gorlov will see real action, like true knights! But I have something to tell you . . . Colonel Selkirk."

His voice was suddenly very low, and he was leaning forward, toward me. Slowly he reached to his own face, put his fingers to his left eye . . . and pulled it out.

I jerked back, so shocked was I—I had never seen an artificial eye in practical use, and had not suspected Potemkin wore one. And while I had witnessed the most horrid of wounds upon the battlefield, and seen the result of cannon shot hurled against the human head, this removal now seemed more garish and unreal than any wound, so clinical and unbloody it was, so nasty, popping it out like an orange seed, here in this room of Turkish tapestries. Pinching the slick round orb between thumb and middle finger, he held it out to the table at his side and dropped it onto a china saucer he had no doubt placed there for that very purpose. The eye fell the two inches and landed with a *clack*! Then Potemkin twisted the eye around, so that the iris part was looking at me. His own eye—that is, the real one, still in his head—he turned on me now, keeping both sets of lids wide, daring me to look away or stare into the empty socket. I faced him.

"Do you know how I lost this eye?" he asked, pointing to the empty socket and smiling, then pointing to the eye upon the dish. "And gained this one? Oh, but there I go again, asking you nonmilitary questions! I shall tell you, simply! Grigory Orlov was the Tsarina's lover. He and his two brothers assisted and protected her in the transition, when her impotent and insane husband was removed from the throne and Catherine proclaimed the ruler. Orlov inhabited these rooms in which we now sit. Those steps there"—he pointed to the spiral staircase at the back of the room—"lead directly into the Tsarina's bedchamber.

"Orlov was unfaithful and broke her heart. That surprises

you, doesn't it, that Orlov could seduce her, and help make her Tsarina, and then openly reject her and take other lovers? Ha! Orlov was a bold man. And jealous, too! I myself was bold," Potemkin said, pointing—not at himself, but at me. "I did as you. I volunteered to go to the war against the Turks. And Catherine was impressed. So impressed was she with me that Orlov and his brothers provoked a fight with me during a drunken billiard game and beat me, the three of them, so badly that I lost my eye. Nevertheless, I went on to the war. When I returned, I met Orlov again. And I asked him, 'What news is there?' And he answered me, 'No news—except that you are going up, and I am coming down.' "

Potemkin batted both lids slowly shut for a moment, then opened them both again. "Now I am the Tsarina's favorite, Colonel Selkirk. I am quite happy to say so, for I love her more than anyone else could, and she loves me. She has been generous with me! She gave me this eye, in fact," he said, pointing to the one in the plate. "She had it manufactured specially for me, by the manikin makers of Paris. She has given me much else besides the eye, of course . . ." He smiled. Then the smile vanished. "She has given me the power to see. Do you understand, Colonel Selkirk? I can see many places."

Potemkin leaned back in his chair. He began to look sleepy; as the alertness faded from his real eye, the orb in the plate seemed to sparkle all the brighter. "I have given my eye for the Tsarina," he said in a low voice, "and she has given me this new one. And it helps me watch everywhere. I am watching you, Colonel Selkirk. With both my eyes. This one, that stays in my head, and this one, that can go anywhere."

He then stared at me so long—from both eyes—that I said, "Am I dismissed, General?"

"Yes. You are dismissed."

I stood and saluted. He did not stand, but he returned the salute in a manner that was so theatrical and precise as to be mocking.

Chapter Twenty-five

EARLY the next morning a messenger from the Royal Ministry of War arrived at the White Goose, bearing papers that designated General Sergei Gorlov as the leader of the corps who were to ride south to reinforce the beleaguered forces already contending with the rebel Cossack Pugachev. Colonel Kieran Selkirk was to ride along as cocommander.

As we were directed to depart St. Petersburg on the morrow, Gorlov and I plunged immediately into the work of organizing our regiment. The task was not so difficult as it might have been, in that we were made to understand that ours was not to be a force commissioned from the ground up, as they say, but a replacement contingent, augmented by such cavalrymen as the military collegium might send to the Crimea along with us as reinforcements. Thus we had only to select from our existing list of applicants a small group of officers, no more than five, to serve as general staff. MacFee was a great help in this regard.

Throughout the day, even as we were interviewing and

appraising the various officers whom we might pick as the most promising leaders, I kept thinking of Beatrice. I wanted to call upon her, and as the day wore on I grew more and more anxious to do so, but I could think of no good excuse. I found it hard to concentrate, and I was relieved when Gorlov announced that we'd done enough for one day, and we returned to our rooms for the evening.

A few minutes later a knock came at my door. I opened it, and to my surprise found Tikhon, who entered with Gorlov behind him. Gorlov was frowning, but with the kind of scowl that covers the urge to smile; Tikhon was a bundle of twitches. The boy stammered, "I . . . I . . . sir! We . . ." He looked round at Gorlov, who nodded to him; and then turning back, he began again. "Sir! We . . . my mother and I . . . request you to come dine with us this evening, if . . . you have nothing better to do, sir."

I looked over Tikhon's shoulder at Gorlov. He was smiling.

"I have many things I might do, Tikhon, and many people with whom I might dine. But none better than you. And no one I could possibly be more honored to meet than your mother."

The boy's chest, inflated by anticipation to the point of popping, sagged, inflated again, and then began to bounce with: "Come then! Right away! Pyotr! Pyotr is outside, and Count Gorlov is coming, too, and my mother has made a meat pie, and we shall be so happy to . . ." And thus he continued as I drew on my cloak and followed down the stairway. Gorlov gripped my shoulder as I passed him in the doorway.

Pyotr was indeed waiting before the house with one of Gorlov's old carriages. We climbed in behind, the three of us, and barreled off through the falling twilight. The sky hung lavender; the air lay still. The streets had dried enough that the carriage wheels clattered upon the bricks; the sound delighted me and made Tikhon happier, if that were possible. Pyotr knew the way without being directed, and he had us soon in a mercantile part of the city: certainly not rich, but the houses and shops were neat, and a few bore paint—a sure sign of diligence in St. Petersburg. We stopped before one of the white-washed fronts, over the door of which hung a sign painted with a hand holding a threaded needle. Pyotr discharged us and rattled off to one of the local liveries. Tikhon walked to the door and stopped. He cast an arched-brow grin at me, and an open-mouthed glance at Gorlov, who nodded back to him in reassurance. The boy led us in.

A bell tinkled as he opened the door, and again as he closed it behind us. The shop was a carnival of cloth: bolts, remnants, swatches, scraps, balls of thread, gouts of ribbon, piles and racks of material jamming the tiny room and giving it an odor of woven cotton, napped felt, clustered woolens. The room itself was unlit, the shutters to the front windows drawn. The only illumination slanted through an open door leading to the back of the building. *"Matya?"* Tikhon called.

A feminine voice answered, beckoning us, ordering us in, I thought. And something else whispered across my brain for the first time: the voice seemed familiar. Tikhon led us through the open doorway into a room where candles burned upon a small wooden table. A woman, her back to us, was placing a platter of steaming potatoes upon the table. We stopped inside the doorway. She kept her back to us, arranging the table, though surely she knew we stood there. *"Matya!"* Tikhon insisted. She turned around. I was struck dumb. It was the seamstress—the one from Mitski's, the one who had made our uniforms.

"Welcome, Colonel Selkirk," she said. "Tikhon! Have you been certain of our acquaintance?"

"But—"

"Tikhon!"

The boy gathered himself under his mother's glare and said formally, "Monsieur . . . Cap— . . . Colonel Selkirk, this is my mother. Mother . . . Colonel Selkirk."

"Madam!" I exclaimed, bowing to kiss her hand. "I am honored to see you again! And delighted to . . . make your true acquaintance."

She nodded with a composed smile; her face stiffened as she said to Gorlov, "And so, General? You were able to come again?"

Again? I wondered.

"I assumed I would not be driven away," Gorlov answered.

"I believe I have enough extra prepared," Tikhon's mother said. But there were already four places set upon the table.

I sat that night at dinner across from Tikhon and next to his mother. Gorlov sat opposite the lady, whose name was Martina Ivanovna Shevlova, and whose husband had been killed ten years before in the Crimea, and who said of him that he "was a complete fool, running off and dying like that; but while he was here he was kind enough to my son and to me," and who proved, within the sharpness of her words, that she had loved the man a great deal. (I should explain here that the Russian middle name is derived from the first name of the person's father, with "ovich" added for men, "ovna" for women; use of this fathername in personal address is a matter of respect and formality; Gorlov never addressed the lady before him as anything but "Martina Ivanovna" or "Madam.") Tikhon watched her whenever she spoke. I studied her, fascinated. But it was Gorlov who observed her most closely, for he pretended not to be watching her at all. As evidence, I cite this exchange, between Martina Ivanovna and Gorlov:

"Count—or should I say General?—what is wrong with your sugar beet?"

"Wrong? Nothing! It is wonderful! Adequate, at any rate."

"And how would you know, since you have not yet touched it?"

"I . . . wait for you to eat yours first, madam."

"It is my custom to eat sugar beets after I have had my meat pie."

"Do you expect of me something different? I always dine in a certain progression." (This was a lie; Gorlov fell to meals like a wild dog, and a man could lose fingers by reaching in front of him when he was truly hungry.) "Besides, it is good manners to follow the hostess, is it not?"

"It is, of course! Perhaps it is only that I am surprised by good manners—from you or any other Russian nobleman."

"If you are so keen that I eat your beet, madam, I shall do so now! Grrnn! Hmmm! Unnn! Yes! That is an excellent beet! I will say so publicly."

"So you do know good cooking, as well as good manners. This surprises me even more."

Tikhon sat breathless through all of this. He rolled his eyes back and forth from Gorlov to his mother and was captivated by their jousting. Gorlov, it seemed to me, broke his lance at every encounter, while she rode away each time in plumes and banners; but perhaps Gorlov was not, in fact, the loser. When Martina Ivanovna was clearing away the dishes, and Tikhon had gone into the kitchen to help her, and Gorlov and I were warming our legs by the fire, he leaned close to me and whispered, "Magnificent woman, isn't she?"

"Unquestionably," I said.

"Do you know," he said rapidly, and with great ebullition, "I visited here yesterday."

"You knew Tikhon was her son?" I broke in.

"No! I did not! I inquired of Mitski for her address! I . . . simply wanted to thank her for having done such a job with the uniforms. That was all. Truly. I was simply proud of mine, and I wanted to thank her."

"Gorlov, I thought we had no secrets from each other. But you have been a busy man."

"Do you—" He broke off as Martina Ivanovna burst back into the room to remove the last platter from the table; Gorlov stared at the ceiling and rocked back and forth upon his heels until she was gone again. "Do you think I lie asleep all day, while you are playing your intrigues at Court?" he resumed. "Anyway, anyway, I came here, you see! And who should come popping out of the door just as I was about to knock upon it but Tikhon! Home on his morning off! And then I remembered his mother was a seamstress, he had said. Well! . . . Tikhon did all the talking, as I met her the second time. She just watched me. I told her how I liked the uniform . . . I said it was an acceptable garment, considering it was ordered on such short notice, and I said I would like to pay her a bonus from monies that had just come to me. And do you know what? She refused! *Refused!* 'I was paid my fee,' she said. 'That is the price I have accepted. I will take no more.' What a woman she is, she—"

Gorlov was interrupted again as our hostess reentered the room, carrying a tray. It bore a steaming samovar of tea and strawberries in cream. The strawberries were tiny and wretched, indoor grown, but I cannot say I ever enjoyed a dessert more.

We left with Martina Ivanovna standing in the doorway of her shop, holding her hand upon Tikhon's shoulder while the boy waved furiously. As Pyotr drove us away, Gorlov was humming.

And so Gorlov had found what every soldier desires on the night before he rides off to battle: a glimmer of love to carry in his heart, with the hope that someone on the face of the whole broad earth will grieve if he should die, and rejoice if he should return.

※

Chapter Twenty-six

AT noon the next day, the rattle of snare drums pulsed through the cold bright air, and mounted hussars, with Gorlov and me at the head of the column, rode in silent formation through the streets of St. Petersburg. We wore blue campaign uniforms supplied from the royal stores; on our flanks, the color-bearers unfurled the battle flags, and the people lining the streets cheered. Loudest of all were the troops of the Tsarina's regular army, marched that morning from their encampments around the city to stand in ranks along the route of our parade. Their shouts for us were lusty, even joyous, and as they saluted our departure I could not help turning to ask Gorlov, riding beside me, "This does not strike you as odd?"

"What?" He sat tall in the saddle, bathing in the attention he seemed to feel was meant solely for him.

"Three hundred mercenaries ride off to fight, and twenty thousand Russians stay behind?"

"They're afraid of the Cossacks," he said, with his usual shrug.

"Do they know something we don't?"

Gorlov threw back his head and laughed.

The column passed the palace, where Catherine and Potemkin watched from a balcony. On a shouted command from Gorlov, we drew our sabers in the cavalry salute: blades vertical, with tips touching the brims of our hats and edges turned forward. This brought the loudest cheers of all from the dignitaries, diplomats, and royal guests who had gathered around the palace to view the spectacle of the Tsarina dispatching her army to bring order back to her kingdom.

Marquis DuBois stood beaming, next to Charlotte, who called out our names as we passed. The other court ladies were also there; sliding along the edge of my vision was Anne, then Nikonovskaya, and then I saw Lord Shettlefield. But instead of attending to his mistress, he was leaning away from her, listening to the whispers of Montrose, who glared up at me as he spoke. Whatever his words were, I was sure their point was that if we should return victorious, we would be hailed as heroes—and then my opinions would carry added weight with the Tsarina. Just how he and Shettlefield felt about that possibility was evident in their stares as we rode past.

On another of the balconies just lower than that of the Queen stood the Mitskis, and those I took to be their relations.

Among this party was Beatrice, attending Natasha. Beatrice watched me as I passed, but I could only dart my eyes toward her once. I thought—or was it only my imagination?—that she held back tears.

I wanted to look at her again, but I forced myself to keep my eyes toward the horizon, as we rode out of the city and toward the south, and battle.

GORLOV and I, having set sentries, walked toward the center of our encampment where we intended to set up our own tents for the night. Hoping to find Cossack outlaws, dispatch them quickly, and get back to my real business in Moscow, I was frustrated by our pace the first day and told Gorlov so. "We make camp five miles from the city?" I groused at him. "At this rate it will be next winter before we reach the Ukraine."

"Don't be so impatient. Our men will go faster once they've forgotten the parade."

I was about to tell him that it was his job to drive the men harder when we heard one of our sentries shout, "Horses coming!"

The men around us reacted as professionals should, grabbing muskets and drawing swords; but what came pounding into our camp was not Wolfhead and his raiders but rather a sleigh full of young palace ladies. Natasha and Charlotte stood at the front of the sleigh, calling out and waving to the young soldiers.

"This . . . this is a military camp," I sputtered.

"This is Russia, haven't you heard?" Gorlov shot back, trotting to catch Natasha, who dived from the open sleigh into his arms. Charlotte and the other ladies spilled out behind her, laughing, leaving the sleigh empty, save for the single cloaked figure sitting motionless in the far corner.

Gorlov sat Natasha onto her feet, and she swayed back into his arms. "We came to say good-bye in person!" she called out, her voice sibilant from wine, and she kissed Gorlov full upon the lips. The other young ladies moved among the laughing officers, whose chests swelled as the feminine fingers played along the shoulders of their uniforms and touched the handles of their sabers. Charlotte giggled like a schoolgirl, tripping up to Laarsen and gushing, "I remember you—but I forgot your name! . . ."

I moved to Beatrice, still sitting alone in the open sleigh.

She did not look at me, but she did not turn away either. "Won't you join us for a moment?" I asked.

"I am not noble like them," she answered, in a quiet yet steady voice.

"Neither am I. But I can smile, if you're here."

She turned, enough so that the light from our campfires penetrated the shadows of her cloak and I could see the shine of her eyes. "Please, Captain," she said, "don't do this to me. I am beneath you. You know that."

"You misjudge me."

"I do?"

"You do! I respect courage, and faith, and tenderness. I respect dignity, not by their measure—" I nodded toward the giddy court ladies "—but by my own."

She paused, staring into me. "That is hard to believe," she said. "You go to war, alongside other mercenaries, all seeking glory, rank, money. Men like that want women like Charlotte, and Natasha, and Anne."

I ignored the inclusion of Anne, though Miss Shettlefield was not among the visitors. "There are things about me you don't understand."

"I understand war. Some men don't come back. I hope you do."

The ladies came piling back into the sleigh, laughing at the supplications of the officers that they stay the night, enjoying the expressions of desire that their brief visit had been intended to fan.

Natasha's driver, at her orders, urged the horses into a quick trot, and the sleigh made a sweeping turn through the camp, the ladies whooping and the officers laughing, then sped back the way it had come. I watched the sleigh disappear, hoping Beatrice would look back, but she did not.

WE rode south through great sweeps of endless forests, across streams swollen by rains, the roads frozen hard at dawn and sundown and heavy with mud in between. As we rode we drilled in the techniques of cavalry movement, in order to transform our motley group into a unified fighting force. We endeavored to stay alert, ready to attack as well as defend. But we found only cold and rain. The Cossacks who had raided the north and seemed on our last journey toward Moscow to be lurking in every shadow had now vanished silently like the snow melting into the earth. Perhaps the depth of mud in the roads, as the weather grew ever warmer, annoyed them as much as it did us.

After days of riding, we came upon headwaters of the Volga River. The Volga, a highway of ice in winter, was no less convenient now. Reaching it, we cut great firs from along its banks and lashed them together to form rafts capable of supporting both men and horses, and drifted down in convoy for more than two days, south, ever south, toward the Ukraine.

Our second night on the Volga the sky cleared of clouds, and Gorlov and I sat on blankets, sharing cold food and staring at a sky full of stars, with the moon shining on the surface of the river as we drifted along. It seemed that our raft and the water suspending us were dead still below the frozen stars, with the great trees skimming by us on moving riverbanks. We sat for a long while in the beauty of that drift, needing nothing, wanting nothing. Now unpressed by any duties, I thought to ask Gorlov something I had wondered but never questioned. After a while, "Gorlov," I said, "every man here is a professional soldier, and all but you are foreigners. The Tsarina has a huge army; why didn't she just send them?" Franklin had given me his opinion on this, and I wanted to hear Gorlov's.

"She couldn't trust them," he said.

"They just fought the Turks for her, fought them for fifteen years."

"But Cossacks are different. Russians fear them, and love them. In our hearts, we all wish to be Cossacks."

"Why is that?"

He sat in silence for so long that I thought only the silence would be his answer, like another of those great mysteries of Mother Russia.

But then Gorlov filled his lungs in a deep sigh, and I thought him about to speak. Instead, he began to sing. It was a low, reverent melody, sung in such a dreamy bass that only the raftsman nearest us heard it, and he cocked his head and gazed at the moonlight sliding down the top edge of his pole, as if he had touched something on the river bottom and the voice rose from the water itself. Then this man, too, began to sing along, in reverberant baritone, and one by one, all up and down the length of the raft, the polers joined in, gently, never breaking the steady rhythm of their strokes. It was a ballad of passion and bravado, of mourning and joy. How I wished I had known the tune and lyrics beforehand, to sing it with them. Sometimes the voices all rose together and split into harmonies, the basses rumbling, the tenors blaring; sometimes only Gorlov sang a verse, his voice fervent as a prayer. Then the song ended in one a cappella chord, the harmony vanishing into the night air, and the raft slipping silently again through the water.

Now I sighed.

" 'The Ballad of Stenka Razin,' " Gorlov said, a smile opening his teeth to the moonlight. "Once there was a Cossack chieftain named Stenka Razin. Like all Cossacks he was a great rider, a great warrior. There are those who will tell you that Cossacks fear nothing, but that is not true; they fear being afraid. If they see fear, they attack it, as if it is a contagious disease that might spread. You've seen their courage already—and their respect for courage. Stenka Razin was admired, and he was followed by a great band of men. One day he led them on a raid into a village, where he took a beautiful maiden as prize. He and his men moved to the Volga, and built a great raft, and let the river carry them just as we are doing now. And Stenka's fellow Cossacks began to complain that he had a woman, but they did not. So he got tired of their complaining and began to sing..." (Here Gorlov quoted the song, which I translate to make rhyme, as it did in Russian.):

"There should be no dissension
Among men so brave and free
Volga, Volga, Mother Volga
Please accept this gift from me ...

"And then," Gorlov said, "he threw her into the river." Gorlov paused, looking up at the stars. "The boatmen say that sometimes, on a moonlit night, they can see her eyes, just below the surface of the water, watching them."

I looked out across the water.

"And yet," I said, "we go to kill them." I paused, and he looked at me. "They are men, Gorlov. And they want to be free, as I do. We are Cossacks, Gorlov, you and I."

"Is that what has been bothering you, making you so quiet ever since we left St. Petersburg?"

He knew me too well—for he was right. The knowledge that I was going to fight men who seemed too much like me, men who were rebels, had haunted me since we had set out. Gorlov was seeing that very split in my spirit now; and that division, along with my heart's other tumults, had made me a miserable companion over the last days.

"It's easy to admire what is wild, and refuses to be tamed," Gorlov said gently. "But if you are having second thoughts about fighting Cossacks, just wait."

Gorlov covered himself with his blanket. I did the same. Soon Gorlov was snoring, but I could only lie there on the raft, sliding on the water beneath the stars. Hussars. Russian knights. *Kazaki!*

Chapter Twenty-seven

IN another week we reached Moscow. We did not, however, enter the city itself, but bivouacked in a military encampment on the outskirts. Such self-denial was extreme but agreeable to the men, all of whom considered their contracted salaries as but a minimal guarantee against the rewards they might win for gallantry in the field—prizes forever forfeited should the campaign end before we could arrive. Among the other soldiers in the camp—mainly Kremlin security troops, who lived in permanent huts with their families—rumors abounded that the Cossacks had already surrendered and been executed by the thousands. These stories, told in grisly detail, found rebuttal in equally vivid accounts of the routing of the government forces and the butchering of nobles, including captured army officers. Gorlov determined that he, perhaps, should make a visit into the city, to seek out more credible authority than he could find within the camp and gather the latest intelligence on the location of the most recent fighting. So at sundown on the day of our arrival he rode off toward the onion domes, glowing orange on the horizon as the clouds broke for the first time in days.

Well past midnight, I awoke to the sound of a wooden wagon rattling to a halt outside our tent, and I emerged to find an artillery cart there, with Gorlov's horse tethered to the back of it. The two laughing majors upon it—noblemen's sons, for neither was more than seventeen—hoisted a burden from the cart bed, dumped it down to me, saluted giddily, and cavorted away.

The burden was Gorlov, drunk beyond his senses.

B U T General Gorlov was awake early the next morning and broke us away from camp and onto the road south just after dawn. This decisiveness I construed to indicate specific knowledge and planning on Gorlov's part. I did not question him, nor did he volunteer his confidence.

We rode ever southward, sometimes with a western drift. We followed the Volga briefly out of Moscow, then shifted to pass through Ryazan' to pick up the Don. The rivers had thawed and surged strong, the waters frigid, not yet muddy. From the first day out of Moscow we began to encounter government army stragglers: men with fever, deserters (who always claimed to have fever), and wounded. None of these bore the marks of battle, but they had sustained their wounds, I assumed, in drunken falls from artillery carts.

The third day, our advance guard—we went ahead now in force—took a Cossack prisoner, a boy scarcely in his teens, who wore riding leggings but had been unhorsed weeks before, to judge by his dilapidation. He was cowering in short brush when the vanguard, who had seen him run from the road and hide at our approach, caught him up. Gorlov interrogated the boy personally, received nothing for his efforts except a frightened nod of the head in response to each of his questions, and finally released the boy, telling him to go home. No man with us showed any ripple of objection.

We pressed on, the hours now an endless quilt of sunshine and rain.

ONE evening, as we were making camp in a copse of trees beside the road, we encountered another soldier coming from the south. But this man was no deserter; he wore a Russian lieutenant's uniform with fur cap, rode erect though he was muddy and the horse lathered, and came straight toward our fires, not avoiding us as others had done. He stopped as soon as the pickets challenged him, then dismounted and followed them gladly. Brought to where Gorlov and I stood before our tent, he saluted us smartly and said in French, "Sirs! I am so very happy to see you!" He wore one of those thin Parisian mustaches that appear as if the nostril hairs have grown too long. Beads of sweat clung to this tiny hedge of manicured whisker.

I bade the man sit, and we each took a block of firewood as support and squatted beside the blaze. Gorlov said nothing, and I then understood that since this man was an officer, but of low rank, I was expected to question him. "From where do you come?" I asked.

"Kazan," the lieutenant said. "With dispatches."

One of the Russian orderlies brought food and drink, and the messenger dug in voraciously, while still sitting upright and clinging to his manners. "Why are you so happy to see us?" I said.

He looked from me to Gorlov, and thought before he answered. He smiled. "Oh, I would have been all right. If they had really threatened me, I'd have given them the blade!

Or simply ordered them away—the Jews try to be peaceful."

"Jews? What . . . among the Cossacks?"

"Among the Cossacks! Ah, no! Ha! Among the Cossacks!" The lieutenant saw from my face that I did not welcome his mocking me, after he had first confused me, and that he would do well to give straight answers. "No, sir. I speak of the residents of Tulk."

"Tulk?"

"The town, sir . . . The one you are about to enter."

"Ah, Tulk! Yes! Well, you see, our maps have been . . . unreliable, and we did not know we were so close. Perhaps we should have pushed on, to make camp there."

"Spend the night in Tulk? I would not advise that! It was a wise decision that you did not push on, sir!" This last bit the lieutenant directed to Gorlov.

"Yes," I said, "the general is most astute in these matters." Gorlov did not look at me. "But tell us why you feared the residents of Tulk. Or why we should."

"Feared? Oh, no, I did not say that. Only that they bear watching, and caution is—"

"Answer my question, Lieutenant."

"Well, the . . . in Tulk . . . the Cossacks were there three weeks ago. Stole, looted, burned. Took everything of value and destroyed the rest. They carried away all the young men and young women—the men for soldiers and the women for—well, you know what the women are for." He chuckled.

"So why do you fear the residents of Tulk?"

"I did not say I fear them!" he insisted.

"No. But you do fear them. And you will tell me why, and answer my questions, or I will take you back there myself."

He crossed his arms and actually tried to sneer at me. "Well! I suppose the people there are unhappy! I know they are, from the way they looked at me when I galloped through. They are fighting one another now for food, and looting from one another what miserable scraps of anything are left. And they have no love for the government forces, whom they expected to protect them, as they have been promised so many times."

I should have deduced that. "So that's why you were glad to see us," I said, to get even. "You feared staying alone on the road."

Gorlov, who had stared into the fire this whole time, now said, "Tell us about the Cossacks. I want to hear about the rebellion—who is at the head of it, and what the status of the forces, both government and Cossack, is now."

This directive pleased the little lieutenant—have I said that he was little?—very much. He asked first for another cup of wine to cool his throat, received it, and began his narrative thus:

"The Cossacks have always been difficult to control, and unhappy to provide the military recruits required by imperial levy, and to pay their taxes, and—"

"We have experience with Cossacks!" I broke in. "Just tell us—"

But Gorlov interrupted my interruption. "Tell us everything, everything you know," he said.

"Everything I know?" the lieutenant said, blinking as if to tell all that would encompass more years than he took to gather such knowledge. But he tried anyway. "Well, the Cossacks, as you know, have a tribal tradition, and follow charismatic leaders, their atamans. They call their groups 'Hosts.' They've always been looking for a true Tsar! Ha! Whoever the Tsar or Tsarina is, the Cossacks hate whatever happens and say that the true ruler is not on the throne! The true ruler would be blessed by God, and God, of course, is a Cossack! And there are many Old Believers among the Cossacks—the Old Believers are those who refused to accept the reforms Peter the Great instituted, when it became a crime to wear beards, and non-European dress, and worship in the old ways. The Old Believers said, 'Fine! We will break the law!' Cossacks, of course, have never minded to be criminals!

"This latest Cossack leader to proclaim himself the true Tsar is a Cossack of the Don region, named Pugachev. He is more enterprising than the others have been. He prints manifestos and proclamations freeing all the Cossacks, and he promises to return them to their old way of life, with free salt, free use of land and fisheries and pastures, and an annual income! In short, he offers to do away with the Russian government, and no matter how ridiculous his claims and promises, the other Cossacks have said, 'Fine! Let's go fight, then!'

"Of course, not every Cossack is so happy to go to war— but they much prefer it to dismemberment, which is what they get if the Cossack force passes through and they don't join! But I get ahead of myself . . .

"Pugachev first marched on the fort at Yaitsk, with three hundred men in his army. The fort commandant had a thousand men, but many were Cossacks who deserted to Pugachev instantly. Still the remaining troops beat off the first attack, and Pugachev went on along the Yaik River, sacking towns and small forts, hanging officers and priests—the priests who had adopted modern reforms. He increased his force to thousands, maybe three thousand, in just two weeks, and laid siege to Orenburg.

"Orenburg being a major stronghold, St. Petersburg was worried enough to send down General Kar from Kazan, along with some detachments from Simbirsk and Siberia. Pugachev smashed Kar, and the general ran back to St. Petersburg! The Cossacks also destroyed the Simbirsk detachment, and hanged their colonel."

The little lieutenant paused here, to let us take in that last aspect of the story. When he went on, his voice had dropped low. "Since then the size of the rebellion has doubled, and redoubled. No regular army units have been able to stand against them. And this, even though Pugachev's army is but a rabble. The wives and daughters of captured government officers are everywhere, having been distributed as booty, and people, even other Cossacks, are executed on the spur of the moment. When we have moved in behind Pugachev, we have found ravines full of corpses."

With this final statement the lieutenant fell silent, and all of us sat in the sudden stillness of the night, and stared into the fire.

When everyone else had gone to bed, I asked Gorlov, "What do you think?"

"What do you mean?" he asked in return, as if the thought of our being massacred did not trouble him.

"They are thousands—perhaps tens of thousands. We are a few hundred."

"They are a mob. They look for someone strong to follow; that's what makes them feel safe. They will follow this Pugachev only until they see that someone else is stronger."

Gorlov pulled off his boots and went to sleep.

Chapter Twenty-eight

THE sunrise revealed upon the horizon three separate plumes of smoke that curled up into the clouds.
The men who had stood watch said they had seen
the fires lighting up the night sky, but had sounded
no alarm because the brightest blaze seemed the most distant,
as though the marauding forces swarmed away from us. This
was logical enough to me; in the presence of an enemy, rest is
precious, and had I known of the fires myself, I doubt I could
have slept. The sight of the smoke itself set us all on edge as
we struck off toward the plumes.

We came upon the debris of the encampment of a regular army patrol and assumed the government forces must be
moving toward the sacked towns as well. Shortly after noon
we arrived at the first of these villages, a place in which there
had once been a foundry. I noticed first of all that dogs still
roamed in this village; three of them clustered and snarled in
the center of the street. Next I noticed that they were snarling
over a human arm.

The report in this village—we found many who would

talk to us—was that a group of Cossacks, no more than a hundred, had arrived the previous morning. They had been calm
enough at first, even official acting. They handed out printed
broadsides, though few in the town could read, and even
fewer of the Cossacks, apparently, for they went through the
streets of the village calling out all sorts of promises—that
taxes were rescinded, food prices reduced, peasants given
land—and waving the broadside as official proof; one literate
peasant had examined the document itself and found it to be
nothing more than a declaration of the divinity of Pugachev,
and when the Cossacks heard the peasant stating this fact to
his neighbors, they declared him a wizard and gouged out his
eyes.

The only fire they set was to the foundry, and the only
men they killed were the four who had been the overseers
there. These they pulled apart with horses. The rest of the
foundry serfs, fifty-four in all, joined with the Cossack party
and rode away with them upon every last draft horse and
donkey the village had owned. They took a number of
younger women as well; no one was sure, or would say, how
many.

We discovered, too, that a government patrol somewhat
smaller than ours had been through the village before us, just
after ten o'clock that very morning. They had not stopped to
ask questions or to give aid, but had simply galloped on.

We had a German with us, a former captain of artillery,
whom MacFee had chosen for our unit because he also had
some training as a surgeon. Gorlov ordered him to leave an
ointment for the blinded peasant. I accompanied the German
into the peasant's house, where the old women of the village
had darkened his room with curtains and filled his eye sockets with a poultice of moss, mud, and duck feathers. They
seemed willing enough to accept our medicine until they
heard us converse and recognized the tongue as German; then

they crossed themselves repeatedly, spat all about between their fingers, and howled us away.

Our column left at a trot, chased by disgust and not danger; but when we got out upon the wooded road, we settled our horses into a walk—or they settled us, for I remember no command. A heaviness weighed upon us all, soaking down from every man's brain to the hooves of his horse. The air was dank and raw with cold. Death lay behind us, and waited before us, and we drifted on. I knew how vulnerable we might be to ambush when all any of us watched was the slow sliding past of a muddy road, and all any of us saw was a severed shoulder tapering down to lifeless gray fingers. Yet I lacked the spirit to do more than order out the vanguard, and keep four riders back to picket the rear, and bark halfheartedly to the others to mind the flanks.

Then MacFee turned to me and said, "Colonel Selkirk, sir, could ye geev me a hand wi' me pack? Not that one, sir, Ah mean the one there on the croup." MacFee had traveled with a second bundle tied behind his saddle; I had asked him once what it was, and he only grinned at me and winked enough times to make me uncomfortable. But now I leaned and undid the lashings for him and handed the bundle forward; he unwrapped the oilskin, exposing a set of bagpipes. He winked at me again, inflated the bag, and began to play.

Never have I seen a more rapid and thorough change come upon men as when the sound of those pipes quivered over us. In our company were eighteen Scots, not counting MacFee (or myself—which omission MacFee would have taken as blasphemy), and they came to life and started their horses prancing. Along with them rode a dozen or so Irishmen, and they, too, sat upright and pranced along with the Scots. The Russians found the sound mystical, the Finns, Danes, and other Scandinavians thought it curious, and the Germans took the occasion as one for straightening spines, spreading out elbows, and squaring formation. MacFee blew well, I thought; a low vibrating chord flowed steadily from the drones while a high liquid melody rose and fell from the chanter. The sound cut the air. I had heard other soldiers say that bagpipes were the perfect military instrument because no other sound could so penetrate the noise of battle; I believed it now. One of our vanguard riders, hundreds of yards at our fore, even galloped back for a bewildered look at what was following him where a normal Russian mercenary column used to be, and the sight of his stunned face made the men in the front of the column laugh, and the ones farther back cheer. MacFee played for half an hour, then tucked the pipes back into the oilcloth and had me help him stow them away again. "Ye cannae geev 'em too mooch at once, like more than one barthday pudding. Spoil th' surprise!" He winked at me again. I winked back.

The day was coming when I would lie in ambush for a British column, and they would come down the road marching in kilts and playing the very tunes that MacFee played that day, and the memory of it would haunt my heart forever. But that was my future. All I wanted at this moment was to be done with the Cossacks so that I could get back to St. Petersburg and find my chance to speak for my countrymen. Almost as if I had willed it, a trickle of peasants, swelling to a stream, appeared on the road before us, refugees from the city of Kazan, which the Cossacks, they told us, had sacked the night before, as we slept.

Chapter Twenty-nine

THE city of Kazan is—or was—on the next hill," Gorlov said, his voice loud enough to be heard by all, and yet deep and steady, telling us facts that held no fear for him. "There is a low plain between us and the higher ground where the Cossacks are. We are a few hundred. They are thousands. But they are a rabble; they've been drinking and raping all night long." Gorlov paused and looked around at the faces watching him. They were professional soldiers and had come here voluntarily; but still Gorlov, I sensed, wanted them to make one more affirmation before the battle, so he presented to them the choice he himself faced. "We could pull back and send for more reinforcements from Moscow."

No one else spoke, so I did. "How many more cities will they sack if we pull back and wait?"

Smoke, and the trees around us, obscured from our view the hilltop where the city lay, but the sounds of drunken singing, and the intermittent screams of women, permitted no doubt that we must fight now.

"Once we engage them," Gorlov said, "they will not allow us to break off and run. They will slaughter us, or we will slaughter them. But remember this: They are untrained, and not used to fighting. We are the government forces, and those peasants out there see us as tenfold larger than we are. This Cossack Pugachev is trying to show his own army how much greater their numbers are than ours. He has ravaged estates and hacked nobles to pieces and sacked towns where most of the defenders were Cossacks or Tartars who deserted to his side anyway. He has not beaten a regular government army. And he will not today."

THE grass had come out all rich and green across the plain. It cushioned the horses' hooves and soaked up sound so that the world lay hushed as we rode slowly forward, out of the shelter of the trees and into the open. Gorlov, with a look, drew me up to ride beside him.

The smoke on the hilltop appeared thicker the closer we came. The wind had shifted so that smoke was drifting down across the plain; in some places we could barely see ten paces ahead. Still we pressed forward, keeping our horses quiet. Eerie sounds filtered down to us from the village, a strange cacophony of laughter and crying, of the shouts of rape and revelry. But the din of destruction seemed to be changing; the laughter was dying out, there were distant shouts and the rattle of weapons.

"They know we're here," Gorlov said quietly. Then in a louder voice he ordered the men behind us to form ranks, spreading out twenty abreast. As our cavalry moved smartly into position we heard other sounds drifting down through the smoke. We held our breath to listen and heard singing; the Cossacks were raising their voices in a battle song. It was lusty, joyous, unafraid.

MacFee and Laarsen, the officers whose skill and valor we most relied upon, Gorlov had positioned in the center and at the rear, one upon the left flank and the other upon the right, so to steady those with less experience. One of these, still in his teens, sat pale upon his horse next to Gorlov, and said aloud, "Thousands! What chance do we have?" I shot a glance at Gorlov; he made no acknowledgment of the panic beginning within our lines.

A breeze picked up, chasing some of the smoke away, and now we could see men pouring out of the shattered ruins of what once had been the collection of prosperous shops and tidy homes known as Kazan. Closest to us were a crazed rabble carrying farm implements as weapons—axes, scythes, hay forks, even rakes. Mixed in among them were Cossacks mounted on horseback, and these looked like dervishes; they were drunk, wild men, with straw in their hair and beards. We sat in our saddles and watched the massive, murderous mob grow on the hill before us.

"Their numbers keep increasing," the panicky young man next to Gorlov said.

"Yes," I answered, "but the Cossacks on the horses are having to whip their peasant infantry forward. See there!" I pointed to the rear of the mob, where mounted Cossacks were using the flats of their sabers to slap the backs of the peasants who were already trying to shrink away from the battle. It is great encouragement to know that one's opponents do not truly wish to fight; I added, "That's a good sign!"

"Yes," Gorlov said quietly to me, "but that isn't." He nodded to where, along the crest of the hill marking the Cossack lines, another group of Cossack riders came galloping. The man at the head of this newly arrived cavalry was unmistakable.

"Wolfhead," I whispered.

The Cossacks cheered as they saw him; men around us paled. I tried to figure what to make of his arrival, and my speculations weren't comforting: Wolfhead had kept his men away from the sacking of the city, from the drunkenness and the gorging on food and rape. He was more military than those riders mixed in among rabble, perhaps even noble, as I had known many Cossacks to be. He would not react in bloodlust and confusion; he was dangerous.

Gorlov watched him, transfixed. "Whoever he rides to is the leader of the rebellion," Gorlov said.

We looked on, all of us on that field, royal mercenaries and rebellious marauders, as Wolfhead the Cossack rode across the ridgeline at the head of his band, for such was the majesty of the man. He rode with animal grace, communicating with the slender black horse beneath him, not with his hands but through his knees, and, or so it seemed, through some non-physical connection he had with the beast. The stallion raced along in fluid, effortless speed and came to a sudden yet relaxed stop amid a nest of Cossack cavalry. In their center was a massive, overfed Cossack in a robe of purple satin trimmed in fur; his face was florid, and, even at the distance from which I saw him, he appeared both drunk and fierce. He nudged his horse forward and embraced Wolfhead in a bearish hug, and I knew that we had at last spotted the rebel chieftain Pugachev.

The mob in front of us had continued to deepen and to spread, oozing out to our flanks and beyond; we were in danger of being surrounded. "Save yourselves!" the now terrified young mercenary next to Gorlov shouted, and he started to rein his horse away; with one swipe of his huge hand, Gorlov knocked him from the saddle.

"Do not flee!" Gorlov barked, then turned and called out to the other end of our line, "Do not flee!" He looked at me, his eyes fierce. "We must charge the mob before their cavalry is ready!"

In answer, I drew my saber. Gorlov's eyes held on me, and he smiled; he had always valued my readiness to fight beside him.

Gorlov slid his blade from its scabbard and spun his horse so that he faced his men. "There is a Russian proverb!" he shouted. "'When a man is born he will walk one of three roads; there are no others. On the path to the left, the wolves will eat him. On the path to the right, he will eat the wolves. On the path down the middle, he will eat himself.' " Gorlov raised his saber into the air. "I say to you, 'Eat the wolves!' "

He turned his horse toward the enemy, screamed, and led the charge.

I spurred to a gallop beside him, the others thundering along behind us. The maneuver we now made, we had discussed around many campfires over the previous weeks, had even practiced during our long ride south; I led one group of cavalry into the peasants massed before me, and Gorlov led a second group slamming into the mob just to our left. The first peasant I reached appeared drunk, so insensible from drink that he was not cowed by our charge; he swung a scythe at me, but his swing was late, and I cut him down easily, then chopped to my left and cut another peasant lifting an ax to strike at me. The other peasants were starting to retreat from us, as we had hoped; standing up to a charge of cavalry requires discipline, steady officers, and training, none of which this mob possessed. They were not cowards, most of them, but they were not professionals, either. What they were, though—many of them in the front ranks who moments before had been brandishing bloody weapons in our direction—were murderers, and we cracked our blades into the backs of the heads of all those we could reach as they turned to flee.

I looked to my left and saw Gorlov in the thick of it, cutting men down. He was even more aggressive than I; as the mob shrank back he pursued them, spurring in so that he found himself ahead of the other royals; he also found himself surrounded by the peasants who were so jammed together they could not flee. Some of them realized that he had separated from his comrades, and they surged back around him. Slicing one down and firing his pistol into the face of another, Gorlov shouted, "Charge!" though the two mercenaries closest to him were even at that moment being dragged from their saddles and hacked to death.

I yelled for my column to fall back and regroup, and instead of going with them I spurred toward Gorlov; my horse, a mare with a liquid gate, was the fastest in the battalion, and she knew my thoughts before I thought them; she covered the ground in a few strides, knocking Gorlov's assailants down with her chest as she bowled through them, and I slashed with my saber. We reached Gorlov and found him in a fighting frenzy, still hacking with his blade though the peasants had backed away again. I seized his bridle. "Gorlov!" I yelled to him. "Back! Back!"

I pulled Gorlov's horse, leading him and the survivors of his charge away from the Cossack lines. All of us, his half of the men and mine, regrouped in our original positions. "Reload pistols!" I shouted to the men.

"Don't be so late next time!" Gorlov roared at me.

"If you would actually fight," I bellowed back, "instead of riding around waving your sword in the air, we would break this rabble!"

"I? I've never seen a rider more concerned with looking graceful than you!"

This shouting at each other in the heat of battle is not recommended doctrine for cavalry leaders, but not unusual for friends who have seen each other almost killed by the enemy. Both Gorlov and I fought to gain control over our emotions, and we ordered our men to reform. The men obeyed smartly, arraying behind us in ranks. I looked toward the Cossack leaders, barely visible to us through the drifts of smoke floating down to us from the town.

"The Cossack riders have to come soon," Gorlov said, "to show their army they are not afraid!"

"Let them come," I told him.

We watched Wolfhead rise in his stirrups to wave his men forward; the burly, satin-robed Cossack next to him, the one we knew had to be Pugachev, reached out an arm to stop him. Pugachev seemed to be smiling, though at this distance I could not be sure. He waved to his own cavalry, on the opposite side of him from Wolfhead's men, and these young riders spurred their horses and screamed forward in a charge.

For a moment we watched them come, and in the second I took to study them, I had the impression that they were like the foot soldiers we had already been fighting that day; they looked drunk, they rode loosely and without formation, and yet they were screaming, some of them howling as if they wished nothing more than to be Wolfhead and fancied themselves to be him already.

We yelled and galloped to meet them, sabers high, horses rippling, men screaming. The two charges slammed together.

We rode right through them. I say this without pride, only as a statement of fact. But no, as I think on it I am proud— for we kept our ranks, we rode as a disciplined unit, in such a formation that every rider in our unit felt the support and protection of every other rider. Such discipline is not easy in battle. The professionalism of our battalion showed, and we knocked the mounted Cossack rabble aside and once more slammed into the massed mob on foot behind them.

The wild infantrymen were gathered thick, here in the center of the Cossack line. Panic was rising through their ranks, and the confusion was even greater with this second clash, as terrified men in the front of the rabble army tried to flee to the rear and collided with their still bloodthirsty brothers who struggled to push their way forward to fight. Laarsen was knocked from his horse, but MacFee and I were able to get to him; MacFee held his reins and I slashed the Cossacks to keep them back as Laarsen remounted.

We killed many and lost few, but our men were growing exhausted with the exertion. "Form up!" Gorlov yelled; I repeated the order to the men behind me, and the Royal Cavalry rallied around us. We did not have to fall back; the Cossack lines had done that for us. They had seen us charge twice, and two swaths of their dead lay littered on the field. For months they had been pillaging and raping, killing and burning whatever they did not wish to steal, then marching on, always moving under the growing myth of their invincibility. Suddenly all that was gushing away.

"Their riders are amateurs," I said to Gorlov.

"Wolfhead's are not."

A hush fell over the field; it was as if every man there, mercenaries and marauders, professional soldiers and peasants alike, had come to the realization that the mesmerizing Cossack had yet to throw his weight into the battle. When the first shock of fighting has passed, deeper instincts emerge, causing each warrior to judge the direction of victory. Our charges and the ineffectiveness of the mob before us had emboldened us and discouraged our enemies; now the mob teetered, like the savages that all men become when they are afraid and have no model of courage. They looked to the most vivid symbol of bravery they could find, and saw Wolfhead.

He had risen in his stirrups to his full height; he was a tall man, and lean—unlike the overfed rascal Pugachev, crouched motionless on the horse beside him. Wolfhead threw back his head and howled.

The sound from his lungs froze the mob in place. They did not run anymore, nor did they attack; they simply stopped and waited to see what would happen.

I do not know what possessed me to do it—perhaps it was

the energy of fear mixed with my natural defiance—but I rose in my own stirrups and howled back.

This surprised Gorlov and others around me; it outraged the Cossacks. One young rider, part of Wolfhead's band, screamed what must have been a Cossack curse and spurred his horse toward me; at the same time one of the Cossacks who had been among the peasants trying to drive them forward, and who possessed a pistol, leveled it and fired a shot in my direction. I felt something slap into my right side, hitting me like a boxer's jab just above the waist. I put my fingers to the spot and was surprised to find blood there. But I had no time to consider the wound; I felt little pain and told myself it was hardly more than a scrape. All I could see was the young rider flying toward me. I spurred my horse, and she leapt forward to meet the charge.

The Cossack was screaming; I must have been, too, though I remember hearing no sound, not the hooves of the horses or the wind or even the pounding of my heart. The motion around me slowed to a crawl, and I saw the event in minute detail: the lips of the Cossack's horse pulled back from its teeth as the rider tugged the reins in his excitement, causing the horse to dart and unbalance him; the Cossack rising to his full height as he drew back his blade to slash at me, his eyes wild and focused on my head. I realized in that elongated moment that he burned to separate my head from my shoulders, and the thought occurred to me, actually formed clearly in my brain though such clarity seems impossible for a moment of such infinitesimal duration, that this Cossack knew who I was, and that I was the very soldier who had beheaded one of his brothers.

Knowing where he intended to slash gave me every advantage. I, too, rose to full height, then used all my momentum to hack down and across, not in a long swing but in a compact movement that used both the speed of the blade and the sharpness of its sliding edge. His saber flashed over my head; mine bit through muscle and bone.

I sailed past him, knowing I had never felt anything like the sensation through the handle of my saber as the blade had chopped into something, and then burst into free air. I pulled the mare up and wheeled, looking for my opponent to do the same.

I could not find him. Then I saw his horse, not pulling up behind me, gathering to charge again as I expected, but running erratically, the poor animal confused and frightened—for on its back was the lower half of a man, anchored to the saddle by the feet still caught in the stirrups. The other half of the Cossack lay lifeless on the open ground between me and the rest of the Royal Cavalry.

The disoriented horse carrying its grisly burden began to lope in slow circles, and as it passed before the Cossack host, the marauders sank to the ground upon their knees and crossed themselves. I spurred my own horse to Gorlov, who said to me in a hushed voice, "I've heard of it being done. I never believed it was possible."

We looked back to the Cossack lines. The loose horse, seeking comfort, had returned to Wolfhead's side. Pugachev, his face flushing redder, lifted his sword for the first time all day and yelled orders. Not one of his men moved in response. Wolfhead's sword flashed out and knocked the blade from Pugachev's hand, and suddenly the mob was all over their former leader, dragging him from his saddle.

We sat still upon our mounts, transfixed by the spectacle of the mob putting down their weapons with pious reverence, as if more than military might but the Almighty Himself had worked against them. Now I felt the pain in my side, and felt the blood again, hot and thick. Gorlov, seeing the scarlet on my fingers, said with alarm, "Is that his blood, or yours?"

Before I could answer, MacFee spoke sharply, "They're coming!"

We readied ourselves for a charge, but the Cossacks moving toward us had dismounted and lowered their weapons. They were dragging Pugachev. They stopped before us and dropped him, dazed and battered, at the hooves of my horse. One of them chattered something.

"What are they saying?" MacFee asked Gorlov.

"He says they are loyal servants of the throne of holy Mother Russia."

The peasants began dispersing, drifting away in groups, heading back to the estates from which they had come.

I felt a strange lightness, as if my body had no weight. Images swam before my eyes, but I have a clear recollection of Wolfhead riding into the smoke with his men, back toward the forest from which they had come. Then I felt Gorlov put his hand to my back, feeling the hole where the pistol ball had exited. "You've been shot!" he snapped, as if angry, and then earth changed places with the sky, and all the world went dark.

Chapter Thirty

I REMEMBER that we were on the road back to St. Petersburg.

I remember that I lay in a cart.

I remember that Pugachev, wrapped in chains, rode in another cart behind the one that carried me, and that the whole procession was surrounded by the Royal Cavalry.

I remember agonizing pain in my side, and then a fever so deep it spread that pain throughout my body, like hot liquid through a limp sponge.

I remember that the journey lasted forever. And yet, for an ordeal so long, I recall little more of it than this.

But one moment of it has stayed in my mind. I can still see the trees passing overhead as I lay on my back looking at the sky; then Gorlov's face above me as he leaned over from his horse to look down upon me. He must have done this many times, for even now I see the worry on that big, brash face, swimming repeatedly out of the fog of my fever; but the details of this one moment I recall with clarity. He spun away from the cart and snapped an order. "Faster! We must go faster!"

"We are pushing the horses as hard as we can!" came a voice—MacFee's, I believe. "And you said yourself we will kill him if we bounce him harder."

"Ride ahead! Fetch a surgeon from St. Petersburg to Count Berenchkov's estate!" Gorlov barked.

Then another voice, unmistakably MacFee's, said, "He'll never make it, even that far."

"Ride!" Gorlov exploded. The hooves of two horses pounded away. Then Gorlov spurred his own horse to the front of my cart, and I lifted my head and saw him grab the traces of the cart horses and try to pull them faster.

I dropped my head back upon the hay and understood then, even through my agony, that Gorlov knew I was dying.

I lost consciousness after that.

I REGAINED consciousness at the estate Berenchko; at least I was aware of our arrival there, and the hope that the pain that had seemed to increase with every bump of the cart would somehow lessen if I could be placed upon a bed. I knew it was day because the light oppressed my eyelids and vibrated in my head. I heard Gorlov speaking quickly with the good little Count Berenchko, and the voices of MacFee, and that of another man who told Gorlov, with a Scottish accent, "I am Stewart, Catherine's personal surgeon. The Tsarina sent me when she heard the news."

I opened my eyes when I heard that—they were carrying me into the house at that moment—and I saw Gorlov's face. Even through my pain and fever, I could see that my friend believed that it might already be too late for hope.

And then I glimpsed another face behind him. It was Beatrice, her cheeks flushed from the exertion of a long ride, for she wore a cloak for horseback, though she had thrown back her head covering and was stretching her neck for a look at me. Was she a hallucination from my pain? I could not be sure.

I fought to stay conscious, even through the agony I felt as they bore me into a bedroom and lay me out upon the bed. Gorlov was muttering, patting my head like a mother might to her son. "You'll be fine," he said, trying to sound cheerful. "The Tsarina's personal doctor is here! Think of that, how important you are! All this attention, for a tiny wound." And Beatrice, if it were really she, and not a dream, slipped in behind them and stood watching from the far corner of the room.

I looked at the doctor, praying for relief, but the doctor, the moment he pulled back the dressing at my abdomen, saw no hope. He and Gorlov withdrew toward the door. The doctor spoke quietly, but the whole house had fallen silent, and I could hear him when he told Gorlov, "Keep him comfortable, give him water if he wants it."

"And he'll be all right?" Gorlov asked.

"He'll die tomorrow."

"No. He will not."

"He will not, only if he dies tonight."

Gorlov grabbed the doctor's throat, nearly crushing it as he lifted the man off the floor. The doctor tried to claw Gorlov's fingers from his windpipe and choked out, "There is no cure for gas gangrene!"

And then Gorlov's fingers just fell away.

The doctor coughed twice, rubbed at his neck, and tried to recover his dignity. "I must send a report to the Tsarina," he said, and left the room.

Gorlov moved to my bedside. "Get some rest," he whispered to me.

"Gorlov . . ."

"Sleep now!"

"I . . . smell the stench," I told him. "I know . . . what it means."

Gorlov could not argue; he moved away from the bed, and then I heard him with Count Berenchko, in the hallway.

My dream Beatrice drifted to the bedside and lifted my fingers in her hand. She squeezed; she was real. "How . . . ?" I began, through my pain.

"Shhh—"

But her presence turned my spirits away from my suffering. "No, tell me. How did you come to be here?"

"I was with Natasha at the palace. She and the other ladies were playing a masquerade game with the Tsarina when a rider was brought in. He was filthy and exhausted, and still they brought him in directly to the Tsarina."

"MacFee," I said, and the thought of Beatrice, tucked anonymously among the women of the Court as they played their games, struck me by its discrepancy, its injustice. It fired my blood, and stirred it.

"Yes," she said, "that was his name. The one with the odd accent. He announced victory, the Cossacks' revolt broken, the new chieftains pledging loyalty. This excited the Court. Then Mac . . . Mac . . ."

"MacFee."

"MacFee said you had cut a Cossack in two. But you had been wounded yourself, and required a surgeon." She paused and I saw how this news had affected her. "The Tsarina asked where you were, and when he told her she saw at once that he was too exhausted to make the trip back. She wondered aloud if anyone else knew the way to this estate. And Natasha said, 'My handmaid does.' "

She had ridden through the bitter cold at breakneck speed, to lead the surgeon to my bedside. I looked up at her eyes, rimmed now with tears, and squeezed her fingers.

OPENING my eyes again, I saw Gorlov standing over me, and next to him an ancient woman, gaping a smile at me. The teeth on the right side of her mouth were green; those on the left were gone. The crone looked familiar. I may have seen her in Berenchkov's barn; she could as well have been reminiscent of some nightmare. She held a sack, decorated like a Russian Easter egg with multicolored stacks of painted zigzags. She laid the sack at my side and crossed herself. Beatrice had withdrawn two steps from my bedside, lingering close enough to watch over me.

"See here! I must protest this!" the doctor blurted through his handkerchief as he burst in. Count Berenchkov followed, walking softly on the balls of his slippers. Receiving no response from Gorlov, the doctor turned on the count. "How can you say you dispel superstition and ignorance among your serfs when you tolerate such stupidity in its nastiest—"

Whatever Gorlov did—probably glared—halted the doctor. The royal physician turned upon his heel and left with Berenchkov, but not without saying loudly to him, "I have done all I can do! I cannot be responsible, if you wish to kill him! I shall be in the library, having *whiskey*!" He named the drink as if to down it was particular revenge.

The room quiet again, Gorlov nodded to the old woman, who had smiled throughout the doctor's tirade, understanding none of it anyway. She loosened the neck of the sack, reached in, and slid out a stiff raven, several days dead. Its eyes were closed and crusted, its breast bloated. She laid the bird upon its back beside me on the bed. Gorlov looked on with one brow up and one down; he pursed his lips and nodded in satisfaction. I expected some kind of incantation.

The crone did cross herself and pray, but with her lips only. She withdrew from the sack a rusty old blade, like a discarded kitchen knife. Here Gorlov interrupted, offering her his own bright dirk. This she took with a pleased smile.

Crooking her wrist down, she plunged the point into the raven's breast, and it split like a melon. She wiped the blade on the sheets and handed it back to Gorlov, who wiped it again before restoring it to his belt. Then the old woman dug her fingertips into the bird's open breast and withdrew a handful of white curd. The curd was moving, alive. Maggots. Beatrice stifled a scream and flinched.

The crone pressed the whole mass of maggots into my open wound.

She scooped another quivering mass from the bird and pushed it into my side again before I closed my eyes and tried to die.

I sank. I cannot say I slumbered. The pain and loss of blood stole my consciousness without admitting sleep. I moaned. I sweated and screamed. My thoughts danced with the blackest images of death and worse than death.

I AWOKE without opening my eyes in the room where Gorlov had writhed in the grasp of Nikonovskaya's poison. I stretched my right arm down, and my fingertips touched my side. I heard Gorlov's laugh. "Surprised?" he said.

I opened my eyes and saw him by the window, eating soup. He stirred his spoon around the wooden bowl and licked the beads of liquid on his mustache. Beatrice sat in a chair beside the bed. She had been dozing; she got to her feet as my hand moved again, and I prodded delicately at my wound. It hurt, but with the raw tenderness of healing. "The maggots . . ." I said weakly.

"Completely scientific!" Gorlov boomed. "The doctor will probably take credit for it, and will receive a royal medal. They eat the dead flesh and clean out the wound. The treatment is good for Russian horses."

"I will kill you both," I said, "if flies come out of me."

A grin burst upon Gorlov's face. He ran out of the room, and in a moment I heard him shouting to the world, "He lives! He lives!"

I turned my smile at Beatrice, but before I could find words to speak to her, she had slipped from the room and was gone.

Chapter Thirty-one

M A G Y A shrieked and ran from the inn to the carriage, wiping her hands upon the white apron as her skirt flapped behind her. Gorlov had already dismounted, and he now tried to keep her from dropping to her knees in the new snow upon the street. But she was too fast for him and crossed herself three times before he could pull her up. She looked at his face, exclaimed as if she had just that moment recognized him, and looked to heaven. She saw Pyotr, gasped in surprise, and dropped to her knees again upon the snow. As I banged open the carriage door, she raised her hands once more, but cut herself off in midpraise when she saw my bound side. Gorlov could not restrain her; she raced to me and tucked herself up under my arm, to crutch me to the inn.

"Magya, you—Svet! You shouldn't be—" Gorlov began, and gave up.

Intent as I was on moving around, I did not want Magya taxing herself; but she was strong, and she did bear me up through the tenderness I felt with every step. Once inside the door of the White Goose she spoke so rapidly in Russian that I could understand not a single word, gathering from her gestures that she meant me to rest in the inn's parlor until she could be certain my room was perfectly prepared; she sat me down on a sofa and shoved my shoulders until I yielded and lay down. Then she trotted upstairs. Tikhon lurked at the doorway and smiled at me, but he, like the rest of the White Goose's staff, hung back. I gathered they had been ordered to do so. Somehow Gorlov, through messages sent ahead of us, had managed to commandeer whatever facilities of the Goose he deemed necessary for my complete convalescence, and I could only imagine what influences he had brought to bear to enforce that situation. Still, I did not believe the Goose was quite prepared for Magya; I heard her yelling now, in the kitchen.

Gorlov strolled into the parlor, gazing about the place to reacquaint himself; he smiled when he saw me, but then looked down the hallway and frowned, saying, "Magya, you should not be racing about! Stop, I beg you!"

Short of breath, gasping, she mumbled some response, and I heard her scurry away again. "Magya!" Gorlov called after her, but she rattled through the kitchen door. Gorlov, seeing me getting to my feet again, exploded. "What, everyone wants to commit suicide here? Sit down, you cretin! Magya insists on an invalid to nurse, and she will become one herself for the pleasure of it!"

"See here, Gorlov, look! I am fine on my feet!"

"What are you doing?"

"Climbing the stairs! I don't intend to—oooff!" Gorlov snatched me by the collar, threw an arm behind my knees, and swept me up, carrying me like a child. He stomped up the stairs and deposited me in my room.

"You ass, you've made me bleed on the coverlet!" I yelled at him.

"Another chore for Magya!" he fumed. "She will be so pleased."

Gorlov was right. The seepage of my wound upon the coverlet seemed to bring Magya deep satisfaction, and she wrestled off my shirt and changed the bandages as if I were a baby. In another hour she had Pyotr lug a table into the room, and laid out upon it food for a dozen. Gorlov had bathed by this time—I was forbidden that pleasure, as Magya insisted a bath was bad enough for Gorlov, but would certainly finish me altogether—and he completed the table setting by carting in the samovar. "I should have left you in the parlor," he rumbled. "She wants now to bring the whole kitchen upstairs. Pyotr! Come on, we'll eat here! We should invite the regiment over—there is food enough!"

I felt ridiculous, propped in the bed eating while Gorlov and Pyotr balanced their plates upon their knees, the table too full of serving dishes for them to find a place at it. Magya herself would not eat, but she did grow still. She began to stare at me. *"Reeba,"* she said.

I looked at her. She had said the Russian word for "fish."

"Reeba," she repeated, and reached an arthritic finger to the dish before me and tapped the salmon upon the fin.

"Reeba," I said.

"It is not a vocabulary lesson," Gorlov barked. "She means for you to eat some."

"I have already eaten some!"

"She means for you to eat some more."

I smiled at Magya and said, *"Nyet. Spaceeba. Ya . . ."* I could not think of the word for "full," and patted my belly to show her the best I could.

"Reeba!" she insisted.

I took some more of the fish.

"Kleb," Magya said.

"Gorlov, please tell her I don't want any more bread. And

that I see everything in front of me, and appreciate it, and assume I can take as much as I wish."

Gorlov translated, more or less, my declaration. Magya winced, her brows bunched in the center of her forehead, and her eyes watered.

"All right!" I said to Gorlov. "I'm sorry. But I want her to understand I am capable of knowing when I am hungry." I took another slice of the loaf, as Gorlov conveyed my sentiments to Magya.

"*Myasa,*" she said, and pointed to the roast.

S VET, the Marquis DuBois is here."
Pyotr had just pulled the table away from the bed, storing it for Magya's next onslaught, and I was wondering whether I might survive gangrene only to die of gluttony.

Gorlov went out and returned with the marquis. "Monsieur!" DuBois said, whisking in and clicking his heels, tapping the ball of his cane to the brim of his hat before setting both on a chair and swirling off his cloak to drape over them. "You have once more prevailed over danger and death."

"We did what we could," I said, glancing at Gorlov.

"I understand you captured Pugachev! Once more we owe you thanks," DuBois said. But instead of expressing gratitude, he paused. Gorlov, for all his lack of subtlety, reacted to the Frenchman's hesitation by saying, "I had better check on Magya." He strode out, leaving the door open.

DuBois went to the door, closed it softly, and returned to my bedside. "My sources within the palace inform me that the British have increased the number of troops they are requesting to thirty thousand."

"Thirty thousand troops . . ." I muttered. "Are you sure?"

"Sir!" He acted hurt. I knew his source was Charlotte, and I knew his information must be correct.

"Thirty thousand! Then . . . there is war already in the American colonies."

"Not yet. But it shows how serious the trouble is in America, and how much the British are willing to pay to stop it."

I felt nauseous. Thirty thousand Russian troops, hardened by years of savage warfare against the Turks, let loose upon the populace of America? They would be as brutal as Pugachev's Cossacks had been.

DuBois stood at the window, holding one hand to his elbow and the other to his lips. To him it was all a diplomatic problem. He kissed his knuckle a moment and then said, "You see, Catherine and the British have continually competed with each other while putting on a show of the greatest cooperation. France, England, Prussia, Austria—all have hoped to play Russia against the other three. But Catherine has just forced the Turks to sign a treaty that makes Russia king of policy in Europe! A year ago she had two wars—with the Turks and the Cossacks. Now she has none, and her armies are sitting idle. She would love to have a piece of the North American continent, and the British are tempting her; their request for her troops is a suggestion that they might cede her territory there, perhaps a block of the western coast, in the California region claimed by Spain."

"Can France help us?"

"I don't see how. If Catherine's troops go to America, France is out, out of the entire conflict. The British know that, and that is another reason they want troops from Catherine. France will fight England, but we will not kill Russian soldiers because it is not in our interests to fight Russia."

"America will be left all alone."

The marquis nodded, considering the problem as coolly as he might ponder a wine with his palate.

"Marquis, I am no diplomat, but I can see the ruin this will be for my country. Who else can help us influence Catherine? Someone in Russia? Potemkin?"

"The English own Potemkin."

"Potemkin is one of the richest men in the world already, just from what Catherine has given him! How could the British buy him?"

"They allow Potemkin to ship goods upon their vessels. Anytime a British oceangoer docks in St. Petersburg, it may take on special cargos—sail duck, mast timbers, anything. The profits from the sale of these go to Potemkin. When entire fortunes are made based upon the profits from one voyage, you can imagine the money Potemkin must reap from these sidelines."

"How much more money could he want?"

"I see you have not known many rich men."

"Is there anything he could be offered diplomatically?" I was grasping for any hope. "Perhaps Franklin could devise something—"

"The British have already agreed to support Potemkin's governorship over the territories Catherine has taken from the Turks by her conquests. This will essentially make Potemkin King of Poland. Can your Mr. Franklin offer him something greater than that?"

I had no answer. I was in despair.

When I looked to DuBois again, he was smiling at me. "I just wanted you to understand the problem," he said.

"Why?" I said bitterly. "There is nothing I can do."

"On the contrary. There may be a great deal you can do. When the Tsarina learned of your wound, she gave orders to Potemkin that he make sure you recover completely—without incident. Thus, she knows the danger to you. Now she is going to Moscow; she has scheduled three weeks there to reorganize the governing of the provinces where the revolt took place. She will return for the execution of Pugachev in St. Petersburg. I have been told that upon her return, she desires a private audience with you."

DuBois looked at me, in my sober wonderment that Franklin's plan had worked. "The interval," DuBois went on, "will give you time to recover, and prepare."

And with no further explanation, he left me.

Chapter Thirty-two

A F T E R parading him through the towns of Russia, all the way up from the Ukraine, they beheaded Pugachev in a city square of St. Petersburg, as a single bell tolled a dirge of death. Catherine herself, resplendent in her imperial crown and jewels, sat enthroned upon the tall wooden platform, surrounded by her retinue. Gorlov and I, in our new uniforms and medals, stood on the platform close beside her, along with other officers from the campaign.

Pugachev was led in chains up onto the platform, then cast down onto his knees in front of the Tsarina. She stared down at the Cossack. His eyes cut toward her, pleading, but her stare was without mercy. She looked toward the executioner, a man as tall and broad shouldered as Gorlov, with a hood upon his head and an ax upon his shoulder. The executioner shunned the use of assistants; with his left hand he gripped Pugachev by the hair and slung him onto his face, then dropped the ax with his right, severing the head at one blow.

The crowd was cheering. The executioner lifted the head by the ears and raised it high for all to see.

Marquis DuBois slapped me happily on the back and nodded his approval. I felt no sense of victory. I stood for a moment watching the Tsarina, surrounded by her retinue, stepping primly down the stairs of the execution platform to her waiting carriage. I again felt a hand on my shoulder, and turned, expecting to see Marquis DuBois still there, but he had moved away and Potemkin was in his place. "Congratulations," he said. He went on quickly, with the directness of one who has already planned exactly what he is about to say. "There will be a ball of celebration at the palace, the day after Christmas. You are invited, as guest of honor. Come prepared."

"Prepared for what?" I asked him.

Potemkin only gazed at me for a moment, then moved away. I turned and watched the Tsarina's carriage leaving, its gilded sides reflecting golden light upon the streets covered in new snow. Everyone else was watching her, too, everyone except Lord Shettlefield, and Montrose beside him; their faces caught my attention from within the crowd, because they were turned toward me. They had seen Potemkin speak with me, I was sure. Shettlefield appeared concerned, but Montrose had a different look. I did not know what it meant at the time, but later I realized that his focused expression was that of a man who has just made a lethal decision.

I looked back toward Gorlov; he and Potemkin were moving away, to the carriage Potemkin had brought, a conveyance of polished wood encrusted with jewels, perhaps not as eye-catching as that of the Tsarina, but just as costly. Gorlov stepped into the carriage behind him, and the two of them drove away together.

※

BEATRICE sat beside a window of the Mitski mansion parlor, sewing a gown of Natasha's. She glanced up when she heard the tap against the glass; seeing me standing there, outside upon the rear veranda, she froze, then quickly dropped her sewing and reached for her bonnet. She moved to the door to admit me, covering her head as she came. As I stepped inside she said, "They are all away."

"I know," I said. "I came to see you." She stood as still as a tomb. "I never thanked you."

"Thank me?" she said, moving back to her chair and picking up the lace she had been stitching around the bodice of Natasha's dress. "For what?"

I followed her and stood before her, waiting for her to look up, but she kept her eyes upon the needle and the cloth. "You rode for hours," I said, "through countryside you knew to be dangerous, to save my life. And you did save it."

She shook her head in dismissal. "All I did was guide the doctor to you, and the doctor was useless."

"I'm not talking about the doctor. I'm not even talking about what I knew after I was wounded, but what I knew before."

"And what is that?"

I knelt, to the level of her eyes, though still she did not look at me. "That your presence has the power to make me want to live."

"Please," she said, "stop this. I am a servant, I—"

"You are not a servant to me." Now, for the first time, she truly looked at me. "Soon," I told her, "I am going home, back to America. When I do, I want you to come with me. There what matters is not what your parents did before your birth, but what you do after."

"There is no place on earth like that."

"There can be. There is. All we have to do is believe it."

She was staring into my eyes. "I wish I could believe that," she said. "I wish I could. But there is no place in the world like that. There never has been, there never will be."

"We can make it so."

She pulled her eyes from mine and fixed them on the lace she was sewing. I put my hand upon hers and stopped her fingers.

"Beatrice," I said. "Beatrice," I repeated, and finally she looked up again. I saw something in her eyes that I had never seen before, and I have no words to describe it. There was an uncertainty in them, and yet a recognition; it was as if her eyes and mine were doing the same thing, both searching and finding all at the same instant.

We kissed. My face pressed down to hers, and hers lifted up to mine, my hand touched her cheek and neck, our lips melted together.

How long the kiss lasted I cannot say. I felt the blood rushing within my own body, and hers; then, as our lips parted, I became aware of the whispering of servants in the next room. I realized they were eavesdropping, and I did not care.

"Beatrice," I whispered, "how long does it take to make a gown?"

TIKHON was waiting for me at the door of the White Goose, holding the message that Gorlov had sent for him to give me. I read what Gorlov had written, then frowned at Tikhon; the boy shook his head, understanding nothing further than that he was to give me the note immediately upon my arrival. I strode at once out of the Goose and back down the side alley to the public stables, where the grooms had not yet unsaddled my horse, then I remounted and did as Gorlov had instructed me, riding out to the fifth house upon the river road, the same shabby mansion that Gorlov had stopped to stare at the night of the Tsarina's torchlight parade.

What I found amazed me; I thought at first that I was at the wrong place, but indeed I found myself on the very lane winding through leafless hardwood trees to the same huge old house Gorlov had shown me the previous winter. And yet the house looked new. Its sideboards wore coats of fresh paint whiter than the fresh snow, the chimneys on either side of the three-storied structure showed clean brick and emitted twin plumes of smoke from fires that must have been burning brightly, for the roof had melted the snowfall so that its new cedar shingles peeked through. I rode toward the place, completely intrigued.

Tucked among the trees to the right of the house were covered stables made of lumber so freshly sawn that it was still fragrant of pine. As I rode my horse into its shelter, I spotted Gorlov's gelding in one of the stalls, with an immaculate saddle hung beside it, smelling richly of oiled leather. Pyotr's sleigh stood covered in an adjacent shelter. Two enthusiastic young grooms accepted the reins of my horse and promised to feed her.

I crossed the snowy yard and climbed the steps. Through the ornate glass of the carved door I saw Gorlov, his back to me, standing in the foyer beneath a dazzling chandelier. He lifted his head as I knocked but did not turn toward me until he had wiped at his eyes, then he moved to the door and let me in. "This is incredible," I said, gazing about in wonder at the restored magnificence of a structure that, last I had seen it, had appeared ready for demolition. "What has happened here?"

"Nothing. And everything," he said. "This was my family home. I played toy soldiers on that floor. . . . My father read to me in that chair. . . ." His eyes still glistened. But then Gorlov's face, always liquid like the lava of his volcanic emotions, flowed from soft reverie to hot brooding. "Potemkin brought me here," he said. "Drove me out in his own carriage.

Stopped at the road, to let me gaze at what his workers had accomplished in the time since our victory. My lands have been restored to me as well. My reward. For loyalty."

Whatever his thoughts were at that moment, they sank from my view, into the dark core of his Russian soul. I was uncomfortable in the silence. But there was something I needed to tell him. "Gorlov, my friend . . . It does my heart good to see you so satisfied. It will help ease my spirit, when I leave."

"Leave?" His attention rose from the depths and focused on me, his brows knitted into a frown, as if the concept of my ever returning to America was unthinkable. He spoke to me as if I were an idiot. "As they have rewarded me, they will reward you."

"My reward is to finish what I came here to do, and then go home," I said softly. He still stared at me. "I am sorry to leave you," I added, "but I am glad to see you so complete."

I hugged him then, and felt my own sadness welling up. He seemed ready to speak, but I left him quickly, not wanting to think too much about how rare a friend I knew him to be, and how hard it would be to bid him farewell the next time, perhaps forever. I made my way quickly back to his new stables, and rode away, trying not to rush so much as to show my sorrow.

W H E N I arrived again at the public stables behind the White Goose, I found no grooms waiting to take my mare. There were other horses in the stalls, and hay forks leaned against the walls as if they had just been set down; I supposed the stable keepers had just stepped away for hot tea or a crust of bread. Certain they must return soon, I tied my own horse, removed her saddle, covered her with a blanket, and stepped out into the alley that lay in the shadow of the inn. Sounds of loud talk and laughter rose from the inn's tavern room around the corner, evidence of life nearby, but still there was none near at hand. I called out in French, in German, and even in a few words of Russian that I had learned, but no one answered or showed himself, in any direction. This seemed odd, but I dismissed the unsettling feeling it gave me as but an echo of my memories of Marsh having been murdered on this very lane. I paused a further moment, then made my way through the powdery snow, toward the front of the inn.

Halfway up I thought I heard the soft crunch of a footstep upon the snow; I looked behind me but saw nothing. There were several doors behind me, opening into storerooms, but all were silent. I turned again and was almost to the corner when I heard a sound of whistling and an impact of meat and bone. I spun around, ducking, sidestepping, and reaching for my sword.

But drawing it was unnecessary. Montrose stood a few paces behind me, a knife in his hand. His eyes were wide with surprise, his jaw fixed as if he needed to draw a breath but could not take one in. His eyes rolled down to look at the point of a saber that protruded a good eight inches from the front of his waistcoat, and he fell forward onto his face, dead.

Gorlov was behind him, still sitting in his saddle on horseback, from which he had hurled his blade to save my life. Gorlov slid quickly to the snow, moved to me, and retrieved his saber from Montrose's back. He wiped the blade on the dead man's coat and returned the saber to its scabbard. "Who was he?" Gorlov asked, as he looked about to be sure no one else had seen.

"I—I don't know," I lied. I was shocked, and trying to buy myself time to think.

Gorlov glared down at Montrose's body. "Looks English.

Well dressed, not a robber." He looked at me. "Why would anyone want to kill you?"

"I don't know."

Gorlov nodded as if he would accept that answer. He glanced about again, then suddenly seized me by the throat with one hand, his fingers tightening like iron around my windpipe as he slammed my back against the wooded wall. His strength was enormous; I tried with both my hands to pull the fingers of his one hand away, but I could not budge them. He spoke quietly. "I came here, followed you, because you're not telling me something. And when you risk your life, you risk mine."

He eased his grip enough for me to breathe. He lowered his hand from my throat but did not step back; his eyes were spots of black fire above his grizzled face. I had often pondered how I might reveal to Gorlov my true mission in Russia; I had never expected to do it with my best friend ready to break my neck and the blood of an assassin blossoming into the snow beneath my boots. "You know . . ." I began, stopping to massage my windpipe, "I believe in democracy."

He snorted in laughter.

"Ridiculous to you," I shot back, "but not to me. Or to those who sent me, sent me to reach the Tsarina. To speak to her for my country. To convince her not to help our enemies. This man you just killed is the agent of those enemies—of the British government, who would treat me and my countrymen as less than men, less than free."

Gorlov's stare narrowed, his brow knotted tighter, his chest heaved in angry puffs. "So!" he spat, "you come to Russia, convince me to join you, act as a spy, in my country, without ever telling me?"

"Well . . ." I said simply, "yes."

Gorlov blinked for a few moments, then shrugged. "Just checking," he said. He started back toward his horse, then stopped and turned to me again. "I told you that a powerful man seduced my wife, but I was the one disgraced."

"Yes?"

"That man was Potemkin."

"My God."

"Don't forget this is Russia. And don't forget what I did to the merchant."

He mounted his horse and rode back to the manor house that Potemkin had just returned to his ownership.

Chapter Thirty-three

I WAS in the upstairs sitting room of Gorlov's house, poring over a stack of books I had found in his library, volumes full of French, Greek, and ancient Roman writings on the philosophy of government, when I heard the bell below, and Charlotte's bright voice as Magya admitted her. I heard Magya say that Gorlov was not at home but that I was, and there was a moment in which I thought to flee anyway, climbing out a window or even crawling beneath a bed to hide. But I stayed seated as she dismissed Magya and showed herself up to the second floor. "Bonjour, Svet!" she sang, pecking me on the cheek as I dragged myself to my feet; she had adopted Gorlov's nickname for me. "Where is Gorsha?" Apparently she had also coined a name for him.

I settled back down upon the couch and pushed aside the books, knowing my preparation for the audience with the Tsarina would make no progress as long as Charlotte was present. She dodged about the room as she always did every other, drawing back the curtains to peer at the street, then readjusting them to suit her taste, now frowning at the ceiling panels as if Gorlov might be clinging to them, now turning up the wick of the lamp upon the mantel. "He is not here," I said stupidly. "Gone somewhere, I don't know."

"Why do you sit in the gloom, with the fire burned down, and you so far away from it?" She was smiling.

"I . . . just had not bothered . . ."

"Perhaps Gorsha will return for the midday meal! It is almost time; have you eaten?"

"What? Eaten? Me . . . uh, no."

She frowned; Charlotte could furrow her auburn brows above her green eyes and still appear beautiful; she knew this, I think, because her frown was always as quick as her smile. She did not speak at first, but watched me as she came slowly from the hearth and sat down beside me.

"Do you know where I think Gorsha is?" she inquired, glancing sideways at me.

"No. No, I don't. Where?"

"I think he has gone to his wife, to confront her with their divorce."

"His *wife*?" I exclaimed, turning sharply to her.

Charlotte nodded with the calm of having considered the subject of Gorlov's personal life from every aspect, and now being devoid of any uncertainties on the matter. "Yes, of course," she said, in her seamless alto. "Everyone knows that he was given his rewards with the understanding that they are his alone, not to be shared with his wife, and that the arrangements make evident a royal sanction of his divorce. And—"

"Wait. What do you mean 'everyone knows'? I have heard no one discussing these matters!"

"Dear Svet!" She smiled again, and squeezed my hand. "You do not speak with enough *ladies*! Ha! This is too prized a pastry not to be nibbled on by everybody. Everyone in St. Petersburg is gossiping about it." She shook her head and seemed ready to laugh, at herself as readily as at others—but not at Gorlov. She lowered her voice, leaned her head closer to mine, and, in a voice of conspiracy, said, "No one in Russia can tolerate the woman. Oh, they did at first; they admired her for being so bold as to get what she wanted—lovers, gifts, attention—and to do it publicly. Gorsha they looked on as a fool. The older ladies tell me this; I believe it. But now he has returned, and is so dignified, and reserved, and attractive to so many."

I had thought that nothing Charlotte could say would distract me from my turmoil. But now the question popped straight out of me: "You, Charlotte? You, too, are attracted to Gorlov?"

"But of course! I find him extremely attractive! Do I love him, you mean. Oh, certainly I do, but as a man, you mean. Do I love him as a man?" She stated this as a clarification of my question, as one more service she had to perform for me. "No. That is the answer! I *see* him as a man—I *love* him as a friend!" Pleased with the perfect balance of her declaration, she smiled again.

"But . . . people no longer see Gorlov as a fool." I suddenly wanted to talk with Charlotte—about anything except my own thoughts, but I wanted to talk.

"Gorlov a fool! Oh, no! Certainly it is his wife who has been foolish. Certainly he seemed foolish for a time, and no one would have even considered him as a lover—the ladies do not say this, but I can tell it is so, by the way they protest how sorry they felt for him when his wife so flagrantly betrayed him. But I see their hypocrisy, because they remained her friends while she was fashionable, not his. But now . . ." She bit the tip of her tongue and sucked on her lips, as if debating whether to tell me something. Then she blushed slightly, lowered her voice even further, and said, "Do you remember on our trip to Moscow, the first time . . . and the Contessa Bellefleur?"

It was hardly something I could have forgotten.

"She was there as . . . as . . . Well! Do you know what a 'prover' is?"

"I believe I do."

Charlotte raised her eyebrows and nodded.

I said, "You mean she came along on the trip, specifically for the purpose of . . ."

" 'Proving' Gorsha—or you?" she helped me. "No, not on direct assignment, I don't think, though it may have been that way. Anne thought so."

"Thought . . . what?" I was becoming more and more confused.

"When the Contessa Bellefleur joined the party, at the last minute, inviting herself, really, Anne believed that she was sent specifically to test you. Test. Yes. Don't look so perplexed! It is an examination of one's prowess as a lover."

"I understand that," I said, trying to sound steady and unabashed. "Anne told you this, that it was her opinion? But you did not agree?"

"Well, of course, we talked about it! We talked about it with the contessa! She would only smile. But I think her assignment was not specific. The way it works is that Potemkin approves a new lover, a potential lover for the Queen after that man has been proved, to determine if the Queen would be satisfied with him. But even then it is not a sign she will accept him. She—"

"Wait. Wait a moment. Are provers the concoction of the Tsarina, or of Potemkin?"

"Mmm. That is a good question. It is hard to tell the difference between their wishes sometimes."

"Excuse me, go ahead."

"Oh. I was just saying that the Contessa Bellefleur sometimes looks for lovers, that she might recommend someone. If she were to discover a wonderful lover and pass him along to the Queen, then surely she would be rewarded with wonderful favors in return."

"So . . . Contessa Bellefleur came on our journey as a prover. To come to Moscow, or to . . . prove us."

"Well the contessa told me, that second night, when Gorsha had become so ill from drinking and eating too much, that he was such a pleasing man she doubted she could ever give him up. She told that to everyone! So you see, Gorsha's reputation has been saved. He is a success, and a proven lover—thus, only his wife can be blamed for her infidelities."

I sat staring at my hands.

"The contessa discussed all this with everybody . . . even Beatrice?" I phrased this question haphazardly, with no point in mind except to introduce Beatrice's name into the conversation—for it was clear to me from the timing of Charlotte's visit that she had come to lecture me in response to the news she had surely received about my encounter with Beatrice at the Mitski mansion.

"Beatrice," Charlotte said, "is a Pole."

I could have had no clearer declaration of the contempt in which Poles were held than these four words from Charlotte, delivered so comfortably and in such absence of active animosity. To Charlotte, Beatrice's Polish origins explained completely that whatever she might hear or not hear could be of no consequence to anyone. Had I asked about Zepsha, or some servant besides Beatrice, I would surely have received a direct answer. A dwarfess, a Russian peasant—these mattered. A Pole did not.

I might have argued that Beatrice had, in fact, a Swedish father, and as for her mother, who knew?—for the whole of Europe had at one time or another raped Poland. But I could not say that because I knew Beatrice would not have said it. Western Poles could call themselves German, those of the east could use Russian spellings of their names, and the Poles who struggled into the upper ranks of society in Moscow and St. Petersburg could claim whatever circuitous ancestry they wished; but Beatrice said plainly that she was a Pole. The very thought of this caused me to flush in hostility toward Charlotte and stirred in me a warmth for Beatrice that tormented me more.

"Listen, Charlotte—"

"Svet." She placed her yielding hand over both of mine as I gripped them together, and stopped me. "I know," she said softly. "We all know that you have taken a kind of notice of Beatrice. You admire horseback riding, and Beatrice did this like a man on the day you saved us from the Cossacks. But you cannot—"

"On the day I saved you? Is that what you said?" I spoke right over her, as she tried at first to prevent my interrupting and then sat calmly, tolerantly, as I pushed my words at her. "For I tell you this minute, Charlotte, this minute, and before God. None of us would be here now, had it not been for Beatrice. Gorlov and I would be dead, and you and all the other fine ladies. . . ." I could not go on—not from inability to imagine what Cossacks would do to noblewomen, for I had seen that with my own eyes, but from a sudden bitterness I felt at everyone in Russia, even myself.

Charlotte nodded, and smiled. "I know, I know. You have made this point before. You have made a point of making this point—to Prince Mitski and Lord Shettlefield especially, and the whole of St. Petersburg for that matter. We all admire you for it. Dear Svet, I love you for it! It is the kind of gentleman you are! But let us not allow our gallantry to distort our perceptions, eh?" She brushed at the yellow satin of her skirt, as if flicking away foolish perceptions.

Whatever I might have said then I do not know, for the door downstairs suddenly flew open, and we heard the high strained voice of a woman, her words on that hysterical edge between laughter and tears. "Shall not!" echoed through the marble foyer. "Shall not!" bounced to us, as we stood and walked to the top of the stairs.

We peered down and caught glimpses of a lady moving back and forth within the foyer, still shouting, "Shall not!" Noticeable even from the top of the stairs was her physical presence, full of vigor and sensuality, both buxom and small-waisted, with a shock of black hair, lightly streaked in gray. Her hair was thrown back from a face that, were it not reddened by rage, surely would have appeared beautiful. And then we saw Gorlov, behaving as if the woman were a nonpresence, a specter in someone else's mind perhaps but not his own. He handed his hat, cloak, and gloves to the bewildered houseman, then vanished from our sight for a moment, and returned with a pipe he had retrieved from the humidor in the front parlor. As Gorlov had no habit of smoking, I took his absorption in tamping down the leaf and routing out the stem to be a display of unconcern for the woman who, for every four steps he took, took two of her own, and kept stopping at some length away from him to thrust her rigid arms down at her sides, better to propel the words, "Shall not!"

I exchanged a dumbfounded look with Charlotte, and she nodded, wide-eyed, and whispered, "Countess Gorlova." The couple disappeared, she lurching after him toward the dining room, and we heard her screams, always the same words, following through the corridors.

Straining as we were to hear, we caught a noise from outside, and I tiptoed to the window to see one carriage—Gorlov's—rattling off, and a second carriage remaining. So distracted had I been in my conversation with Charlotte about Beatrice that I had not noticed their driving up; but it seemed to me now that Gorlov had ridden through the streets of St. Petersburg, returning stoically home, as his wife tore after him, standing to bellow, "Shall not, shall not!" as she did now.

As the sounds had ebbed, they now flowed back, the couple reappearing at the foot of the staircase. Gorlov, carrying a long-necked bottle of wine with a single crystal goblet in one hand, and his pipe in the other, turned and started up. Charlotte and I, in the sudden embarrassment of our eavesdropping, drew back and searched frantically for concealment. Finding none, we finally sat idiotically upon the same couch from which we had risen, and pretended to be locked in the same conversation, happily ignorant of any shouting.

The absurdity of our position became increasingly painful as Gorlov reached the top of the stairs, his wife bounding up behind him and shrieking, "Shall not!" in deafening tones. But he pretended not to see us, and I think she truly did not; the intervals between her volleys were not, in fact, silences, but fairly bulged with the quieter spasms of hysteria—now breathless sobs, now sinister giggles. Gorlov marched placidly by, the wine bottle swinging slowly at his side and clinking against the glass, all the way to the door of his bedchamber.

Gorlova's shouts became even more convulsive, and began to fray at the ends: "Shall naaahht! Shall naaaaa!" But Gorlov did not stop. She staggered after him; but the closing of the door before her face brought a dead stillness to her, and to the whole house.

This silence lasted but a few seconds, and was broken with such sudden violence that Charlotte flinched and seized my forearm; Gorlova had recovered her tongue, and a bit more vocabulary, which she punctuated with kicks and strikes of her fists against the door. "You swore! Took a vow! 'I shall not leave you!' Shall not! Shall not!"

I thought to take Charlotte away, to steal back down the stairs ourselves and save any of the parties embarrassment—though in truth neither Gorlov nor his wife had bothered with such a feeling, and Charlotte and I had looked on in shameless fascination—when Gorlova backed away from the doorway and once more froze the house, this time not with silence, but with words. "You are a liar," she said, with slow, searing heat. "You are just like your father."

Another interval, like the quiet descent of a cannon charge—and then the explosion. The door burst back, the top hinge twisting, and there stood Gorlov in all his wrath. Gorlova squealed sharply, but stood her ground, as if resolved to defy him. Gorlov himself was spattered along his left sleeve with the wine—I truly believe he had crushed the glass he was holding when he heard those words—but the stains of the wine were not as crimson as his face. The bottle he still held in his right hand, and, dashing it against the doorjamb, he raised the neck and jagged shards above his head like a dagger, and advanced upon her.

"Gorlov!" I screamed. And he stopped, but not because of me, if he had even heard. His wife faced him, her face as red as his, her hands upon her hips and her hips thrust forward so that her head cocked back and she stared down her nose at him.

"I say it again," she hissed. "A liar! Like your father!" And she spat.

Gorlov lowered the bottle. His face turned slowly pale. Wine covered his right hand, and something thicker and redder—blood—trickled from his left. Then he raised both hands—almost lazily, it seemed to me—and locked them about Gorlova's throat.

If, seeing the resolution of Gorlov's face and hearing the breath so crushed off within Gorlova, I could have any doubts that she was a dead woman, they were dispelled as I hammered at his arms and felt the iron of his grasp. I could not, with the force of my whole hand, break loose a single finger, wildly as I tried, screaming all the while, "Gorlov! Gorlov! In the name of God!"

But nothing could break that grip; not God's name, nor God Himself, I thought, for even if I had been willing to draw the dagger from my boot and stab Gorlov through the heart, I knew he would see the life extinguished from his wife's breast before the last drops of blood beat from his own body.

It was Charlotte who saved her. While Gorlova's arms had already gone limp, and the crimson of her face shifted to purple and then a faint blue, Charlotte put both hands to Gorlov's face and whispered, "Gorsha . . . Gorsha! You shall not kill her!" She kissed him upon the cheek, upon the eye, upon the ear, and whispered there, "Shall not . . . shall not . . . shall not . . ."

Gorlov dropped his wife suddenly, looked at me, at Charlotte; his eyes brimmed with tears, and, turning slowly back into his bedchamber, he closed the door behind him.

We slapped the woman's hands, then her face, yet could not bring normal color there. But the blueness instead of a pallor gave us some hope, and when the houseman peered from the stairs to us on the second landing, Charlotte yelled, "Brandy, you idiot! Hurry!"

The first drops we poured upon Gorlova's tongue slid right back out, but the second dose stayed, and with the third she coughed. She sat up, shoved my hand away as I sought to make her sip, and tried to gain her feet. Charlotte and I caught her as she sagged, and she fought her way back upright, glowered at us both, and, throwing our arms off, raced to the stairs. She slipped over three steps at the top, then stumbled again halfway down and tumbled the rest of the way. She leapt up again, threw open the door, and staggered into the twilight. We heard her carriage rumble away.

Chapter Thirty-four

T HE snows invigorated Gorlov, spiritually as much as physically, and he found joy in living in his old home. He spent many hours with Magya and Pyotr, and many nights went out alone, calling upon old friends.

Then Christmas Eve came, and I went across to the stables of Gorlov's house, where Pyotr was mending harnesses, and drew from him one of Gorlov's mounts. Pyotr protested that there would be *bolshoi snyeg*—a great snow—but I rode out nevertheless.

I made my way first toward the row of shops on the street where stood the Goose. The snowflakes, thick as cannon wad, filled the air, so that at times I could see scarcely twenty feet before me. With the city hidden thus from me, and I from it, and with no companion but a horse, I drifted into a reverie of isolation, of the singleness I felt when a boy, alone with a horse at the dawn or twilight riding across a gray winter field. Between that boy then, in Virginia, and myself now, in Russia, I felt no seam; encased within the blankness of the falling snow, I knew a continuum beyond time and place. It was Christmas, but that was not a day or a season—it was an expectation, a promise of joy and peace, an obligation to pierce the veil of singleness separating me from all the universe, a duty more compelling because of the pregnancy of the night itself, the real Christian anticipation that God Almighty, God Himself, would in the silent moments of that night leap the gap between the divine and the human and commune with us all. An expectation—and a challenge: to find the peace I could not find, to find the joy that was not mine, to forgive and be forgiven, when, in fact, my only sin and my only virtue, then and now, was my aloneness.

I rode to buy gifts for my friends. In Virginia, I rode *as* my gift to my father, exercising all the horses on the day before Christmas so that he could spend one morning of the year before his fireplace, and I there with him. I missed my father now, not from warm memory but rather from that Christmas obligation to unite, to let him know that, whatever pain it was in him that made him sit by the fire, and stare into it uncomfortably, and wish—privately, but clearly—that it was not Christmas and he could be out again among his horses, he was still my father and I his son and I loved him the best I could, which was how he loved me. And . . . God in heaven! My father . . . and I. He, not two years married, and a widower! I, not two years married, and a widower. In all the time since the death of my wife, it had never occurred to me that we were alike in that. My own grief had hidden the parallel from me, or else I was blinded by the single difference—that my child had died, with her mother, and his child, me, had lived. And had I had to rear my own child, without the wife I had loved, then I, too, might have sat before the fireplace at Christmas and looked upon the flames, rather than into the eyes of my child.

Forgiveness! The pain and grief of it knotted around my

lungs, and I was grateful to the snow that hid my face. In two years I had not written to my father. I had grown to be a man without ever becoming a man; I was twenty-four years old, had faced death and inflicted it, had fled from my grief and put behind me the coldness of my own father, only to discover it again in my path, that coldness my own, here on the other side of the world.

I rode on, to buy presents, something for Gorlov, for Pyotr, and for his wife, Magya. I anticipated being alone that night, but I would have something to give tomorrow, and something to keep for myself that Christmas.

When I reached the shops and tied my horse before the tobacconist's, there were two inches of snow settled upon my shoulders. I brushed the drifts away and wished for someone with me, to laugh.

I entered the shop. It was crowded and noisy; several gentlemen and even a couple of ladies were keeping the owner and his female assistant busy with rapid questions and the immediately contradicted decisions of last-hour purchases. As I waited my turn, I noticed the assistant's face and found her oddly familiar. I had never been into the shop, so why should I have a vague recollection of this woman's face? And then I realized where I had seen her; she had on several occasions visited the tavern room of the White Goose, to sell herself as a prostitute to my fellow mercenaries. I was surprised to see her, in a setting of honest work and respectability, and I wondered if her visits to the Goose had been out of desperation.

I found myself wondering about her as I wondered about myself. Who are we really? Are we who we are at our worst, or at our best?

Without the rouge, and in the apron of the tobacco clerk, she looked so different, but it was she. She was not what I would have called pretty, either with the facial paint or without, but I did see a softness in her, as well as the lines of someone who had known hunger. "And now, sir, what is your choice?" she said to me before glancing up and stopping. She apparently had recognized men before who knew her, for though she paled she kept her composure.

For Gorlov and Pyotr, I chose two pouches of Virginia leaf, the finest they had, tobacco that had been brought by British ships, but was grown in my country, nonetheless. She wrapped them in brown paper for me, accepted my money, and made change sharply. "Have you worked here long?" I asked casually. "You seem familiar with the leaf grades."

"I have been here a month. Tobacco sells best in winter. I enjoy the aromas of the leaf. My nose makes me expert," she said. I smiled. "Happy Christmas," she called to me as I was leaving. "God bless you."

"And you." Back out on the street again, I felt the snow a celebration. The presence of this girl, at work respectably in a crowded shop, lifted for a moment every possible cynicism of humanity for me. In the flush of that spirit I plunged into the cutlery shop next door, where I purchased two clasp knives of Swedish steel—again one for Pyotr and one for Gorlov. (I have never had the best imagination for gifts.) I also found there a display of mustache dye and waxes, and bought a supply for Gorlov, as I thought this humorous, and also wanted to give him something extra. At a confectioner's I found a jar of French brandied cherries for Magya. Then I crossed over to a vintner and bought Laarsen a bottle of wine, and the finest whiskey they had for MacFee.

My easier shopping completed, I stepped out onto the street again and watched the snow falling, lit in the twilight by the bright shop windows. My horse shivered, and snow collected on the saddle; but I wanted to walk a little longer upon the street. Not far down I passed a jewelry shop, and I paused to peer through the mist of its window. Draped around the black velvet form of a feminine neck hung an ivory oval, carved in a virginal cameo and surrounded in gold. I entered.

The lady of the shop, a rotund, dark woman, sat in her corner reading, following me with her ears. I pretended to browse for a few moments, and said finally, "That locket in the window . . . may I see it please?"

The woman slid from her stool and waddled to the window, where she drew out the pendant, sighing from the effort. But she wound the chain delicately around her fingers and suspended the pendant in the light for me. "Here is another," she said, "with a different but equally beautiful face. The sisters, I call them." She dangled a second pendant beside the first.

"How much for both?" I asked.

"One hundred rubles."

"Thirty."

She stared at the corner, at the ceiling, at the floor; she pursed her lips and said, "Forty rubles."

In possession of two pendants, I crossed the street again, my arms full of purchases, and reentered the tobacconist's. The girl came to me again, as I rested my bundles upon the counter. "Did you forget someone, sir?" she asked.

"I come to ask a favor. I am trying to buy a gift for a friend, and don't trust my own judgment. She is a lady. Could you help me, only for a moment?"

She glanced at the owner, then back to me. "A lady? I . . . cannot be of much—"

"Your opinion would be valuable to me. I have just found these, across the street." I withdrew the two pendants, and held them out. "I must choose which to give to a young lady, whose affection is precious to me. Could you not tell me which is the more appealing?"

"A lady," she muttered again. "I . . . could not . . ." But she did look at the ivories, slowly and gently, and then shook her head. "I would help you, but I cannot say. They are both of equal beauty."

"Yes," I said, taking from her hand the one that first had caught my eye. "That is what I thought. So this one, I will give to the lady of whom I spoke. That one, I give to you."

I took up my packages and walked out, too quickly. I was embarrassed by my own reach for goodness, and chased by the fear that I had been ostentatiously good, and thus not good at all. I did not look back. But when I mounted my horse, and cantered off through the snow, I was not sorry.

I rode first to MacFee's and found him not at home, so I left his present upon his porch.

As I took the road again the flurries had subsided a little, even as the darkness fell, and I could see to the tops of the fir trees as the flakes floated by and caught in their crowns. The horse's hooves fell muffled, and he was docile and warm with exertion as I reached the house of Prince Mitski. I sat in the saddle, within the silence of the snowfall, and watched the house, the windows all ablaze with candles. I turned and rode away. Then I stopped, turned back, and spurred toward the house.

I rode directly to the front door. This time no one was watching for my arrival; no one came out to greet me. I dismounted and moved to the door, knocking sharply.

The door opened, and a perfumed French butler stuck his head around it. "Yes, monsieur?" he wondered.

"I . . . I wish to see Beatrice."

"Beatrice? Beatrice?" He tried two different pronunciations, as if the name itself was unfamiliar.

"The attendant of Princess Mitski. Of Natasha," I insisted.

"Ah. Ah, yes," he said. He appraised me for a moment as if I might be a thief, then added, "You may wait indoors, please."

I stepped inside and stood in the foyer. The house was quiet except for the sounds of muffled laughter coming from the kitchen. The servants, it seemed, had already begun their Christmas celebration.

"Well, General Selkirk!" Natasha entered from the parlor, her voice sharp and without warmth, like her look.

"Natasha," I said with as much cheerfulness as I could manage, "I've come to speak with Beatrice, if I may."

"Beatrice. Ah. Yes. Beatrice. Come with me."

She led me through the length of the house, and she was humming; it was, I thought, a Russian Christmas melody, and yet it seemed mirthless, cutting off all conversation as we made our way through the hallways, back toward the kitchen. Natasha stopped outside a doorway, fixed me with her eyes, and pushed the door open.

Beatrice looked up. She was on her knees, upon the bare wooden floor, scrubbing. "Beatrice," Natasha said to me with a vengeance, and she walked away.

For a moment as she had seen me, Beatrice had frozen. Now she went back to scrubbing, her face lowered. I knelt to Beatrice. "Happy Christmas," I said.

"Yes, of course," she answered, still scrubbing. "Happy Christmas."

"I . . . have . . . uh . . . Here!" I drew the package from the pocket within my cloak and handed it to her. She slowly put down the scrub brush and held the package. "Open it. Please."

She still hesitated, but then she tore off the wrapping and studied for a moment the velvet box. I thought her fingers trembled; her lips did. But they were pale, in anger it seemed, and I did not understand.

"Please," I said softly, "I hope you will like it."

She opened the box and gazed at the pendant.

"Do you like it?"

She said nothing.

"What is the matter?"

"I was just wondering," she said, "why you did not give it to Anne Shettlefield."

"Beatrice! I—"

She closed the box and extended it back to me. "I am sorry," she said. "This is a gift for a lady." She forced the box back into my hand, grabbed up the brush again, and attacked the floor.

"You are to me."

"Not the kind for balls and dancing."

"I . . . don't . . ."

She stopped, and her eyes flashed at me. She said quietly, "Charlotte DuBois expounded on every detail of your romance with Miss Shettlefield as I stood brushing the Princess Mitski's hair—before I was threatened with having my hands cut off for being too brutal with her scalp!" There was laughter from the room next door, and then a sudden hush; once again the servants in the kitchen were eavesdropping. I lowered my voice and said, "I have no romance with Anne Shettlefield."

Beatrice went back to scrubbing and would not look up.

"Beatrice . . ."

"Get away!"

I stood. I reached to touch her.

"Just get away," she whispered.

As I left, I thought she was crying. I know the housemaids, cooks, and lackeys in the kitchen were laughing.

I rode away from the Mitski mansion, beneath a thickening gray sky that seemed to be descending onto my shoulders, and I told myself that I would never understand the female spirit. I had professed my love to Beatrice, and at that moment she had believed me utterly; now, in another moment, having encountered the opinions of other women, she had decided I was a liar, with the romantic sensitivities of a dog.

But the closer I drew to Gorlov's house, where he had invited me to spend the holidays, the more it seemed to me that Beatrice's reactions were characteristic not just of women, but of all humanity. We hope and dream; somewhere we find faith. Then doubt spreads through us as a dark liquid stream, fed not so much by the world outside us but through some source within our own souls. Faith and doubt appear in our lives like two visitors—coming uninvited and leaving at their whim. We feed them both, and when they leave us by ourselves we remember the voice of each and ask which one spoke our true hearts—when both did.

GORLOV was not at home when I returned, and I was contemplating a night alone. The house boasted a fine library, containing even a few books in English, the livelier of which I had selected for the evening. But they lay unopened on the bed. I stared out the window, at the snow blotting out the ground.

There was a shout somewhere in the house, far below. I heard it again and went out into the hallway and to the top of the stairs. "Come on!" Gorlov boomed. "We will be late! Svet! Where are you? Magya! Pyotr! Come on! If we hurry, we can be stranded in just the right place!"

"What are you talking about, you fool?" I yelled down to him. He had been gone all day, and I had grown angry with him for having other friends.

"Come on, heathen! It is Christmas! We have been invited to dinner with Martina Ivanovna! All of us!"

With coaxes, threats, teases, and tickles, Gorlov made Magya to understand that she must come immediately, for we were all going together. He ordered us to bundle up, and we were soon plunging through a foot of new snow in a sleigh, with Magya huddling against Pyotr's arm on the box and Gorlov and me clinging to the sides, stretching out with lanterns to penetrate the blizzard. Pyotr took wide turns, running us nearly off bridges and through hedges, all to make

Gorlov swear and Magya squeal—for he made wild, out-of-control movements with his body, but never twitched once through his reins, and his wry craftiness lifted my spirits and made me call out frantically to beware.

We reached the seamstress's shop, and Tikhon staggered through the snow to meet us as Martina Ivanovna stood erect in the open doorway. Tikhon hopped into the box with Pyotr as Gorlov assisted Magya down and Martina Ivanovna bowed her welcome. The seamstress allowed me to kneel before her and kiss her hand, and when I rose she smiled at me with her eyes alone, as if to say, There. I *will* love your friend. And now you know it.

Martina Ivanovna had already made tea spiced with cinnamon and oranges; but Magya insisted on going into the kitchen with her as if nothing were prepared. Gorlov and I sat beside the fire, even stoked the blaze higher. Gorlov threw logs into the hearth as if they were his own. "This is where you have been coming so many nights since we returned from the Cossack wars, isn't it?" I said. He did not look at me.

We sipped our tea. "What is keeping Pyotr and Tikhon?" I said when they had been gone nearly a half hour. "Can they have gotten stuck between here and the stables?"

No one answered. Martina Ivanovna took a particular interest in the bottom of her teacup.

The door opened. Beatrice entered, followed by Pyotr and Tikhon. It was obvious from Beatrice's face that she was as surprised as I. But I am sure my eyes popped wide, while hers narrowed.

We had a feast that night; Magya was distressed because everything was done and she could only sit and eat. Tikhon was allowed a sip of vodka after dinner—a thimbleful, by his mother's measure—and though I had seen him quaff a man-sized ale when supping at the Goose, he played his role suitably and choked during the Christmas toast.

Beatrice conversed quietly with the others, but she did not speak to me. Nor would she look at me, but as the night wore on she did not look away so steadfastly either.

WE sang carols; they taught me the Russian. They told stories of enchanted bears, and Grandfather Frost, and the Angel and the Magpie. Martina Ivanovna related the story of the birth of Jesus, and Magya wept—all this in Russian, and all of which I understood, or seemed to, in the mix of spirits both ethereal and liquid. Afterward we dressed as lords and ladies, Martina Ivanovna draping us in silks and laces, and irritating Tikhon when she tried pressing him into service as a prince to dance with her, and then as a wealthy virgin to be Gorlov's partner, as he had been so reluctant in the other role. Then she danced with Gorlov, and Pyotr and Magya spun round together before the hearth. I stood from my seat beside the woodpile, walked to Beatrice on the opposite side of the fire, and held out my hand. She reluctantly accepted it, and watched my eyes as we stepped about each other. Still we did not speak.

The ladies insisted on retiring to the kitchen to clean the dishes. Gorlov and I sat beside the fire while Pyotr settled in beside the window, sucking dreamily on his unlit pipe. Tikhon, still wearing the scarlet cloth remnants Martina Ivanovna had draped upon him, fell asleep upon cushions in the corner. I stared at him a moment, then looked into the fire. I felt Gorlov watching me.

"What are you thinking?" he asked. When I did not answer he said gently, "Of your child?"

I looked at him. "No. Of my father." I looked back to the flames. My last Christmas with him, as we sat by the fire after I had ridden the horses, he pulled from his pocket a tiny cross he had whittled. It was oak, and only a man with hands as strong as his could have fashioned it. "You have given me so much," he said, "and I wanted to give something to you." Then the tears had come to me so suddenly, I had been unable to stop them. Except for the extra chores on Christmas mornings I had never presented him with a gift of anything, for he, in his economy, had forbidden it, saying he needed nothing except for me to continue to be the young man I already was. That blessing from my father had always been gift enough. The day I left I asked him to keep that cross for me, as a promise of my return. Now I sat in Russia, thinking of my father, sitting at his fireplace alone, holding—I hoped— that cross in his fingers.

Gorlov, with that mystical sense he always seemed to have, stared into me. "He has a gift this Christmas," Gorlov said. "I am sure."

Gorlov looked at the flames. Then he looked at Tikhon.

I said, "I am also thinking that I was married on Christmas Day." I sighed. "What is it about Christmas that makes us dredge up our memories, our shortcomings and our sorrows?"

"At Christmas we count our treasures, and there is no such thing as a shortcoming or a sorrow. We are as God made us, and we have what He has given us," Gorlov said.

There by the fireplace I thought I understood what he meant.

In the kitchen Martina Ivanovna, Magya, and Beatrice had begun to sing some carol, in soprano harmony. They sounded as angels. Gorlov and I sat listening, and I said to him, "I ceased long ago to believe it, but wouldn't it be a miracle . . . a wonder, beyond words . . . if it were really true that God Almighty, God Himself, would on this night become such a creature as man, if for no other reason than to touch his world? And . . . and maybe that is the meaning of Christmas— that a Christian is someone who would find that thought beautiful, and could believe it because of its very beauty, and because it moved him?"

Gorlov looked at me and smiled.

The blizzard did catch us. The snow was three feet deep against the door when we opened it at midnight to gaze up at the sky. The street was still, the snow settling silently. Gathered in the doorway, watching Christmas fall across the world, we sang a Russian hymn. I hummed the bass—beautifully, I thought.

The women all slept in Martina Ivanovna's bed. Tikhon remained in his corner. Pyotr, Gorlov, and I curled up before the fire, with bolts of cloth as pillows, and went to sleep, serene in the hope, for that one night, of the coming of God.

Chapter Thirty-five

T H E passing of Christmas seemed to have precipitated some crisis with Gorlov; for the entire day following, I heard him pacing about, and when I went downstairs the next morning to have breakfast, I caught sight of him peering out at me from his doorway. He was wringing his hands. I was about to bid him good morning, but he suddenly closed his door.

I took a ride, arranging and rearranging the way I intended to present my thoughts to the Tsarina. Gorlov must have been listening for my return, however, for as soon as I had come back upstairs he knocked and tossed my door open without waiting. "Svet!" he said in a shaking voice. "Friend . . . !"

"Gorlov! What is it?" The sight of his bloodless face warmed me with concern.

He spoke in volleys, pacing in bursts like a chicken. "I must ask . . . assistance as a second! That is it! . . . You must be my second! It . . . it must happen now. Now! Or . . . it will never happen!"

"As a second!" I cried. "You have been challenged? My God, Gorlov, a duel! Who is he?"

But Gorlov would answer me nothing. He seemed unable to speak at all, and he flushed crimson. His jaw worked, but his voice did not, and in frustration and fluster he grabbed up my cloak, tossed it over my shoulders, and pulled me out with him.

In the stables behind the house we found Pyotr, oiling the sleigh harnesses. He looked up when he saw Gorlov, and me with him, and stared fixedly at his master's face. He put his rags down slowly and, without a word from either of us, shoved the sleigh out onto the snow and hitched up a filly. Gorlov staggered into the open rear box, and me behind him. Wherever we were going, Pyotr knew; no one called a destination, and we were off like the wind.

It could have been my imagination—that capacity being sorely stimulated at that time—but it seemed to me that even the children on the streets stopped their playing and sensed something grave about us as we flew by. And Pyotr *was* flying, cracking the whip above the filly's head and throwing a spray of snow behind us as we went. *"Nye toot bistro!"* Gorlov cried out suddenly; then, sinking back into his seat, he repeated the order in three languages, beneath his breath: *"Non celer! . . . Nicht so schnell . . ."* and even a stab at the English: "No zo fass."

I had never seen him so frightened.

And then I saw why. We stopped at the front door of Martina Ivanovna's shop. The filly, aroused and lively, snorted. Pyotr waited motionless, then turned around and looked Gorlov dead in the face with an air that was absolutely haughty. Gorlov swallowed. Pyotr turned away again. His shoulders sagged in a taunting sigh.

"We . . . must . . . here . . ." Gorlov muttered, and stepped out. I tumbled out behind him, and rushed to his side as he banged at the door. He did not pause for anyone to answer, but kept pounding until Martina Ivanovna slung open the door and faced him. She was scowling at this brusque behavior, but her face cleared as Gorlov stammered, "In . . . inside! In here!" She took my cloak from me, laid it over a stack of cloth bolts, and walked beside me as I followed Gorlov into her sitting room.

Tikhon had apparently just returned home for his supper; he was standing beside the grate where a few sticks burned, and was unwinding his scarf from beneath his pink cheeks. I thought again how much I liked the boy, working at a tavern when other lads his age built snowmen. Gorlov drew himself up just inside the door and said, "Tikhon! Go . . . outside! Play somewhere!"

Tikhon looked up but stood still, so surprised was he. Gorlov motioned with his head as if to chase the boy, but Martina Ivanovna said, "No." Squeezing by Gorlov, still plugging up the doorway, she walked to where Tikhon stood and took up a stance beside him at the hearth. "You have brought your second," she said to Gorlov. "Tikhon shall be mine. What have you to say?"

Gorlov's eyelids fluttered for at least a minute. "I have . . ." he began. "I have come . . . to . . . to . . ."

"You have come," Martina Ivanovna repeated. "You have come to . . . what?"

"P-p-pro-pro," Gorlov stammered.

"Pro*mote*? Pro*tect*?" she pressed. The conversation was in French, and not literally the exact image of the English, but the effect was the same, as she formed her lips in the shape of the words he could not make himself utter, and said them for him. "Pro*pose!*" she shouted, and Gorlov nodded vigorously. "Propose what?" she demanded. "A business arrangement? An outing in the country?"

Gorlov, apparently grateful for her help, though it was harsh, shook his head.

"Could you mean marriage?" Martina Ivanovna inquired.

Gorlov nodded fiercely.

She nodded slowly and pursed her lips. "You must tell me why."

His eyes fluttered again. "I . . . I . . ." he said.

"You what? You want me?"

This threw him. At first he nodded; but then, decisively, he shook his head.

"No? Then . . . you are saying you want me as your wife . . ."

Gorlov nodded.

" . . . because you like me?"

Gorlov shook his head.

"Because . . . you love me?"

Gorlov paused. "More!" he blurted. "More . . . than . . ."

Martina Ivanovna waved him to silence, strode quickly across the floor, and seized his hands. Her head cocked back, her eyes blinking, she said, "You love me. That is enough."

"Pyotr!" Gorlov shouted, recovering all his old vigor. He ran to the front door, poked his head out, and boomed the name again. But the sleigh was gone. He shouted "Pyotr!" a third time, loud enough to shake windows across the way, and sure enough up slid the sleigh, containing Pyotr and a priest. When they walked in with Gorlov, Martina Ivanovna looked at the bald little clergyman and nodded. "Yes," she agreed. "Here. We shall do it here."

"No. Not here," Gorlov said. "In the church of this neighborhood. Tomorrow! We shall invite everyone. Make the arrangements now."

And that quickly their roles had shifted; Gorlov was strong in leadership—going just the way Martina Ivanovna wanted him.

※

IT happened as Gorlov said: they invited everyone, and everyone came. The church was too small to hold them all, and many of those who came late, especially the nobles like Prince Mitski and Natasha, were left standing outside, which insulted them and made Gorlov especially happy. Lord Shettlefield did not attend, but Anne came, sitting with other court ladies—and her presence did not trouble Beatrice, who sat in the front pew, weeping with happiness. Charlotte brought Marquis DuBois. And Nikonovskaya. And many persons of the Court, even Zepsha. And many more soldiers and acquaintances from the German quarter around the Goose, which was but a few streets over from Martina Ivanovna's shop. I even thought I saw the hungry prostitute, from the tobacconist's shop. Most of all there were neighbors of the seamstress, dozens of them, gathered in the church and out in the snow to cheer as the nuptial couple emerged from their vows.

They held the celebration outside in the street, fixing torches to the posts of buildings along the lane (the seamstress shop and church being but a few hundred yards from each other) and shared food produced from various kitchens about the neighborhood and vodka and wine placed about in barrels for everyone to tap. Gorlov got thoroughly drunk, amid the torchlight and the singing and the dancing that wore the snow away right down to the frozen earth. Martina Ivanovna was intoxicated as well. And even Tikhon was drunk, but not from the wine, as I at first thought. He and Pyotr danced together, and the boy had two new fathers.

Chapter Thirty-six

I F air can sparkle, it was sparkling then.
Dueling ranks of dwarfs, exotic dances, music, stunning gowns, jewels, food, drink—all spilling, twisting, shining in the atmosphere of the palace, until each lungful of breath made every visitor feel near bursting.

Four great halls of the palace received diners, each hall split with rows of tables, the tables stacked with candelabra, silver utensils, gold goblets, painted plates—but no food, for that flowed on trays like barges in rivers of servants from the table of the Tsarina in the imperial dining room. At each place at every table sat jewel-encrusted ladies and men in uniform—military or civilian: sashes and braid, pomade and boot polish.

We arrived late, after the vodka and champagne and wines had already lubricated the laughter of the guests assembled first in the ballroom, and they were taking seats now at the table. It had not been our design to miss any portion of the evening; Martina Ivanovna had refused to depart until she had redone the ribbons upon the shoulders of the second of the two gowns she had made for the evening. The timing proved to our advantage, for we had a single, unified audience. As the palace ball master searched for and found our names upon the guest list, I whispered to Gorlov, "You go first."

He did, Martina Ivanovna upon his arm. Following the waiter to their assigned place, Gorlov swaggered, while Martina Ivanovna gripped his bicep and twisted the fingers of her other hand into the satin of her skirt. The master of the ball called out, "General Sergei Gorlov, and his escort!" and the guests looked up to see them move to their seats. Many applauded, and though I was sure that some of the women noticed Martina Ivanovna, as it is the feminine tendency to look at other women first, it was clear that Gorlov, the arriving hero, was the focus of that royal society, and his guest, despite her beauty, was noticed as no more than the accessory of his arm. Gorlov held the chair for her, but the respectful applause at their entrance did not change until Gorlov acknowledged their ovation with a bow and settled to his place.

It was at that moment that I knew how I must enter.

The idea required a quick whispered conversation in the foyer. I quickly explained what I wanted to the ball master, who faltered only a moment and then sang out, "Colonel Kieran Selkirk!" The applause rose—I believe the diners had already turned to look, in anticipation of my arrival after Gorlov's—and I strode quickly and alone to my place at the table. I did not sit, but rather drew out the empty chair next to the one intended for me, and waited.

The women, I am sure, understood first; but the men were no less curious about who would take that place, and when the ball master called out, "and the escort of Colonel Selkirk," every eye in the room fixed on the doorway as Beatrice entered.

Martina Ivanovna had outdone herself, by refusing to

overdo Beatrice. The gown she had made was simple, white, with the only color the red bows upon the shoulders and the band she had sewn with a cameo around Beatrice's throat. The rest she had left alone, confiding to Gorlov (who, of course, passed the comment along to me): "Why compete with what God has given her? I struggled for years to give noblewomen the breasts and waist and shape that He had denied them. Now I can simply show what He has done." Thus was I able to understand Martina Ivanovna's answer when, upon viewing the gown, I suggested that it showed too much of her bosom. "It is all to the glory of God," she had said.

Pride. Pride and arrogance. I was full of both. But I felt a debt, too, a debt to Beatrice for the times she had covered her face as a handmaiden, and the times I had thought of my own birth as too humble.

Heads turned. Couples looked at each other, conversations ended in midsentence, new conversations began suddenly in faster, whispered phrases.

And no one knew her.

It was to me a shocking example of the effect of expectation upon human perception. The breathtaking woman floating before those royal guests like a swan effortlessly crossing a palace pond appeared so noble that they literally could not conceive that she might be anything other than what they imagined her to be, some mysterious royal beauty who was gracing me with her presence because of my recent notoriety. There were many in that room who had seen Beatrice before, and yet it is fair to say that they never had truly looked at her. Certainly her hair was different, brushed full and away from her face, and the rouge of her lips and blush of her cheeks had not been there before. Yet I saw in her what I had always seen, while they, it was clear, had never seen her at all.

I kissed her cheek as she reached me; we took our seats, and we dined.

We laughed too much, perhaps, the four of us—but that was easy to do, with eyes upon us from both ends of our table, and glances cast over shoulders from the other ranks. And I remembered Benjamin Franklin's observation to me, that someone born poor is the best spy among the rich, missing no nuance of manner or breeding, for Beatrice demonstrated the most impeccable style in the lifting of her glass, the replacing of her knife and return of her right hand to her lap before she should raise the fork with her left.

Men stared, women whispered; and still, no one knew her.

The courses changed; the waiters flowed. Dishes vanished; more appeared. A herald stepped to the doorway of our hall and announced, "The dance begins!" causing everyone else to stand and abandon their places at the table.

I stood and held a gloved hand out to Beatrice; she took it and rose, as Gorlov and Martina Ivanovna did the same.

Toward the ballroom the company crowded, raising a din of voices. "Kieran!" exclaimed a lady behind us, and I turned to see Charlotte, who had been sitting at the far end of our table. "You must introduce me to your new friend!" As Charlotte said this she looked toward Beatrice, and I saw curiosity but only vague recognition. It was perhaps the deepest of insults, or it was a compliment; Charlotte did not connect the woman she saw before her now with the serving girl.

"Good evening, Charlotte," Beatrice said.

"Do I . . . have we . . ." Charlotte began.

"Kieran has told me about you," Beatrice replied.

We reached the ballroom, and Anne approached, greeting not us but Charlotte. They kissed, cheek to cheek. "I've planned a surprise ball for the Tsarina, in her chambers, after this one," Anne said loudly. "Can you come?"

"Oh, yes!" Charlotte replied, with equal volume and enthusiasm. "I heard about it. What a delightful idea. I have anticipated attending, trusting you would invite me."

"And who is this?" Anne said, turning to Beatrice and me. She saw something; she squinted slightly.

"Will you dance?" Gorlov interrupted, gripping my shoulder. "Or must I take your companion from you?"

"Excuse us, ladies," I said to Anne and Charlotte, and led Beatrice onto the floor.

"Kieran," Beatrice whispered into my ear, as I drew her close for the dance, "I cannot do this."

"It is nothing. You hold me and walk."

"Not the dancing; that is no problem for me. I had to learn to be Natasha Mitski's partner for practice. But this charade is bad."

"Why?"

"Because we humiliate them."

"That is true."

"It is wrong. It is . . . dangerous."

And yet we did dance, and our steps were as light as the air.

T H E Tsarina did not attend the ball. This, Gorlov said, was not unusual. Her aides said she was busy, her ladies-in-waiting said she was tired, and everyone else said she had a new lover.

But while I did not have the opportunity to show off Beatrice to the royalty, I did encounter another face whose presence both chilled and comforted me: I saw the Lady Nikonovskaya. She was dancing with Lord Shettlefield, and speaking to him subtly as they moved. She appeared even more vivid at a distance, having blackened her hair, whitened her face, and reddened her lips and cheeks, while he seemed to have faded, his hair growing paler, his chest sinking.

I wanted to approach them. I hesitated, thinking the sight of me might be a shock to her. I was wrong. She saw me, dropped Shettlefield's arms immediately, and marched straight to me. "You're a fool," she said.

"You are a remarkable woman," I told her.

"I know."

"Nikonovskaya, I wish you to meet someone . . ." I began, turning toward Beatrice, who had drifted off a few steps.

"Meet? You don't need to introduce me. I already know Beatrice. I always knew you loved her, as well. Don't look at me that way. Why be surprised? If you had not loved her, you would have loved me. I would have found a way to make you—though it would have been futile, for you are a dead man."

She turned away and rejoined Lord Shettlefield. I dodged slowly through the crowd back to Beatrice and gripped her hand. Gorlov moved up beside me and whispered in my ear, "What a woman Beatrice is, Svet. So tough. And look how Martina Ivanovna watches and admires her. If those two were men, we would not want to butt heads with them in a tavern."

"Even as they are, I wouldn't want to—" I began, but stopped at the sight of a single face appearing at the edge of the group of ladies and immediately flushing. Natasha, the Princess Mitski, grasped the shoulder of the friend on either side of her, sucked in a great breath of air, screamed "Beatrice!" and fainted.

I remember the entire room falling silent, and yet it may be that I lost all impression except sight; the entire room, it seemed, had turned to stone but for the eyes of the ladies snapping from the limp Natasha to the frozen Beatrice. And it was Beatrice who broke the silence, moving to Natasha, lifting her head—the princess's royal friends holding her uselessly by the arms, so that her neck flopped back like that of a rag doll—and took over her resuscitation, patting her cheeks and speaking to her in the voice she had so often used to soothe Natasha's spells of dramatic fainting.

If the sight of Beatrice's instinctive support of the woman

who had treated her so thoughtlessly touched anyone else be-sides myself, Gorlov, and Martina Ivanovna, I could not per-ceive it; for the other ladies it was as if the scales had fallen from their eyes and they once again saw the world in the reassuring clarity of their own superiority. The musicians still sawed away in the balconies above the ballroom, the chandeliers glittered upon their gowns, and Beatrice was no longer a mystery, sim-ply a puppet in a play held for their own amusement.

I saw Lord Potemkin move up and speak to Charlotte, whispering into her ear with the arrogant calm of the charade master who holds all of the strings. At that moment someone touched me by the arm; I turned to see Lady Nikonovskaya. Her eyes were strangely still, and—it seemed to me—sad. "You have been granted an audience with the Tsarina," she said. "A private audience."

"Yes," I said, "but when?"

"Now. Follow me. I will show you to her." She turned and walked away a few steps, then looked back to see me hesitat-ing. "Now," she repeated emphatically.

I looked to Beatrice. Charlotte had crouched down to her and was whispering something; I thought she surely must be telling her that I was off to see the Empress and would be returning soon. I looked to Gorlov; he was alert, his mind spinning. "I go to the Tsarina," I said softly, and followed quickly after Nikonovskaya.

At the door of the ballroom I looked back at Beatrice. She had turned to find me, and her eyes were bright and rimmed with tears. I stopped, wondering what was the matter; but Nikonovskaya grabbed me hard by the arm, snatching me with surprising strength. "You cannot delay!" she ordered.

I followed her, and now I see myself as the only one in all of Russia who did not understand exactly where I was going, and what was expected of me.

Chapter Thirty-seven

I PACED in the palace corridor, rehearsing my speech to Catherine.

"Your Majesty . . ." I began again, trying to find a voice that sounded strong, assured, comfortable, trustworthy, instead of like the tense and smothered monotone I kept hearing in my own ears, "Thomas Jefferson has written: 'I have sworn upon the altar of God eternal enmity against every form of tyranny over the mind of man.' And if we consider what Voltaire has written . . ."

But it was all just words.

"You are an eloquent man," Franklin had told me.

And I had responded, "No man is as eloquent as the soldier who stands his ground." What fine defiant words those had been, and I had put my life on the line in conviction of their truth. But I had never had an audience with an empress, or spoken with anyone who with a word alone could launch armies, or disperse them. If I could say the right thing this evening, appealing to the mind and heart of the Tsarina, then I might save the lives of untold thousands of my countrymen, might save even the hope of democracy for my nation itself. . . .

If I could only say the right thing.

"Your Majesty . . ." I muttered to myself once more, still trying to find the right voice.

Nikonovskaya, who had ordered me to wait while she moved down a dimly lit corridor, returned quickly and led me down the way she had just gone. We had walked only a few steps when Potemkin, flanked by his personal soldiers, stepped from the shadows. "So," he said, smiling, "you have gotten what you wanted. An audience with the Tsarina." He leaned so close that I could smell the meat from his dinner as he breathed into my ear. "If she is pleased with your encounter, I will give you riches, influence, everything you desire. If she is displeased, you will die."

I was stunned and baffled; before I could react, Potemkin stepped inside his office, his soldiers blocking the door, and Nikonovskaya tugged me into another hallway.

There I balked and shook off her arm. "I don't understand what—"

She ambushed me with a kiss, pressing her lips hot and full against my mouth and pulling away just as suddenly; as I stood there blinking and stunned, she shoved me backward, through a revolving panel of the corridor wall.

The panel clapped shut, plunging me into darkness. "I don't understand! What are you trying to—" I called out, trying not to sound too angry, for it seemed I had become a player in one of the Court's planned farces, like those of the giants and dwarfs, and I was expected to relax and keep a good humor; I warned myself to do so, lest all would be lost.

I had little time to consider the game, in fact, no time at all. Another lady, who may have been Contessa Bellefleur, for she wore the same scent, swam out of the darkness and pressed herself against me, kissing me as Nikonovskaya had, then nibbling my ear and moaning as if in the ultimate moment of passion. She spun me around and with a hard shove sent me staggering into a whole swarm of feminine arms; hands flew about me like lusty bats in the darkness, mussing my hair, stroking my belly, my legs.

They spun me first one way and then another. My eyes were adjusting to the dim light, and I saw a masked woman— the mask covered only her eyes; her bosom was completely bare—step from the shadows. She presented me with a goblet. It was full of dark liquid: wine, by its aroma. Wanting to keep all of what was left of my composure, I looked up to hand the cup back to her, and just as my face came up, the masked, half-naked woman kissed me ferociously. One of the other ladies must have grabbed the goblet, for I do not remember it falling, though it may have; I was bewildered and dizzy from their ambush, and I see now that this was exactly their purpose. "What—" I tried to say; but before I could form any other words, they shoved me once more, and I staggered backward through a curtain.

I found myself in a room lit with hundreds of candles. Silvery furs lined the floors, sablelike carpet.

A voice from behind me, sultry and low, said, "Colonel."

I turned and saw her—Catherine, Empress of All the Russias. She was sitting at her writing desk, regal in a mantle of white sable fur that blanketed her from shoulders to ankles. Around her throat dangled a ruby choker, at her wrists hung diamond bracelets, and laced through her mane of black-gray hair was a chain of sparkling jewels, and yet it was her eyes that shined the most. "Or may I call you Kieran?" she asked, as if there were any question that she could do whatever she desired.

"Please . . . do, my-my lady . . ." I stammered.

She offered her hand, and I moved quickly to her and touched my lips to the backs of her fingers; she surprised me by gripping my fingers in return and looking straight into my eyes. "I want to thank you," she said, in a voice both deep and soft, "for everything you've done for me. A queen is nothing without the achievements of her people. And you have achieved much."

It struck me that she had just referred to me as one of her own people; I was calculating this as an opportunity to bring up America and the new notion of its nationhood, when she startled me by kissing my hand. I stared at her: the Tsarina, ruler of an empire, standing in front of me and gazing directly into my eyes.

There was a tap at the door, and I jumped. The Tsarina laughed, seeming to find my nervousness a novel delight. "Come in," she called. A team of servants streamed into the room and in a matter of seconds had placed a table, chairs, and a whole setting of food directly in front of the huge hearth. "I thought we might eat here," she said to me, "if you are hungry."

Of course I had just eaten, but the table was laid and the servants had vanished. So I pulled her chair back for her, then edged too quickly to my own. As I sat I knocked over my wine glass and grabbed at it reflexively, managing to knock over one of the candelabras.

"You are nervous," the Tsarina said.

I must have resembled a startled deer as I looked up at her. But her smile showed such ease and delight that I found myself smiling, too. "Yes," I said, and cleared my throat. "My trip into this room was a bit . . . unusual."

"Did my ladies toy with you? I must speak to them. What those naughty girls do is really inexcusable."

She averted her eyes from me, fixing them on the fire, and I saw that she was trying not to burst out laughing; she had orchestrated everything that had happened to me that night. "I'm sure you'll find your balance," she said, returning her eyes to mine.

"I hope so, m'lady," I answered, my voice growing husky.

"Perhaps it would be easier if you called me Catherine." As she said this she undid the throat clasp of the sable mantle and let it fall to the floor, revealing bare, athletic shoulders above a low-cut crimson gown that accentuated her breasts.

I felt myself being played like a helpless boy, and I did not like the feeling. Instinctively, I countered. "Catherine," I said, "but that wasn't your name when you came to Russia, was it."

Her eyes took on new sparkle. She saw that I was not asking a question, but stating a fact—and declaring my intention to meet her on more equal ground. "No," she answered. "It was Sophie."

"And you weren't always a queen."

Her voice took on an edge—not a threat, exactly, more like a warning. "No one . . . ever . . . talks to me about that."

"I don't mind being unique."

I saw that I had surprised her. "You are brash . . . Kieran," she said, telling me how she felt about such brashness by using my given name.

"I've tried to prepare myself to meet you," I answered. "I've learned what I could about you, I've read your favorite books. But yes, I'm nervous. I don't rule a nation of people; I can't imagine what that's like. So I try to remember that you once knew what it is to be in someone else's palace."

"Are you trying to disarm me?"

"You would see through that." And she would see through me, to judge by her stare.

"How much do you know about me?" she asked, with no threat and no anger, just directness.

"I know what books say. And I know that books are only books."

She lifted her wineglass and took a slow drink. "I lived in a village in Germany. I was fifteen years old. I was distantly related to royalty. I owned one nice dress." She paused for a moment, realizing, as I did, that she had determined to answer my honesty with honesty of her own. "One of my uncles in the German Court heard that the Tsarina Elizabeth was look-ing for a match for her son, Prince Peter, heir to the Russian throne. My uncle had submitted my name as a candidate, and the Tsarina wanted me to come to Russia."

I was drawn in, already fascinated, and could not resist interrupting with a question. "Did you know why she chose you?"

"Not at the time. I found out the prince liked German girls. His mother was hoping to make him happy." She paused again, and I had the feeling that she had not told this story often, if she had told it at all. "My parents didn't want me to go, but they saw it was my chance. So my father agreed. But before I left he made me promise him two things. One: that I would remain a Lutheran. Two: that I would not involve myself with politics."

I could not help smiling at this, and the corners of her mouth lifted in response. But then her smile faded. "I never saw my father again," she said. "I came to Russia. I met the prince. He was a pig. He was educated in Germany, and he hated everything Russian—its language, its religion, its ruler . . . his mother. Then they led me in to meet the Tsarina Elizabeth, the daughter of Peter the Great."

Now in her face, lit by the orange glow of the logs crack-ling in the brass grate of her palace bedroom hearth, I could see the vulnerable girl she used to be. "And I looked into her eyes," she went on, "and I saw that she perceived what I had seen—that her son was weak. And I knew then that I would never be allowed to leave Russia with that knowledge. And so I said, 'M'lady, I have two requests: that you teach me Russian, and confirm me in your faith.'" Again, she paused. "Three months later, I married her son. A month after that, she had him strangled. And I became the Tsarina."

The story had enchanted me; but it had, it seemed, put Catherine into a trance of loneliness and vulnerability. She reached for my hand, where it lay on the linen of the table-cloth, and held it.

I pressed her fingers in return; it seemed natural, accepting such a simple request to comfort the vulnerability of a lady who had just shown herself to be a woman first, before she was anything else. And then I realized she was staring into my eyes.

Her stare was magnetic; a beautiful woman, full of the loneliness of power and the power of loneliness, smoldering in her. She suddenly plunged across the table, knocking it over, locking her lips against mine.

Among all the other thoughts exploding in my mind was an awareness that some of her servants—from the guards who protected her to the servers of her food to pets like Zepsha who came whenever she wished—would be just outside the door and must have heard the crash of the table. In those crazy moments I actually feared they might rush in and assume I was attacking their queen; and, at the same time, I knew they would not interrupt at all, for there was no doubt that Catherine was doing exactly as she wished to do.

She kissed with playful passion, pushing me backward out of my chair and wrestling me onto the sable rug in front of the fire. Straddled across my lap the way she would ride a horse, she sat up, holding my shoulders and staring down into my eyes.

She jerked at my tunic, sending buttons popping every-where, and plunged her mouth down onto my chest. "Wait!" I managed to say. "Please wait!"

She paused and grinned. "No need to wait, Kieran. I'm ready."

She smothered me with another kiss—but suddenly I sat up, holding her off.

"What's wrong?" She frowned, truly baffled. I sat there staring, blinking, drawing unsteady breath, looking, I am sure, like a man who has just opened his eyes from a ruthless dream. "What is it?" she wondered.

"I thought . . . I was coming here . . . to talk to you about America."

"We can talk politics all you want," she said. "In the morning." She kissed me again, tried to grope me, but I rose to my knees. She paused, then realized I was indeed stopping; she snatched my collar in fury. *"Don't you do this to me!"* she shouted.

She hurled me onto my back, and tried to straddle me again. I grabbed her wrists and wrestled her onto her back. Suddenly she was smiling, thinking she was about to get what she so clearly wanted. But when she realized she was wrong, she opened her jaws to scream.

I clamped my hand over her mouth, caught both her wrists in one hand, and tried, in that wild moment, to think; here I was atop the Tsarina of Russia, and her eyes were popping with fury. It was as if I had grabbed a cannon shell, and the moment I let go, it would explode. "Your— Your Majesty . . ." I stammered stupidly.

Her eyes burned even hotter. . . . I winced, aware that of all the choices of how I might address her at that instant, those words were the last she wished to hear. I spoke more firmly. "I am dead, the moment I let you go. So I may as well say what I came to say." I looked directly into her flaming eyes and answered their anger with anger of my own. "If you send soldiers to America, we will kill them. Not me, I won't make it back. But men like me. We don't want to kill your soldiers, or King George's, or anybody's. But we will fight for what we believe."

In her rage and her struggle, she was sucking air so loudly through her nose that I at first thought it likely she had not heard a word I had said. But now her eyes looked less wild, more fixed and still, with that furious intelligence of hers that took in everything.

Even so, I realized I was speaking for myself, whether she understood me or not. I went on: "I . . . am a man. You hear me? A man. I have a choice. And I won't give up my choice because a king . . . or a queen . . . has a whim. Or even . . . a need. I have been a fool. But I have crossed the snows of half the world. I have fought wolves and wild men to be here, to say what I'm saying now."

I glanced toward the door. Catherine was no longer struggling, and her eyes were locked on mine. "I'm going to take my hand off your mouth," I told her. "You can call your guards and cut off my head, the way you cut off the head of Pugachev. But if you do, then I will know that you are no more the True Ruler of Russia than he was."

I removed my hand from her mouth. We looked at each other for a long moment. "Leave me," she said quietly.

I wanted to say something else, some word of apology or regret; I was not sorry for a syllable I had spoken, but I hated leaving any lady looking as she did now. I opened my mouth but found no way to express—

"LEAVE ME!"

I stood and moved to the door, trying to fasten my tunic on the way. I stopped at the door, hesitated, then left without looking back.

But I could tell, without seeing her, that she had rolled over toward the fire, her face away from me, and was weeping.

I WAS not the only one that night to feel the ground of my known world open into an abyss beneath my feet.

While I was visiting the Tsarina within her private bedchambers, the Court ladies had gathered into a tight circle of their own. Bellefleur and Nikonovskaya, along with other young beauties, clustered around Natasha, who recovered enough to glare at Beatrice, even while insisting that she remain close by, since, as Natasha put it, she was "now one of them." And Charlotte, returning from the hidden hallways near the bedchamber, gripped Anne Shettlefield by the arm and drew her into the group, so great was the feminine instinct to form their own perimeter at that moment.

"So!" Charlotte said with hushed excitement. "It is done."

Beatrice was growing more pale by the moment, as the blood drained from her head and her heart.

"Congratulations, Anne," Natasha said, emphasizing the name even as she glared at Beatrice.

Now Anne felt everyone's attention upon her. As she felt her cheeks flush hot, she saw in the faces of all of them, all but Beatrice, that they were certain she was the one due the prize for having found the Tsarina a new lover. Then Anne Shettlefield spoke two words she would regret the rest of her life.

"Thank you," she said.

B EATRICE was standing in an alcove of the palace's great hall, having removed herself as far as possible from the revelry of the other guests, when she saw me appear, barging through the diners and dancers, looking for her. When the provers noticed me, they were shocked; Charlotte and the Lady Nikonovskaya were standing close to Beatrice, and I overheard Charlotte whisper, "So soon? What went wrong?"

I spotted Gorlov, pulled him close, and muttered rapidly into his ear. Then I pushed my way toward Beatrice.

Guards, coming from the direction of the Tsarina's wing

of the palace, moved in to cut me off. "Beatrice!" I called. I tried to shoulder my way through to her, but the confused crowd was blocking my way and the guards were grabbing at me. I was close, but could not reach her.

"Go with Gorlov!" I shouted. "Get away from here!"

"What have you done?" she called back to me.

The guards swarmed me. Gorlov jumped in, pulling one of them off and slamming him through a table before the razor-sharp pikes clustered around Gorlov's throat, and more arms grabbed me.

Mitski appeared among the guards. "Hold your tongue, Gorlov—and keep your head," he said.

"This man is an officer!" Gorlov protested, as the guards punched and clubbed upon my ribs and shoulders.

"Not anymore!" Mitski spat. "Lord Potemkin has denounced him as a spy."

Even with several men on my back, trying to drive me flat against the polished floor, I lifted myself to full height; I saw Gorlov looking on helplessly behind the pikes as two of Potemkin's guards quietly flanked Beatrice and whisked her away without a sound. Then something struck my temple, and the world went black.

Chapter Thirty-eight

I DRIFTED in unconsciousness, floating away from pain like a planet in dark space. Then a cold stone floor flew out of the blackness and slammed against me.

I awoke upon it, to realize I was totally naked, in a windowless stone dungeon. I turned my head enough to see gray light slanting through the open iron door, and the boots of the two brutes who had done what their sergeant had said would be an interrogation, though no one had asked me any questions through the beating they administered. They left, closing the door to leave me again in complete darkness. I lay on the rough stone, and wished that they had killed me.

I was allowed no glimpse of the sky, nor the remotest access to the outer world, so that I had no reference for the passage of time. After what I took to be a day they told me I had been in the wet stone room for a week; after what I took to be a week the jailors said it had been a day. They tried to extinguish my dignity by coming in to watch whenever I had to evacuate my bowels—which I had to do upon straw in the corner of my room, and which I did agonizingly often because of the rotten food they gave me. Most of all they looked to rob me of hope; they laughed when I asked any question; they left me for long periods to convince me I had been forgotten; then they would begin a series of beatings with ever shorter interludes in between, to make me experience life as an existence of escalating pain. But even in this I saw a contradiction, for they never beat me on the face, inflicting pain on every other part of my body instead. It seemed they wished to avoid leaving permanent marks, and because of this I told myself that they must suspect that I might someday be released; thus, I clung to hope.

I WAS lying naked and shivering upon the stinking straw of the stone floor when the two jailors banged open the door, came in, fell upon me suddenly, and trussed me round and round so that my legs were pinned together and my arms pressed to my sides. I could move only my head and toes. My toes they did not care about; my head they pressed to the rough stone floor. Then they began to pour icy water into my ear.

When I was a child, I once plucked a broomstraw and poked it into my ear opening in pursuit of some flying summer insect that I fancied had secreted himself there. The pain was so sudden and sharp that I chose it preferable to let the invader (imaginary, it turned out) raise offspring inside my head rather than go after him in that fashion again.

The pain of the water was similar—except it felt as if they had thrust in the entire broom instead of a single straw. When I screamed, they stuffed a foul woolen sock into my mouth. The agony of that was twofold; the stream of water filled my ear and flowed across and into my nostrils so that I was smothered as well as strangled.

Every fifteen seconds they poured again. I thought my brain would freeze. I hoped it would. But not even the feeling inside my ear would deaden; it grew ever worse.

I tried to fight. I tried to succumb and faint from the pain. I could not.

How long this continued I cannot say. They eventually turned me onto my right side, and when I expected the pitcher—so cold I thought it must have been dipped into a hole cut in the river ice—I felt instead the lips of a man who whispered: "Confess . . . confess . . ." Then the frigid water shot in.

They worked on my left ear for a time. They turned me back over and left me alone long enough for me to hope it was over; then they began again on the right. All the while they repeated, "Confess . . . confess . . ."

I mumbled in the sock; I screamed through it. Finally they pulled it from my mouth like a slobbery cork, and I was able to draw enough breath and feel enough relief to blurt, "I confess I am a better man than you!"

They laughed, and resumed the torture.

Chapter Thirty-nine

THE Kirov Abbey stood with its back to the stone hill from which it was carved. The abbey itself was cold and stark, beautiful in its isolation. A low spiked wall surrounded it, with but a single iron gate as entrance or exit. In its courtyard, solitary nuns wandered through the snow to its chapel and storehouses.

Tsarinas had died there, imprisoned by husbands who no longer loved them, or hated by brothers who competed with them for the right to succession, or mistrusted by sons who feared their own mother's influence; when a royal woman faced internal exile, it was to the Kirov Abbey that she came.

Beatrice knew nothing of the Kirov Abbey; she had never read of it, had never heard it mentioned. The very existence of such a place—a convent prison, with nuns and castrated monks as attendants and loyalist soldiers as guards—had been beyond the realm of her experience or imagination. When the Tsarina's bodyguards had taken her from the palace, still dressed in the gown Martina Ivanovna had made for her, they had thrown a soldier's cloak over her shoulders and a blindfold about her eyes. When they removed the blindfold, after an hour-long carriage ride, she found herself in a huge rectangular room, with a bed at the far end and a single barred window set into one wall. There was a chair and a writing desk, but no paper, only a copy of the Orthodox Bible. Beatrice still had no idea where she was. The place, though barren, was oddly regal.

The nun who removed her blindfold left silently and latched the door behind. From the sound of the latches, they were quite strong.

Beatrice sat for a moment and tried to collect herself, but the room offered no help in that. She stood, finally, and made her way to the window. It had no curtains over the bars, and she was eager for the view.

What she saw was no comfort. The room Beatrice now inhabited stood but a few feet away from the granite cliff against which the abbey had been built. Set into the wall just opposite her window were iron bars where in the past bodies of traitors had been hung, apparently as objects of meditation for those imprisoned within the room. Birds had been allowed to feast upon the unfortunates, and what Beatrice beheld on her first look from the window were the remains of the last victim—a weathered skeleton picked clean except for a few remaining tufts of long hair; the last traitor, apparently, had been a woman.

Beatrice recoiled from the window, certain that she would never look out of it again.

WHILE I lay on the floor of the prison, three riders galloped through the snows lying deep in the woodlands surrounding St. Petersburg. In the gray light of winter, both horses and men slid through the shadowed forests like phantoms, then burst into a clearing where stood the weathered structures of a community of woodcutters.

Most of the villagers who inhabited the hamlets in the extreme north of Russia had never seen Wolfhead or his followers, but every last one of them had listened in terror to the stories of him, had heard him described in minute detail, often by others who themselves had never seen him either. Thus, they immediately recognized the apparition who burst upon them from the shadowed woods, as if emerging straight from the dark legends of Russia.

The villagers screamed and ran for cover as Wolfhead reined his horse to a stop in the center of the road that ran through their cluster of huts, all built around a church, a magistrate's office, and a central well. The Cossack seemed to be searching for something—or someone. Although they could see only the lower half of his face, they could tell by what they saw that he was both powerful and ferocious. He bellowed, with a voice like a rusty casket hinge, "Who is the Tsarina's magistrate?"

A terrified peasant woman who had frozen in the street pointed out a fat little man cowering behind the woodpile next to the magistrate's office; the shuddering little man attempted to flee, but Wolfhead spurred his horse masterfully to a trot, caught the running peasant by the collar, carried him to the center of the village where the well was, and dropped him into the snow beside it. While the two filthy Cossacks riding with him sat easily upon their horses and laughed at his antics, Wolfhead slid from his saddle and jumped onto the wooden walls of the well so that he stood above the awed villagers like Pugachev had stood on the platform of his execution. "Citizens of Russia!" he shouted. "The rumor that I fled to Siberia is a royal lie! Here I am, and I will have my tribute! You have ignored me and paid the royal magistrate instead!"

With this, Wolfhead dropped his handsewn trousers and

pissed on the back of the magistrate. The townspeople peeked from their homes; some gasped, while others tried to conceal their treasonous snickers behind their hands. The Cossack then retied his trousers and jumped onto his horse, his huge graceful body landing lightly on the saddle. He spurred his horse away, and his men followed, disappearing instantly and utterly.

The very next day the magistrate Wolfhead had pissed upon stood quivering before the Tsarina. It was bad enough that they had made him come here in person, to her throne room; it was even worse that they had made him tell the story again, exactly as he had told it before; but the very worst of all for the already terrified little peasant was the sight of the rage that filled the Tsarina's eyes. She turned those eyes on her cowering generals. "How can you find nothing, with my whole army? Not even a trace of a camp?"

One of the generals tried to say, "He vanishes—"

But the Tsarina cut him off. "Nobody vanishes! I sent a handful of mercenaries to the Ukraine, and they brought me Pugachev, defeating a whole army of Cossacks to get to him! Now you cannot capture the leader of one tiny band of Cossacks, trampling through my own back garden?" Her rage had grown as these words spilled from her, and the men in the room, who had seen others tortured for having demonstrated incompetence, found themselves growing as frightened as the peasant magistrate—for the little peasant was not the only village official to have encountered the marauders. Raids by Wolfhead the Cossack were being reported all around St. Petersburg, and they were an enormous embarrassment to Catherine; they seemed to show that the defeat of Pugachev and the subsequent celebrations of the Tsarina's victory were little more than a pompous sham, and that true power still lay with the wild riders who could defy her and do whatever they wished, in a countryside that was more theirs than hers.

✳

HOW much Lord Potemkin concerned himself with the reports of Wolfhead's reappearance, I cannot say. But I can write with much more conviction concerning his interest in the potential alliance of Russia with Great Britain for the suppression of American independence, and of his relationship with Lord Shettlefield. I have reason to believe that the British diplomat visited Lord Potemkin in the latter's personal chambers at the Royal Palace, during my imprisonment, and this is the essence of what transpired:

Potemkin, always confident, was self-satisfied to the point of quiet elation; he felt he had masterminded a situation and so was a master mind. Shettlefield, a natural pleaser of the powerful, saw this celebration in Potemkin and fed it, saying something along the lines of, "I bow to you. Beside your ruthless brilliance I am an amateur. For once Catherine chooses her own lover; by showing her lover to be treacherous, you make her doubt her own judgment and make her even more dependent on yours."

"I must admit that I've impressed even myself," Potemkin returned.

"Now," Shettlefield observed, "all you have to do is prove Selkirk's treachery. But I cannot help you. I must appear impartial."

"I don't need your help," Potemkin informed him. "I will have a confession—one way or another."

"Then why did you call me?"

"We have a problem with your daughter." Potemkin handed a note, written in a feminine hand, to Lord Shettlefield. "She sent this to Kirov Abbey. I believe it is time your daughter went home."

Shettlefield read the note with rising anger.

✳

BACK at his home Lord Shettlefield confronted his daughter. He was trying to smile, having told himself that he might seem more calm that way, thus making himself appear so furious as to be on the verge of madness. Waving Anne's note in the air, he said, "You use the Tsarina's royal seal to try to get a note past Potemkin's guards? That is treason! In this country and in ours!"

Anne felt neither disgrace nor despair, but only disappointment that her note had not reached the person for whom she had intended it. "I was trying to be faithful to a higher law," she told her father.

"A higher law?" He read the note aloud to her, as if she did not know what she'd written. " 'Beatrice, I burn with shame. I have sinned against your spirit. I lied about the man you love. About the man I love. But he was not my lover. I wanted to be a part of things. When everyone thought I'd had him, and envied me for it, I lacked the courage to tell the truth. You were braver, better, than all of us. Forgive me.'"

Shettlefield lowered the note and raised his voice. "My God!"

"What troubles you, Father? That I apologize? Or that I love?"

"Love?"

"Does that shock you? You encouraged affection between me and Selkirk."

"I encouraged an acquaintance, not for you to act like— like—"

"Like a woman? He is admirable, Father. He is brave, and noble. He is—"

"He is an agent of the American rebels."

"I don't believe that," Anne said defiantly.

"Benjamin Franklin sent him here to gain Catherine's favor. If he flattered you, it was only to get to her."

"Thank you for flattering me." She stood to leave.

"Anne, I—"

"He did not court me, Father. He sought nothing. If I admire him as a man, perhaps it is because he is the first real man I have ever known."

She left her father alone in his study.

Chapter Forty

A F T E R two weeks of imprisonment, Beatrice had a visitor. It was Zepsha.

Beatrice knew what it was to play the role that every servant must play, to show happiness, interest, excitement, or concern, as called for by the mistress. She recognized Zepsha's extraordinary talent for this role; the dwarfess, far from resenting her position in life, relished the opportunity to please and entertain the royals, and because they so embraced her for her skill at doing so, she considered herself part of their circle. For not lamenting her physical shortcomings, Beatrice admired Zepsha; for convincing herself she was more master than servant, Beatrice distrusted her. She knew that Zepsha possessed neither the affection for her nor the authority to visit her of her own accord, so she knew the dwarfess had been sent; Beatrice assumed it had been at the initiative of Natasha, whose heart was as shallow as her mind, and yet was without malice.

Beatrice sat with her back to the awful window as Zepsha unpacked the fruits, candies, and scented soaps she had brought in a pouch beneath her dress. She had told Beatrice that the guards wanted to search her, but when she had defied them in the name of the Tsarina, they had simply laughed and let her through. "The Tsarina sends her condolences to you, with these gifts," Zepsha said, her voice reedy and musical, like an oboe. "You poor dear. But don't worry, I've heard them talking, and you'll be out in six months, if you act agreeably."

"Six months?" Beatrice said, shocked. No one had ever explained the reasons for her imprisonment; certainly no one had given her any idea of when she might be released.

"Well, it is routine," Zepsha said, shrugging, as if everything at Court was within her knowledge. "You consorted with a spy, after all."

"A spy? He is not a spy."

"Dear girl, don't blame yourself for being naïve. The man was a natural seductor. Not just you, and Anne, but also Charlotte, Nikonovskaya—"

"Anne? . . . Charlotte? . . ."

"They endorsed his prowess as well."

"But Natasha said—"

"Natasha! The only one he didn't sleep with! You didn't know that?"

Beatrice wanted to believe none of this, and yet Zepsha exuded certainty. Her face was painted as it always was, chinbones white with powder, cheeks rosy with rouge, eyelashes enormously long around her bright eyes. She studied Beatrice from beneath those slowly batting lashes, her expression one of helpful concern. "If you would sign a statement about his attempts to find out information about the Tsarina, she would release you immediately."

Beatrice looked down at her hands upon her lap. "I would never sign a statement. Whatever he is."

Something hardened within Zepsha, but Beatrice was still looking down and did not notice it then. "Is?" Zepsha piped.

"Was. I thought they had told you. He was beheaded yester-day." Zepsha paused as Beatrice's heart crumbled within her. She hopped from her chair and moved to Beatrice's side. "You poor thing. Perhaps this place is just what you need." She stroked Beatrice's hair, then moved to the door. She paused there. "Visitors are allowed once a year. I will come again next winter." With that, Zepsha stepped out and left Beatrice alone, the door as it closed exhaling a draft of air from the dark stone corridor, like the last breath of a lost wanderer, dying from cold.

T HE abbey watchmen—soldiers handpicked from Potemkin's personal corps of bodyguards—came shortly afterward, to tell Beatrice that she would be allowed to take an evening stroll about the grounds; they told her she would not be permitted to walk close to the abbey's gates, but she could climb the bell tower if she wished. They then moved out of her room and left the door open.

Zepsha must have been watching from some concealed cranny as Beatrice stepped into the corridor; certainly Beatrice did not see her and would not, at that moment, have imag-ined that she might still be lurking somewhere, even if Beatrice were characteristically clear-headed and sensitive to her surroundings, which she was far from now. Beatrice, in a state of utter distress, drifted like a sleepwalker to the winding stone staircase and made her way up, up, up to the top of the tower.

There, her back to the bells and her face to the forests of Russia and to a dream of freedom she felt no hope of pos-sessing, Beatrice stopped. She believed herself to be utterly alone.

She was not. Behind the bass bells, Zepsha waited and

watched, begging all the dark powers within her own breast that Beatrice would surrender to despair and step out to the death that waited upon the paving stones so far below. Zepsha held her breath, afraid to make a sound and so distract Beatrice from thoughts of doom.

Beatrice's shoulders sagged in grief, and she sobbed.

But it was not in her to kill herself. The winds stung her face and drove her back from the edge of the tower.

That one step back must have been what triggered Zepsha; of course, no one could ever say for sure. As she peeked at Beatrice from behind the bells, she must have thought about the poison she might have used, and how dangerous that could be, for the right doctors could read its signs and the Tsarina had access to the right doctors. A suicidal leap from the bell tower would have been the end of it, perfect for Potemkin, perfect for Zepsha—and the opportunity must have seemed just too close to resist. Zepsha scrambled from behind the bells and raced forward, screaming with the effort and wild energy she had always used to amplify her strength and her stature.

Beatrice heard the sound behind her, and with the same reflexes that enabled her to ride so nimbly, she stepped aside.

Zepsha missed her entirely and fell with her arms flailing the air, her tiny hands grasping at nothing.

It took a moment for Beatrice to realize what had just happened. Hearing the shouts from below, she peered over the edge of the low wall to see Zepsha broken upon the ground below her.

In that moment, Beatrice knew for certain that I was alive.

POTEMKIN was polishing his eye as his guards ushered Gorlov into his private chamber. He carefully placed the glass orb back into its socket and waved his guards out. Then he stared at Gorlov, his living eye grown larger beneath its raised brow. "I have had some difficulty obtaining a confession," he said to Gorlov, with a voice that tried to be casual and yet nevertheless sounded strained. "You are going to have to help me. My eye sees that your friend Selkirk revealed to you that he was sent to Russia on a secret mission to destroy monarchy, in America and everywhere else."

"And what else does your eye see?" Gorlov asked, making no effort to hide his contempt.

"That you will tell this to the Tsarina. And that for your loyalty you will not only keep what you have now, but will increase your reward." Potemkin paused, and looked away, then turned toward him again, while the other eye remained steadily in place. "And if you do not do this, then all you have will be taken away."

Both Potemkin's eyes remained on Gorlov for a very long time.

AND he confessed all this to you?" the Tsarina asked Gorlov, after hearing him repeat the words Potemkin had told him to say. The Tsarina's tone was like that of a judge who has heard so many lies that even the truth sounds false.

"Yes, Your Majesty," Gorlov said quickly, perhaps even a bit too quickly. "The day of your ball. The one to celebrate victory over the Cossacks." Gorlov stood at attention, with Potemkin and Lord Shettlefield hovering behind him.

"And why did you not come to us sooner?" she demanded.

Potemkin was ready for the question. "General Gorlov

was confused, Your Majesty. He fought beside Selkirk, he thought the man was loyal and brave. Selkirk was seductive. Anyone, even Lord Shettlefield's daughter, could have been taken in."

The Tsarina sifted Shettlefield with her stare, then her eyes darted back to Gorlov. "And you come forward now, after Selkirk was arrested?" she offered, as if to give Gorlov the opportunity to explain why he who had once seemed so wild and brave now behaved like a coward and an opportunist. Gorlov said nothing and lowered his eyes. When he raised them again, he thought he saw disappointment in her. Catherine the Great had seen many men brought to heel. It did not seem likely that she would be dismayed by Gorlov's acting as so many others in her world had done, embracing those on the ascent and denouncing those who fell from favor. Her gaze drifted down, and her thoughts receded far from the jeweled throne room around her.

Potemkin smiled and nodded for Gorlov to leave. As Gorlov started for the door, Shettlefield took a hesitant step forward. "Your Majesty," the Englishman said, "Selkirk is an example of the treachery we face in America. I feel responsible for him, being a British subject. We will hang him for you if you wish."

"What?" Catherine said abruptly, and she seemed to replay the statement in her own mind, before she responded. "It . . . it is up to Lord Potemkin," she answered. She looked at Potemkin. "What do you wish to do?"

"We should not hang him," Potemkin said. Gorlov, paused at the door, listened openly to all this; Potemkin, if he knew Gorlov was there, did not mind at all that he should hear. "We will behead him, in the Russian way. We will do it at dawn tomorrow."

As Gorlov left, Catherine was still sitting motionless upon a golden chair, gazing at the floor.

GORLOV stopped off at the White Goose, where he sat alone beside the hearth and stared into the flames. Several acquaintances noticed him there and tried to speak with him, but he answered not a word, and seemed not to be sensible of anyone else's presence until MacFee and Laarsen saw him there and moved over to join him. The three of them talked but a few moments, and Gorlov then left, the first and only time of his life when anyone could remember his visiting a tavern and leaving without having consumed a drink.

He rode directly to his grand house, the one whose price of ownership had just been established as requiring the payment of his own soul. He did not enter the house to bid greeting or farewell to Martina Ivanovna or to Tikhon, but went directly to the stables, where a handful of chickens were roosted, providing the new family with fresh eggs. Gorlov, with the snatch of one of his huge hands, seized a rooster by the feet and swung it against a stall post, killing the bird instantly.

Taking a lantern from the stables, he mounted his horse again and rode into the deep woods. Reaching a spot among the trees, he set the lantern down, slit the chicken's throat, and spread its blood upon his arms and legs. Then he doused the flame of the lantern and sat down to wait.

He did not wait long. Nor did he flinch when the first howl sounded, or the second, closer by. They closed in on him from two directions.

Gorlov was ready.

Chapter Forty-one

I HAD lain upon the floor for many hours, undisturbed by visits from my brutal jailers. During that period I rested, actually fell into a slumber, so exhausted had I been by the tortures that taxed my spirit more than damaged my body. As part of their plan to break me, my tormentors had intentionally deprived me of rest; now sleep washed over me.

When I awoke, still in cold and darkness, I found myself hungry, and I took this as a sign of health, for my body would not crave food if it were shattered internally, or ill. When I stretched out my limbs, every bone and muscle screamed in pain, and yet that too was encouraging, for I could feel, though the feeling was agony; all my appendages, even fingers and toes, had movement.

After more hours of being neither tortured nor fed, I began to sense that something had changed about my imprisonment. Though it appeared that I had been utterly forgotten, I knew this was not the case; on the contrary, I began to fear that someone had made a decision about my future, and that this decision was anything but good. I stood and took a few agonizing steps, staggering at first but finding my balance. I moved to the iron door and pressed my ear against it but heard nothing; I lay flat upon the floor and tried to peer beneath it, but saw no shadows interrupting the light of the lantern glowing dimly in the prison corridor.

I rose and moved back to the far wall, where I sat down and tried to suppress the anxieties rising within me. How much greater my fears would have been, had I realized that the wagon of the executioner had, at almost that very moment, entered the courtyard of the royal prison.

THE executioner's carriage was a sight that chilled the guts of grown men, and disturbed the dreams of Russian children. It could well have been that this was its intent, since increasing the terror of a prisoner about to be executed is a short-term effect, but instilling it in the populace has broad and long-lasting implications. Pulled by four ebony horses whose manes tossed like wounded ravens as they ran, the carriage was black and boxlike, with covered windows, since on its return journey it served as hearse. Bristling from the racks at its rear were a collection of sordid axes and other implements of inflicting a death that was meant to be less than merciful. Old women spat between their fingers and crossed themselves when it rattled past; children covered their eyes and ran. I myself had glimpsed this very carriage at the beheading of Pugachev; the jailors at my prison had seen it often, and yet even they were loathe to look at it for long. The executioner himself I had judged to be a sadist, for at the execution of Pugachev he seemed to inflate with excitement as he lifted the massive ax and drove it through the bones of the Cossack's neck.

It was the hour before dawn when the sinister carriage rattled through the prison gate and came to a stop in the center of the gray courtyard. The guards had been told it was coming and so they were not surprised by its arrival, or by the creaking open of its main door. Yet they did find it odd when, from the shadows of its interior, there emerged not the hulking body of the executioner, but only a powerful arm, its sinewy hand beckoning them closer.

The guards glanced at one another; the ominous gesture was repeated, impatiently. Two of the guards drifted toward the door as enthusiastically as they might approach an open crypt.

A foot, encased with a riding boot wrapped in fur leggings, slammed full into the face of one guard, snapping his head back and dropping him senseless to the paving stones. The second guard froze as the body of the executioner, his throat cut from ear to ear in a huge grisly smile, fell to the ground at his feet. Leaping from the shadows of the wagon came Wolfhead the Cossack.

His hands moved with animal speed and grace; in a single fluid motion he knocked down the second guard, then seized one of the axes from the racks at the rear of the carriage and hurled it into the back of a third guard who was running to close the gate to seal off the courtyard. The two men perched in the driver's box of the wagon flung off their black lackey's cloaks and revealed their wolf-pelt shoulder wraps and their necklaces of teeth and claws.

"Cossacks!" a watchman on the wall shouted in panic. "Cossacks!" There were a dozen soldiers garrisoned as guards in the prison; most of these were still in their sleeping quarters in the predawn darkness. They tumbled from their beds and grabbed at their weapons; two of them ran headlong into the courtyard where they were instantly cut down by the two Cossacks from the carriage perch. The other guards, jolted from slumber into terror, not knowing the size of the Cossack force attacking them, and having seen several of their number so expertly eliminated, immediately barred the door of their barracks and took up positions of defense.

Wolfhead never slowed down. After throwing the ax he ran directly into the cell block, where the two bullying jailors, still intoxicated from the vodka they had been drinking all night, proved no match for him; he slashed the neck of one and punched the chin of the other with the butt of his saber.

I had heard the shouts, had followed the terrible sounds as they grew nearer. Now the whole prison seemed to echo as the iron bar blocking my cell door was kicked away, the door thrown open, and there, his figure huge and silhouetted in the lantern light, stood Wolfhead.

I think I tried to raise my arms to fight; in truth, I cannot remember clearly. I know that I was shocked and frightened, and that my instincts told me to fight and my mind shouted to my body that it must. But if I offered any resistance, Wolfhead knocked it instantly away, snatching me by the hair and dragging me out of the cell like a child might run with a doll.

We reached the outer courtyard, and all the world was a tumbling blur to me. I clawed at the arm that was pulling me, but only aided Wolfhead in tugging me to the carriage, where he slammed me against its side, so hard I lost breath and nearly lost consciousness. I saw two Cossacks cutting the traces of the carriage horses and holding one steady. Wolfhead slung me onto its bare back, as the two Cossacks with him bounced with the grace of born horsemen onto the twin blacks they had just sliced loose, leaving one mount remaining for Wolfhead.

Somehow the feeling of the horse beneath me was a comfort; my fingers curled instinctively into his mane, and I leaned low against his neck; the horse turned with those of the

Cossacks as they scrambled into the open gate, and stopped, wheeling.

The Cossacks were waiting for Wolfhead, but he was in no hurry—far from it. As I looked back I saw him draw himself to full height there in the courtyard and glare defiantly at the prison itself, and the guards who were meant to man it, now barricaded in fear within their own barracks. He glimpsed a figure quivering in the shadows beside a rain barrel only a few feet away from him and must have noticed the royal insignia on the man's collar, for Wolfhead snatched him and flung him face-first to the cobblestones at his feet. I recognized the man as the chief interrogator who had tormented me through the last two weeks.

Wolfhead tugged down his own trousers and pissed upon the interrogator's back. He took his time; the faces of the barricaded guards, at the windows of their barracks, were pale with fear. The terrifying Cossack then leapt onto the fourth horse, wheeled to join me and the others at the gate, and boomed in a voice as deep and dusty as a tomb, "I am Wolfhead! I claim the right to execute this man among my kinsmen, for killing my Cossack brothers!" He shouted in Russian, and yet I understood his words; and though they offered me no hope, I was eager to ride away from the prison.

Still Wolfhead was not finished. He started to spin away, then reared his horse, turning back again to shout, "And tell the Tsarina she is nothing but a plump bitch with big tits!"

He dug his heels into the ribs of his horse, and all of us galloped away, as the sun was just cracking the edge of the horizon.

W̲OLFHEAD thundered in front, and the other two Cossacks rode at my left and right, hemming me in so that I had no chance to dart and try to flee. We crashed through the trackless forest, not slowing until the horses were fully winded. Wolfhead drew his horse to a walk and led us straight to a small opening among the trees, sheltered by dense underbrush. Four fresh horses stood tethered there.

Wolfhead slid from the back of his spent mount, and the other two Cossacks did the same. Naked and shivering, I mimicked them docilely. But as they seemed to relax I jumped, as quickly as I could manage, back toward the horse I had just dismounted. They were ready for that; one Cossack grabbed me instantly by the hair, and he and his companion had me sprawled out and pinned against the snow-covered floor of the forest. Their leader, towering over me, pulled the wolf's skull off his head, revealing his face.

It was Gorlov.

Chapter Forty-two

THEY had wrapped me in blankets. MacFee and Laarsen—for indeed it was they who had ridden in with Gorlov to free me from the prison—had removed their wolf-pelt headgear but otherwise remained in their Cossack disguises as they heated tea and soup upon a covered fire.

"Where is Beatrice?" I asked Gorlov.

"You must eat," he said. He extended a twist of jerked beef to me.

I knocked it away. "Where is she?"

He took a deep breath, then said it quickly: "At the Kirov Abbey, awaiting execution." He let me absorb this grim news, and studied me, appraising the effects of my imprisonment. "You are better than I feared you might be, after two weeks in that hole."

So it had been two weeks. I tried to think, tried to make sense of everything, but my fears were overwhelming. "Gorlov—" I moaned.

He put a hand upon my shoulder to steady me. "They will

hunt us first," he said. "I mean they will hunt Wolfhead. His legend is our advantage. The royal patrols will move south, to search for him among the other Cossacks."

The implications of all this, not only to Beatrice and to me, but to these my finest friends, swept over me. "Gorlov," I said, "you are giving up everything."

"I had nothing to give up," he said. "Eat. I have a plan."

I F there is anything in life I know to be true, it is that life itself is a matter of the spirit. A man with a broken spirit, whose soul nourishes nothing except the belief that the poison within his own heart is shared by the whole human race, and hopes nothing beyond the desire that everyone he meets will share in his misery, is sick indeed, and his body, however healthy in its potential, is on a path toward corruption; but the person with a purpose, warmed by the impression that, for all of his other shortcomings, something resides within him that is capable of loving and of being loved, can bear all things, believe all things, endure all things. That person's body will heal faster than medical minds imagine. It will overcome pain; in many cases, it will not feel it at all.

Such was my state, after Gorlov's talk with me. My friend had risked his life, a life he had come to value, in order to preserve mine; he had saved me, to rescue the woman I loved and return with her to the homeland I would fight for. Though I had spent two agonizing weeks in the Tsarina's prison, I felt the healthiest, most potent man alive.

T H E Kirov Abbey stood silent, the dawn light casting fog-muted yellow across the eastern faces of its walls, its bell tower still in the frozen air. Behind it rose the cliffs into which the monastic architects, using forced slave labor, had set the abbey's foundations, and from which they had quarried its stone slabs; all around, sloping away from its encircling wall, stood the carpet of an evergreen forest, breached only by the narrow road north from St. Petersburg. A chill wind drifted down from the arctic wastes beyond the cliffs; the abbey looked like the loneliest place on earth.

The four of us—MacFee, Laarsen, Gorlov, and I—sat upon our horses, in the shadows of the trees, a musket shot away from the abbey gate. It was open. A wisp of cooking smoke drifted up from one of the buildings within the walls; otherwise, there was no sign of life. "If I am right," Gorlov said, "the abbey will not be reinforced."

"If you are right," I said, "it will be the first time." I coughed and spat, the cold burning my lungs and the movement of breathing scraping at my ribs; but Gorlov's eyes brightened. He smiled at me. In spite of all my worry, I smiled back.

All four of us now wore wolf-pelt disguises. Theirs looked utterly convincing; I could only hope that I appeared as authentic as they. The horses we now rode, the ones Gorlov had brought into the forest before hijacking the executioner's carriage, were the same ones we had ridden into the campaign against Pugachev; they were scarred like Cossack horses, and Gorlov had even dressed them out with the Cossack saddle and bridle ornaments Laarsen and MacFee had brought back as souvenirs, so even our mounts appeared wild and half insane.

We drew our sabers. Gorlov looked at MacFee and Laarsen, and then at me. "Eat the wolves," he said.

"Eat the wolves," I answered.

We spurred our horses and charged toward the abbey gate.

✳

THOUGH the oaken gates of the abbey stood wide, we did not ride through the opening, but leapt our horses over the low wall, hoping the unexpected direction of our attack would multiply its surprise. Better still, such tactics were characteristic of the Cossack raiders we hoped to be taken for.

Our horses came to earth within the abbey compound, and a monk—for there were still such devotees in that unholy place—dropped the pottery pitcher he was carrying to the well, stared at us in a moment of shock, and fled back to the kitchen building.

The soldiers at the gate were no less shocked, but they were more awake than those at the prison had been, if for no other reason than that the hour was fully day. They grabbed at their muskets and raced for cover; Laarsen and MacFee had anticipated their defense and rode them down quickly. Gorlov and I cut down soldiers running at us in the courtyard, the men here being remarkably aggressive, their comfortable duty at the abbey having been their reward for valor in the Tsarina's battles.

Gorlov lifted a torch from a courtyard flambeau and rode into the abbey stables, where he ignited the hay there; I spurred my horse up a stone staircase winding to the heart of the building beside the bell tower, where Gorlov had informed me the important prisoners were by tradition held. Beyond this fact, he had been able to tell me nothing; I was prepared to search through the whole building, probe every cranny of the abbey itself, to find Beatrice. I knew my three friends, even aided by the shock of our attack and the diversion of smoke and flame from the stables, could not for long hold off the counterattack that would surely come as the guards rallied; but I would not leave without her.

I reached the second floor and rode into an enclosed passage, the ceilings arched high above me, the stone echoing the hooves of my horse. A soldier, emerging from a staircase that must have led to the bell tower, ran straight down the corridor at me, and had almost reached me when he looked up in surprise to see me there. Instead of retreating, he tried to raise his musket, and I spurred my horse and chopped him down as the flintlock discharged into the floor.

The sound of the blast was deafening within the stone corridor; my horse shied and the acrid smoke of the gunpowder swirled in the air.

Beatrice, within her chamber, heard the shot.

I was steadying my horse and trying to orient myself when I heard a door open behind me; I spun around in my saddle and saw her. She gasped and jumped back toward her chamber. I realized she saw not me, but the Cossack raider I pretended to be. "Beatrice!" I shouted.

The door came open again; she looked out in disbelief.

"Beatrice!" I called again, and tore the wolf-pelt disguise from my head and shoulders. "Come on!"

She ran to me, reached her hand to grasp my arm, and swung herself up behind me on the horse.

We galloped back along the passage, down the stairs, and out into the courtyard, where musket balls buzzed through the air like frantic bees.

In that moment I almost ruined everything. Gorlov, MacFee, and Laarsen were hugging the perimeter of the courtyard, riding between doors and windows to throw burning hay through every opening, and so to distract and suppress the musket fire of the soldiers sheltered inside the buildings. I came within a heartbeat of yelling, "Gorlov!" But I caught myself and screamed a high, Cossack shriek instead, and so saved the chance that Gorlov, as well as MacFee and Laarsen, might remain in Russia with their deeds of this day undiscovered, and their rewards intact.

Gorlov heard me; he shouted to MacFee and Laarsen, and they galloped toward the gate. MacFee and Laarsen came through first, Beatrice and I followed, and Gorlov came out last, still magnificent as Wolfhead.

A marksman on the second-floor balcony of the abbot's residence was taking aim at Gorlov's back when a pistol ball slapped into his forehead and killed him, the shot fired by MacFee, who had turned back to cover Gorlov's escape.

With that last bit of magnificent luck behind us, we galloped away.

Chapter Forty-three

M A R T I N A Ivanovna and Tikhon had ridden to the lodge with Pyotr in their own separate sleigh, bringing blankets and food. But they had been unwilling to risk alerting anyone to their presence in the lodge by building a fire, and they looked blue with cold. This was not the way I wished to remember them; I moved to the hearth and lit a blaze there. Doing so distressed Beatrice more than comforted her, for this close to escape she thought it unlucky to take any chances. "This is our last meal in Russia," I told her, "with friends who have risked their lives for us. So let us be warm to eat it."

Pyotr, who had stood guard outside all night, smiled at me.

As the logs began to snap in the grate, Gorlov, who stood in the corner of the log lodge and kept peering out through the murkiness of the mica windows, said, "I think I will take one more ride around."

I moved up beside him. "Do you see something?" I whispered.

"No. I will take just a ride."

I followed him outside. "What is the matter?" I asked.

"I have had the feeling we have been followed. I had it even in St. Petersburg, but I thought it was because we were in the city and I was anxious about our ruse. But I still have the feeling. Even after leaving the camp, I thought there was someone with us—in front, behind, somewhere."

"Who?"

"I don't know." Gorlov frowned uncertainly at the line of trees encircling the lodge. "Just a little gallop around. I will be right back."

Beatrice helped prepare the meal. I marveled at her composure after all she had lately been through. I moved to her and tried to hug her waist from behind as she laid food upon the table; she touched my hands but moved away quickly, as if afraid to pause, and I realized then how tense she was, how anxious to get on our way. I thought then that Martina Ivanovna was tense as well, and that the paleness around her lips was from more than cold.

Gorlov returned, sullen and silent. When Tikhon pressed him for what he had found, Gorlov said, "There are riders on the road, an hour to the east; I saw the birds rising in the line of the highway, as I watched from the hilltop just there."

"Royal cavalry, moving in the wrong direction," I hoped aloud.

"Probably," Gorlov said, scowling.

We ate the cheese, dried beef, and fruit that Martina Ivanovna had for us. The food was good, but the conversation stilted. We tried to talk, but every imagined noise from the outside hushed us; even the quietness of one of our number would cause all the others to think the one not talking had heard some sound; it was a tense meal, soon ended.

"So. That is that," Gorlov said. "Shall we go?"

"Yes," I said. "Yes. Is the sleigh in place?"

Pyotr nodded; it was he who had driven the sleigh from

St. Petersburg a week before, hidden it deep in the woods, and brought the horses back secretly.

We scattered the fire and drowned the ashes. Beatrice swept them up.

"That is not necessary," Gorlov said. "Come on."

"There is a death penalty for peasants caught using the Tsarina's property," she said.

"Peasants! We are nobles!" Gorlov said.

"The next person to visit this lodge with the Tsarina won't know that," Beatrice said. "And they may accuse some peasant, if they find ashes here."

The place tidied, we all walked out into the cold, still air. Pyotr had concealed the sleigh cleverly beneath a pile of brush that looked like woodcutter's refuse. We uncovered it and harnessed up the two extra trace horses Pyotr had brought out with the lighter sleigh when he had driven Martina Ivanovna and Tikhon to the lodge the night before.

Beatrice paused, touched Tikhon's head, and turned to Martina Ivanovna. "Have a safe trip," Martina Ivanovna said. "And God speed."

"And you," Beatrice said.

They embraced. I did not think Martina Ivanovna emotional, until I saw her eyes. She assisted Beatrice into the sleigh, tucked blankets around her, and then handed me a parcel she had carried with her from the lodge. "Warm cloaks," she said. "Nuts. And cheese. You must eat cheese until you can find fresh milk."

She threw her arms about my neck and only then burst into tears.

Pyotr, having quickly traced up the horses, scrambled into the box and took up the leads. I turned to Gorlov, who held the reins of the saddled mare I had been riding.

"So," I said, my voice thick. "Letters will come to you, from a merchant in England, or a lady in France . . . written in different tongues, by different hands. But they shall be to you, from me. And if I have a son, I will name him after you. If I have a *daughter,* I shall name her after you!"

"Go on," Gorlov said. "Go."

I reached for his hand; he threw his arms about me in a hug that would have done a bear proud; he whispered into my ear, "She is just the woman for you." When he let me go, we could not look at each other.

"Tikhon," I said, and shook the strong young hand of the boy, growing more every day like Gorlov, his true father—not of blood, but of heart. "I will never forget you," I told him, and tears rolled down his cheeks.

I turned, and tapped Pyotr upon the shoulder. He lifted the reins. But before he snapped them down upon the horses' backs, he went rigid.

Before us, among the trees, sat a man on horseback. The horse was poor, bony. The man's pants were torn and patched many times; his boots were encased in rags. Upon his shoulders lay the tattered remnants of a fur shawl. Upon his head, with the snout pulled down before his eyes, lay the skull fur of a wolf.

"Gorlov," I said, loudly, though he was right at my side, "Who is it?"

"The real one," Gorlov whispered, the tone and reverence of his breath declaring, *Russia will not be mocked!*

I was afraid beyond any fear I had ever felt. Confusion and disbelief beat together like the twin wings of a bat bashing about my brain as I tried to make sense of the horseman who had materialized before us. *Russia will not be mocked!*

I cannot say how long we stared at him, and he at us. Our silence was profound, Gorlov surely feeling the surprise as intensely as I; having revelled in the ruse of impersonating him, we had so discounted the real Wolfhead that he had almost ceased to exist for us. But here he was, and no apparition.

"A madman!" I tried. "Some peasant who has fantasies . . . I . . . I will kill him with my saber!" Yet I could not draw the blade, so shaken was I, so stunned in finding the perfect music of our plan suddenly turned raucous.

The others, too, had lost power of movement. Beatrice sat gripping the blanket with one hand, the sleigh side with the other, and not blinking, not breathing. Gorlov stood breathless, his mouth half open, his hands frozen upon the reins of his horse, and mine. Tikhon and Martina Ivanovna also were motionless, though I could not see them behind Gorlov; and Pyotr sat upon the box like a dead leaf, so fragile a breeze could blow him away or crumble him. Wolfhead—for it was he, no other—sensed this fear in us, knew it in his instinctive depths. He urged his horse toward us, in a walk at first, then quickening into a trot, the quiver of his hands turning into the fast, sharp movements of a man on a battlefield about to charge.

He drew nearer. He spurred his horse to a gallop and came on screaming, a smiling demon, flapping rags and tatters, his fangs bared.

He stopped twenty feet before us. Not one of us had raised a sword, but we each had stood our ground; I did not understand until later that he surely paused only because we had not fled. He had tested us, instinctively, like a wolf might test the fear of his prey; now all of us hung there frozen, he gawking at us from black hollow eyes, seeing us gazing back just as wildly at him. Then he spoke, his voice thin and tubercular, with words of unschooled Russian that I struggled then to comprehend and can translate only thus: "Why you chase me now?"

None of us could answer. I could not believe he had spoken. Nor could I, still blinded by the beating bat's wings, readily comprehend the figure I saw before me.

"Gorlov!" I whispered. "He was alive all this time. Hidden like an animal. We . . . we . . ."

"We flushed him out," Gorlov completed for me.

I looked at Gorlov. "Tell him I am Selkirk, who sliced a Cossack in two."

Gorlov shouted this out in Russian.

After a pause, Wolfhead's answer echoed back. Gorlov translated. "He says he knows your legend. He wishes to drink your blood."

"If he is the true Wolfhead," I answered, "I will fight him now, and he will taste a hero's blood—or his own."

Gorlov frowned at me. "That's a bit flowery, don't you think?"

I glared at Gorlov, and he shrugged, then shouted the translation toward the Cossack.

Wolfhead drew his saber.

I leapt into the saddle of my horse, took the reins, and drew my own blade.

"Kieran!" Beatrice said, the fright in her voice. But I had no choice. I gave her the most reassuring look I could manage, wheeled my horse, and spurred him toward Wolfhead.

The Cossack was already galloping toward me, riding with a liquid grace like I had never seen. He bore straight at me . . . and time crept nearly to a stop.

For a long slow instant I thought our horses would collide, so direct was our charge at each other. We shot by, right side to right side, and our sabers clashed.

My slash felt quick, perhaps too hurried; but when I looked back I saw that his blade had snapped with the impact. I reined up and waited for Wolfhead to wheel and flee; with his sword broken, and facing an experienced rider, it could hardly have been considered cowardly for him to do so. But instead the Cossack threw down his useless blade and galloped at me barehanded.

His recklessness surprised me—but I could not let myself hesitate. I spurred forward and raised my saber for the stroke;

but Wolfhead slipped down along the flank of his horse, twisted his hip on the saddle like a gypsy acrobat, and caught me full in the chest with a two-footed kick, knocking me cleanly from the back of my horse.

Wolfhead popped back up onto the saddle and reined around, fifty paces away, to face me. Struggling to catch the breath his kick had knocked from me, I groped for my saber, but it was not at hand. I rolled to my feet and saw my blade lying between Wolfhead and me. I ran for it; Wolfhead spurred his horse and beat me to it, slipping halfway off the saddle to scoop it up from the snowy ground.

Gorlov started forward to interfere. "No!" I shouted, and he stopped, too far away to help anyway.

On foot, unarmed, I faced Wolfhead.

He charged.

I dodged, snatched Wolfhead's broken saber from the ground and tumbled as the Cossack tried to ride over me; I slashed below the horse's belly, cutting the cinch of Wolfhead's saddle. He fell in a heap. In an instant I was on top of him, one hand on his throat, the other raised to drive the broken blade into his heart.

But in our struggling the wolf-skull headgear had tumbled off the Cossack, and I now saw not the snarl of a wild killer, but the sunken, half-starved face of a man in his seventies.

I froze.

By this time Gorlov had run to us, and he saw Wolfhead the same as I: an ancient warrior who had the courage but not the strength to face a man a third his age. "An old man," I muttered.

Wolfhead said something in Russian. Gorlov translated. "He says it is an honor to die by your hand."

"And a greater honor to let him live," I said, standing.

Gorlov translated this into Russian for the Cossack, and I lifted him to his feet. He tried to kneel in homage, but I pulled him up again.

And then the unimaginable—unimaginable anywhere but in Russia—happened: Wolfhead, the legendary Cossack, his eyes brimming with emotion, gave me a Russian hug.

"This is all very touching," Gorlov interjected, "but—" He stopped suddenly, and then I heard it, too, a rising, terrifying noise. "Horses!" Gorlov said.

"Lots of them!" I said.

"Which way?" Gorlov said, his head swiveling. "I hear them everywhere!"

And he did; crashing from the woods on all sides of us came the entire royal bodyguard, maneuvering as four prongs converging on the clearing and streaming around us in a complete encirclement. They stopped and faced us, sabers drawn, in a clear signal that anyone trying to run would be cut down.

"This is bad," Gorlov said quietly.

"This is very bad," I agreed.

Pounding down the main road to the lodge, the road we had been about to take for our escape from Russia, came Catherine the Great, riding sidesaddle. Potemkin rode at her side. Lord Shettlefield sat perched on one of the horses behind them.

"This is worse," I said.

"Much worse," Gorlov said.

Then no one said anything. Catherine dismounted, leaping from her saddle without assistance, yet still looking regal in a riding cloak that reached nearly to the snow at her feet. With her long hair blown back and away from her face by the ride, she appeared even more fierce. She looked around—first at me, then at Gorlov, who studied the sky and chewed his mustache. The Tsarina's hot gaze swung to the sleigh where Beatrice sat, with Martina Ivanovna, Tikhon, and Pyotr close by. That gaze then burned again on me.

"Seize them!" Potemkin commanded, and the royal cavalrymen grabbed me, Gorlov, and the others, ignoring the real

Wolfhead, who, without his headgear, looked as some reclusive peasant we had recruited to help us in our ruse.

"No!" Catherine's voice cut through the frozen air, and everyone stopped dead still. "No need to grab them, where are they going to go?"

Potemkin, eyelids fluttering and mouth agape, like a child caught in a lie, pointed to the traveling sleigh, where Pyotr was muttering rapid prayers in Russian and crossing himself furiously. "To—to the border, apparently!" Potemkin sputtered. "Treason, deception, espionage, lying, unfaithfulness—"

"Love." Catherine said this quietly, but once again her words brought silence.

She walked to Gorlov, and everything was so quiet that the crunch of her footsteps in the snow was ominous. "General Gorlov," she said. "Who lied. Who pretended to be a renegade Cossack. Who terrorized my subjects. Who pissed on my magistrate."

Gorlov shrugged and shriveled, gesturing like these were minor infractions.

But the Tsarina's anger was rising, to judge by the tone and volume of her voice. "Who made speeches against me and defied the Throne of Holy Russia!"

Gorlov's mustache danced above his twitching mouth like a tube of black caterpillars roused to an orgy.

"All out of loyalty to a friend," Catherine went on. "Hoping to gain nothing. Risking everything." She paused. "Russia needs men like that."

Gorlov's mustache ceased dancing, and his eyebrows stopped bouncing, locked in their uppermost position. She held his gaze with her own, then turned her stare to Potemkin. "Prince Potemkin . . ." she said, letting his name linger for a moment upon her lips. "I think it will do you good to rest at a monastery, where you may meditate on the wisdom of making arrangements whereby you profit personally, at the expense of my kingdom."

Potemkin turned white as the bark of the birch trees. His own guards grabbed the reins of his horse, and, without ceremony, they led him away, riding off quietly back down the road from whence they had come. Catherine watched him go, and I thought I saw a hint of regret on her face, but any remorse in her look was certainly dominated by an unbendable anger.

The sight of Potemkin, the most powerful man in Russia, being led by his own guards into exile, however temporary it might prove to be, mesmerized everyone there—except one. Wolfhead, with the instincts that had kept him alive for so long, seized the moment to drift, as silent and natural as fog, to Pyotr's side, where Pyotr himself slipped a blanket about him in a gesture utterly unremarkable to those who viewed them simply as two peasants, but that would intrigue me for many hours in the future. Before Potemkin had disappeared in one direction, Wolfhead had vanished into the trees of the other, leaving behind only the headgear I had knocked off him.

When I looked back up from the wolf-pelt skull lying on the ground, I saw Catherine staring directly at me, pondering my face as she had done before. Once more her eyes darted to Beatrice, hung there a moment, then came back to me. "Queens," the Tsarina said, "have everything in limitless supply. Everything except love and honor."

She paused again, pondering—not considering her next action, for she seemed to have decided already on her immediate course of action; but in the distance of her stare I thought she gazed toward the future, not just that of her own kingdom but of mankind itself.

And then I realized how naïve we had been to think we could deceive her. Strangely, I wanted to laugh. "You knew," I said. "You knew the Cossacks who saved me were impersonators, and that we would free Beatrice."

"Of course I knew," she said lightly, almost amused. "I knew everything. From the beginning."

"From the beginning?"

"I knew you were coming to Russia. Not you personally, of course, but someone sent by Benjamin Franklin. I have studied the man, and he is anything but stupid. Your British friends knew this, too."

Lord Shettlefield had slid from his saddle as Potemkin had been led away, better to be ready to intercede with the Tsarina should her anger turn against him as well. Yet she ignored him, and Catherine looked back at me. "Yes, Mr. Selkirk," she said, "since my pleasures are no great secret, I expected Franklin to send an appealing young American to try to sway me, and I was quite looking forward to it. I just did not expect him to send me you." She tapped her lips with her fingertips, in a gesture befitting a queen or a barmaid. "You know, it was quite brilliant, what he did. He sends a young man full of ideals, religion, principles—knowing I am not at all interested in the principles and yet will be disarmed by the sincerity. The principles, you see, are ridiculous. Democracy will never work."

Shettlefield spouted, "That is right, Your Highness!"

"But Your Highness—" I shot back.

"Do not interrupt me! Either of you! Not ever," the Tsarina said, the volume of her voice tapering from sudden anger to a fine quiet point of danger, and both Shettlefield and I held our breath.

"Democracy," she went on emphatically, "will *not* work. I have heard many men prattle about its principles. But I have never seen such a willingness to die for those dreams." She was studying me again, still looking into the future. "Those closest to me have shown no scruples; they were willing to betray anything while you were willing to betray nothing. You could have had wealth, women, and power. You chose something greater. In doing so, you *have* won."

"Your Highness . . . !" Lord Shettlefield pleaded.

"Our deal was already over, Lord Shettlefield," the Tsarina said sharply. "Your efforts to suppress American independence will not succeed."

"They will! If you send us men!"

"No," she answered, shaking her head. "If I sent soldiers to America, they would be slaughtered."

"That is not what King George thinks!"

"King George has not had such men in his bedchambers," the Tsarina answered flatly.

She stepped directly in front of me, and we exchanged a long look. "You treated me not as a queen but as a woman," she said. "And it is as a woman that I give you this."

She slapped me so suddenly and so hard that the men in her own cavalry flinched. Then, slowly, she smiled, and kissed me primly on the spot she had just slapped.

She moved closer to Gorlov and fixed a hard stare on him. "So," she said. "A plump bitch. With big tits."

"But, Your Highness . . ." Gorlov said. "I *like* plump bitches with big tits."

Again the Tsarina smiled.

I do not know when Martina Ivanovna decided to move up next to Gorlov, but suddenly there she was beside him, gripping his arm and glaring back defiantly at the Tsarina. Catherine nodded to her respectfully, then turned back to her horse. Two of her young guards leapt from their saddles, helped her into her own, then rode away behind her, the Tsarina's eyes fixed on the road ahead.

We were left again in silence. I glanced to Beatrice, then watched her climb into the sleigh to wait for me.

I turned to Gorlov, and we looked at each other for a moment. I reached to the ground, lifted my saber from the place where it had fallen, and tossed it to him. He caught mine, then drew his own and tossed it to me. We smiled.

"So," he said, "you have eaten the wolves."

I stepped to the sleigh, climbed in beside Beatrice, and Pyotr snapped the reins.

The runners grabbed but once, as Pyotr lashed the horses and they tugged the sleigh across a still-thawed ditch at the roadside. But once upon the refrozen surface, they whisked, and the sleigh began to slide toward the west; the wind caught our faces and froze my tears.

Gorlov, with Martina Ivanovna and now Tikhon, too, by his side, watched the sleigh as it pulled away, a Russian sadness in his eyes. He raised my saber into the air. "Hussars of the Tsarina!" he shouted.

I lifted his saber and raised it high, in sad, sweet farewell.

Acknowledgments

I am grateful to so many who have enriched my life and work, and some who have touched me most profoundly will not be listed here; but a few, because of their direct involvement with this novel, deserve special mention.

Rob Weisbach has served as editor for this novel, and his service in all areas of this book's life has been extraordinary.

Dave Wirtschafter became my principal agent twelve years ago, at a time when I had no recognition, no financial security, and indiscernible professional prospects. Since that time he has exhibited courage, wisdom, integrity, and friendship. And Mel Berger has carried forward that same spirit in championing this novel in the world of book publishing.

Danielle Lemmon Zapotoczny and Stephen Zapotoczny have participated in all aspects of this book's life, performing with creativity, persistence, intelligence, humor, unshakeable values, and love. Jill Rytie has been stalwart in managing the mechanics of this manuscript and the madness of life. Sue Ritchie and Jim Lee have contributed mightily in sharing with me and with others their exuberance for this book.

My mother, Evelyn Wallace, always seemed to like this story best, and my sons, along with the rest of my family and friends, have loved me through the long silences of my life. And Christine Wallace contributed in all sorts of ways to keeping this novel alive.

Hilda and Michail Pavlov showed me Russia, through its language and literature and their own hearts. Reynolds Price and Doris Betts lifted the light of their teaching upon the darkness of my writing.

My father taught me what a man is, and something of immortality, for his death brought all of us who loved him a new experience of life.

There are many others to thank; I am grateful to you all.

About the Author

RANDALL WALLACE directed, produced, and wrote the screenplay for the Vietnam drama *We Were Soldiers,* based on the *New York Times* bestseller. He received the Writers Guild of America Award for Best Original Screenplay for *Braveheart,* as well as Academy Award and Golden Globe nominations. He subsequently wrote, directed, and produced the 1998 MGM drama *The Man in the Iron Mask* and wrote the blockbuster *Pearl Harbor.* Wallace has published six novels, including the novel of *Braveheart* and the *New York Times* bestseller *Pearl Harbor.*